THE
SECOND
WOMAN

Charlotte Philby worked for the *Independent* for eight years as a columnist, editor and reporter, and was shortlisted for the Cudlipp Prize for her investigative journalism at the 2013 Press Awards. A former contributing editor and feature writer at *Marie Claire*, she has written for the *New Statesman*, *Elle*, *Telegraph*, *Guardian* and *Sunday Times*, and presented documentaries for the BBC World Service and *The One Show*. Charlotte is the granddaughter of Kim Philby, Britain's most infamous communist double-agent, the elusive 'third man' in the notorious Cambridge spy ring. This is her third novel.

Also by Charlotte Philby

Part of the Family
A Double Life

THE
SECOND
WOMAN

CHARLOTTE PHILBY

THE BOROUGH PRESS

The Borough Press
An imprint of HarperCollins*Publishers* Ltd
1 London Bridge Street
London SE1 9GF

www.harpercollins.co.uk

HarperCollins*Publishers*
1st Floor, Watermarque Building, Ringsend Road
Dublin 4, Ireland

Published by HarperCollins*Publishers* 2021

1

Typeset in Adobe Garamond Pro by
Palimpsest Book Production Ltd, Falkirk, Stirlingshire

Printed and Bound in the UK using 100% Renewable Electricity
at CPI Group (UK) Ltd

MIX
Paper from
responsible sources
FSC™ C007454

For Xander

'Let the die be cast!'

Plutarch

Prologue

London, the day Anna dies

It is dusk. The road is not yet dark but the early evening glow of the streetlamps casts pools of light, like fingerprints, along the pavement. The figure moves quickly, heartbeat rising as the house comes into view. The wisteria that had burst with new life just a few months earlier now clings to the brick like sinew, exposed beneath the skin of a corpse.

From this vantage point at the bottom of the tiled front steps, it is possible to see through the panes of glass in the front door that the hallway is dark. At the back of the house a wall of glass overlooks the perfectly manicured lawn rolling down towards the Heath, the moonlight blotted out by the shadows of the trees.

The children are not home yet, but they will be soon. There isn't much time.

Hearing the faint sound of the car doors closing in the street, the figure takes a step up towards the front door, flinching at the brushing of rope against skin as the men from the car pass by and disappear up into the shadows beside the entrance, just out of sight.

When they have taken their positions there is a sharp intake of breath, and then a single knock.

The voice, as it calls through the letterbox, is firm.

'Anna, it's me. Open the door.'

When she does, her expression transforms. 'What are you doing here?'

PART ONE

Harry

London, the inquest

The journalists gathered inside the Coroner's Court are growing restless. Through the arched window of the courtroom the leaves of the oak trees in the Vestry of St Pancras sway against a clear blue sky. But in here, there is no fresh air.

The jury benches are empty, giving a ghostly quality to the room. There have been no jurors present since the inquest started. There seems to be no need in a case such as this, the inquest serving as little more than a rubber stamp to officiate an inevitable conclusion.

Beneath dark beams that line a gabled roof, with blood-red ceilings and matching carpets, the twelve or more reporters squashed together along the mahogany pews at the back of the room are agitated from the heat. The coroner, seemingly unfazed at the front of the room, continues to consult her notes. On the table in front of her, which is reserved for family and friends, two women sit: the older one perfectly still – the dead woman's mother, her body closed in on itself as if in retreat from the world. The younger woman sits beside her but set slightly apart, her spine poker straight, making no effort to push back the red curls that fall around her face. Behind them the father-in-law, who wears a fedora hat, even in this heat, coughs into his sleeve. The woman next to him pulls a tissue from the pocket of her immaculate trouser suit, handing it to him and giving his elbow a comforting squeeze.

'I'll now call my final witness.' The sound of the coroner's voice silences the ripple of impatience moving along the press benches. A young woman stills the pencil she had been absent-mindedly drumming against her notepad. Harry, a few seats along, bites his lower lip, eyes fixed ahead. His fingers touch the outline of the old NUJ card hanging from a lanyard around his neck.

The summoned witness is small and sharp. He wears glasses, his nose like an upright skimming stone. The eyes of everyone in the room follow him intently as he moves towards the microphone, his manner suggesting he is savouring every moment with his captive audience.

When he reaches the stand, he pauses, adjusting his microphone before repeating the oath.

'I solemnly and sincerely declare and affirm that the evidence I shall give will be the truth, the whole truth and nothing but the truth.'

'Thank you, Dr Blackman,' the coroner says. 'And will you please explain to the court your relationship to Marianne Witherall?'

'Of course. I am a psychiatrist. I am – I *was* – Ms Witherall's doctor in the final two years of her life.'

The energy in the room changes. Beneath the silence of the crowd, there is a fizz of excitement.

'When you say you were her doctor . . .'

'I was employed by the family. There was an intervention, if you will, not long after the birth of her twin daughters. David, her husband, was worried. So was her father-in-law, Clive Witherall.'

The doctor glances briefly at the older man in the hat, seated in the benches.

'Anna – sorry, *Marianne* – had been suffering from postnatal depression.'

'And you treated her for her depression, Dr Blackman?'

'That's right.'

'And what did that treatment involve?'

'It was a combination of talking therapies and medication.'

'What sort of medication?'

'She took an SSRI, sertraline specifically, owing to the fact that Ms Witherall was still breastfeeding at the point of commencement.'

'It was you who prescribed the drugs?'

He pauses. 'Not at first. It was the hospital who suggested them initially. I oversaw the increase in dosage. She'd started with 50mg per day. When that failed to have the desired effect, the daily intake was gradually increased to 200mg.'

'Why was that?'

'Ms Witherall wasn't coping. She was detached. She was struggling to bond with her children. My suggestion at this time was that she ought to seek in-house treatment, but she refused. And David, her husband, was keen to support that decision.'

'How long did you treat Ms Witherall for her depression?'

'Just over three years, until she . . . Until she died.'

'And did you prescribe any other medication during that time?' the coroner asks.

Dr Blackman pauses, running his tongue over his top lip.

'No.'

'And in your professional opinion, do you believe that Ms Witherall was of a mental state that she might have taken her own life?'

Dr Blackman sighs regretfully. 'I do.'

There is a scuffle on the press benches, the excitement too much to contain. Although whichever way, this is a story that will continue to elicit plenty of hand-rubbing on Fleet Street. Either she took her own life or she was murdered. However you look at it, the story of the beautiful fallen heiress is gold dust, and this lot will continue to pick at the remains until there is nothing left, or until they are distracted by the smell of fresh blood. Whichever comes first.

'Thank you, Dr Blackman,' the coroner says, crisply. 'Please return to your seat. The court will now adjourn for a short while so I can prepare my conclusion. If the family would leave first, and wait in the family room. Members of the press, owing to your volume, please wait outside the court until you are called back.'

The journalists have barely finished their second cigarettes when the coroner's officer calls them into the courtroom for her conclusion. Harry doesn't join them, slipping quietly away to the corner of the adjoining gardens until he hears the crowd being summoned back in.

The coroner sits still at the front of the room, studying her hands while she waits for the final reporters to shuffle back into their seats. The woman with the red hair has her arms held protectively in front of herself. Even now, he won't let himself say her name. Anna's mother looks as though she has not moved since the onlookers cleared out, before piling back in again.

'I would like to start by thanking the witnesses for their time. I am satisfied that I have reached my conclusion in reference to the circumstances of the death of Marianne Witherall. In a case of suicide, there needs to be clear evidence so that the coroner is sure beyond all reasonable doubt that the deceased intended to take their own life. This is different from other conclusions, where we just have to be sure on the balance of probabilities. Based on the presence of the note, which as we have heard was confirmed to be in Ms Witherall's handwriting by Consultant Graphologist Hannah Birch, along with the testimony of the police officers who first attended the scene, Sarah Marshall, who found the body, the forensic officer who studied the body, and Ms Witherall's psychiatrist, Dr Blackman, I confirm that I am fully satisfied with the conclusion that on the date in question, Ms Marianne Witherall died by suicide.'

The woman with the red hair slumps slightly, her posture softening at the news. The older woman barely flinches.

Focusing her attention on the table in front of her, the coroner continues, 'I would like to offer, on behalf of the court, my sincerest condolences to Ms Witherall's family, not least her mother and her daughters, Stella and Rose. The inquest is now closed.'

Artemis

Greece, the Eighties

The sun was already stretching over the port when Artemis came to, perhaps awoken by the sound of her own moaning. Or maybe it was the cloying damp of the sweat on her forehead that caused her to shiver and stir, her heart tapping out a rhythm against her ribcage.

She had been deep in dreams of the earthquake – the same dream, mutated over time: the earth cracking so that the ground opened up beneath her, preparing to draw her in. Screams quickening into a shrill vibrato.

Artemis sat upright and gave herself a minute, taking in the scene, as if half-expecting to find herself in the old cot-bed she had slept in as a child, in the village at the top of the mountain rather than where she had passed out the previous evening, safely tucked up down by the water in the same house she and her family had lived for the past twenty years. Ever since—

She paused her thoughts there.

Reaching for the Walkman on the side table, she pulled the headphones over her head and pressed play, hearing the click before the music seeped in, Simple Minds' 'Don't You (Forget About Me)' instantly blotting out the world around her.

Sinking back into her pillow, she closed her eyes and drank in the sounds, dozing for a few minutes before standing to face the day, dressing quickly and heading out into the sun-bleached morning.

It was a Saturday, mid-July. On the street she turned right, away from the corner window of the bakery where her mother would have long been at work, away from the fishing boats bobbing at the edge of the water. She stretched her hands above her head, then reached into her bag for her Walkman. Pressing rewind, she yawned as she moved up the mountain path, towards the old village and the freshly emerging tremor lines that she could not yet see.

The old village, which stood at the top of the mountain, rang with the intermittent sounds of new life that summer. Twenty years after the earthquake that had taken their home and what lay inside, her father, Markos, behaved as though this act of nature had been a cruel and cunning ploy orchestrated by foreign developers seeking to take hold of the island on which his family had lived for generations. Even now, he refused to come up here, too scared of the ghosts that lingered among the olive trees, repelled by the steady churn of diggers as Europeans – from across Germany and France predominantly – snapped up property that had lain abandoned for two decades.

Artemis despaired of and loved her father in equal measure for his unshakeable loyalty to a past life. In the two decades since the house had fallen, taking with it his youngest child, the carcass of the building now symbolised for Markos a physical and spiritual sacrifice. Unable to focus on the true horror of his loss, the earthquake represented not just the event that had taken away his three-year-old daughter, but had become an emblem of a world – *his* world – that was now under threat from the emergence of a frivolous new Greece. To his broken mind, the earthquake was no longer an act of God but a threat to the foundations of the land he loved.

It wasn't rational, of course, but then what would be an acceptably rational response to the death of a child? This wasn't a question his fellow villagers were willing to take time to consider. So many people had lost so much that night, and in refusing to come together with his neighbours in his suffering, unwilling to conform to their collective grief, Markos had outcast himself and – by association – he had cast out his family, too.

The last time Markos ventured to the old village, he had returned with a look of dread. Rena had held out a hand to comfort him but he pushed her away.

'Perhaps regeneration is exactly what this island needs,' his wife had tried softly. 'A bit of fresh life – for all our sakes.'

'What are you saying, Rena? You think we need to *move on?*'

She barked back at him and Artemis had snuck away, leaving them to scrap like dogs over the bones that lay buried in the rubble.

Artemis walked with no particular direction in mind this morning, running her fingers along the mottled stone of the narrow alleyways, past flashes of the original Venetian walls and an old Byzantine church, her head bobbing occasionally to the beat of her mixtape. The morning sun brushed lightly against her skin, warming her.

Athena would be working all day. They had agreed to meet that evening at the opening of Nico's, a new restaurant that was launching in the village's central square. Now that foreigners had started to trickle in for the summer, Athena was keen to hang out in the places where she imagined some loaded, far-flung visitor might step in and whisk her off her feet. This was despite her on-off relationship with Panos, the boyfriend Athena was head-over-heels in love with one minute, and in total denial about the next. Absent-mindedly, Artemis scuffed the dusty path with the toe of her shoe as she walked her usual route to Carolina's shop. Athena had no idea what she had; more to the point, she had no idea what it was like to be Artemis and to be considered an untouchable, even among boys like Panos; nice boys. And God knows those were few and far enough between.

It wasn't that Artemis needed, or really actively wanted, a boyfriend. But there was something about the idea of someone wanting *her*. Objectively speaking, she was attractive. On the island, though, she was branded for life – partly due to her father's idiosyncrasies, and partly due to manifestations of her own trauma, which ranged from the nightmares to, when she was younger, wetting herself in class; both irresistible fodder for the bullies who smelt her weakness, along with the urine that had sometimes streaked down her legs suddenly in the middle of a lesson, causing her to freeze.

And then there was Jorgos.

Artemis shuddered. Pulling out a cigarette and lighting it, she stopped and inhaled sharply, perching on the edge of a low wall where the side of the mountain tumbled down to the sea, grateful for a sudden gust of light wind.

It was early still and the few tourists who might follow the sign guiding them from the street at the top of the village, through Carolina's grocery store and out towards the makeshift gallery in the back-room where Artemis' paintings hung against stone walls, would likely still be asleep. She could afford to take a moment. Reaching into her bag, she pressed stop on her Walkman and closed her eyes, breathing in deeply as the ghosts rose up around her.

There was something soothing about sitting here, letting that night play out on loop in her head. In wakefulness, she could control the way her mind worked through the memory in a way that she couldn't in sleep, though she never found the answer to the same question that came up again and again. Up here, in the middle of the day, the heat prickling against her skin, Artemis could try to make sense of what had happened – why she had survived while her sister, Helena, who had been sleeping just a few feet away, had not. It was the same question she would sometimes see flash behind her parents' eyes when they looked at their remaining child. The question that vibrated silently between them when they fought.

It was a morbid pleasure, returning to this spot, one that offered the same eerie solace now as it had then, when the bullying was at its worst. Back then, Artemis would sneak out through the back door of the school at the end of the day, running all the way up the path to the ruins of her old family home. It was here that she would sit and wait until she knew the boys who would otherwise have taunted her all the way back to the bakery would have grown bored and headed home to their mothers. No one, not even Athena, knew that she came up here, back then or now. There weren't many things she had to herself on an island as small and as incestuous as this one, but this spot was her own private world.

Reaching into her bag, she pressed play and turned the volume up to full before pulling out a sketchbook and pencil. As the tip of the lead touched the paper, she felt a hand on her shoulder. The unexpected contact caught her off-guard and she lurched away from it; feeling herself about to fall, her hands gripping the inside of the wall.

The man touched her shoulder again, this time to steady her. 'Whoa. Are you OK? I didn't mean to scare you . . .'

He spoke in English.

'I'm fine.' She shook her head. Something about the look of concentration on his face made her expression soften into a reluctant half-smile. 'Oh, it's you.' She paused. 'Honestly, I'm fine . . .'

'Bloody hell, you speak English?' he said.

'Better than your Greek,' she replied, rubbing her arm where he had grabbed it.

'Well, it's all Greek to me.' He laughed, without blushing, and she remembered the self-belief on this man's face as he'd asked her about one of her paintings in the gallery, the previous Saturday. He was a few years older than she was, maybe twenty-eight or twenty-nine, and a commanding presence in every respect. Twice he had been into the gallery in the past couple of weeks, poring over the strokes of her brush on the canvas. It wasn't unusual to see the same faces again and again at the height of summer, given the scale of the island, but something about this particular face had caught her attention.

'I was actually going to ask you directions,' he ploughed on. 'I came for a walk and I appear to have got a bit lost.'

'Really? Where are you staying?' she asked.

'I'm not quite sure. That's the thing about being lost, you see,' he replied, rubbing his chin. 'I've bought a house here. I say *house* – it's more of a shack, really. Just over . . .' He looked at her and shrugged, as if where it might be was no longer of relevance. 'Somewhere over there.'

She laughed, despite herself. There was something vaguely ridiculous about the prospect of this man ever being lost.

'What's your name?' he asked.

She paused. 'Artemis.'

'Artemis.' He repeated it, enunciating each syllable, and she felt a chill brush over the backs of her knees.

'Clive, Clive Witherall,' he replied, reaching out a hand and holding her with his eyes until she had to blink.

Madeleine

London, two days before Anna dies

Madeleine wakes to the sound of the cleaner hoovering in the apartment below. The same time every week, as if anyone is ever around to drop a crumb. As if those bloody Saudis hadn't simply bought the place as a convenient means to shaft excess cash into the ever-obliging anals of the British banking system, and perhaps while away a weekend or two every year in a city in the throes of a housing crisis. Did she mean *annals*, Gabriela had attempted to correct her when she complained about her new neighbours, the week they arrived. Did she hell.

Where is Gabriela, she wonders, inserting a Nespresso capsule into the machine and slamming at the handle with her palm. There is something going on with her, but then when isn't something going on? Madeleine should call her, but Christ, she's only just home from Krakow and there is so much to catch up on and she is *tired*. Of course, she wouldn't dare utter such words to her friend – tiredness, after all, is Gabriela's personal domain; woe betide a woman without children who claims exhaustion.

But the fact is, the past weeks away have been relentless. As always, while she was in Poland, meeting with her international counterparts, she had felt an emboldening, a willingness to focus on perceptions of progress: on the women's lives being saved, the meting out of justice. But back in London, she finds it harder to be optimistic.

Sipping at her coffee, she thinks of her office at the National Crime Agency – the lack of resources and the absence of actual investigators – and feels herself physically slump. Not that she can talk. She didn't join the NCA from its previous incarnation as the Serious Organised Crime Agency, or any other part of the police force, but from – cue all manner of imaginative hand gestures from her colleagues – the Foreign Office. Not that it really matters where they all hail from: they're in it together now, not so much making shit happen as pushing shit uphill.

Rolling her shoulders and cracking out her back, Madeleine picks up her phone from the counter along with her cup, scrolling through her emails as she moves back into the bedroom, pulling out an outfit from the rows that line the walk-in wardrobe. Dropping her heels into her handbag, she slips on a pair of trainers and strides out of the house, turning right onto Marylebone Lane, towards Oxford Circus tube.

It is a few minutes' walk from Vauxhall station to the NCA: a faceless grey building just metres from MI5 – a markedly different affair from the organisation's glossy old headquarters on the fringes of St James's Park. It is hard to know whether they are being closely monitored by their new neighbours, or simply not considered worth the flashy postcode. Either, or perhaps both.

It could be a worse location, though. The office is situated opposite a wall of bars and gay clubs that have been shamefully sanitised since her days on the scene. Those days feel like a lifetime ago now, but the proximity to these memories serves as a reminder of what is possible, even if the memories have grown woefully faded. More's the pity. Is there anything sadder than a lapsed tart? The lack of sex certainly isn't for lack of want, it's just that there's no time these days. She will make time, she tells herself as she strides into reception, then shoves the thought to the back of her mind where she intends to pick up on it again later.

Madeleine has paperwork to catch up on, keeping the international agencies abreast of where they are at since their recent intervention: sixteen girls brought across the border in the back of a van from Vietnam, eight of them dead on arrival. She is pulling a croissant from her bag when Sean from Intelligence pokes his head around the door.

'Can I get your eyes on this?'

Madeleine looks up, taking a bite before speaking. 'Depends what it is.'

Sean walks towards her, holding a case file. 'It's kind of between us. Official and unofficial. It's about Vasiliev . . .'

Madeleine talks as she chews. 'Remind me.'

In the three years since she had joined the agency, gratefully relinquishing her position in the anti-trafficking department at the FCO, Madeleine has only spoken to Sean a handful of times, but from their fleeting communication she has drawn the conclusion that the title Sean from Intelligence is something of an oxymoron.

'Irena Vasiliev. She's a Russian national. We've been investigating her for years on various charges, with a number of international police forces, but with the assistance of Moscow she continues to evade arrest. Her name came up again recently in an investigation we're working on relating to an international VAT carousel case worth billions. You're not in on that, are you?'

Madeleine shakes her head. 'Nothing to do with me.'

'OK, well these so-called carousels are incredibly lucrative and notoriously hard to arrest on. Fraudsters claim the reimbursement of VAT from the tax office, for tax they never paid in the first place. Legally, VAT is only supposed to be paid by the final buyer of a product, but in cases like this, by trading goods between EU member states several times and exploiting the fact that no VAT is due on cross-border trades owing to different member states having different VAT rates, criminal organisations can play the system.'

Madeleine looks at him with an expression of feigned disbelief. 'What, our system? But surely not, it's so robust!'

Sean rolls his eyes. 'So, in this case money is being made from selling mobile phones, video consoles and – strange as it sounds – certificates for carbon dioxide emissions . . . And there are British companies involved too. The way they make money is this: for example, a man in Germany buys, say, a mobile phone in France at zero per cent VAT. He can then sell it on to another trader in Germany with a nineteen per cent surcharge. Now officially, he is obliged to pass that money on to the tax office, but instead, he keeps the money. And by the time the tax office in any given country has noticed, the trader – read: thieving bastard – has disappeared.'

Madeleine nods. 'Got it.'

'Which is why he is called a missing trader, and this type of crime is also known as "Missing Trade Intra-Community" or MTIC – you know how we love an acronym.'

Madeleine winks at him. 'Don't I just.' She looks at her watch. 'I don't mean to be rude but—'

'This Irena Vasiliev,' Sean ploughs on. 'At the time we started looking into her, she was running eleven businesses, mostly registered in other people's names. The money she made, which amounts to billions, comes, in part, from the tax she stole by moving the merchandise in circles across borders. Without paying VAT, she tricked the authorities into paying herself and her partners money they were never owed. Crimes of this sort are estimated by the EU Commission to create an annual tax loss of around fifty billion euros. Now these deals involve highly sophisticated lawyers and bankers in order to help engineer the trades. In this case, a London-based lawyer – one James McCann – registered to an office on Queen Square . . .

'Anyway, they're litigious bastards and we have to be careful how we come at this, but, while the MTIC case is moving painfully slowly, thanks to a number of factors – not least trying to tee up with our international counterparts – another investigation is looking more hopeful.'

'Remind me how I fit into this?' Madeleine asks, taking another bite.

'The problem is – and it's this I wanted to consult you on – when we were looking into Vasiliev on these other charges, another name came up . . . Vasiliev's man in the UK is a guy called Ivan Popov. Heard of him? No reason why you should have. He's a slick one. Rich as Croesus. Has a big house on the river over in Richmond, runs a couple of above-board companies here in London – but his main source of income is as Irena Vasiliev's front man. What I haven't yet mentioned is that among her many sidelines, Vasiliev is also into human trafficking. And as part of that revenue stream, her man Popov is the one supplying student visas to traffickers, facilitating their movement between countries.'

'OK, so human trafficking *is* very much my department's remit,' Madeleine says.

'Exactly,' Sean nods tentatively. 'And that's the *official* reason I came to you . . .'

Madeleine stops chewing. 'And the unofficial reason?'

Sean pauses. 'There are corruption charges we're working on, too; they should be easier to make stick . . . Popov's housemaid is working for us; she's been tapping his phone lines and has uncovered all sorts of conversations involving bribes to government officials abroad, in return for accepting their business relating to their seemingly more legitimate energy companies . . . But something else has come up. Popov has a girlfriend; they have a baby together . . . The woman, she's ex-FCO.'

Madeleine's eyes light up. 'You're fucking kidding me.'

'I'm fucking not.'

'Well, that was worth waiting for. Is she in on it?'

'I don't know yet. I just spotted her name. Wanted to bring it to you in case you had ever worked together in your time on the dark side . . .'

Madeleine rolls her eyes. 'It's no darker at the FCO than it is

here, let me tell you. Just with budget for slightly better lighting
. . . Is that her?'

The file is upside down as he hands it over. As Madeleine turns
it towards herself, she feels her stomach drop.

For a moment, she says nothing as she stares at the photo,
processing what is unfolding in front of her. It is as if the rest of
the world has dissolved, her attention entirely fixed on the image
of the woman walking along Richmond High Street, her hands
wrapped around the handles of a pram: even beneath the sunglasses,
she is instantly recognisable, the same mass of hair falling in front
of her face.

And then Sean's voice breaks the silence. 'So, do you know her,
this Gabriela Shaw?'

Madeleine pauses, wishing to slow down time, to give herself
adequate space to think this through. But when she looks up again,
a moment later, Sean is staring at her. The only answer she can give
is the truth.

'Yes,' she says, taking a seat. 'I know her.'

Artemis

Greece, the Eighties

Clive's place stood a few metres from the road. She eyed him with a narrow gaze as they approached the spot where the path thinned, growing knotted with trees.

'I lied,' he said brazenly. 'I wasn't lost. I saw you sitting there on the wall and I decided to speak to you . . . You come up here a lot.'

'You've been watching me?' Something about this quiet invasion of her privacy both thrilled and unnerved her.

He didn't answer and she inhaled the smell of burnt pine, enjoying the muted sounds of the island, little clouds of dust rising at their feet as they padded along the dirt track, which gave way to olive groves and a small house.

'It's where we lived. Our house was back there,' Artemis said, by way of explanation for why she had been sitting on the wall. Clive stopped.

'Really? Before the earthquake, I take it?'

She took the hairband from her ponytail and shook out her hair, looking away from him. Why had she brought it up?

'Don't worry, I was only five. I don't remember it, not really,' she replied, obscuring her face with dark brown curls. 'It's a nice spot for painting, it's peaceful . . . At least it was, until you came along and tried to push me off the edge of a cliff.'

'Yes. Sorry about that,' he said. 'But you didn't fall, so that's the main thing.'

She smiled, a fluttering in her chest as her hand brushed accidentally against his. 'That's OK,' she replied, emboldened by his attentions. 'As long as you don't try it again.'

Clive's cottage stood over two floors on the edge of the mountain, with painted blue shutters and a small Juliet balcony overlooking untended olive groves rolling down towards the edge of the mountain, and the sea beyond.

It was impossible to fathom how this tiny house had survived the earthquake when every other building around it had been blown apart, and something about its survival gave it an otherworldly quality, as if it existed in isolation, untouched by the vulnerabilities of the rest of the world.

Artemis felt her head lower, almost reverentially, as Clive led her into the cool shade of the dark stone kitchen, which had just enough space for a cooker and a couple of shelves along the far wall, a small dining table to the right of the door. It smelt of wood and citronella, and against the left wall was a recently erected staircase leading up to the mezzanine level. As she looked up at the stairs, Artemis felt a sudden chill.

'The stairs and the upper floor were the only things that were damaged, amazingly,' Clive said, following Artemis' gaze around the house.

She wrapped her arms against her chest for warmth. 'Did you rebuild it yourself?'

Clive nodded proudly. 'Want to have a look?' Noting her expression, he added, 'Don't worry, I have insurance, in case you fear the robustness of my treads . . .'

'I trust you,' Artemis replied, placing a tentative foot on the first step. In that moment, she had no reason not to.

There were two rooms upstairs. The second was empty, the first sparsely furnished with a neatly made bed, a copy of a book entitled *In Search of Excellence* placed on the pillow.

She felt him moving close behind her, the hairs on her arms lifting in the relative cool of the house.

'What are you reading?' she said.

Clive grimaced. 'Ah yes, that. Not very alluring, I'm afraid. It's a business book, by a couple of Americans. It's . . . well, it's all very American. But what can I say? I've just started my own company and I'm looking to expand so I need all the advice I can get.'

Artemis was impressed. 'What sort of business?'

'Import/export, trading. All *highly* sexy. But it keeps me busy and I get to travel.'

'You work alone?'

'For now. My old pal Jeff does the accounts, and we share an office in London so I have some company.'

'And this place, you're not planning to live in it?'

'God no,' Clive said and then caught himself. 'Not that . . . Sorry. It's an investment. But I suppose it's more than that. A contact of Jeff's suggested looking at this island as a place to invest and something about it . . .' He stopped and held her eye. 'Well, the whole thing is quite enchanting.'

Artemis felt her cheeks burn. Turning away from the intensity of his gaze, she placed her fingers on the handrail. Did she imagine it buckling under her weight?

'And where do you live the rest of the time?'

'In London. My parents both died within a year of each other and I inherited their house and some money and I decided to start my own business. I was working in the City before . . . But enough about me, I want to know about you.'

She visibly clammed up, imagining the words spilling from her lips: *I watched my sister die in an earthquake and did nothing to help her.*

She swallowed. 'There isn't much to tell. I grew up on the island. I was born in a house in the old village and then after the earthquake my parents moved down to the port and relocated their bakery. I work there five days a week, and . . . there's little more to say.'

'I don't believe you.'

Artemis glanced up at him, her cheeks growing hot.

'You paint,' Clive prompted her, after a beat. 'And you speak excellent English. I mean, you could have warned me when I was trying to make small talk with you in my finest pidgin Greek.'

Artemis laughed. 'Why? It was entertaining. But yes, I'm interested in languages.' She paused. 'Reading is a good escape from reality, don't they say? And I like to sketch and paint. Carolina, who owns the shop in the old village, lets me take the room at the back for free every Saturday in summer. Out of pity, I suppose—' She broke off.

'You're very talented.'

Artemis looked unconvinced.

'What, you think I'm trying to seduce you by pretending to be interested in your artwork?' He smiled. 'Why would I bother? You're already in my bedroom.'

Clive held up his hands. 'I'm joking – honestly, I'm joking. Sorry, poor taste. My mother was an artist, actually. Not professionally, but after the war, when she and her family escaped to England, she used to sketch. And honestly, your paintings . . . They're mesmeric.' He looked at her without breaking eye contact and she felt her cheeks flush.

His tone changed then. 'I tell you what, I was thinking of hiring a boat for the day tomorrow, but I'll need a skipper. Why don't you come with me? You can bring your paints.'

'I don't know.' She shook her head. Her heart was thumping in her chest, for reasons she couldn't explain.

'Why not? You've already told me you don't work on Sundays . . . See, you're giving away too much already . . .'

Artemis got the sense this was a man who got what he wanted. But for all his assertiveness, and yes, she saw it now, his *arrogance*, there was something magnetic about him. The men she knew of her own age were just as arrogant, and yet most of them with far less reason to be. And some of them weren't just arrogant, they were cruel.

She returned his gaze, a sense of anticipation building inside her. Why shouldn't she go out with him? The sensation in her stomach was part excitement, part nerves. And yet what reason did she have to be nervous?

She looked down, shaking her head in amused surrender. 'I tell you what, a new restaurant is opening tonight and I'm meeting a friend there for dinner. You could join us.'

Harry

London, the day before Anna dies

Harry has no way of recognising the woman he's due to meet, but as soon as he spots her walking towards the park bench where he sits waiting, her coat drawn against the biting wind, he knows that this is Maria.

Feeling his foot thrumming self-consciously against the tarmac, he stills his body, suddenly aware of how much he could give away. Pulling a cigarette from the packet and tapping it, out of habit, against the box, he lights up and sits back.

The conversation from earlier that day has been replaying in his mind ever since he received her call. It had played out again and again in his mind as he made his way to Regent's Park, the ramifications of what had been said rushing at him as he waited, with a growing sense of restlessness, to meet this stranger who knows a worrying amount about his life. And now she's here, walking towards him, and the only thing he can do is to pull himself together and listen.

Looking away, having a word with himself, he processes the few details he already knows of her, aside from her name – or at least the name she had given him. From this distance, he can see that the woman appears to be in her late twenties. He already knew from her accent on the phone when she rang him yesterday and asked to meet, that she was probably Greek. The call had been made from a payphone in Hampstead according to the number he had found when he re-dialled later, so even if she hadn't told him upfront

27

that her call was connected to Anna, he would have guessed at it. But he still couldn't be sure what the connection was, or who had given this woman his phone number.

'Harry?'

He looks up at her, his eyes automatically moving over her shoulder, sweeping the park for signs of anyone else who might have been following at a distance, but the area is clear.

'Maria,' she says, reaching out and shaking his hand. 'Like I said on the phone, I'm a friend of Anna's. I also believe we have another person in common.'

'Another person in common, you say?' Harry replies, taken off-guard by the lack of foreplay. He softens his voice before taking a drag of his cigarette, hoping she won't see his fingers trembling.

Maria sits, taking a moment to gather herself.

'Yes. I think until now, you and I have been working from different angles, towards the same common goal. And I think we could help each other if we joined forces.'

Harry keeps his eyes on her, not yet sure how to play this. Does she know about the meeting he has just come from? She can't, otherwise she wouldn't be here. 'Is that right?' he says simply, waiting for her to play her hand.

She looks down for a moment and then lifts her head, staring back at him. 'If you're anything like me, you're not going to want to see him get away with it. After everything we've given to bringing them to justice . . .'

'We?' He pauses, working through the various meanings.

'Yes, we . . .'

'What are we talking about here?'

Harry works hard to keep his expression cool, taking another drag of his cigarette as he looks out across sculpted hedges circling an ornamental fountain.

'I assume you've heard about David,' Maria replies, not quite answering his question.

Harry raises an eyebrow, his voice measured. 'I read something about it.'

Maria leans forward, her voice quieter.

'David's not dead.'

Harry's expression drops.

She half-laughs. 'Now you're listening? David is alive and is fleeing to the Maldives – tomorrow evening – where, as I'm sure you know, there is no extradition treaty, so once he is there, he's free. MI6, they're no longer interested. The African authorities, from what I gather, because of Nguema's involvement and how much influence he has there, aren't in a hurry to prosecute. If anyone does try to fit him up for it, there is a plan to lay the blame on Anna. So the way I see it, there are only two people left on this earth who care about bringing Clive to justice. And one of us has been asked to accompany David to the Maldives, as his mistress.'

Harry cocks his head, feeling a wave of panic rising up inside him. What the *fuck* is going on?

Attempting to hold it together, to extract as much as he can whilst giving away as little as possible, he exhales a long line of smoke. 'Well, I certainly didn't get the memo. OK, now I'm listening.'

'Anna is due to meet with Clive's solicitors about the will. David and I are meeting at the airport tomorrow afternoon. He wanted to be sure everything went smoothly in terms of Anna's reaction to the meeting she is due to have with his father's solicitors tomorrow morning, so he has been lying low at his father's flat, "getting his ducks in order", that's what you say. Right?'

Harry looks at her, trying to read her expression. She's beautiful, her direct gaze suggesting both a steeliness and a reserve that is the exact opposite of Anna in almost every respect.

He laughs tightly. 'I definitely don't say that.'

Maria pauses then, her expression changing, so that now she is the one surveying him. 'Why did you do it?'

'Do what?'

'All of it. I mean, there must have been easier ways to make money . . . Seriously, I'm intrigued. I know why *I* did it, but I can't work out . . .'

Harry pauses, his mind running over the events of the past few years, his memory hovering over the image of Anna the night he asked her to be involved – the look of triumph that passed over her face.

How much of all this does Maria know, and how long has she known it? He doesn't have time to contemplate it now. Besides, it's not important. Something surges inside him and he blinks hard, rearranging his expression into a wistful smile.

'But life's not like that, is it?' he says. 'It's not that straightforward. You must know that as well as I do. You make decisions as and when situations arise; you take steps and you never really know where they will take you. You just do what you think is right in that moment; sometimes you're right, and sometimes—' His voice stops abruptly, his face hardening as he thinks about what comes next. 'Well, maybe I was right, maybe I was wrong. Maybe we all were. It just depends what angle you're looking at it from.'

Artemis

Greece, the Eighties

Athena was late. Artemis was sitting at a table nursing a beer by the time her friend finally arrived for the opening night's celebration, a shield of bougainvillea acting as a screen between the garden of Nico's restaurant – where locals and foreigners bustled between checked tablecloths – and the outside world.

She winced inwardly at the sight of Athena's hair as she moved between the checked tablecloths and baskets of bread. Artemis recognised the hairdo as an attempt at replicating the andro-gynous bobs the girls had pored over in a copy of American *Vogue* they'd found discarded on the beach a few days earlier. Inevitably, given the coarseness of Athena's locks, the look hadn't quite translated.

'What do you think?' Athena asked, tossing her head as she pulled up a chair. Torn between brutal honesty and the preservation of her friend's feelings, Artemis prevaricated for a moment before spotting Clive walking up the steps into the restaurant.

She felt her attention gratefully drift. Following Artemis' gaze, Athena turned and they both watched him enter the bar, dressed in a pair of chinos and a pale-yellow polo shirt.

'Who is that?' Athena spoke slowly, to herself as much as to anyone else.

Artemis sat straighter as Clive moved towards them.

'Apologies I'm slightly later than planned,' he said. 'I got held up talking to one of the builders. You know what they're like: why do today what can feasibly be put off until tomorrow?'

Without hesitating, Clive leaned in and kissed Artemis on the cheek. She felt a shiver as their bodies touched.

Athena coughed and on cue, he turned towards her, his hand outstretched. 'I'm Clive, you must be Athena . . .'

Artemis watched her friend flush, and for a fleeting moment she was grateful for what Athena had done to her hair. But then as Clive turned back towards her, focusing his full attention on her face, she felt any sense of schadenfreude dissolve. It was her he wanted.

'Can I get you both a drink?'

Clive moved to the bar and Athena spun to look at Artemis, her eyes glistening. Artemis shrugged coyly. 'We met this afternoon, in the old village. He's bought a property here; he lives in London and has just started his own business. I hope you don't mind that I invited him along.'

Watching Athena's gaze swivel and follow him to the bar like a hawk marking its prey, Artemis cleared her throat.

'He's rented a boat, we're going to take it out for the day tomorrow.'

'Really?' Athena attempted to toss her hair but it barely budged. 'What time are—'

'Just the two of us.' The firmness of her tone surprised them both.

'You came,' Clive said the following morning, opening the door with a smile that stretched from ear to ear, his eyes bright despite the volume of drink he had knocked back the night before.

'Did you think I'd change my mind?' She leaned against the doorframe, breathing in the same faint smell of citronella.

'I hoped you wouldn't,' he said, leading the way inside and picking up a bag of supplies.

'After seeing your dancing I can understand your concern.' She bit her lower lip mockingly.

'Oh please, you loved it,' he retorted, his self-belief undented. 'Now, I have absolutely no idea what I've bought. I thought this was some of that smoked ham you lot do so well but on second inspection I think it might be raw bacon.'

Clive held up the packet for her to read the label and Artemis laughed. 'Yes, you might want to leave that one in the fridge.'

There was a motorbike parked in front of the house, Artemis noted as she followed him back outside.

'So the boat will be waiting for us when we get to the beach?' she asked, putting on the helmet he passed her. 'And you definitely know how to drive it?'

Clive nodded. 'I bloody hope so. Don't you have a bike? How the hell do you get around this place?'

'I have one. I just prefer to walk, unless I have to drive,' Artemis replied. She didn't add that she wasn't going to risk being seen going around the island with a strange man on the back of her bike. Not with the eyes and loose lips that lurked everywhere. And yet part of her wanted them to see what she had, what they had never believed she was capable or deserving of achieving.

Clive smiled. 'OK, well you navigate. And don't forget to hold on – these roads are laced with potholes.'

Madeleine

Madeleine arrives first at lunch the next day, ordering a large glass of wine, feeling a stab of pain as she spots her friend teetering on the pavement on the other side of the road.

Holding her fingers tightly around the stem of her glass to hide the shaking, Madeleine watches Gabriela cross towards the restaurant, looking left and right and then left again, once more than necessary, as if expecting a freight lorry to emerge from behind the blind bend and crush her beneath its weight. Does Madeleine imagine a hint of skittish excitement in her movements as Gabriela curls a handful of hair behind her ear? The truth is, she's really not clear what she sees when she looks at the woman she had until that morning considered one of her closest friends. At this point she might as well be a total stranger – and how much easier it would be if she was.

Gabriela pulls open the door to Daphne's restaurant and Madeleine feels herself flinch. Her friend moves towards the booth, a smile breaking across her face as she leans down to kiss Madeleine on both cheeks. Her skin is cold and Madeleine pulls back, moving into conversation before she has a chance to give herself away too soon, shifting her gaze to the table where her fingers cling to her glass.

'What will you drink? Wine?'

The waitress appears but Gabriela speaks directly to Madeleine. 'Actually, I think I'd like something stronger. A brandy?'

There is something almost vibrant about her face, the life bursting from it as if in a final flourish.

As the waitress disappears, Madeleine speaks more quickly than she'd intended, purging herself of the words. 'Talking of something stronger, I've just been in your old neck of the woods. I drank so much vodka I think I can still feel it in my liver.'

'Moscow?'

She doesn't even blink. Holy shit, you're good at this, Madeleine thinks. You're far too good.

'What were you doing in Russia?' Gabriela asks, her tongue running discreetly over her top lip. Madeleine holds her eye, willing her to crack, to show a chink of weakness, of remorse. Anything.

'What am I always doing? Work,' Madeleine says. 'Is there anything else in my life apart from work? God, sometimes I wonder if I'm getting this living thing all wrong. But no, I shouldn't say that, not now when things are finally coming together.'

'That's good to hear.'

Was there a shift then, almost imperceptible? An uncrossing of the legs, a rearrangement of hands under the table?

'Anyway . . .' Madeleine smiles stiffly. 'We always end up talking about my work. I'm such a narcissist. Tell me about you, what's going on?'

There it is, a flicker in the left eye. As the waitress arrives and starts to dole out their drinks and a selection of starters on the table in front of them, Gabriela's mask drops just a fraction. Not so much that Madeleine would have noticed it if she hadn't been looking, but she is looking now – albeit too late – and yet she still can't be quite sure what is staring back at her.

Gabriela's voice is slightly higher pitched when she speaks again. 'No, tell me about Moscow. I'm interested, it's been so long since I was there.'

'Has it?'

Gabriela looks up too quickly, her gaze meeting Madeleine's and then focusing immediately away again, her cheeks turning red. It would be wrong to say that Madeleine is enjoying this, but at last she feels something start to tear, her fingers catching hold and pulling gently but persistently enough to rip through to whatever lies beneath.

'Well, I shouldn't tell you this, but we always share things with each other, don't we?'

Does Gabriela notice, Madeleine wonders, the catch in her voice?

'Besides, who are you going to tell, right? So you know how I told you we were closing in on some of the peripheral figures? Well, one of those is a Russian-owned company . . .'

Madeleine pauses, giving her friend one last chance to intercept, to launch in with the truth – but the rocket has already taken off. They are both already flailing through space, the air thinning, and time to attach their oxygen tanks is running out.

'But there are a few things we need to tie up first,' Madeleine says, and Gabriela doesn't even look up this time as she replies.

'Right.' The colour drains from her face, a single vein pulsing above her left eye.

'Aren't you going to ask which company?'

Madeleine doesn't wait. 'Oh, it's one of those intentionally oblique ones – offers a breadth of legitimate services, specialising in energy supply, I believe. But like so many of these companies, they dabble in sidelines. After all, that's where the money's at, right? As well as bursts of philanthropy. In this case, a children's orphanage, no less.'

Madeleine watches as the fork slips from between Gabriela's fingers and crashes against her plate. When Madeleine speaks again, she can barely suppress an acid note of scorn.

'Gaby, is something wrong?'

Artemis

Greece, the Eighties

She had dreaded the sex in the lead-up to the first time with Clive, unable to distil the prospect of the act from the image of the teenage boy's face above hers, his rhythmic grunts drowning out her protestations. But when it finally happened, in the bed upstairs in Clive's cottage, the moonlight spilling in through the cracks in the shutters, Artemis felt herself give into him in a way she would never have thought possible.

It was more than relief that flooded her body as she lay silently in the bed next to him, listening to him catch his breath, the sweetness of the scent of their sweat overpowering her. There was something restorative about that time together, as if this level of intimacy could atone for all the years she had been alone.

After that, she craved those moments together, as though with every thrust she was pushing the memory of Jorgos deeper inside herself until she could no longer feel it.

The day Clive left the island after their initial month together, Artemis convinced herself she would never see him again. He'd had his way with her and now he was gone, and she was grateful that she'd ever had him, even if only for a brief moment.

It was hard to tell if Athena was disappointed or secretly jubilant when Clive left. While Artemis' best friend could hardly conceal the thrill she felt in Clive's company, making a fool of herself with her constant vying for his attention, she must have felt some relief when he was gone again and equilibrium between her and Artemis was restored. It wasn't that Athena was a bad friend, it was just that things had always been a certain way. The balance of power between them was delicate, if basic. To Athena, it didn't matter that Artemis was the more beautiful of the two because as far as the boys on the island were concerned, she was untouchable. She had no power here and therefore she was no threat.

If years of watching Artemis being taunted for the regular accidents in class, as well as for her father's eccentric behaviour in the village, hadn't been enough to put the boys off, then Jorgos' recounting of what had happened between them that afternoon certainly had. Artemis could never be sure exactly what version of the day's events he had told the other boys, but she recognised the shapes of their words perfectly when they saw her after that. Slut. Whore.

Their taunts haunted her for years – until she met Clive. From then on, his wanting of her pushed out any sense of shame.

The only boy who had been kind to her after what happened with Jorgos was Panos. Briefly, she had wondered whether he might like her in the way that boys her age liked other girls in her class. But of course it had been Athena he was interested in all along. Artemis had felt foolish for reading something into the occasional kind glances he had given her, for having thought, even for a moment, that they had meant anything more than pity.

Over the years, Artemis had become accustomed to never being the one who was chosen. But then there was Clive and he did choose her – and the shift that came that first summer with him marked a fracturing in the foundations of her friendship with Athena that could never be fixed.

The first time Clive showed up after that, lingering outside the bakery one afternoon out of the blue after months away and not a word, Artemis felt her skin tingle with fury and desire.

'What are you doing here?' she hissed at him, walking past and waiting for him to follow, leading into a sliver of alleyway between two buildings opposite the port, away from prying eyes.

'What kind of welcome back is that?' he asked, amused, turned on by the subterfuge. 'Nice hat, by the way.'

She pulled off the hairnet she wore to work, her cheeks hot with more than the hours she had spent in front of the oven.

'You didn't tell me you were coming back.'

'Yes, I did.'

'OK, well I didn't believe you and you didn't say *when* . . .'

He looked baffled. 'I have a house here. Anyway, even if I didn't have, how could I not come back for you? You need to have more faith in me.'

He looked at her and leaned in for a kiss, taking her face in his hands.

'Fuck, I've missed you,' he said and she kissed him back before pulling away.

'I can't, not here.'

'Why not?'

'Go up to the house, I'll meet you there in a while.'

She felt him watching her as she walked away, pressing her fingers against her lips, her pulse vibrating so that she could barely breathe.

'How was London?' she asked, once they were alone, her body turned towards his on the bed. Clive ran a finger down the line of her arm.

'Lonely.'

Artemis looked away from him, desperate to know but unwilling to ask if there had been anyone else between then and now.

'How long are you staying for?' she asked quietly.

'Depends,' Clive replied. 'I have a few meetings planned. I'll have to see how those go.'

He ran his finger down her chest towards her belly button. 'Anyway, I'm here now, so let's make the most of it . . .'

Over the following months, Clive came back to the island intermittently. Every time he would hunt her down within hours of arriving. He missed her, he was not too proud to say it, and she missed him, too – she missed his confident reassurance, the way he looked at her like what she said actually mattered. She missed the way that when he was there, it was like being pulled out of her own mind and dragged into another world – a world inside which she could imagine she was someone else entirely.

'Where are you going?' Artemis asked one morning after she woke in Clive's bed. She sat up, wrapped in his bedsheet, as he walked up the stairs towards her, dressed in his signature chinos and polo shirt. A shard of light from the window illuminated his face so that she could hardly make out his features. He smelt of freshly laundered washing, his hair slightly shorter since he'd returned to the island this summer.

'I didn't want to disturb you . . . I'm going to meet someone in Skiathos. I'm catching the Dolphin across in half an hour.'

'That's OK, I should get up anyway.' Artemis smiled, stretching her arms above her head. 'My parents will be wondering where I am.'

'I thought you told them you'd stayed at Athena's,' Clive said, leaning across from the bottom of the mattress to kiss her.

'I did. But still . . .'

Artemis was twenty-four years old; she was a grown-up. Contemporaries from school were already married with kids by now – even those who didn't deserve such happiness. Jorgos' face flashed in her mind. She didn't know if he was married or not – only that he had moved away. That was all she needed to know. The sense of relief after all these years of terror – knowing that she could walk outside without having to scour the streets for him – was indescribable. Though the memories he had left behind were harder to shake.

There was no reason to introduce Clive to her parents. To Markos, Clive – a foreigner – represented the very thing he believed, in his irrational mind, was responsible for the dead weight inside him. Her mother would simply either worry or have her hopes unnecessarily raised and then dashed. Either way, it would not end well. This was a short-term arrangement, and Artemis knew that was all it could ever be. She wasn't so naive. Clive would be gone again soon, and what was to stop him returning the next time with a girlfriend or a wife on his arm?

'Artemis?' Clive's eyes were fixed on her. 'Are you listening?'

'I was just thinking,' she said, lifting off the sheet and walking over to meet him on the landing. 'If you give me five minutes, I'll walk part way with you.'

'God, you're beautiful,' he said, looking her up and down, and she smiled, despite herself.

No, it could not last, but she would enjoy it while it did. She would be hurt when it was over, but that was already an inevitability; she might as well immerse herself in their time together while she had it. After all, she had no way of knowing what she was being drawn into, or how deep she would be dragged.

Artemis and Clive split paths at the top of the track that led behind the baker's, half an hour later.

'So who's this friend you're meeting?' Artemis asked as Clive leaned in to say goodbye.

'His name's Francisco,' Clive replied. 'He's not actually a friend as such, more a business acquaintance . . . he's an old university pal of my accountant, Jeff's wife – which sounds far more convoluted than it is.'

'Francisco? Is he Spanish?'

'No. Francisco Nguema . . . He's from Africa originally but studied in London and now he has a business based in Greece. Very cosmo-politan. He is the guy who recommended I try investing here, so I have a lot to thank him for . . . Are you around later?'

Artemis shrugged, with a wry smile. 'Might be.'

'Come to the house,' he said. 'I'll make dinner.'

'Really?' She cocked an eyebrow.

'Of course not, I can't cook for love nor money, as you well know. But I do know how to purchase a takeaway, and the food at Nico's is second to none.'

'My mother would challenge you on that . . .'

'Well, she'll never know, will she? If you won't introduce me to her.'

He turned away and Artemis watched him move along the dirt path to the main road that swept down to the port. As he disap-peared, she imagined him standing at the dock waiting for the passenger boat that would take him west back towards Skiathos, the horizon swallowing him whole.

'How did the meeting go?' Artemis asked that evening as they tucked into a spread of souvlaki and moussaka in the dusty olive grove behind the house, stretched out across a picnic blanket she had stolen from the bakery when her parents weren't looking, along with a basket of pastries.

'Good,' Clive said, tearing at the bread with his teeth. He always ate like he hadn't been fed in days, ravenously sinking his teeth into whatever was laid in front of him.

'So what sort of business does this man have, in Greece?'

'Francisco? Well, he runs it between here and Equatorial Guinea. Boats.'

'Boats?'

'Sexy, isn't it? Tankers, mainly. The reason he is willing to meet me is that he wants me to use his vessels to move my goods – except at the moment we are hardly working at a scale where it would make logistical sense. According to Jeff, he has a few tricks up his sleeve and wants to invest. It will help us expand and ensure him some good business. Savvy chap by all accounts.'

'Wow. How do you feel about that?'

Clive looked pensive. 'About expanding? Pretty positive, I think. He's seems like a good guy, as much as one can tell. He's a good businessman anyway. And that's what matters.'

Artemis hesitated. 'And would that mean you would spend more time here?'

Clive looked up at her, uncharacteristically coy. 'I think it might.'

He reached his hand to her face. 'I like spending time with you. You're lovely and you're beautiful. What I can't understand is why you don't already have a boyfriend.'

She felt her back stiffen. Moving herself into a different position on the blanket, she looked away from him. 'Have you met any of the men my age here?'

He laughed. 'Actually, I met one today. He's been working as a driver for Francisco – it's how he knew about this island, apparently. So really this man is responsible for us ever meeting.'

Artemis took a bite. 'Really?'

'Nice guy. I don't suppose you know him – his name's Jorgos Constantine.'

Madeleine

London, the day before Anna dies

There are so many things Madeleine wants to ask, but there is no time. For now, above all, a single question needs answering.

'Did you know?'

One look at Gabriela's face gives her the answer she needs.

Madeleine closes her eyes, overcome with relief and contempt. It is almost worse, in a way, that her friend clearly had no idea who she was getting involved with. How could you not have known? Madeleine wants to ask. She wants to take Gabriela by the shoulders and shake her. *How could you not have looked more deeply and discovered who he really was?* And yet, even if she had dug, what would she have found? These people are sophisticated, they know how to cover their tracks. Besides, in order to find the truth you had to be willing to believe it.

A woman who is willing to live a double life, to betray her children as well as her partner – could she be counted on to ask the right questions of herself, let alone of anyone else? Madeleine curses herself for such a misogynistic judgement, but it is true, and she, for one, is willing to look the truth in the eye, even if she hates what is staring back at her.

'We met at a restaurant, the one Emsworth always took us to—'

Madeleine pictures their old FCO boss, Guy Emsworth, at the Italian bistro on Crown Passage, his unofficial second office.

'Madeline. I—' Gabriela attempts to take her hand.

Madeleine pulls her fingers away sharply. She doesn't raise her voice, she doesn't even look up, leaning into her bag and extracting a pad from which she tears a single sheet of paper. Without looking at Gabriela, she scrawls down an address.

'I'm going to show you this and you need to memorise it – then I'm going to tear up the paper.'

Gabriela nods.

'You will drive as soon as possible to where I need you to go. You will tell Tom and the children to meet you there. Someone will meet you here.' Madeleine indicates towards the name of the British ferry terminal scrawled on the paper she is holding up. 'He will tell you what you need to do next. Have all your passports.'

'When?'

'Soon. I'll call you with further information. You need to go straight home and gather your things.'

Madeleine doesn't want to commit with details just yet, not only because she can't be certain Gabriela isn't being bugged – much as she thinks that Gabriela isn't in on it, she cannot wholly trust anything she says. How can she? But it's also a matter of logistics – she has not yet decided who she can trust with this task. Too many lives are at stake.

She had discussed it directly with Sean, not long after the big revelation. After admitting she and Gabriela had worked together – keeping the details brief – they had agreed that for the safety of the children, at the very least, this couldn't be handled in-house. There had been too many leaks already; it was impossible to think Vasiliev didn't have a man, or woman, on the inside passing information back to her.

For all her anger towards Gabriela – and there is plenty of that – Madeleine is desperate to get this right. Whomever Madeleine chooses to be the one to usher Gabriela to safety has to be the right person, and Sean, to his credit, understands that Madeleine is the one to seek that person out. So she had been wrong about Sean, she had conceded as she made her way home from the office after his revelation, and yet that was hardly surprising. We are wrong about people all the time. People can surprise you, for better or for worse. That is one fact of which she can be sure.

She has to act quickly. Once Popov is arrested, Vasiliev will be targeting Gabriela and her family, culling those who might speak out.

'Have you memorised it?' Madeleine asks, signalling towards the words on the paper she is holding up.

Gabriela nods.

Without another word, Madeleine stands. She hesitates for a second, blinking hard as she tears the paper into tiny pieces. As she turns away from the friend she will never see again in this lifetime, she closes her eyes and feels the burn behind them.

Madeleine pauses for a moment, waiting for Gabriela to say something, but she says nothing. She doesn't even say thank you.

Madeleine clutches the door handle for the duration of the taxi ride from Daphne's restaurant to her flat on Bulstrode Street. It is only when the car stops that she notices she is doing it. For a moment she simply sits, holding herself there in the sudden stillness of the vehicle, not ready to process what has just happened.

'We stopping here or what?' the driver asks, the sudden burst of noise over the speaker in the back of the cab puncturing the silence.

'Yes,' Madeleine says, steadying her voice, righting herself again, ready to take action. Reaching into her handbag, she notices the indentation of the door handle on the skin of her palm as she pulls a twenty-pound note from her purse.

Her heels make a clattering sound as she steps out onto the pavement. Moving towards the front door, she blocks out the sound of afternoon life bustling on as ever along Marylebone Lane.

Gabriela will be back at home by now, Madeleine calculates as she enters the townhouse. She'd had it divided into flats after her father had died – it was one thing living in the house she had grown up in, between stints abroad as part of her father's diplomatic career, but quite another to do so with her childhood ghosts hanging around to bother her. There had been a time she had wanted to sell the whole thing, to start anew, but what would be the point? You didn't get two chances to purchase a pad like this, right in the heart of Marylebone, certainly not with stamp duty and all the other taxes that would soon eat into any profit. So when it was suggested that she split it into two apartments and sell one off, she didn't think twice. Just as she hadn't thought twice at the time about handing over the keys to owners who would never use it. It was one thing having a moral high ground in the abstract, and another refusing a shit-ton of cash when you needed it. She is a hypocrite, she accepts that fact mournfully. We all are.

She thinks of Gabriela without emotion, forcing herself to push her own feelings aside. There is no time for that. The children will still be at school, which will give their mother time to gather their things without causing alarm. Tom might be home, but what she does or doesn't tell him now is none of Madeleine's concern. As long as he goes with her, which surely even with all that is happening he will have to understand is necessary . . . That is all that matters now.

But first, Madeleine has to get a plan in place, to sort out the arrangements, as promised. Beyond that, Gabriela is on her own. She has to be: her life depends on it.

Artemis

It had been Clive's idea. He had said it like it was the most obvious thing in the world, so obvious that Artemis had been stunned into submissive silence. A baby? They were sitting on the boat, bobbing on the surface of the water seemingly miles from shore, the stretch of beach behind them coming in and out of focus like an optical illusion.

At first she had stared at him in disbelief. How would that even work? They were still living in different countries, with Clive visiting every few months, and when they were together they would conduct their relationship in the privacy of the old village, Artemis still refusing to risk being exposed.

It was a charade, of course. However careful they might have been to stay away as much as possible from prying eyes, the island was like a fishbowl. There was no way her parents hadn't heard the rumours that would no doubt be crackling across the parched scrubland, but so far Rena and Markos had chosen to ignore them – or at least they had chosen not to confront them head on. Athena, who had done little to conceal her jealousy over her friend's ensnaring of exactly the kind of man she had wanted to snag for herself, had simply refused to acknowledge their relationship. As far as she was concerned, Artemis and Clive as a couple didn't exist, despite all the evidence to the contrary.

'OK, where would we live?' Artemis said after a while, taking a swig from a bottle of beer, playing along.

'London.'

'I can't just move to London.'

'Why not?'

Her jaw went slack as she tried to think up reasons, beyond the obvious fact that she had no more connection to the place than she had to the moon.

Clive pushed again. 'You'll love it.'

Would she? She tried to picture it: the heaving crowds at Camden Market overlaid with the stench of incense and cheap meat; the gigs at the Dublin Castle, the pub Clive had described one night as they lay between the trees, staring up at the stars.

He had sent her a letter not long after he'd last returned to London – a single sentence, 'I miss you', on a sheet of white A5 paper. Inside, was a photo of a house with tiled steps leading to the front door, wisteria hanging over the arch. On the back of the photo, Clive had written, 'In case you wanted to picture where I am now.'

There was something so intimate about the gesture, something so tender . . . the house itself was beautiful, and yet something about it had unnerved her.

She dismissed the memory now, focusing on his question: *why not?*

It was a fair enough question, in a sense. There were certainly alluring details in the world Clive described – the homes of John Keats and Sigmund Freud, all within spitting distance of Clive's family house. Irresistible snippets of history embedded in his beloved corner of North London, and yet when she tried to picture the scene beyond the framework of the house itself it was all too vague, too fanciful ever to try to place herself within it.

Maybe she just wasn't trying hard enough. Was she really intent on spending her whole life here, on the island? When she thought of staying, her blood ran as cold as when she imagined what it would mean to leave.

Though the prospect of seeing Jorgos again had plagued her for a while after Clive mentioned their meeting, Artemis had pushed it to the back of her mind. As far as she knew, he was still living on Skiathos, and the likelihood of him coming back to the island to visit and her bumping into him was no greater than it had been before. Besides, there was no reason for her to be afraid of him, was there? He couldn't hurt her. Not any more.

Clive's voice interrupted her thoughts. 'What's here for you? I mean what's *really* here – beyond your parents and the job at the bakery? You want more than that, I know you do, even if you deny it. You could open a gallery in London, a proper gallery . . .'

'I don't want to talk about it,' she said, turning away from him. Could he not understand what a betrayal it would be to leave? She was the only child her parents had left. And yet, was Helena's absence really the reason she felt compelled to stay?

'I brought you something,' Clive said, reaching into his bag and pulling out a small black leather box. He opened it to show a necklace resting on a bed of cream-coloured silk. For a moment, Artemis was reminded of the image of Snow White laid out in her coffin.

'It was my mother's,' Clive said, without looking up at her.

She closed her eyes as he clasped the amethyst necklace around her throat.

'It's perfect,' he said, letting the hair fall against her back. 'It's as if it was made for you.'

The necklace felt a little tight as she breathed in but it would be wrong to mention it. Instead she turned and leaned into him.

'Thank you, it's perfect.'

Madeleine

London, the day before Anna dies

The house throbs with heat. Madeleine must have forgotten to turn off the radiators and radio before leaving this morning, and the sound of a Chopin nocturne rings out of the speakers. Moving across the room, she slams her palm on the off-button and pulls her phone from her handbag.

She hasn't spoken to Harry in months and for a moment she wonders if he might be bunkered down somewhere, already undercover, his phone strategically abandoned in a drawer on the boat where he lives. Scrolling through to his name, she presses call, closing her eyes and opening them again when the phone starts to ring.

'To what do I owe this pleasure?'

Her body sags with relief at the sound of his voice.

'Harry. I need a favour. It's important. Are you around tomorrow?'

Gabriela hadn't even said thank you.

This is the thought that criss-crosses Madeleine's mind as she makes her way to King's Cross the next morning.

Even after Madeleine had slipped the papers across the table to her, giving her time for the words to sink in as she read.

Mr Ivan Popov is director of a number of global companies. One of them is GEF Energy Ltd, a business engaged in the provision of renewable energy and solar power. The ownership of GEF is divided between an investment company and another company, the Stan Group, registered to the British Virgin Islands.

Even after Madeline had explained about Gabriela's partner Popov being implicated in bribery related to his efforts running one of Vasiliev's companies outside of Russia. Even when she had told her that Vasiliev had had Gabriela tailed by investigators and that when Vasiliev had confronted Popov with evidence of Gabriela's other life, he hadn't believed her, it hadn't occurred to Gabriela to show any gratitude. Madeleine had told her this out of kindness, out of a misplaced sense of duty to an old friend. Even then, Gabriela hadn't said thank you to Madeleine for saving her neck.

Madeleine sometimes wonders about the men she encounters in her line of work: the traffickers, the paedophiles. So often, when she gets them face-to-face, they display signs of what she can only describe as a God complex: an unwavering belief that their needs are paramount, that they are wholly deserving of the life they chose, and that they will get away with it. With Gabriela, it is hard to know if she is deeply narcissistic or just naive. And yet whatever she might have been planning, long-term, Gabriela no longer has a choice, either way. Not any more. Vasiliev knows who she is and the moment Popov is arrested, which will be any minute now, before he can flee to Moscow, Gabriela's life – and those of her children – will be in terrible danger.

Even Gabriela will have to understand that. For as long as they live, she and Tom are shackled together – and there is nothing either of them can do to escape. They may never have married but they, more than anyone, were wedded together: until death do them part.

Artemis

The speed with which Artemis became pregnant shocked them both, though perhaps there was an inevitability to it. Clive approached sex with the same hunger that he showed for food. She had heard people talk about submitting to their partner in bed, but that suggested an element of coercion or one-sidedness that didn't resonate with her own experience. What surprised Artemis about the physicality between them was how fiercely she wanted him back. When she thought about the fact of her pregnancy, once it had happened, she saw it as an inevitability; there was an urgency to the energy that ran between them that would result in producing a new life – a life over which, once born, she had no control.

'I'm not sure about this,' Artemis said suddenly as they approached the port, when the day finally came to share the news with her parents.

From the footpath where she and Clive now stood, she could just make out the outline of her father's body under the awning. Her mother was seated beside him at the table where they were due to have their first meal all together, away from the house. Markos had resisted at first – why go out and pay to eat when Rena's cooking was better than any restaurant could produce? But Artemis had been uncharacteristically insistent and her mother, sensing the importance of it, backed up her daughter's arguments. She was tired, Rena said, not in the mood to cook. They should go out. Artemis had shot her a grateful look. It was as though Rena intuitively understood that this conversation, whatever it might entail, had to happen somewhere outside of their four walls – somewhere that wasn't Markos' domain.

Her parents had met Clive a few times by now. Despite her apprehension, they had accepted his presence in their daughter's life in a way that made Artemis believe things might be OK after all.

When she saw Rena and Markos waiting for them now, her mother dressed in her smartest clothes beneath the awning of Yannis' bar, she realised it wasn't apprehension she was feeling, but rage. Rage for all those years when Rena and Markos must have heard her crying at night but never came to ask her why she wept. Rage for the times they placed their own trauma at the loss of their dead child above the needs of the one who had lived. The fury that suddenly rose through her as she stood watching them in the black-ness of the evening, her parents' faces illuminated under the lights of Yannis' bar, was shocking. After everything she had been through, not only had they failed to offer the warmth she had so badly needed in the years after Helena died, but they had trapped Artemis here, enabling her fear; allowing her to believe it wouldn't be fair on them for her to go.

She felt her heels press down into the tarmac, as if pushing against what had been and, instinctively, what was to come. Feeling her resistance, Clive squeezed her fingers inside his. He stopped and turned to face her, his eyes moving discreetly towards her belly.

'You're not having second thoughts?'

'No, of course not.' She held his gaze. 'I just, maybe it would be better if I spoke to my parents alone . . .'

'Don't be ridiculous,' Clive said reassuringly. 'We are doing this together. What are you so scared of? You're twenty-six, you're not a child. Besides, it's happy news . . .'

He applied further pressure to her hand, before releasing it. 'Come on. Let's not keep them waiting.'

Clive stepped ahead of her, stretching out his hand as they approached. 'Markos.'

Artemis saw her father's posture stiffen at the presence of the man who had stepped in and stolen the heart of his daughter. Artemis had always thought of Markos as a big man but she watched him physically shrink in Clive's presence. Everything about her new paramour commanded space and attention, and even Markos could not resist compliance.

'Rena . . . *Kalispera.*' Clive saved a special smile for Artemis' mother, kissing her lightly on both cheeks, trying out one of the few Greek phrases he had learnt over the intermittent months he had spent on the island.

Keeping her attention on Clive, Artemis kissed her parents hello, neither seeming to notice the energy that was coming off her like fat in a pan.

With little mutual language to bolster the group in small talk, Artemis waited only as long as it took for the appetisers to arrive before she delivered the first part of the news, avoiding eye contact as she spoke. There was a brief silence and then her mother cried out, in relief. A grandchild! Even out of wedlock, a grandchild with a foreigner was better than no grandchild, and they could marry before the baby arrived. She was not so old-fashioned; they were not the most religious family. Whatever God they might have once believed in had abandoned them one night more than twenty years earlier.

And a baby was a gift . . . Rena's eyes brimmed with tears. She understood all too well what a precious gift a baby was.

Artemis couldn't stay furious with her mother as she shared the second part of their news. Once she had spoken, Rena's face dropped.

England?

Artemis hardly dared look at Markos. When she did, he stretched his mouth into a tiny smile, the best he could manage. For the first time since she was a child, she saw tears form in the corners of his eyes.

'*Yamas*,' he said, his voice gravelly, as if something was stuck in his chest. And then, in English, his eyes fixed on hers, 'To your health.'

Athena was less diplomatic when Artemis told her the news the next day. 'What do you mean, London? But you've barely even been further than Skiathos. You never even wanted to—'

'Can't you just be happy for me?' Artemis snapped at her friend. 'We're having a baby together, we have to live as a family. Clive has a job, a business in London . . . and what is there for me here? My mother's bakery? You think I want to spend the rest of my life doing the same—'

She stopped, realising what she was saying. 'I'm sorry, I didn't mean . . . Maybe you could come and stay with us . . .'

Athena turned angrily and wiped away her tears. This had been her dream for as long as either of them could remember, to find someone and move away; to start a life apart from the island. As far as Athena was concerned, Panos was only ever a stopgap, even though they had been together on-and-off since school. Artemis resented how dismissive Athena was of him; Panos was a good man, he deserved more respect, but it wasn't Artemis' place to say anything, certainly not now. After years of dismissing her friend's ambition, rolling her eyes – a self-preservation tactic to defend herself against the prospect of her best friend leaving the island – Artemis had taken Athena's dream for herself. And what – now she expected Athena to be happy for her? She was a traitor, and she knew it. In leaving, she was abandoning the only people who had ever really loved her, as well as the person who could never leave. For a moment, she let herself picture Helena's face – fair skin, the cupid's bow, the details diminished over time.

She turned away then, allowing her mind to fix in the present.

There was a ripple of satisfaction when she thought of herself leaving, a sense that she was transforming from an ugly duckling into a swan, and all those who doubted her were being forced to watch. After so many years of being complicit in her own entrapment, she was escaping the version of herself that always defined her, a version she had not chosen. So why was she shaking?

'Hey,' Artemis said, taking her friend's hand, struggling to find the words to finish the sentence. When the words came at her, what she wanted to say was that she was scared – that if it was up to her she and Clive would stay forever, even if she hated it here in so many ways. She wanted to tell Athena that there was nothing for her in England, other than the father of her child.

'Look, Clive's business is just starting to take off and for now he has to be based in London. But who knows . . .' she heard herself say instead.

'Don't,' Athena replied, pulling her hand away. 'Don't pretend you're coming back.'

Harry

Harry is shaking as he leaves the park, a wind creeping in as he walks towards the crescent of Nash buildings that line the street, Maria having gone ahead, taking with her the letter she had watched him write.

He moves slowly, letting his thoughts sprawl in front of him. This is his last chance to think.

Does he trust her? His mind darkens. Does *she* trust him? Neither of them has much choice, she must have surmised. As far as she's concerned, they are the only ones left who can help Anna.

He thinks of Clive's face earlier that day and stops dead, finally processing what is going to happen next.

Artemis

Greece, the Eighties

'You look beautiful,' Athena announced with just a hint of jealousy, as Artemis stood in front of her wearing the dress Rena had pulled out of storage and given to her daughter the week before the wedding. Maid-of-honour duties appeared to have stymied the fallout Artemis had been expecting when she told her best friend of the plan for a shotgun wedding. *Their* plan, rather – Clive and her parents. Artemis, after all, had barely been part of the conversation as the decision was made and a venue booked for before they were due to leave for England, and soon people she hadn't spoken to for months were stopping her in the street to congratulate her on her engagement.

'We need to think about the Stefana crowns . . .' Athena continued, bustling towards her and fiddling with the neckline of the dress.

'This feels a bit tight; I wonder if we can take it out a bit here. We don't want you squashing the baby.'

She pulled at Artemis' waist.

'It's not going to get squashed, I'm only going to be wearing it for a day. And I don't need a crown; Clive and I don't want something so traditional . . .'

'Rubbish,' Athena retorted. 'I know it can't be a formal religious ceremony in the traditional sense, what with . . .' she pointed at Artemis' stomach. 'But other than the vows, everything will be traditional enough. Rena and I are arranging it all, with the help of Clive's cheque book. We need to think about the menu – for the *youvetsi*, do we want lamb or beef? I think lamb.'

She answered her own question, scrawling something on the piece of paper she was holding.

'How many of Clive's friends or family are coming, has he confirmed?'

'Oh,' Artemis shrugged. 'I don't know, I hadn't thought about it.'

'I'm sure he mentioned that novelist who bought a place down by the beach would be coming. You know, the American one? I'll talk to Clive about it.'

Artemis could tell the idea of colluding with her fiancé pleased Athena. Not that it bothered her. If anything, it was flattering, her friend's little crush on her husband-to-be; she liked knowing that other people wanted him and he only wanted her. But the wedding guests? This question unfurled in front of her like an unknown flower. Who were Clive's friends? Beyond his deceased parents, did he have any family to speak of? Why didn't Artemis know these things? When she considered it, what did she really know about him at all?

Harry

Harry wakes to the muffled sound of his phone ringing. He is covered in sweat; the sound of the radio bleeds into the shift in consciousness from sleep to wakefulness as he sits up in the living area of the boat.

Pulling himself upright, he feels around for the phone which is vibrating somewhere beneath him on the sofa where he had fallen into a fretful doze that afternoon. Instantly he thinks of Maria.

Prising the phone from between two pillows, the name on the handset fills him with a rush of hope followed by fear. Why is she calling him *now*? It will be to offer him work, he reminds himself, reaching for calm. And he couldn't be more in need of a job – both for the money and the distraction it will provide.

He doesn't let himself think any further. Whatever it is that she wants, she will know where to find him.

Inhaling, resetting himself, Harry presses answer.

'Hey, Madeleine . . . How's things?'

Artemis

Greece and London, the Eighties

The night before the wedding Artemis stayed at Athena's house, kept awake by nervous excitement. Her chest vibrated with it as she listened to the occasional gasps of the sea through the gaps in the shutters.

Clive had arranged a car to take her to the venue. As Artemis stepped out of the house, she saw the driver waiting, holding the door open for her, and stopped dead.

Walking ahead, Athena spoke first, her face breaking into a smile. 'Jorgos! What are you doing here?'

Jorgos grinned back at his old school friend. 'I'm your driver for the occasion, madame.'

Athena laughed. 'I thought you were living on Skiathos these days – too hotshot for the likes of us . . .'

Jorgos turned his attention to Artemis. 'I'm doing some work with a contact of Clive and he asked if I would do the honours today. Seeing as we go back . . .'

Artemis felt bile rise in her throat. Reaching for something to steady her balance, she felt herself falling though her body remained upright. The memory was pulling her down so that she was suddenly back there: the anniversary of the earthquake. She could see it perfectly, the port bustling with people – villagers who had lost their homes coming together in the streets to mark their unity in the face of what had happened to them. She could smell the fish,

62

all sizes and shapes laid out by the fishermen just returned with their catch, as she peered in from the edges of the celebration.

Markos and Rena pointedly refused to come to these occasions on the basis that they made light of their tragedy – or rather Markos refused and Rena knew better than to argue with him on this subject, at least. Artemis had been about to go home when Jorgos stepped in front of her, blocking her path. Immediately, she took a step away from him, this boy who had taunted her mercilessly over the years. But as he stepped forward that afternoon, he had appeared contrite.

'Are you not coming to the feast?'

She shook her head, hardly daring to look at him.

'Me neither.' He paused. There was a moment's silence while she glanced warily at him, crossing her arms across her chest. He bit his lip. 'Look, I'm sorry that I was mean to you. It's just that I like you and I was embarrassed.'

She felt her guard drop, a moment of doubt instantly replaced by a flicker of hope.

'I don't suppose you want to go for a walk?' he asked.

'I can't.' She took a step away from him, her body working separately from her mind.

He held out his hand. 'Please. I'm sorry. I know I was nasty to you but I'm not really like that. Please, give me a chance?'

She inhaled, years later, coaxing herself out of the memory, struggling for breath as she returned to the present. But seeing him there, in front of her, at her wedding, she felt herself being pulled back below the surface. He was older by now, his hair pulled back in a ponytail, but his eyes had not changed. The same eyes that watched her resist as he pinned her to the spot. She could still smell his breath on her face as she kicked and screamed, the scent of bubble gum mixed with cigarette smoke.

'Artemis?' Athena looked between her friend and Jorgos. Artemis' fingers tightened around the side of her mother's wedding dress, nausea churning in her stomach. How could Athena not understand how wrong this was? Especially after she had told her what had happened . . . Except how much had she actually made clear, once she had got away from him, the day of the feast, only the skewed angle of her skirt hinting at what had just happened? She remembered the swell of sound from the port as she approached the door to the bakery, the music and voices of the celebration just streets away. She couldn't go home. Her parents would be there and there was no way that she could face them. And there was no way she could face being alone – she couldn't risk him coming for her again.

She had run from the bakery, praying that her friend would be home, and she was, filling an old water bottle with wine from her parents' fridge at the kitchen counter.

'Shit, you scared me!' Athena jumped when she heard Artemis walk in. When she saw her face, Athena's expression changed. 'What's happened?'

She tried to tell her but the words wouldn't form properly. It was as if she was underwater, the sounds turning to bubbles in her mouth, only certain phrases forming. In any case, Athena hadn't wanted to hear what she was trying to tell her, not properly.

'Jorgos? You *slut*. It's OK to feel regret. No one likes their first time. Anyway, you've done it – no one can call you a virgin any more . . . Here, have a swig of this.'

Artemis had felt sick as she drank and now, despite the intervening years, she could still taste the memory of the retsina in her throat that afternoon, as she looked at the man standing in front of her.

'Artemis?' Athena spoke again, impatience lacing her voice. 'We need to go, we're going to be late.'

Artemis felt a final surge of nausea as the car swung around the bend before closing in on the venue. Woozy, she reached for the door as the wheels came to a halt on the gravel. Light-headedness was a common side effect in this stage of pregnancy, she reminded herself, concentrating her attention on Jorgos' face as he opened the door, releasing her into the crowd.

Half the villagers seemed to have turned out for the occasion, rats crawling out of the sewers. Artemis kept her eyes on Clive where he stood on the far side of the crowd, between webs of white and blue flowers, pleated in arched formations between the tables and chairs. Keeping her focus straight ahead, she was flanked either side by Athena and Jorgos, her guards of honour escorting her to her fate.

Dancing had erupted under the canopies by the time darkness fell, the roof appearing to hem her in like the lid of a coffin. Clive was distracted talking to his friends from London – Jeff and May, and another old friend called Clarissa having descended the day before. Artemis had barely spent more than a few minutes in their company and none of them seemed to notice as she disappeared from their group now, keeping her eyes to the floor as she slipped away to the bathroom.

The sounds of the celebration muted as she closed the door behind her and moved into one of the cubicles. She stood there for almost a minute, pulling deep breaths into her lungs, before she heard the external bathroom door swing open.

'Artemis?'

It was Athena's voice. Before she could reply, her friend spoke again.

'What are you doing in here?'

Artemis opened the cubicle door and walked into the communal space, heading for the sink and splashing her face with water.

'I'm sorry,' she replied. 'I feel strange.'

'It's your wedding day, you're supposed to feel strange . . . You're also supposed to be *at* the wedding, not hiding in the bathroom messing up your own make-up. Come on, the *Kalamatianó* is starting soon – we're needed.'

All eyes turned to Artemis and Athena as they emerged on the dance floor, the beat of the music forming a death knell as they moved towards the circle. The guests clapped out a rhythm, parting ways to draw them into the circle and then clamping it shut again with their bodies.

'Dance!' Athena laughed as the movement started, the women around them locking arms, getting faster so that their bodies were spinning around them in a circle that constricted and expanded around them. The beat seemed to get louder so that soon all Artemis could hear was a rush of noise merging with her own shallow breathing. Standing back slightly from the crowd beyond, Artemis' eyes latched onto one face, watching her now with the same empty intensity that she recognised from that afternoon as he had pinned her down, his eyes inches above hers.

And then she felt herself fall.

Clive's house stood at the edge of Hampstead Heath, a blanket of calm amidst the bustle of North London.

The house was exactly as he had described it, with tiled steps leading up to a traditional Victorian front door.

Away from the busy London streets, the silence inside the house was deafening. She hadn't acknowledged the specific sounds of the island – the dragging of the nets onto the port, the calling out of the fishermen, the jangle of plates from beneath the plastic awnings of the new restaurants that had sprung up to cater for the summer visitors – until they were gone. She'd felt them recede as they stepped onto the boat to Athens, a few days after the wedding, the airport awaiting them like a portal into another world.

'Close your eyes,' Clive said as he guided her through the hallway into the living room.

'Now open . . .'

Looking up, she was greeted by one of her paintings, hanging over the fireplace. The view from that spot at the top of the island, where she and Clive had first met, in dusty strokes of blue and rusty greens.

'What . . . But how did you get this?'

'I had it shipped over, Carolina helped. You're not going to faint again, are you?' he joked, noting the shock in her eyes.

She looked away from him. 'I'm sorry about that, I don't know what happened. I think it's the pregnancy and—'

'I'm joking. All brides are allowed a little freak-out on the big day,' he said. 'I'm just glad you're feeling better. I want you to feel like this is properly your home. The other paintings are on their way; I thought we could hang them along the landing upstairs.'

'Thank you,' she said, casting her gaze away from the image of the island. 'But we don't have to. I'd like to do some fresh paintings, maybe on the Heathland you mentioned.'

'It's already arranged,' he said firmly. 'The shipments will be arriving next week.'

'Well, I was also thinking about what you said before, about me maybe getting a little gallery space, somewhere local . . .'

He regarded her. 'Absolutely. That's a wonderful idea. Once you're a bit more settled into the pregnancy, we will definitely do that. If anything, I think the fainting shows that you need to keep things calm for a while. Besides, you don't have to do anything. All you need to worry about is staying well. Agreed?'

He pushed her hair back behind her ear and she smiled weakly. 'You're right. There's plenty of time.'

'There certainly is,' he said, and she felt his arms tighten around her as she closed her eyes. 'All the time in the world. You're not going anywhere.'

That first night in London, she woke up suddenly.

The bathroom stood a little way along the landing. The light switch was activated by pulling on a string cord. Reaching for it in the darkness, Artemis stopped herself at the last minute, wary of the sound of the attached extractor fan waking Clive. Moving quickly across the room, she pulled open the curtain to let in the moonlight. As she did so, a gust of wind rattled at the sash windows.

Looking out, she could see the wall where the garden gave way to the Heath. In late summer, the branches of the trees that lined the horizon were thick with leaves, casting shadows along the lawn.

Shivering, she pulled the curtain to again and used the toilet, letting her eyes adjust to the dark. When she stood, she caught the rich smell of amber emanating from the crystal perfume bottle Clive had given her the day before.

It was dark in the hallway as Artemis returned to the bedroom, moving briskly, aware of the shadows cast by the bannisters, like prison bars, along the bare wall where her pictures were yet to be hung.

Back in the bedroom, she lunged into bed, closing her eyes and then opening them again to find Clive staring at her in the dark.

His expression was one of concern. 'Hey,' he said, reaching out a hand to her arms, her goosebumps exacerbated by his touch. 'Are you OK? You look like someone walked over your grave.'

'I'm fine,' she said, trying to smile. 'I just needed to use the bathroom.'

She closed her eyes again and tried to slow her heartbeat, focusing her attention on the sound of the trees rustling at the windows.

'Sleep well,' he said, turning away from her. 'I know it all feels new now, a touch overwhelming perhaps. But everything is going to be great.'

Harry

London, the day Anna dies

Parcel Yard is almost empty but for a couple of men in kilts drinking pints in one corner of the pub, a group of office workers laughing too loudly in the other.

Harry arrives first, taking a seat at a table overlooking the train tracks, the sound of King's Cross station rattling around him, surveying the room as he waits, his back straightening as he sees Madeleine appear at the door, teetering across the room on too-high heels.

He doesn't blink, watching her face closely.

'Harry,' she says, smiling, business-like, and leaning forward to kiss him on the cheek. 'Early for that. Shall we walk?'

He looks at his drink before downing it, ignoring her quip. If there is one thing he knows about Madeleine it is that she isn't one to judge.

'Sure, let's go,' he says, and they move outside and through the crowds gathered outside the departure boards, exiting the station and turning right towards Coal Drops Yard.

'How have you been?' she asks, noting the red rings around his eyes. He looks away.

'I've had better days.'

She looks enquiringly at him and he shrugs. 'It was a nice distraction to get your call. What's up?'

'I need you to help move someone,' she says above the drone of the traffic. 'An old colleague of mine . . . She has a family. Three young children and a partner. I need you to meet them at Plymouth tomorrow.'

'Tomorrow?'

'I know it's short notice but I wouldn't ask if it wasn't urgent. I need someone I can trust . . .'

Harry nods. 'I'm touched.'

'I've lined up a people carrier. You'll meet them near the ferry. There will be someone waiting to take their car and get rid of it. You'll continue on with them. There is a house, I've written down the address.'

'A family, though? Jesus, Mads, what is this about?'

Madeleine shakes her head, biting the inside of her mouth.

'They are witnesses in a case the NCA are building.'

'So why aren't you keeping this in-house?'

She shoves her hands deep into her pockets.

'OK,' he says. 'Obviously you're not willing to tell me everything, but I need to know what I'm signing up to. I think you'd worry if I didn't ask . . .'

Madeleine nods. 'You can't report this, ever. What I say now is strictly off record. It can never come out.'

Harry smiles, showing his palms. 'You have my word. I haven't worked for a newspaper for five years . . .'

She doesn't ask why. Pausing, she clears her throat. 'The NCA is building a case against a network of international criminals. They need Gabriela – that's my former colleague – to help convict a woman called Irena Vasiliev. They've been trying to get her for years; they've been working with international agencies, pushing to prosecute offences from involvement in something called a VAT carousel to a number of arguably more serious crimes that are equally hard to pin to her, especially with her legal team as litigious as they are – but this is where Gabriela comes in.'

Harry listens, without reaction.

'Gabriela has been with the same man since they were in their early twenties. A guy called Tom. As far as I knew, they were happy together . . .'

Harry looks at her sidelong. She doesn't meet his eye. 'We worked together at the FCO. Anyway, Gabriela and Tom have kids – a girl and a boy, they're seven and five now. Then one day, almost two years ago, she met this Russian guy, Ivan Popov. Popov is Vasiliev's main man in the UK. Vasiliev is wanted around the world but she barely leaves Russia now, other than to countries deemed safe, i.e. anywhere untouched by Europol or Interpol, or any of the other agencies braying for her blood. Popov met Gabriela at a café in town and they started a relationship. They had a baby together.'

Harry raises an eyebrow. 'So if she's already split up with this Tom guy, how come he's going with her?'

Madeleine pauses. 'She didn't split up with him. They were still together. It seems she's been living a double life, moving between the two families for months.'

'Seriously?' Harry exhales through his teeth. 'Wow, that takes some balls. And no one noticed?'

'Not that I'm aware of.' Madeleine clears her throat. 'Popov's phone was tapped . . . These recordings connect Vasiliev and Popov with a number of crimes.'

'And Gabriela is going to testify?'

'That's the plan. Except Vasiliev knows about Gabriela. She had her investigated, found out about the children and Tom . . . Still, when Vasiliev confronted Popov with the information, he chose to stay with her.'

Harry reaches into his pocket and pulls out a cigarette, offering her one.

'Fuck me, this is really not what I expected you to say when I agreed to meet you . . .'

'Well, you can be sure that it came as something of a shock to me, too.'

Harry holds out the lighter to Madeleine as she leans in. They are interrupted by the sound of Harry's phone. As he pulls it out, he sees the name *Maria* flash on the screen.

Pressing reject, he slips it in his pocket.

'Are you sure you're up to this?' she says. 'I mean, if you have other stuff going on . . .'

'No,' he says firmly. 'I'm up for it. So where am I going?'

Artemis

Clive had lived in the house alone since his father's death. He had suffered a heart attack within a year of losing Clive's mother, Elisabeth, who had fled to this pocket of North London from Austria during the war. She and Bernard had met at nearby Keats House library not long after she'd arrived and together they had bought this house in the early Fifties.

Artemis knew she was lucky to be here – Clive had already impressed on her Hampstead's cultural and geographical significance – and yet the terraced houses, so many lives wedged in against one another in the midst of the city, the lack of sky, made her feel hemmed in.

Sometimes, when she looked out through the kitchen window, she would blink and imagine the ghost-like silhouette of a woman hunched over a sketchbook. In that moment she couldn't be sure if it was Elisabeth she was imagining, or herself.

Clive took that first week in London off work. Arm in arm, they spent their days walking the streets he had described – puffs of smoke wafting in front of them as they navigated the towpath beside the canal lined with grubby, multicoloured boats, past the zoo and on to Little Venice.

They spent the Friday walking over the Heath, the tips of the leaves turning from green to orange, giving the illusion of a fire burning somewhere in the distance. They stopped for a drink on the way home, at the Magdala pub. It was an *institution*, apparently – this was a word Clive used a lot, as if to pre-empt her inability to understand the importance of some seemingly insignificant place or bizarre custom – and the place where Ruth Ellis famously shot her lover before becoming the last woman in the country to be hanged.

Looking around her, Artemis lifted her fingers to her throat as a cloud of cigarette smoke rose up from the table next to theirs.

'We better hurry up with these,' Clive said as he drained his glass. 'People will be arriving soon.'

Artemis sighed, inwardly. She couldn't think of anything she less wanted to do than have Clive's friend's over. She was so tired.

Since arriving in London, her sleep had been broken. It was partly the growing bump in her belly that was preventing her from getting comfortable, but mostly it was the dreams that came for her as soon as she drifted off, the cracking sound, like something inside her breaking, and then the scream . . .

She pictured Jeff and May, him with his overly personal manner and wandering eyes; her with the impenetrable gaze, her entire being shrouded behind layers of fake tan and an excess of perfume. May had been friendly enough the couple of times they had met, but there was a tartness about her, something almost untrustworthy, though Artemis would have struggled to say exactly what, or why this woman made her feel so uneasy. A mother to a baby herself, May should have been just the person Artemis wanted to talk to, the kind of friend that might have become a kindred spirit, but it seemed impossible to connect; besides, May never brought her own child with her when they came out. She didn't know much about Clive's best friends, but what she had understood immediately was how little she had in common with them.

From a distance, through Clive's stories, this world of his had seemed dreamlike and inviting. Up close, she felt like she had been catapulted into someone else's life. Surely when his friends looked at her, they too would see, with all their shared history, that she was not one of them. They would be within their rights to assume that she, a small-town girl from a remote island with nothing to contribute to the relationship other than her womb, was a gold-digger, but she wasn't. For all its initial allure, Clive's relative wealth was something she had come to resent for the imbalance of power it created between them. Even without it, she was already in a position of weakness: in another country, without any friends or family, pregnant, her body transforming into a version of itself she didn't yet understand.

She wished she could speak to Athena. Athena would know what to say, even if her comfort came laced with back-handed compliments and coated in expletives. Artemis had arrived with no autonomy, no real sway in any aspect of their lives. In order for their relationship to work, it was she who had to mould herself to Clive's world, without asking him to adjust in the slightest. His money only added a further layer of dependency – not that he made her feel guilty when she asked for cash for groceries or whatever it was she needed.

And yet, she had never fitted in back on the island either, had she? When she thought of it, she pictured the sun brushing against the path meandering behind her house, the sea glistening at the edge. The horizon filled with a familiar sky that had watched over so many traumas and done nothing to stop them. The truth was, she had never fitted in anywhere.

Although that wasn't strictly true. She had felt a sense of belonging, for a while, she and Clive hemmed in their own little world in that pocket of land just beyond the old village, during those long, intimate summers on the island, before anyone found out. They may not have known each other in the way that only time would allow, but she felt right with him, back then. Together, alone, she and Clive had made sense; she understood then how their disparate worlds folded into one another's. But everything had changed so quickly. Once the circle opened up, everything had poured in – the friends, the new city – so that she felt like she might drown.

'Artemis?'

When she looked up, she saw Clive regarding her with an expression she couldn't quite fathom.

'Sorry,' she said, blushing, as though she had been caught out.

'What are you sorry for? Is everything OK?'

She smiled tightly. 'I'm fine.'

'Good,' he replied, picking up her wine glass and knocking it back. 'We better get a wriggle on; the guests will be here before we know it. You'll need to make a start on lunch.'

Madeleine

London, the day Anna dies

Madeleine has been trying hard, in the hours since her meeting with Harry, to distract herself from the mental image of Gabriela, with remarkably little success. She hasn't called to say she is on her way to Devon and Madeleine knows better than to ring her and risk raising an alarm. According to the plan Madeleine had conveyed in the restaurant, Gabriela was to go straight to her North London family home, spend the night there, then head to Richmond the following morning to collect the baby. From here she should instruct Tom to meet her in Devon with the children.

When Madeleine pictures her friend now she still sees the old Gabriela, sharing gossip and fags in the street outside the offices at King Charles Street. Though it's a terrible thing to think – and of course she would never say it – Gabriela was better before the kids. Some women blossom in motherhood, others wither. Maybe it's simply a matter of confidence. If she was being kind, Madeleine could put it down to a lack of conviction in herself and her decisions that meant Gabriela was constantly questioning her plausibility as a parent. She cared too much what others thought, but more to the point she could never seem to enjoy it. She would never let herself recognise what she had, or what she could have had if she had given in to it a little.

But this? She doesn't deserve this. Not even after what she's done. If she's honest with herself, Madeleine resents her friend for never

77

having confided in her. When Harry raised the question of how no one noticed what had been going on with Gabriela, Madeleine had felt defensive. Because she hadn't noticed either, had she? Sure, she had felt something was off, but she had thought it was probably something to do with the drudgery of domestic life that Gabriela was forever complaining about. There were aspects of her friend's existence that Madeleine simply hadn't paid too much attention to. When Gabriela had said she planned to stay at home rather than find a new job after leaving the FCO, Madeleine had known it wouldn't have been her choice. She had imagined it was Tom's decision, or that being pushed out by their boss, Guy Emsworth, after she had rejected his sexual advances, had knocked her confidence so badly that she was struggling to find her mojo again. But equally it just wasn't the sort of chat they had; their friendship was different, better than domestic small talk, Madeleine had thought at the time. Or maybe it was that she was wary of talking to Gabriela about family life. It grated on her how often she complained about the tedium of motherhood – Madeleine wouldn't go so far as to claim motherhood was a sacred gift, but it was a choice. This wasn't the Fifties; Gabriela had freedom to choose whether or not she wanted to have children. It wasn't a choice everyone had the luxury of.

Her mind moves to Harry. She knows he had simply been asking the questions he needed to ask – the ones she, too, would have posed in his position. But how well does she really know him? Enough to think that she has no reason to distrust him any more than anyone else that she could get to do the job. People are fallible. She relies upon this fact, and pays for it, in her line of work; that people are corruptible is a gift as well as a curse.

There are few people Madeleine trusts entirely; and now with Gabriela, there is one fewer. At least, she reasons sardonically to herself, this latest unravelling proves that she is right to remain vigilant. So no, she doesn't wholly trust Harry, but in this moment she needs someone, and for a job like this it has to be someone outside the agency. Vasiliev is too well-connected; there have been too many leaks over the years, too many evasions. Besides, Harry is a pro. Since their first meeting at an international conference on people trafficking years ago, which he was covering for a newspaper, they have worked together numerous times, always in an unofficial capacity – her offering him leads in return for favours, the sorts of transactions it is best to keep off paper. Harry has never failed to deliver, though admittedly what she has asked of him has never been anything approaching this scale.

'You free?' Sean appears holding two cups of coffee.

'If one of those is for me then I might be. How's it going?'

He hands her the cup. 'Pretty bloody good actually.' He waits for a minute, taking a sip, enjoying the build-up to whatever it is he's about to reveal. 'I've just been having a chat with an old pal, MI6, thinks she might be able to give us some intel on this case.'

'Nice,' Madeleine replies, wondering what this has to do with her – she was only brought in to make contact with Gabriela and arrange the next steps in terms of her vanishing. The case itself is nothing to do with her. For a horrible moment she wonders if Sean is using it as a means to chat her up, but she discards the idea as quickly as it arises. She knows when a man is imagining he might be able to get into her knickers, and Sean isn't one of them. You could say a lot about him, but at least he understands his own limitations.

'Apparently one of the companies Vasiliev is involved with – TradeSmart, it's a multi-billion-pound trading company run by this British guy, Clive Witherall – they were under surveillance for a while a few years back,' he continues. 'Something to do with a chemical spillage they were involved in over in Central Africa. The case was dropped mid-way through, but in the process they had human informants inside the house as well as inside his business, who managed to plant probes and also, I believe, cloned a computer drive. Tons of recordings, emails, you name it. It will take some digging but it looks like we might have some work to do.'

'Right,' Madeleine says.

'She's going to give me a call later today, and, well, because of your connection to Gabriela and the fact that another of the companies we're watching appears to be a front for human trafficking . . .'

'You want me to work with you on the case?'

Sean smiles pleadingly. 'What do you say?'

Madeleine leans back in her chair, taking a sip from her cup. 'I thought you'd never ask. But you might need to buy me something stronger than a coffee.'

They head to Pico's on the Embankment after work, casting their eyes around for anyone from the office, but there's no one there apart from a couple of stragglers they don't recognise.

'So Felicity's background is in fraud,' Sean explains, once they are seated opposite each other, drinks in hand. 'A few years ago, when she was with MI6, she was pulled onto this case involving three corporate criminals. The original reason for looking into them was that they were using offshore companies to commit fraud – all pretty standard stuff. But there was also particular interest in TradeSmart because of its apparent involvement in this chemical spillage in Central Africa. You remember hearing about it? Never made headlines as there wasn't enough evidence, but there were rumours . . .'

Madeleine shakes her head. It isn't that surprising that she missed it; she's spent so much of the past few years abroad, either in Eastern Europe or Asia. When she was here in London, she was head-down in various ongoing trafficking cases.

'Doesn't matter,' Sean continues, unperturbed. 'Anyway, according to Felicity, it looked like there was a hell of a lot more going on in those shipments. One of the guys involved, an African by the name of Francisco Nguema, was using his shipping business as a means to trade arms.' He takes a sip of his lager. 'But then the investigation was suddenly pulled because it transpired that one of the men involved was FCO. They got rid of him in the end, falsified some claims of sexual harassment and sent him out to pasture.'

Madeleine's mind moves instantly to Guy Emsworth, her former FCO boss who had put so much pressure on both her and Gabriela that they had both eventually left, Madeleine for a career in law enforcement, Gabriela for—

'Oh my God.' She feels her heartbeat rise. 'Did your friend tell you this man's name?'

Sean shakes his head. 'Doesn't really matter. The point is she was working with informants tracking everything that was happening in and out of the house of our new mate, Clive Witherall, up until that point, including the woman who looked after his son's kids. Same as Popov and his housemaid. I tell you what, if I was up to some dodgy shit, I'd be a bit more careful choosing who I made part of the family.'

Harry

Plymouth, the day after Anna dies

The car he collects, following Madeleine's instruction, is an old VW Touran. The traffic is light and it takes just over three hours from London to the remote café, hidden behind a seemingly abandoned dairy farm, near Plymouth. The car park is empty other than a small Nissan and a Volvo estate, stationed several metres apart. As Harry pulls up beside the larger vehicle, he spots a woman seated at the picnic table in the forecourt with a baby dozing on her lap, the barely touched remains of two jacket potatoes curling on their plates in front of her.

He recognises her instantly from the photo: the same dark curls and full mouth. From the hats and tinsel it must have been taken at a Christmas party.

For a moment he wonders if she is alone with her youngest child but then he sees the man in the makeshift playground a few metres beyond, pushing a girl absent-mindedly back and forth on a plastic swing. The boy is climbing the steps to the freestanding slide, taking each tread with care as if scared the whole thing might collapse.

Watching Harry warily as he pulls up, the woman sits straighter, supporting the baby's head with a cupped hand. As he steps out of the car, she untucks her legs from the bench and stands.

'Gabriela,' he says and she nods, taking his extended hand with obvious caution.

'I'm Harry. I'm a friend of Madeleine's . . .'

He smiles and holds her eye for a moment before moving his attention to their surroundings. There are no cameras, no other people around besides whomever it was inside the café who cooked and served the food.

'Can I get you something?' Gabriela asks, noting his eyes move to the discarded plates. 'The kids were hungry.'

'I'm fine,' he says, looking towards the playground, where the man has turned to watch them. 'Is that Tom?' Gabriela nods, looking away. Harry raises a hand in acknowledgement.

'And this is your car?' He peers in through the glass. They've travelled relatively lightly, given the number of children. 'Do you want me to help transfer those bags into here?'

Tom approaches and Harry greets him, holding out his hand. Tom ignores it, so Harry addresses the children, who follow at a distance, crouching to meet their eyes. 'You must be Sadie and Callum?'

The girl says nothing but her focus doesn't shift from his face. Callum nods, moving closer towards his older sister.

'It's good to meet you,' Harry says gently before returning his attention to Gabriela. Tom doesn't seem interested in conversation and frankly Harry can't blame him.

'Do you need a hand with the car seats?'

'No,' she replies. Tom is standing away from the vehicle, physically shielding his children. Gabriela moves methodically, aware of the baby pressed up against her chest as she lifts out one of the seats, Harry stepping in to assist her without saying a word.

Once the transferral is complete, he walks over and hands Gabriela the keys to the people carrier.

'Do you have the keys for the Volvo?' Gabriela nods towards Tom.

'He has them.'

'Pal, do you think I could grab the keys off you? I need to take your car . . .' Harry says.

As Tom's eyes meet his, he sees that what he had previously taken for contempt is actually fear or shock or, more likely, both. Tom hands him the keys and moves away again, and as Harry looks down he sees the key ring: an image of the four of them, encased in cheap plastic – Tom, Gabriela, Sadie and Callum, posing in a garden.

'Do you want me to take them off the chain?' he asks quietly. Tom calls back over his shoulder.

'You can keep it.'

It takes less than an hour for Harry to deposit the car at the edge of a nearby field, ready for collection by whomever will be sent to deal with it, before returning to the car park. Gabriela seems relieved to see him again, gathering the children into the VW Touran, Sadie in the far back seat, Callum and Layla strapped into the middle row.

After a moment's pause, she indicates for Harry to go in the front passenger seat beside Tom, before climbing between her youngest children.

'What do you think of the new car?' she says to Sadie in a staged effort at normality once the engine starts. The child's answer, if there is one, is lost in the sound of the wipers reverberating against the windscreen.

It has stopped raining, the sky settling in an oppressive grey mist.

'There's a button just there, to turn them off,' Harry says to Tom, leaning over to point it out, but Tom doesn't react, his expression fixed on the road ahead of him. Harry wishes he had suggested he continue to drive. What is he thinking? He tries to imagine and for a second he pictures Tom veering towards the barrier. That's all it would take, one tiny shift of the steering wheel and they would all be dead.

'This is our turning,' Harry says quickly, overriding his own thoughts.

Tom takes the exit and Harry exhales silently. Christ, he can't wait for this job to be over. He hates everything about it.

But it won't be for long, he reminds himself. Just as soon as they touch down in France, Harry's work here will be done.

'I'm your brother, if anyone asks,' Harry explains as they take their queue for the ferry. 'This envelope has your passports inside. I'll need your old ones . . .'

'Why do you need them?' Gabriela asks.

'I need to get rid of them properly. We can't risk anyone finding them.' He gives her a look across the car that tells her this is not a conversation to be having in front of the children. 'Callum, would you mind passing that to your mother?'

The child hesitates before leaning to take the parcel from his hand. Harry winks reassuringly. When he looks up at Gabriela, he sees her face is suddenly white. In one hand, she holds the envelope of passports; with the other she is holding her throat as if her airways are constricting and she is struggling to breathe.

Shit.

'Gabriela, are you OK?' Harry focuses on her face from the other side of the car. Her eyes bulge as she shakes her head, mouthing the words *I can't breathe.*

He keeps his voice calm. 'You're just having a panic attack.' He leans between the seats so that he is fully focused on her. The car is stationary, vehicles locking them in on all sides. 'Gabriela, look at me. Breathe. OK? Callum, can you open the door, please? That's it, stay where you are – we just need air. Gabriela, you're fine, you just need to breathe . . .'

Sensing her mother's unease, Layla cries out from her car seat.

'Mum?' There is fear in Sadie's voice as Layla's cry intensifies in the seat in front of her.

'Don't worry, your mum's going to be fine,' Harry says before returning his attention to Gabriela. 'Steady, that's it, steady . . . Gabriela, breathe. Sadie, it's OK . . .'

At a loss about what to do with the screaming baby, he leans towards Layla in the middle row of seats, making hushing sounds, briefly glancing at Tom who is not responding, as if he is already somewhere else. For fuck's sake, surely now would be a good time to man up.

'Pal?' Harry says, trying to get his attention. 'Do you think you could grab the baby?'

Gabriela is still struggling to catch her breath, her panic increasing with the child's cry. *Help the bloody baby*, Harry wants to shout at Tom, who remains focused on the windshield, but the less attention they attract to their group from the other passengers waiting in line, the better. Stepping out of the car, Harry moves to the door behind him, opening it, undoing Layla's seat belt and lifting the child out.

He takes a step away from the people carrier, aware of several pairs of eyes watching him as he awkwardly juggles the child. A few moments later he feels a hand on his back and when he turns, Gabriela is there, reaching for her child.

'OK, baby,' she says, taking Layla. 'OK. Come to me, baby. Come to me.'

Artemis

London and Greece, the Nineties

The day David was born, Artemis felt, for the first time since she arrived in London – perhaps for the first time ever – that she had an ally; someone with whom she would side, and who would side with her, through anything. David, with his serious dark eyes and his quiet adoration of his mother, emboldened her and gave her purpose. It was as if the moment she became a parent, she understood her place in the world. From then on it would be him and her against everyone and everything. Until the day she died.

In the months that followed the birth, her body returned to a version of herself that she respected, with its soft, yielding curves. As time passed, Artemis started to carve out a routine for them both, between the library and the playground and the grocer's in South End Green. In doing so, she felt herself taking ownership of a piece of the city that suddenly felt as though it belonged to her. With David's tiny hand cocooned in hers, London made sense. Previously daunting and unnavigable, the Heath became her and David's secret garden, an oasis within the bustle of the city. In the days and sometimes weeks Clive spent away for work, she would roam the paths with the buggy, David taking his first steps on the pavement by Parliament Hill tennis courts.

Even the big rattling house with its emerald-green carpets and heavy Victorian furniture shifted in her mind from being Clive's home to the epicentre of their family life. At the kitchen table, she would spread out a large oilcloth and cut potatoes into shapes, watching David's eyes light up as she helped him squelch the misshapen blocks into a palette of brightly coloured paints, lurching his fist across to the paper, creating amateur masterpieces to show to Daddy when he got home from work.

She never resented it, the long hours Clive spent at the office in town or the meetings with Jeff after he started getting more involved in the business. The regular travelling for work only cemented her belief that their roles were delineated and equally valid. When he was home, Clive would throw his son scraps of attention, marvelling over the flecks of colour in a picture he'd made, pointing out tenuous patterns ('A dog?' 'A hedgehog?' 'A tree?') and David would shake his head, giggling with increasing glee at every erroneous suggestion.

For the first time, Artemis was happy. Despite the uncertain start in the city, her and Clive's life together was good. The foundations that for so many years had been broken, finally felt solid.

The year David turned two, Athena also had a baby back in Greece, a tiny girl with her father's eyes and thick black curls. The women cried as they watched their children side-by-side when Artemis went to visit, taking David to see her parents for the first time.

'She looks just like Panos,' Artemis laughed.

'And she is about the same amount of use around the house . . .' Athena retorted.

'Sweet Maria. How is Panos?'

Athena seemed to bristle at the sound of Panos' name on her friend's tongue. 'Useless.' She paused, and then asked, 'And how is Clive?'

There was a slight strain in her voice.

'Clive is well,' Artemis said, focusing her attention on the children. 'He sends his love. Hopefully he can come out next year, when things die down a bit with work.'

'Sounds like it's going well with the business.' Athena's voice was tight, the jealousy seeping through the space between the words. Artemis knew Panos' lack of meaningful income was one of the bones of contention between the couple.

'It is,' Artemis replied, non-committal. 'He's doing more work abroad. He and his business partner, Jeff.'

'What's Jeff like?' Athena asked.

'I'm not sure.' Artemis didn't feel like talking about him. Right now she wanted to focus on Athena and the baby. 'He's . . . well, he's married, for one,' she said lightly.

'Shut up, so am I.' Athena feigned hurt.

'I'm joking. You're a good couple, you and Panos. I know he's not—'

'Not what?' Athena snapped defensively. Her twisted loyalty was part of her make-up. She could say anything about anyone, but woe betide anyone else speak ill of someone close to her.

Baby Maria winced at the sound of her mother's raised voice. Artemis leaned forward and stroked her head. 'You have such a beautiful daughter,' she said, changing the subject.

'I know,' Athena replied, her voice mellowing. 'She is beautiful. I don't deserve her.'

It was an uncharacteristic display of self-flagellation and Artemis took her friend's hand.

'Don't be stupid, of course you deserve her. And I'll tell you something else, she and David are going to be great friends.' Artemis beamed, looking up and meeting Athena's eyes.

'Yes, they are,' she replied, squeezing Artemis' palm. 'They will look after each other. Who knows, one day maybe they'll fall in love and we can wear matching hats at the wedding.'

'I hope so,' Artemis smiled, turning as Maria cried out, alarmed by something in her peripheral vision that neither of the women could see.

Harry

The Channel, the day after Anna dies

The ramp clatters as the car moves onto the ferry. Once parked up, they head into the stairwell, following signs to the main deck, Harry following behind at a respectful distance. He watches as Sadie tucks herself onto Tom's lap, Gabriela's face pulling away, her daughter withdrawing in a foetal position, as if trying to make herself as small as possible, to make herself disappear.

'You guys stay here,' Harry says, though he is not here as their guardian and he knows that even if that was his job, there would be only so much he could do to keep them safe.

Finally, the motion of the boat lulls the older children to sleep, the two of them curled up on the floor, their heads resting against their bags, Tom seated beside them, his eyes fixed on the grey sea outside. Rain spatters against the windows once more as England disappears behind them for the final time.

Harry leans against the bar at the far side of the room, ordering a beer and sipping at it slowly as the boat makes headway. Finishing his drink sometime later, he orders another. When he glances over again at the family, Tom and the older children are just as he left them an hour or so earlier, but Gabriela is nowhere to be seen. Standing straighter, he keeps his cool – she has probably just gone to the bathroom or to change Layla's nappy. There could be any number of reasons why she isn't here, but something urges him to step away from the bar, to follow the path through from the centre of the boat towards the rain-spattered windows and the darkness beyond.

Part of Harry expects the door out to the deck to be closed at this late hour. But as he pushes against it, the mechanism gives way and he feels the wet sea air sting his cheeks. He spots her instantly, as he turns towards the nose of the boat, her silhouette framed by night sky. The surface of the deck is wet. Harry focuses on maintaining his balance as he moves carefully along the side of the ship, towards Gabriela. She is standing dead centre at the back of the boat, looking over the water so that her back is facing him. Leaning forward, one hand on Layla's head, the other gripped around the ice-cold handrail, she watches the waves churning in the motor.

'Hey,' Harry says, once he is close enough that he could feasibly reach out and touch her.

When she turns to face him, Harry's eyes move to the baby who is pressed against her mother's chest.

If Gabriela is surprised to see him, she doesn't show it.

'How do you know Madeleine?' she asks, as if continuing a conversation they were already having.

'We met at an event. I was a reporter.'

Gabriela seems uninterested rather than placated by his answer.

'She and I worked together at the Foreign Office. She was my work wife. She was better at it than I was . . . the work bit, not the wife bit – although she probably would have been better at that too.' Gabriela laughs sardonically. 'Our old boss, Guy Emsworth, hated us. It was mutual, although I didn't hate him as much as Madeleine did, not at first – apparently she is much better at reading people than I am. Anyway, Madeleine left the FCO and went to the NCA, didn't she? I was just thinking, if I had left then, too, that none of this would have happened.'

Gabriela's voice trails off.

'You know, what's done is done. I don't think there's much point thinking about what ifs,' Harry says. 'We've all done things we're not proud of.'

'Yeah, well it's one thing telling yourself that and it's another stopping your mind from going where it wants to go,' Gabriela replies, jiggling slightly as the baby stirs, before lowering her voice. 'The point is, when I was replaying it all in my head, trying to pinpoint the moment at which it really started, I realised the connection between Ivan and me was Emsworth, my old boss. When I was at the FCO, he always used to take me to this little Italian bistro on Crown Passage, behind Pall Mall. He called it his "second office". Once I left the FCO, I went back there one day and that's where I met Ivan. I always assumed it was random, Ivan and I meeting like that, but what if the reason Ivan was there was that this was where he, too, met Emsworth, to hand over information?

'I'm not saying Emsworth meant for Ivan and me to meet. In fact, I'm sure he wouldn't have wanted or anticipated that at all, but inadvertently, I suppose, this whole thing – this whole situation – is Emsworth's fault, right?'

Harry bites his tongue.

'That was what I was thinking, and then I realised, as you're probably thinking right now, that I'm a fucking idiot. There was no grand conspiracy for me to meet Ivan, no one made this happen, no one is to blame, apart from me. I used to tell myself that this was Tom's fault for not noticing or for not asking the right questions when I claimed to be spending weeks, sometimes months, abroad for work after Layla was born. But that was bullshit. The truth is, I was bored and I had an affair, that's how basic it is. And now I'm taking my whole family on a boat to I don't even fucking know where because our lives are under threat and—'

'Hey,' Harry says. 'Let's go inside . . . The baby will be getting cold. You should try to get some sleep. You must be tired.'

He felt her body tense as he touched her. 'Come on, it's a long drive tomorrow.'

They leave the ferry at Santander at five o'clock the following afternoon. According to the route he had plotted before he left home, the journey will take just over six and a half hours, leading them back into a pocket of France that is closer to the Spanish border than it is to Caen or Calais.

By the time the car pulls past San Sebastian, the city lights twinkling in the distance, all three children are asleep. Harry sits in the front, navigating from his phone, aware that his role now is as much a diplomatic presence, a neutralising force, as it is a chaperone.

There is nothing to mark their crossing the border from Spain to France as they make their way inland but for a small road sign, which flashes by in the dark so quickly that he almost misses it. Obediently, Tom follows the motorway signs for Carcassonne and Gabriela drifts off leaving just Harry and Tom awake in the front.

'Are you OK? I can take over for a while if you want to grab some kip,' Harry says after a while and Tom shakes his head.

'Do you mind if I try the radio?' Harry asks.

'Be my guest.'

There is a blast of Euro-pop as Harry presses the power button, flicking through the channels before settling on a gentler song he vaguely recognises.

Allowing the music to fill the silence, Harry looks out of the window and after a moment, Tom starts to sing along quietly.

'You know this one?' Harry says and Tom almost smiles, speaking more than three words for the first time since their trip began.

'You don't?' His face is incredulous, almost animated. 'Eartha Kitt, man – it's one of her most famous songs – it's a classic.'

He starts to hum along again, a half-smile forming on his lips, as if he is suddenly lost in memory. Harry considers him for a moment before turning back towards the windscreen.

'I don't really listen to music.'

'You don't listen to music?' Tom turns to look at him, before returning his attention to the road.

Harry shrugs. 'Not really.'

'That's fucked up.'

There is a beat's pause and then Harry laughs wistfully, looking out the window. 'You're not the first person to say so.' His mind momentarily retreats to Meg, in the flat in Bethnal Green, several years earlier, not long before she left.

Abruptly, he changes the subject, pushing away the image of her face, a curl of red hair falling across her eye. 'Where you from, then? That's not a London accent.'

'You really are a detective,' Tom replies. 'Edinburgh. Left when I was in my early twenties but some things you can't shake. You?'

'Irish.'

'I guessed that much,' Tom said. 'Where in Ireland?'

'Galway.'

'Nice.'

'It's all right. Like you, got out as soon as I could. What did you do in London?' He didn't really care about the answer so much as he was grateful for the conversation, any distraction from the memories that threatened to smother him, the image of Anna that still lingered, just out of shot.

'I was an architect, until the kids were born . . .' His voice hardened. 'One of us needed to stay at home and . . .'

The sound of the baby stirring cuts him off and when Harry turns, he sees Gabriela coming to, sitting up and reaching forward to comfort her.

'I think she might need a change. How far away are we?'

'Not far,' Harry replies. 'It's just past midnight now. We'll stay the night at a guesthouse in Béziers then drive on in the morning.

The house is only a few minutes from there but it's quite remote and the road can apparently be treacherous, so I don't think we want to arrive in the dark.'

They leave the guesthouse early the next morning, Harry producing a bag of croissants as they pile into the car, like the teacher on a school trip.

No one speaks; the only sound is the occasional ping from the game Callum is playing on the iPad. Soon, long, featureless roads turn into smaller lanes, twisting and turning around the side of the mountain, folding into a series of pretty roundabouts and foot-bridges, before closing in on the village. The main boulevard is drenched in light; the forecourt of the Mairie brims with scooters.

Harry signals to Tom to pull over in front of a small café with an adjoining tabac.

'You speak French, don't you?' he says, turning to Gabriela, without waiting for a reply. 'We're all going to go inside and order coffees. Strike up a conversation with someone there and explain that you're moving here to renovate an old house. The plan is to live in it long-term, once it's complete. You will be home-schooling the kids, if anyone asks.'

'Why?'

'Because we want people to know why you're here before anyone starts asking questions. You want to assimilate without getting too involved. If it comes up, I'm here to help you with the move. OK? Right, let's do this.'

Madeleine

London, three days after Anna dies

Madeleine hails a cab on Marylebone Lane. It is an extravagant way to travel to the office, she concedes, but if she were to take the tube as normal, it would no doubt be while she was underground without phone-signal that the call she had been waiting for all morning would finally come through. As for the bus – she would rather crawl to Vauxhall, and that would probably be quicker than negotiating all those endless stops, even in a tailored pencil skirt and heels.

Ducking into the back, she picks up the newspaper a previous passenger has left on the seat, partly to distract herself from the nerves building in her stomach with every second that her phone doesn't ring, and partly to signal to the driver that she is not in the market for chit-chat. Pulling out the croissant tucked in her handbag, she takes a bite.

It is a local paper, folded somewhere in the middle, and she flicks through the pages with limited interest until she reaches the back page and turns it over. She sees the photograph of a glamorous-looking couple, arm-in-arm, and begins to read:

The socialite heiress and magazine editor Anna Witherall has died at her North London home. The mother-of-two was found hanged at the family house on Parliament Hill in South End Green. Ms Witherall, who was editor of luxury interiors magazine House *at the time of her death, was married to the late David Witherall. The couple leave behind two daughters, aged three.*

David Witherall, who was heir to the global trading company TradeSmart, died just months ago after being hit by a car. Ms Witherall was found hanged at the couple's £3.5m home. Her body was discovered by a friend who had been looking after the children for the day.

An inquest will follow.

Scanning the page, Madeleine's eyes fall on the byline. *ISOBEL MASON.*

Isobel Mason. Madeleine sits forward in her seat, mulling over the name, her mind moving back to the previous week, to the meeting at the women's refuge in Kentish Town. Madeleine and Dana had arrived first. Maureen, who ran the refuge, was an old contact of Madeleine, since her time investigating human trafficking back at the Foreign Office. It was Maureen who had brokered the meeting between Dana, one of Madeleine's informants, and Isobel Mason, a local journalist and friend of Maureen who was looking into an attack on a sex worker Dana had been in contact with. Madeleine hadn't needed to go along but there was no way she was going to let one of her sources, and a woman she cared about, go to meet a reporter alone. If she was honest, she had been reticent about Dana speaking to Isobel at all, but from Maureen's assurances, Isobel was as fine a journalist as one could wish to meet – not that the bar, in Madeleine's experience, was particularly high. Isobel's motives in probing Dana for information, Maureen insisted, were as much about trying to find out what happened to the missing woman as they were about finding a story. At least that's what Maureen had clearly chosen to believe.

'Dana has been working with the organisation to help report suspected instances of trafficking. She has been hugely brave in working with Madeleine, and she thinks she might be able to help you,' Maureen had said by way of introduction once Isobel had arrived.

Madeleine had tried not to look taken aback when she walked in. In the flesh, which frankly she could do with a little more of, Isobel looked about twelve, with rings under her eyes and chewed fingernails – more akin with one of the girls Maureen looked after than an accomplished reporter. Though perhaps her deceptive appearance was part of what made her effective in her job. From the research Madeleine had done ahead of coming along with Dana, Isobel had had her fair share of meaty stories, especially for a local hack who must have been in her early twenties at most.

'I'm not here in an official capacity,' Madeleine had confirmed when Isobel eyed her sidelong. 'Maureen mentioned your enquiries, and I thought of Dana. Maureen tells me you're a brilliant journalist, and very trustworthy. I thought it would be good to meet you, put a face to a name . . .'

And here is the same name staring back at her now, attached to a piece about the death of Anna Witherall who was married to the late heir of a company associated with Irena Vasiliev – the Russian boss of the man with whom Gabriella had been having an affair.

Pulling out her phone, Madeleine dials Sean's number. He answers after two rings.

'Madeleine. How do?'

'Listen,' she says, lowering her voice, though the driver is immersed, tutting along to a radio phone-in, oblivious to her conversation.

'Are you in the office?'

'Sure am.'

'Could we speak when I get in? I'll be twenty minutes or so.' She looks out at the traffic as the car moves along Park Lane. 'Actually, make that half an hour.'

'No prob—'

Before Sean finishes, Madeleine cuts off the call and sits back in her seat, her mind spinning.

Sean smiles as he runs his eyes over the paper Madeleine has flattened on the desk for him to read.

'Please tell me you don't think this is a coincidence,' she says, her words quickening with anticipation.

'It's a hell of a coincidence,' Sean replies, more neutrally than Madeleine had hoped.

'Oh, come on,' she says, prodding him on. 'TradeSmart is implicated in a chemical spillage and for a while has MI6 on its case . . . Suddenly the co-owner dies in a hit-and-run – and then his wife hangs herself?'

'Maybe she was bereft, couldn't cope with life without him . . . They had two young kids. It can't have been easy for her, can it?'

Madeleine kisses her teeth. 'And they all just happen to be associated with Irena Vasiliev, one of the world's biggest corporate crim—?'

It is a moment before Madeleine realises the ringing is coming from her bag.

'Hold on a second.' She pulls out the phone and turns away from Sean as she sees the name flashing on the screen.

Inhaling deeply, she nods at him to hold on a second and presses answer.

'Is it done?' she asks quietly into the mouthpiece.

'Yes,' the voice at the end of the phone replies. 'It's done.'

Harry

Devon, four days after Anna dies

The wind whips off the water as Harry disembarks the boat at Plymouth along with a cluster of fellow foot passengers: bleary-eyed European students, retired couples with ruddy complexions and hiking boots, all, too, returned or arriving from the continent.

As he steps onto firm ground, he has a jolt of memory. He closes his eyes, refusing to acknowledge the face that stares back at him in his mind's eye.

Pulling his phone from his pocket to retrieve the address of the long-term car park in Plymouth where his own car had been moved to, he thinks of the older daughter's expression the final time they made eye contact.

It will be a long journey back to London, he thinks, taking a moment for the signal to adjust to its British service provider; when it does, there is a message from Maria. Pressing delete, he logs onto the BBC homepage out of habit; the headline causes him to stop dead in his tracks.

British Family Vanish in France. Below it, their faces: Tom, Gabriela, Sadie and Callum, smiling in a group portrait – the same image he had held in his hands just a couple of days earlier, encased in a plastic key ring.

The car belonging to a British family has been found, crushed, at the foot of a mountain road in the South of

France. Local reports indicate that the victims, who include young children, had arrived in the area just days earlier. The couple, who have been identified as Gabriela Shaw and Tom Wilson, are believed to have been building a family home on their plot of land near the sleepy village of Villemagne-L'Argentiere, in South East France.

The car, which contained traces of blood, was found by a passing cyclist who alerted the emergency services. The police have started a large-scale man-hunt and the Foreign Office says it is making efforts to reach the victims' relatives.

PART TWO

Harry

It was autumn by the time Harry returned to the offices at South Quay. The secretaries at reception fussed in their seats as they spotted him making his way through the revolving doors.

'Where you been?' the older woman asked, sitting taller as he stepped into the room.

Harry tapped his nose. His hair was longer and more unkempt than when he'd left.

'Here and there, Maggie . . . How are you, ladies? Looking tan, Crystal. Been on holiday? Oh hey, Dev.'

The newspaper's personal finance editor slapped him on the back as the pair moved towards the lifts. 'Hear you caught a big one? You were all the talk at conference yesterday, mate.'

'Don't believe a word of it,' Harry replied, squeezing Dev's arm warmly. 'Let's have a drink soon, eh?'

At his desk, Harry threw his coat down on the back of the chair, letting his eyes move across the office floor with its precarious piles of old newspapers stacked in rows at the foot of a filing cabinet; the familiar drone of the phone that no one in their right mind would ever pick up. God, it felt good to be back, he thought, drinking in that specific combination of freshly printed paper and stale coffee. After six months undercover, it felt great. And he'd done it – he'd got his story. His expression darkened: and he had got away with it, so far.

The editor's PA looked up at Harry as he approached, her face widening into a smile.

Harry winked. 'Hey Khadija. How you doing?'

'I'm good. Feels like I haven't seen you for ages . . .'

'It's been a while. Can I go in?' Harry asks.

'That's fine, they're expecting you . . .'

He tapped his fingers on the edge of the desk before moving towards the office where inside, Eddy Monkton, the paper's editor, and his direct boss, news editor Corinne Russell, were both waiting.

'Bloody hell!' Corinne was unable to keep the smile from her face as he entered the room, stopping short of kissing him on the cheek. 'Don't they have phones west of Paddington? Anyone would think you were in Damascus, not Wiltshire, for all we've heard from you, you elusive bastard.'

'Sorry, Cor.' Harry leaned down to hug her before she could protest. 'If it's any consolation, I imagine the food would have been better in a war zone . . . But I think you'll forgive me when you hear what I got for you.'

Harry moved forward to shake Eddy's hand, noting the speed with which he broke contact again.

'So, Harry, what you got?'

Eddy pushed himself back in his seat on the other side of his desk.

Harry leaned against the wall and signalled Corinne towards the chair. 'Trust me, you're going to want to sit for this.'

'Right, so the top line is: respected British charity who claim to support fair-trade movements across Asia and Africa have provable links with arms traders.'

'Exactly. Though they don't just *claim* to support fair-trade movements, they do support them,' Harry corrected Corinne. 'The vast majority of members are well-meaning, sometimes painfully worthy, campaigners who do a lot of good work. But as ever, where there is access to fractured or vulnerable communities, there are those who seek to take advantage. And yes, I have emails I've intercepted as well as recorded conversations that prove that members of the group are being funded by renowned arms dealers in both Africa and Asia.'

Eddy said nothing for a moment. Harry wasn't sure whether it was awe or contempt that moved across his face. When he finally spoke, his tone was uncharacteristically reverential. 'Well, if this stacks up . . .' He puckered his lips, as if the act of paying Harry heed caused him pain. 'That's a cracker of a story.'

It was almost a week later by the time he had run his recordings past the various department heads in order to close in from all angles, finally getting the sign-off from legal ahead of the planned splash. There were seven of them seated around the table in Eddy's office in that last meeting, a flat-plan spread out between them, adrenaline ricocheting off the walls.

'We've got Carl writing the leader on accountability in the third sector, touching on the other recent exposés around improper behaviour by charity employees. Foreign are working up a map of trade routes used by the arms dealers with whom the charity is known to have connections, together with a brief history of the conflict in the area and the subsequent involvement of international organisations. Comment, we'll need something from you on the white man saviour complex. Maybe get MJ on that?'

Eddy turned his attention to Harry. 'Right, so you'll give us a straight five hundred-word news exposé on charity workers found to be in cahoots with arms dealers, plus another six hundred on the undercover operation; a bit of colour on where you were based, how you infiltrated the group, without giving too much away, obviously. Picture desk, we'll need to pull stills from the button-hole cameras, and mix them up with stock images of the accused . . . Any questions?'

'I just want to be clear: we're willing to risk legal action over this?' Corinne asked.

'No one is taking anyone to court,' Eddy replied. 'These fuckers are all about reputation. There is only one possible response to a story like this, and that's to chop out the rotten parts and fling them as far as possible from the scene.'

'That's a beautiful image,' Harry commented without looking up from his flat-plan.

'We've got nothing to worry about. That's right, isn't it, Dwyer?'

Eddy's eyes lingered on Harry's a moment too long.

'That's right,' he said, holding Eddy's gaze. 'There is nothing to worry about.'

Aside from the night editors, most of the newsroom had already headed home by the time the paper went off stone, just after ten. Five of them remained, skimming over the final words, nursing cans of beer Corinne had pulled out from the mini fridge beside her desk.

None of the pieces associated with Harry's scoop were due to go online until four, ensuring rival papers couldn't pick up on them and run a version of the piece through their late edition, so there was no way he would be hanging around to see them go live.

'Hey, you want to grab a drink?' Harry asked Corinne as they moved out of the office into the brisk night air.

She waved her keys back at him. 'Better not. Iris is sick and the au pair is freaking out. Can I give you a lift?'

'Nah,' Harry said, smiling. 'You get home. I'll see you in the morning.'

'See you,' Corinne replied, heading to her car. 'Hey, Harry?' When he turned, she smiled. 'You did good. I'm proud of you.'

The sound of builders on the footpath outside his window roused Harry from a deep sleep the following morning. It was nearly eleven, he noted without concern, rolling over in bed, reaching for his phone and logging onto the newspaper's homepage. Already there were two missed calls from the office. They would have just come out of conference and would be scoping out ideas for follow-ups to keep the momentum over the course of the week. But come on, he had already filed enough copy to last them another two days, he had earnt a late start at least.

Taking a moment, he stayed in bed, pulling a cigarette from the packet on the floor and scrolling through his story online, noting the numbers of comments and shares that had already amassed since the piece went live just a few hours earlier. Closing his eyes, he held himself there for a moment, letting the peace wash over him. Jesus, after how much he'd risked to get that scoop, he could at least afford himself a couple of minutes' grace, in his own bed, at last.

He felt himself physically lift. After six months of constant guardedness, at last he could breathe. It was over. He had done it. It had been hairy for a minute but it was done, and now he was free. It had been worth it, of course, but it took its toll. These things always did.

When he finished his cigarette, extinguishing it in the dregs of last night's glass, Harry stood and stretched out his arms. Ducking through the bedroom door into the boat's main living area, he filled the kettle and leaned back against the countertop, flicking to his email and ignoring the usual pile-up of unsolicited PR bollocks that had landed overnight. At the top, there were two new messages. One from Corinne and one from Eddy. Both with words to the same effect: *Get into the office. Now.*

Harry worked hard to ignore the feeling that something was very wrong as he pulled on his jeans and a clean shirt, trying to dismiss the nagging doubt. There was no reason to panic, he told himself – not yet. His editors would just be stressed, as ever, from managing their overburdened staff, rather than anything more sinister. It was fine, Harry repeated to himself as he showered quickly and dressed. He grabbed his bag then stepped off the stern and onto the towpath by Millfields Park. Everything was just fine. He just had to keep his cool.

Within moments of approaching Eddy's office, less than an hour later, it was apparent that things were far from fine.

'Hey, Harry.' The faintest flinch in the corner of Khadija's left eye as he passed her gave her away.

'Take a seat.'

Eddy was standing in front of his desk, flicking through a copy of the morning's paper, making a show of it with his fingers. Harry had no need to look; he already knew the headline shouting back at him from the front page by heart, having bought a copy of the paper on his way in, stopping at the newsagent's under the footbridge next to South Quay station while the train trundled on above his head, putting off whatever was coming as long as he could.

Exclusive: Leading Charity in Cahoots With Arms Dealer.

Harry stood where he was, waiting for Eddy's opening shot.

'We had a call this morning, from a Mr and Mrs Conway.'

These were not the words he was expecting, and Harry shifted onto the other foot. Maybe it was going to be OK after all.

Rubbing at his temples with his thumb and forefinger, he tried to think, but he was too strung out. None of this was making any sense.

'I'm too tired for games, Eddy, please just spit it out.'

'OK,' Monkton said, scratching his nose with his middle finger. 'You want me to spell it out for you, I will: you're a nonce.'

He didn't raise his voice but his words cut through the air as though the volume had suddenly been turned up on an old pair of speakers. Harry felt his whole body grow rigid, every part of him so tightly held that he felt if he moved he might snap.

'What?'

Harry turned to look at Corinne, to make sense of what he'd just heard, expecting to find her expression incredulous, willing her to turn to him and throw her hands up at the ludicrousness of Eddy's suggestion, of how clearly he had this wrong.

But as he looked he saw her wince, her arms wrapped defensively around her body, her eyes refusing to meet his. Through the cheap glass wall behind him, he felt the journalists scattered across the newsroom drawing nearer, aware of the heat emanating from the editor's office.

Harry's mind struggled to focus, to process the words.

'What the hell are you . . .' But even as his thoughts spiralled, freefalling in front of him, one of them caught and it was as though it had hooked into his skin.

'Jesus.'

He spoke under his breath, closing his eyes as if to block out the flashes of freckled skin, the whiteness of her eyes, her face tipped back in a smile. The tears the night she came to his room to find him there with his bags packed.

Naomi.

Monkton charged on. 'I tell you what's going to happen. For some reason that is completely beyond me, the parents have agreed with Naomi – that's her name, isn't it? The fifteen-year-old you were fucking while on payroll? It's important to get the details right, as I'm sure you'll understand . . . Well, her parents have agreed – presumably under some duress from their traumatised teenage daughter – not to report this to the police, or even to the PCC. On the condition that you are sacked and that you disappear quietly . . .'

Harry shook his head, too shocked to keep his counsel.

'Naomi? She told me she was twenty . . .'

'I haven't finished,' Monkton continued, savouring the moment. 'They won't press charges on the condition that you are sacked and that you don't write for another paper again. Maybe they want to spare their daughter the ordeal of having to relive it all, or maybe they've read about prosecution rates for rape cases, although one like this – statutory rape – I would have thought that would be more cut-and-dried. Wouldn't you?'

'Eddy, I didn't know . . . I asked her. She told me she was *twenty*—' Harry's voice grew hostile.

He carried on as though Harry hadn't spoken. 'An eye for eye, and all that—'

'This is absurd.'

'You know why I never liked you, Harry?' Eddy's voice was pensive as if he was processing something for the first time and Harry looked away.

'Me neither,' he continued, coming to terms with something strange but inevitable. 'I just didn't. I never trusted you. You were too perfect, I suppose. Too charming. Too handsome. Too fucking smooth for words. I always knew you were rotten, I just didn't know how. And now I see it. But, I have to say, I didn't see this one coming.' He shook his head. 'You're a fucking disgrace.'

'Eddy,' Harry said, raising his voice. '*I didn't know.*'

But it was too late. It was over. And it had only just begun.

When he thought about it later, Harry understood how different things might have been if he had just kept walking when he left the office that day. If he had simply followed the footpath back to the station and away from there. But he hadn't.

He couldn't be sure how long he walked that afternoon, zigzagging from pub to pub. By the time he reached the bar near Canary Wharf, the sky was a dusky grey. Weaving through clots of smokers gathered around outside heaters, Harry moved inside and waited to catch the barman's eye before ordering himself a pint, paying with a handful of cash.

Without waiting for his change, he moved through the bar and out into an otherwise empty garden, away from the hordes of office workers and the low roar of the speakers.

It was dark by now and Harry focused on the soft glow of the fairy lights hanging limply between a couple of barren pot plants; anchoring his thoughts as his mind spun.

There was a shriek of laughter followed by a flurry of voices as the door from the pub swung open, but Harry was so immersed in his own thoughts that he barely noticed the figures fingering unlit cigarettes as they moved outside. It wasn't until one of them stood and walked towards him that he gave them a second thought. When he looked up, the young woman was just a couple of feet away, pushing strands of auburn hair away from her face.

'You got a lighter?' Her Newcastle accent was at odds with those of the friends behind her, a man and a woman both in their early twenties, lurking like members of the chorus in a Greek tragedy.

'Hold on, you're Harry Dwyer,' she said suddenly, her face glinting with recognition. 'I read your story today – we're interning at your paper, Anna and me.' She gestured towards her friend as if this was a great coincidence, a real *hoot*.

He looked back at her, too drained and too drunk to respond properly.

'I'm Meg.' She took another step towards him. His eyes automatically moved over the black tights beneath a tight black mini-skirt and DM boots.

'Come and sit with us?'

He shook his head. 'I'm good, I'm going soon.'

'Don't be like that . . .' She persevered and even though he wanted to be alone, he felt himself standing. He knew girls like this; there would be no getting rid of her without a fight.

'This is Anna and this is David.' Harry nodded.

Someone asked if he wanted a drink and he found himself nodding again. It was such a long way home, and he was not yet ready to face the night bus, the next chapter looming precariously in front of him. At home, he would have to think, to try to work out what this all meant. He wasn't ready to do that. Not yet.

One more drink, he told himself. Just one more.

* * *

Harry woke to the steady churn of the cement mixers, which seemed to have been turning solidly on the building site along the towpath for the past few days. Casting his eyes over the remnants of a kebab stagnating on the table beside an empty bottle of Bells, he pulled open the fridge and closed it again, leaning back against the kitchen counter with a sigh, rubbing the hollows of his eyes with his fingertips.

The boat that had been parked on the opposite bank had moved overnight and through his window he had a clear view of the marshes; dogs of varying shapes and sizes scuttling at the heels of a lone walker, beyond them the grasses moving gently in the morning breeze.

Turning back into the room, he caught sight of his rucksack slung in the corner and he pictured Naomi, her fingers clasped tightly around the straps, attempting to pull him back. He heard himself trying to placate her: *It's over, I'm sorry. I have to leave. I'm sorry.* And he was. But not as sorry as he would be.

Folding his hand into a fist, he cracked his head back against the wooden wall between the window panes, the pain throbbing at his skull bringing temporary release.

The boat was so small, it was closing in on him. He needed air.

It wasn't sunny as he stepped outside into the daylight, but the glare of the sky was harsh, making him wish he owned a pair of sunglasses as he moved along the towpath towards the hill. The nearest shop was only a short walk away and he picked up a pint of milk, coffee and bread from two sparsely stocked aisles, pointing out a bottle of Bells to the man behind the counter. Once he had what he needed, he walked towards the canal, breathing deeply, focusing on the oxygen moving in and out of his lungs, reminding himself that he could do this. He had to do it – there was simply too much at stake not to.

A wave of too-loud reggae and stale beer spilled out from the bar as he stepped inside the Hope & Anchor, ordering a pint and taking it back out to one of the damp picnic benches that lined the canal. He spent a moment watching the rowers, their movements strong and purposeful in contrast to the meandering progress of the coots and the ducks, before reaching into his pocket and pulling out his cigarettes. Shit, no lighter.

For a moment his mind faltered. He had barely left the boat in the past couple of days, where he had been lighting up from the hob, but he could have sworn he had a lighter in his jacket pocket. The image came to him of the girl outside the pub a few nights earlier. She must have pocketed it, or maybe he had left it there on the table, having walked off without looking back after a couple of drinks in the company of her and her friends, tuning out of their conversation as his mind went still with drink.

Right now, drink was what he needed; that blissful oblivion.

It wasn't that he was worried, as such, he told himself as his attention turned back to the present. Worry was a futile emotion; its only power was to hold you back. If he had to name the feeling that followed him as he stood later that afternoon, swaying slightly from the final pint, stumbling towards the poorly lit foot tunnel that led back towards the boat, the echoes of his own movements eclipsed by the sudden rumbling of a train above, the name he would be forced to give would be fear. Fear was different to worry. Fear released adrenaline and adrenaline propelled you forward; in a fight or flight situation, fear could save your life.

It was completely dark when he woke on the sofa a few hours later, the sound of knocking at the canal-boat door so faint at first that he wondered if he had imagined it. Perhaps it was just the purr of the wind brushing through the branches of the trees that lined the water. But the boat was motionless, Harry realised as he stood, glancing at his phone.

It was only 21.09. He was still fully clothed. He had a memory of working his way through the whisky, on this sofa, as the afternoon sun gave way to the moon, bright and lonely against a still East London sky.

All the lights were still on, so there was no way to pretend he wasn't there.

The sound of knocking came again a moment later, too particular this time to be mistaken for the scuffle of the rats who built their nests on the banks here, between the twists of roots that clung to the earth. It was too quietly purposeful to belong to another boater asking to borrow a spare part.

Whoever it was who had come for him could have easily gone unnoticed as they moved towards the canal, passing by a couple of old workers' cottages, and beyond those, up and away from the water, housing estates that lined the vertiginous residential streets towards the main road at Stamford Hill.

In a flash of memory, Harry pictured the night he had cracked the story on the charity's corrupt elements, plying one of the employees with enough booze to loosen his tongue, shifting himself in his chair so that the angle of the button-hole camera in his shirt was pointed at his face while he implicated himself and several other members.

It wasn't like Harry to concern himself with potential reprisals. Exposing corruption, and all that came with it, had its pitfalls – that was his job, it was what he was good at, and if he let himself dwell on the possibility that those he exposed might come seeking revenge, he might have lost his nerve altogether. But that didn't mean he shouldn't be worried at all. That didn't mean there wouldn't be people who wanted him punished. Never more so than now. In this moment there were very good reasons for Harry to fear for his life.

Moving through the boat, the adrenaline finally kicked in, and with it the kind of clarity – even through the cloud of whisky and beer – that made his skin bristle.

Yet perhaps there really was no one outside. His mind flickered between two conflicting states, faltering as it moved from catatonia to wakefulness, because suddenly it was so quiet again out there that he could believe it really was just his brain playing tricks on him. Then there it was again: not a knock this time, catching his attention above the crackle of wood from the wood-burning stove. This time it was movement rather than sound that he sensed on the footpath. The rest of his body completely still, he felt his eyes drawn to the small curtain above the sink opposite the sofa, understanding at once that there was someone approaching the stern. The same person, or was there more than one?

Slowly moving towards the kitchen area, he pulled open the top drawer quietly so as not to give himself away, slowly drawing out a knife. As he turned back towards the front door, his senses on high alert, he finally heard a voice.

'Harry? I know you're in there. For God's sake, man, let me in.'

Aware of a hand slapping against the door, he moved quickly towards it, the blade held out at his side.

'What do you want?' His voice was a hiss.

'Harry?'

There was a pause, and then the man spoke again, and at once Harry knew whose voice it was, and he felt his body sag with relief. Reaching for the wall with one hand to right himself, he felt the other hand loosening around the handle of his weapon.

'Nigel . . .' Harry hissed as he pulled open the door, his voice shaking with the instant shift from relief to fury. 'You scared me half to bloody death.'

Nigel stood in front of him, his angular features half in shadow. 'Aren't you going to let me in?'

Harry

Harry took the overground from Clapton train station the next day, changing at Liverpool Street and standing with his back to the wall on the tube, out of habit, as the Central line shuttled him into Tottenham Court Road. The sun was bright and the chill of the crisp morning air revived him as he walked, admiring the details of the buildings that stretched across a blue sky, making his way towards the address Nigel had given him the night before.

Harry's interest had immediately been aroused as he sat listening to Nigel, the boat rocking steadily beneath them.

'From what we know of Clive Witherall, he started the business as a legitimate commodity trading firm back in the Eighties. Over the years the company has grown to incorporate everything from the trading of oil, metals and minerals to asset management, through a subsidiary company.'

Nigel had topped up their glasses, then continued.

'But it seems that with expansion has come, shall we say, *diversification* . . . Our client, the one who is paying us to look into all this, has reason to believe that TradeSmart is embroiled in a number of trading activities which don't feature under its official FTSE 100 listing.'

'Drugs, you mean?'

Nigel had shrugged nonchalantly. 'The thing is, the client would rather we move into this without external influence. He wants to see what we come up with of our own accord . . .'

Then came the ace card – a truth that when he heard it, Harry could not deny.

'Look, I could sit here all night engaging you from a moral standpoint and that would be perfectly legitimate, but the fact is, beggars can't be choosers. What have they offered you as severance from the paper – three months' pay? You need a job. And I'm offering you one . . .'

Who was Harry to argue with that?

He ran a hand over his hair as he moved through the automatic doors into a discreet but capacious reception area. He had intentionally dressed down in his most crinkled shirt and scuffed boots – anything to demarcate himself. *I'm not one of you*, he wanted them to know, while continuing to tell himself he still didn't know who 'they' were. Newspapers were all corporations these days anyway, their stance dictated by the agendas of the billionaire owners and the advertisers who funded them. What was the difference between that and accepting payment from the coffers of a corporate intelligence agency?

The main difference, it seemed to him in this moment, was the amount of money and the transparency of the transaction.

'Harry!'

Nigel beamed at his former protégé as Harry made his way towards the reception desk.

'Delighted you could make it.'

Harry followed Nigel into the lift and out again three floors up, noting the interior architecture as they passed through the office floor. White walls, sealed meeting rooms, corporate coffee machines all creating the illusion of effective neutrality. Function over form. None of the employees looked up as the two of them walked through the main floor. *Whatever happens in this building stays in this building*, the subtext read. An important message, presumably, to clients whose payments flowed out of bank accounts in the Cayman Islands, Switzerland, the British Virgin Islands, anywhere their provenance could not be traced.

'Can I get you a drink?'

'Wouldn't say no,' Harry replied, looking around the room as he moved towards the table and chairs; a meeting area that could accommodate some twenty attendees, set aside for just the two of them.

Nigel leaned forward towards the phone system and pressed a button. 'Bring us in a couple of coffees would you, Marika? And a bottle of water.'

He sat back and surveyed Harry, smiling.

'Water?' Harry raised an eyebrow. 'Thought you didn't touch the stuff. *Fish fuck in it.* I'm pretty sure that's what you said last time we had lunch – how long ago was that, two years?'

Nigel leaned back in his chair. 'Gosh, I really do have a way with words. Well, that was then, and this is . . . Maybe it's what happens when you get old, and have to have one of your balls lopped off . . .'

Harry winced. 'I heard something about cancer but I didn't know . . .'

Nigel lifted a hand as a middle-aged woman came into the room carrying a tray of drinks, setting them on the table between the men. 'Thanks, Marika.' His face transformed effortlessly into a smile.

'I'm sorry to hear it, Nige,' Harry said once she had left the room.

'Well, so am I. But one bollock is better than no bollocks. And you know what they say, what doesn't kill you makes you stronger. So here I am. Gave up the newspaper game, moved over to the corporate dark side – sold out. And bugger me, I'm making more money than ever, and I have a woman who delivers me coffee. It's awful.'

He smiled and Harry frowned. 'So you're a journalist for hire these days, Nige? Who would have thought it?'

Nigel made a so-shoot-me expression. 'What journalist isn't for hire? It's just a matter of who's doing the hiring – and what they're prepared to pay.'

Harry looked up at him. 'Well, I wasn't going to bring it up, but now that you have . . .'

A crooked smile formed at the edge of Nigel's lips. He reached into the bag by his feet and pulled out a wad of A4 papers, neatly stapled together.

'As you'll appreciate, our clients expect the highest levels of discretion.'

'Is that an NDA?'

'It's a contract,' Nigel replied, sliding the papers in front of Harry. 'It's all there.'

Harry looked down, flicking through the pages until he found the one he was looking for.

'That's how much we're prepared to pay . . . More than enough to buy yourself some help, should you need it,' Nigel confirmed.

'Holy shit.' Harry spoke before he could stop himself. When he looked up, Nigel was grinning back at him.

'Couldn't have put it better myself . . . Once that's out of the way, we can set to work.'

Reaching back into the bag, half an hour or so later, Nigel pulled out a series of photos, which he spread across the table.

'So now that's all sorted, this is Witherall with his right-hand man, Jeff Mayhew. Nominally, Mayhew is just the money man, but he's also in charge of the ethical foundations and, from having put the feelers out, it seems he's a bit of a live wire. Might be worth looking into. That one there is a minder, Jorgos Constantine . . .'

Harry cast his eyes over the image. From the suits and sunglasses and the champagne glasses in hand, he imagined it must have been taken at a party. In the background were mountains, and a flash of blue sea. As his eyes moved away from the figure of Jorgos, his dark hair pulled back in a ponytail, he felt his attention settle briefly on the younger man on the other side of the photograph, in conversation with someone just out of frame.

He felt a bolt of recognition.

'Who is that?'

Nigel sensed the urgency in his voice.

'That?' He turned the photo to face him, leaning in to get a better look. 'That's Witherall's son, David.'

'Fuck.' Harry sat up and fixed Nigel with his eyes. 'I've met him.'

Nigel smiles, leaning back into his chair. 'I know.'

Harry

Harry approached the front of the building with a glance up at the window above the kebab shop. Behind him, Camden High Street bustled with life as he pressed the buzzer. Waiting a moment, he looked up again and saw a flicker of movement.

A few moments later, a voice sounded over the intercom.

'Hello?'

The four of them had been out last night, to the club on Delancey Street. He spoke into the intercom. 'Anna? It's Harry,' he said and then, after a pause, 'It's bloody cold out here – are you going to let me in?'

Making his way up the flight of stairs towards the internal front door, Harry listened out for the sound of a second voice inside the flat. Nigel's words that day at the office haunted him as he moved up the steps.

'You know, Harry, I would have thought of you anyway,' his old boss had told him moments after pulling out the photo of David at the office. 'You would have been my first port of call for a job like this, in an ideal world. But you know what you're like, you're always busy so it didn't occur to me at first. That's right . . . And then, as if by some sort of divine intervention, David turns up a couple of nights ago at the pub and who do you think ends up having a drink with the man we've got eyes on?'

Harry had sat back in his seat without saying a word.

'And then it turns out you've just been fired?'

Harry's eyes narrowed in disbelief. 'What are the chances?'

Nigel had thrown up his arms. 'You tell me.'

There was a pause like the moment before a boxer lands a blow and Harry had looked at Nigel, searching his face for what was coming next. 'You've lost me.'

'What were you doing there? You can't be telling me it's fate that we're watching the son of a corrupt criminal and you just happen to turn up on the scene.'

'He was in the pub just around the corner from my office, the night I was fired.'

'Right you are, but . . . you can see why I might find it a little too coincidental . . .'

'Wait, Nige, are you interrogating *me?*'

Harry pushed himself back in his chair, eyeballing his old boss.

Nigel shook his head. 'I'm asking you to tell me the truth. And I trust you to do that.'

'I'm sorry, I don't understand your question.'

Their eyes held one another's without blinking.

'My question is: had you ever met or heard of David Witherall before that evening?'

Harry didn't hesitate, replying truthfully, 'Never.'

Watching Nigel's deadpan expression, Harry continued. 'What I can say is that I don't believe in coincidence either. If I'm honest, I'm not liking this much . . .'

Harry looked at the clock on the wall. It had been almost forty-five minutes since their meeting started and they had reached deadlock.

Nigel breathed in sharply, leaning back in his chair. 'So what do we call this – the exception that proves the rule?' His face twisted into a smile. 'Or I suppose we could just call it destiny.'

As Harry reached the top of the stairs, he heard the front door click open.

When Anna opened the door, it was clear she was alone. Her hair pulled back in a bun, she wore an ill-fitting T-shirt and the same leggings Harry had seen Meg come and go in a couple of times over the past few weeks.

'What are you watching?' he asked now, following Anna to the sofa, in front of which the TV screen flickered soundlessly.

'A film,' she replied, moving towards the kitchen counter, her back turned to him. He could almost feel the embarrassment coming off her. She must have known he'd seen her the previous evening, groaning, sick stains on her vest top as Meg and David carried her outside.

'You alone?' he asked casually.

'Yeah. Would you like tea?'

'You feel like shit, right?'

'I don't know what happened, I'm not usually—'

Harry laughed. 'Course you're not. I'm just glad you're OK. That's what I came to check . . .' He was good at this, thinking on his feet. He enjoyed it, too, these little games of cat and mouse, even – or especially – when the other player had no idea of the game he or she was engaged in.

He settled on the sofa, mentally scrolling through potential excuses to hang around until Meg came home. Anna talked on and off, Harry replying willingly at first and then suppressing his irritation as time wore on. He had expected Meg to be back by now. She was working today, she'd told him the previous night, as she lifted a bump of MDMA to his nose in the corridor in the club, their lips just about to meet when Anna came crashing around the corner, her body swaying with drink.

Surely she wouldn't be long.

'Have you eaten?' he asked Anna, looking for reasons to prolong the visit, an idea popping into his mind.

'I still feel pretty sick,' she replied.

Harry stood. 'You've got to eat. And have a drink. Trust me, it will make you feel better.' He winked, taking a sip of his tea and passing it back to her.

'I'll be back in ten.' He paused, his eyes moving to the table. 'Actually, are these your keys? You sit. I'll just let myself back in.'

By the time he returned from the shops, Anna seemed to have settled into herself.

She sat on the sofa, taking a slice of pizza while he made hot chocolate, its sweetness sharpened with a strong dose of brandy.

'How long have you guys known each other?' Harry asked, passing her the drink, watching her wince as she took the first sip.

'Me and Meg? Since university. We lived in halls together and then moved into a flat, just the two of us.'

'In Brighton?'

Anna looked up at him. 'Yeah. Did I already say that?'

'Meg mentioned you were both at Sussex,' he lied, taking another bite. 'With David, right?'

Anna nodded. 'He was our Residential Advisor in the first year. So how's work?'

Harry sat a little straighter, the two of them facing each other on the sofa. 'Well, if you really want to know, I've been sacked.'

It made sense to tell her everything, within certain constraints. About the investigation, about Naomi's allegation. Not the whole truth, of course. But enough to pre-empt the rumours Meg was bound to hear in the office.

'It's bullshit, you should know that. I mean, Jesus . . .'

At that second, there was a jangle of keys in the lock and then Meg was there, her expression unreadable as she looked from Harry to Anna.

'Hi!' she said unnaturally brightly, looking down and placing her bag on the table. Was she regretting their almost-kiss the night before, or was she simply annoyed by his unbidden arrival?

Sensing this was not the time, he stood and smiled at Anna. 'I'm glad you're feeling OK.'

Anna stood, too, brushing her hands self-consciously against her thighs.

'What are you guys doing next Friday?' he asked before he left. 'I'll be working near here in the afternoon if you fancy a drink afterwards?'

Harry intentionally looked at Anna first, to prove to Meg he wasn't asking her out on a date. 'Bring your friend David, too, if he's around . . .'

It was a Monday morning, a month after that night in the club, when Harry sat in the window of the coffee shop across the road from the flat, his gaze fixed upwards, watching occasional shadows move across the window as the women got ready for work. He knew from their most recent night out together that both would be leaving early this morning. Meg was going back to Newcastle for a couple of days while Anna headed to the magazine, which was gearing up for a bumper Christmas issue.

David hadn't joined them the last time he met up with the girls and Harry wondered fleetingly if he had started to pick up on what was going on between him and Meg. It wasn't possible, he reminded himself. They had been so discreet. Nonetheless, David wasn't as daft as Harry might have hoped he would be; he could tell from the way he looked at him, sidelong, that he was suspicious – not that he knew anything specific, but rather he simply didn't like having him around. Harry had vowed to be careful. It would be counterproductive to drive a wedge between Meg and David, but equally he needed to get close enough that she would bring him into the fold. In that respect, at least, things were going well.

Given how aloof Meg had been the night Harry showed up at the flat, he had been surprised when she texted the following day. They had agreed to meet early at the Crown and Goose, before the others were due, and as they sat facing one another, Harry felt the tip of Meg's shoe running up his shin. He could see that she enjoyed it when he suggested they should keep anything that might happen between the two of them private – not least owing to his reputation at the newspaper where she was now staff. It wouldn't do either of them any favours, she agreed.

He could see that she loved it, secretly stroking his thigh under the table as the four of them sat together, her eyes giving nothing away.

Harry felt a shiver of excitement thinking of it as he watched the building from the road this morning. Anna emerged first, wrapping her coat tightly around her waist as she stepped out on the street and turned right towards the tube. When Meg appeared, she had a wheeled suitcase at her feet, a second bag clutched chaotically under her arm. She stopped briefly to light a cigarette, a curl of red hair falling in front of her face, dangerously close to the flame, and then she turned left towards the bus stop, presumably to catch the bus to King's Cross where the train would shuttle her back up north.

Harry waited another twenty minutes before leaving the coffee shop. Checking the stretch of the high street in both directions first, he weaved between the stationary traffic before arriving at the front door and pulling the key from his pocket. It was the one he had had copied at a Timpson down the road in Chalk Farm that evening at the flat with Anna, ordering a Margherita by phone and then jumping in a cab to the locksmith, collecting the pizza on his way back and handing the original key straight back to Anna.

Approaching the door, he had no idea what he was looking for, but it was always a good idea to have something in reserve, just in case – and you could always find something.

The lock gave way after a few seconds' struggle. There was a musty smell in the hall as Harry made his way up the stairs. Inside, a radio had been left on, music rattling out from one of the bedrooms. Following the sound hesitantly, though he knew no one was in, he approached Meg's room slowly. Pausing for a second, he breathed deeply before moving inside towards the sound of the radio.

The room was strewn with clothes. Beside the bed in front of the window was a desk with a drawer beneath. Without knowing what he was looking for, Harry moved through the space towards the desk. When he opened it he found the drawer was filled with the usual female detritus: tampons and dried out pens side by side with receipts and old photos. In one there was Meg as a child, her arms wrapped around a German Shepherd, the sky grey and sodden behind her. In another, slightly further down the pile, was Meg as a pre-teen, next to a woman who must have been her mother, in a wheelchair.

Rifling further, Harry's fingers brushed against the soft metal frame of a digital camera. As he pulled it out, he sat back on the bed, pressing the on button and watching the screen come to life. The date in the corner told him the images were a few years old, and as he flicked through, he smiled at the sight of Meg in what would have been her first year at Sussex. It was part of a series, all taken on the same night, featuring various faces. But the ones that came up again and again were of Meg and David. He flicked through, until he found one that caught his attention: Meg holding the camera, the lens turned to face the two of them, their tongues outstretched, pupils blazing. Then another, taken by someone out of shot. Anna, perhaps? Meg leaning into David, her hand moving towards his, passing a tiny folded pouch of paper that was clearly a wrap.

Bingo.

Pulling out his phone, Harry angled his lens at the screen of the camera and took a photo. Returning the item to the drawer, he pushed the contents around until he pulled out a notebook. Inside, the pages were roughly gridded by hand, in pencil, with three titled columns: Names, Amount, Tick? Smiling to himself, Harry pocketed the book and then stood. He was about to leave when he gave a final glance from the doorway and spotted the corner of a ring binder poking out of the bed.

He felt a brief pang of guilt as he opened the file and saw a wad of medical forms. On top, an information pack on applying for Carer's Allowance. Below it, details of various medications related to long-term MS. Returning the folder to where he found it, Harry walked out of the room and headed for the front door.

Harry

Harry met Meg the day after she returned from Newcastle, at the Captain Kidd in Wapping.

He could tell she was on one from the moment she walked in, several faces in the room looking up and watching her cross towards the crowded bar, the energy coming off her like warning shots.

'Sambuca or tequila?' she asked without taking off her jacket, rubbing her hands together in fingerless gloves.

Harry tilted his head. 'Maybe. You all right?'

'Fine. Fucking Newcastle, man. Boring as fuck.'

Harry leaned towards the barman and signalled for two tequilas, hesitating before handing her the glass, watching her neck tense as she leaned back and let the liquid run down her throat.

'Has something happened?' he asked and Meg frowned.

'Like what?'

'I don't know,' Harry said. 'You just seem jumpy.'

'Jumpy?' She sneered. 'I told you, I just don't like going home. But I'm back now and I'm fine, so get us another one of those shots.'

They moved from pub to bar, making their way back towards Bethnal Green. At the off licence nearest the flat, Meg picked out an armful of gin and tonic in tins. Harry paid and they walked towards the apartment the agency had given him occasional access to, in a handsome Victorian mansion block on a quieter street behind the main road. As soon as they were upstairs, Meg pulled out the wrap of white powder she had been snorting bumps from all night using her house key, and Harry thought, with a flicker of regret, of his time in her flat, the ring binder full of information about carers and medication.

He watched her now as she cut out a series of lines.

'Haven't you got any music?' she asked. She rolled a note and inhaled one line and then a second.

'I can sing to you, if you like?' Harry joked, taking the note from her pale fingers and hoovering up the last of it.

'What the fuck's wrong with you?' she said, tilting her head back, wiping the remains of powder from the base of her nose and sniffing hard. Her pupils were small and sharp. 'You can't trust people who don't listen to music. Why don't you have a girlfriend? You're too old to be single.'

'Jesus.' Harry rubbed his temples. 'Anyway, who says I don't have a girlfriend?' He stared back at her and then he shrugged, leaning forward and touching her face. 'I don't know why. Maybe because I'm never here.'

She pulled away from his touch, moving around the living room, which was largely bare aside from a few books and a couple of soulless photographs framed on the wall. After a moment, she stopped and turned to him.

'So where are you?'

His eyes narrowed. 'Is that an existential question?'

'Anna told me you were fired from the paper. For fucking a teenager. Is that true?'

Harry's face stilled. Christ. He had assumed from the lack of confrontation before now that Anna hadn't said anything, or that the gossip-mill at his old paper had long since reached her and she wasn't bothered.

'Do you think it's true?' He was genuinely intrigued.

Meg started to walk around the room again, picking up one of the cans from the table and cracking it open with a hiss.

Harry was about to speak again but Meg interrupted.

'Don't you ever get bored of this shit?'

'Bored of . . .?'

'Life. All of it. It's so fucking *mundane*. I had this idea, you know, that I would become a *journalist* and work at a *newspaper* and do shit that mattered, that I'd make a difference. But it's just bullshit, it's all bullshit, isn't it? I'm just there making cups of fucking tea for entitled old men who don't give a shit about me or what I can do, pretending that I don't mind being their fucking lap dog.'

'I didn't know she was fifteen,' Harry said. He needed her to know that.

'What's the difference. Fifteen, sixteen, eighteen. You're all the fucking same, it's just what you can get away with.'

She tipped the last of the gin and tonic into her mouth and scrunched up the can. 'I just want to do something. You know? What am I even saying, of course you don't.'

'Yes, I do.' Harry's voice was even. 'Traditional journalism is bullshit. I know it. Why do you think I got out?'

'Cause you were fired?'

She looked amused by her own quip.

'I was fired because my editor wouldn't back me, even though he knew I was right. My story stood up regardless of the other shit. The story should be what matters, irrespective of the means by which it is obtained. The PCC, advertisers, they're all calling the shots so that the freedom of the press – or rather the substance of the story in its purest form – is compromised.'

She stopped pacing.

He was on a roll now. 'There's always an agenda. The problem with newspapers is that the agenda isn't always clear. There is always a reason why one story is pursued or ignored at the expense of another. There is no objective truth in journalism. The transactional nature is necessarily polluted – but it's dressed up as neutral.'

'Jesus. Remind me never to give you coke again.' Meg rolled her eyes, moving back to the wrap and racking up another couple of lines with the side of her credit card.

'You can take the piss if you like, but you know I'm right.'

'So what's the answer?'

'Depends what the question is . . . If the question is how do you uncover truth and do so in a way that is untainted by false ethics and a hypocritical code of conduct, then the answer is that you make it a purely financial transaction.'

Meg looked up from her task.

'What the fuck are you on about?'

Harry studied her face for a reaction. 'There are companies that hire journalists, lawyers, people who are expert at uncovering the truth in all its magnificent, fucked up glory – people like us. Unlike newspapers they pay extremely well, and there is no hidden agenda dressed up as a moral code.'

This was a lie and he knew it. The agenda in this instance would be set by the client who was picking up the tab, whether or not he knew who that person or organisation was.

Meg sat back on her calves, watching him.

Harry paused. 'If you were interested, I could bring you in.'

'You know I'm interested,' she replied without hesitation.

'Good. The case I've been hired to work on at the moment involves a corrupt company. It's my job – and could be yours, too – to find out information about this company.'

'Why me?'

'Because you're smart. Because you're dedicated. Because . . .' He took a deep breath. 'Because the company is connected to someone you know. Someone you know well.'

Harry

Harry soon realised the basic mistake he had made.

Meg had gone away 'to think' and he hadn't made plans to see Anna and David that night, the night things became clear. The moment he spotted the two of them moving up the street towards him, unaware of his eyes on them, he finally understood. How had it taken him so long? He had been right about Meg and David, in a way – Meg was indeed in love with David. But what he hadn't realised until now was that David only had eyes for Anna.

There was something else, too, which was obvious as he walked towards them, smiling by way of hello. Something that explained Meg's reluctance to go back to her and Anna's shared flat during their months together, as well as her coolness towards him the night he'd turned up there after the episode at the club. It was only as he found himself face-to-face with Anna and David in the street outside the Crown and Goose that night that he saw it properly.

David wanted Anna – but Anna's eyes were fixed on Harry.

Meg was sitting at her usual table in the Crown and Goose the next time he saw her, the following week, her back to him as he walked through the door. It was two weeks since he had asked her to spy on her friend. There had been a moment of silence, which seemed to Harry to last several minutes though it was no more than a couple of seconds, before Meg spoke again. When she did her voice was scathing. 'You want me to help you get information on *David*?'

She'd moved to the other side of the room, pausing, and then pacing again. 'You want me to help you spy on my friend? How long have you . . .'

His voice had remained firm. 'Meg, sit down. Calm down.'

'Calm down?' She'd taken a step towards him. 'How fucking *dare* you? Who the fuck do you think you are? Who do you think I am?'

As he approached now, he saw both feet drumming against the wooden floorboards.

'You didn't say you were back.'

She jumped at the sound of his voice. Her whole demeanour was twitchy; she looked like she had already stuck half a gram of gak up her nose and it wasn't even dinner time.

'What the fuck are you doing here?' Her eyes moved around the room as he sat in front of her, picking up a bar mat and moving it between his fingers.

'I thought you were going to call as soon as you were back. Once you'd had time to think properly.'

She flinched as he sat in front of her.

'But then I didn't hear from you. Are you meeting someone?'

'No.' Her fingers pressed and released against her glass.

'You're a shit liar, Meg.'

The door opened and her head turned towards the door.

'What time are they coming?'

'I just want you to leave me alone,' she said, any defiance in her voice fading to a plea. 'Please, Harry.'

He smiled with genuine regret. 'I'm sorry, but I can't do that.'

If he was honest, he was almost relieved to see Meg gone. She was a live wire, that one. He hadn't realised quite how much at first, but it would be simpler without her around. And there was no way she would come back, not after the threats he had made.

Harry

Nigel hadn't liked the switch when it came, but he had no choice. Besides, he knew how good Harry was. He'd never let him down before and there was no reason to believe he would start now, not with so much at stake. What did it matter whether it was Meg or Anna? They had to be pragmatic. This case was too important – until suddenly it wasn't.

One minute, Harry was relaying to Nigel that Anna had been approached by MI6, who were asking questions about David and Clive. The next, the whole case was being pulled.

Nigel had been jittery when they met at a bench in Regent's Park overlooking one of the ponds, tourists milling along the path in front of them, their bodies huddled against the wind.

'The client was Francisco Nguema. It was he who was paying to have the case investigated, presumably to see how easily he could be implicated in the chemical spillage.'

'I don't understand,' Harry said.

Nigel kept his eyes fixed ahead of him. 'You don't need to. All you need to know is that it's over. You got your money, and you're safe. There's one thing outstanding – Anna. Can we trust her to stay quiet? She's not going to have a sudden burst of remorse once the money stops and feel the need to get things off her chest with David, is she? Because that would not go down well with the client.'

Harry lowered his voice. 'We can trust Anna. I'll let her know how important it is for her to keep her lip buttoned. Anyway, they have children together. She has a good job. I imagine if anything she will be relieved.'

Even as he said it, he felt a pang of guilt. He wasn't so blind that he couldn't see how deeply Anna had felt about him. But this was the best possible outcome, for all of them. As he walked back across the park later that morning, Harry felt a sense of unravelling, as if casting off layers that had bound him for so long.

'Well then, it's over,' Nigel had said. In that instant, they could both have been forgiven for believing it was.

Harry

It was a month or so after that, once he had resolved to cut all contact with Anna for the final time, that Andrea stepped into his world, in a bar in town.

He'd been at a meeting with Madeleine about a small job connected to her new position at the National Crime Agency. Harry wasn't CHIS – not officially. No, his role was always off the books, just as he liked it. He was a 'sole trader', an expression he felt suited him, only ever paid off the record to do background investigations into *persons of interest*. Madeleine was a delegator, and he got that. Plus, she had shit-tons of money, Harry could tell just by looking at her. She had the balls of a woman who'd never known poverty, who knew what she wanted, was willing to pay for it and expected to get it. And she usually did.

In the end it was nothing much to get excited about – just a matter of digging into a person of interest in a trafficking case she had been working on in Eastern Europe. Madeleine's rate was pitiful but it was some cash at a time when Harry had none coming in. And who knew what else it would lead to in the future? There was enough left in the kitty for now, but it wouldn't do to become complacent. Especially when his usual journalistic revenue streams had dried up permanently.

He had just ordered another whisky when he felt the presence of a woman to his left. Glancing up at her, he took in the dress, nipped in at the waist, the perfectly blow-dried hair. She was more dolled up than his usual type, but when she turned and smiled at him, her fingers clutching a gold Amex card, he felt his jaw clench with desire.

They fucked in the recess of a doorway in the alley outside the bar, her dress hitched up around her waist – and then again back at her flat overlooking the river.

'Where did you even come from?' He asked as she dressed in front of the window, and she turned and smiled.

'That would be telling.'

He woke at Andrea's the next day, the morning sun stretching above the Thames. It was hard to believe this was an extension of the same canal on which his little boat bobbed. From here, London oozed with money and promise, the possibility reflecting on the surface of every building.

She had kept him up half the night, and he needed coffee. He was pulling on his trousers when she turned in bed to look up at him.

'Where are you going?'

'I thought I'd better be off.'

'Why? It's still early.'

He stopped. 'I just assumed—'

'You know what they say about assumption,' she said, pulling the sheet away from herself.

They were preoccupied when Harry's phone rang. It was only afterwards when he pulled it out of his pocket and checked the missed calls that he saw that it was Anna.

'Who's Anna?' Andrea asked, propped up on one elbow.

'No one.'

'Good.'

That was the last time he heard from her. He had every reason to think that chapter of his life was over.

When Andrea first mentioned that the firm she worked for was putting on a charity auction the following February, Harry had recoiled. He didn't know much about her job at the bank, but he knew enough to be confident that it would not be his choice of an evening out, surrounded by stuffy blokes in expensive suits making a show of their generosity for the women hanging from their arms.

But the truth was, more than ever this was exactly the sort of place he should be heading for: an event pulsing with wealth and status, with stories and loose tongues. You never knew who you might meet. And he needed to start thinking about new ventures.

As they moved along the Strand, Andrea spoke to the taxi driver. 'It's just here.'

The car stopped in front of great revolving doors.

'Don't worry,' Andrea said, leaning in to kiss him. 'We don't have to stay long. I just need to show my face. You know what it's like.'

Inside, the atrium lights were too bright, the ballroom pulsating with noise and male sweat. Andrea led Harry to a table laden with bottles of champagne, taking her seat on the opposite side of the table.

'Let's go back to mine,' she said a while later, approaching him from behind as the auctioneer took bids on a Caribbean cruise. He smiled, grateful to be released from a devastatingly dull conversation with the husband of one of the firm's partners.

'You head out and get our coats. I'll say goodbye and meet you out there in a minute,' Andrea said.

He was almost at the door from the ballroom into the atrium when he heard a sudden swell of noise at odds with the heckling of the crowd. Turning, he saw them, the man's hand gripping her wrist. From the way she held herself unsteadily on her feet, it was clear that she was drunk.

He watched them for a moment, frozen to the spot by a rush of blood to his head.

'What are you doing?'

Harry turned towards Andrea's voice. Did he imagine the sharpening of her gaze as she followed the direction in which he was looking?

'I thought I saw someone I know . . . knew. Come on, let's get our coats.'

'I'm going to visit the ladies quickly,' Andrea said, once they had collected their belongings from the cloakroom.

'Why don't we just stop somewhere on the way back?' Harry said and Andrea looked at him, as if gleaning his obvious discomfort.

'No, I need to go now,' she said firmly, pressing her coat into his hands. 'I won't be long.'

Harry lingered as close to the wall as he could, resisting the temptation to look back through to the dining hall to check Anna and David weren't coming through here.

He didn't so much hear her presence as feel it. When he looked up, their eyes met and he saw her physically lose her breath. For a split second neither of them spoke and then Anna broke the silence, her voice cracking.

'What are you doing here?'

Before Harry could answer, he heard another voice, 'Are you ready? Oh . . .'

'Harry,' Anna said, appearing to gather herself. 'This is my husband, David. You know Harry . . .'

What was she saying? For fuck's sake, Harry wanted to shake her. Of course he knew David. Was she so drunk that she had forgotten which part of her life was real and which was imagined?

'My God,' she said, 'but it has been years.'

David hardly flinched. 'Harry, of course. Good to see you.' And then he looked to Harry's right. 'Andrea?'

Harry watched them. 'You two know each other?' He struggled to think of what to say next, to fill the silence that opened up between them.

'Andrea works for the firm who put on the charity ball,' Harry said finally.

'Of course,' David replied, apparently unperturbed by this unlikely connection. 'That's my old firm. Andrea and I, we did work experience together back in the day.'

Harry regarded them both as David moved forward and kissed her on both cheeks. 'This is Anna, my wife.'

There was a moment's silence and then David spoke again. 'We'd better be off, our taxi . . .'

'Please,' Harry said, relieved, the room suddenly spinning around them. 'Good to see you.'

'You know David Witherall?' Harry said quietly, as Andrea took her coat from under Harry's arm.

Andrea widened her eyes, moving in conspiratorially. 'Not a fucking clue. I'm usually good with faces, but that guy I can't remember ever having seen before in my life. *Awkward.* Did I make a convincing job of pretending? And what was with his wife? She couldn't take her eyes off you, or maybe she was trying hard not to fall over. She was *rat*-arsed.'

Leaning out a little, Andrea straightened up, her eyes responding to something in Harry's expression.

'Are you OK? Was Anna an old girlfriend or something?'

'No,' Harry said. 'Nothing like that.'

He put a hand on the small of her back, a cold wind rushing through the hallway as David and Anna moved out onto the Strand.

'Let's get out of here.'

Harry

It was almost twenty-four hours before he checked his old phone. There was no reason for him to do so, it was obsolete, and yet something had made him hold onto it, even after cutting Anna off. Something told him to turn it on and wait for a message to appear on the screen. The sight of Anna's number, when it appeared, sent a chill through his chest.

He read the message three times, digesting its meaning with a growing sense of panic.

> *Dear Harry,*
>
> *I don't know if you're reading this, but after seeing you again I've realised the guilt is too much. I can't do it any more. For so long, I've been lying to so many people. I have let everyone down. I can't see any way to absolve my guilt other than to be honest with the people who have stood by me. My family. I'm sorry if that means I've let you down too, but I suppose that makes us even.*

He moved quickly into the kitchen and poured a drink, pacing the room while he worked out the plan. Half an hour later, he threw on his jacket and strode towards the Hope & Anchor, the speakers booming as he walked towards the bar.

'Mimi?'

The barmaid looked up at him and smiled. She'd always had a weakness for him, though after Naomi he had resolutely steered clear of women who were under their mid-twenties; it wasn't worth the trouble.

'I need to ask you a favour. It's urgent.'

He met Mimi just down the footpath from the pub the following day.

'This is fucking weird,' she said as he ran over the plan once more.

'Well I'm paying you for it – and you're a drama student, aren't you?'

'I know, but—' She broke off. 'What time are we meeting this Anna woman?'

'Twenty minutes,' he said, looking over his shoulder. 'She'll be waiting for us on one of the benches at the top of the park.'

'As if she's going to fall for it, though.' Mimi looked unconvinced.

'You don't need to worry about that. You've memorised everything I need you to say.'

'Of course. I'm a professional . . .'

'Right, and you've nailed the accent?'

'I mean, I've tried,' she said. 'I've Googled it. You know my family is from Jamaica, yeah? I know we might all look the same to you, but it's been a few generations since any of my family were from the Motherland.'

'Well I'm sure you'll smash it.' He held her with a look that made her slightly recoil. 'All you need to do is persuade her that your brother was one of the men in Equatorial Guinea who was part of the chemical spillage, and that he was killed by the villagers in retaliation for what he did. Just stick to the script, you'll be fine.'

'What's all this about?' she asked.

'I've paid you handsomely,' Harry said. 'This is a job for you, nothing more. It's best you don't ask questions. Right, you ready? Let's go.'

Harry

If only she had left when he told her to, and she almost had.

Christ, Mimi's performance had been persuasive. It was so good he too had nearly fallen for the story he had concocted on her behalf about the brother in Equatorial Guinea, a poorly paid delivery driver who had been instructed to dump the waste near the playground, and who had later been killed in order to cover tracks. He had been proud of his cunning strategy to convince Anna to flee, once it had become clear that she was more of a liability than he'd been willing to see. He was doing it for her own safety, as much as his. If she was really on the brink of telling David, as she'd said she was, then her life was in jeopardy. And to his credit it had worked, nearly.

She had made it as far as Greece before Clive and his people managed to lure her back with the story of David's death – which faced her with the prospect of the twins left alone with no family left to look after them but Clive.

She had left him with no choice, hadn't she? Together, they had whittled away the line between the impossible and the inevitable, until it hung by a single thread that was too weak to withstand the slightest tug.

Harry

London, the day before Anna dies

Harry watches the building for just over an hour before Clive appears, figures from the lunchtime crowds on the other side of the Central London square passing in flashes between the winter-faded hedgerows.

He's frailer than Harry had imagined, his body already riddled with cancer. His expression hardly shifts when Harry steps out in front of his door. Holding out a hand to forestall the doorman who immediately steps in, Witherall considers the figure in front of him with an almost amused expression.

'So you came,' he says after a moment.

'Looks like it,' Harry replies.

Clive's nose twitches. 'Good. I thought you might let me know – I wasn't sure my message had reached you.'

'Well, I'm here, so I guess it must have,' Harry says. 'Shall we go inside?'

'I was just leaving. I do wish you'd given me some warning.' Flicking his eyes back to his apartment, he turns and ushers Harry inside, closing the door behind them.

In the apartment, a windowless corridor leads through to the living room. In one of the rooms to the left, a housemaid swills plates at the sink.

As they take their seats on opposing sofas, Harry feels a pang of pity for the old man, lowering himself with the help of an expensive walking cane.

Harry isn't letting his guard down yet – after all, he has no idea what he has been summoned here for, and despite appearances, Clive is a dangerous man. And yet if he means to hurt him, he could have done so immediately rather than summoning Harry to a meeting. For now, they are alone, apart from the maid.

Clive lowers himself carefully into his throne-like armchair, pointing with his stick to the sofa opposite.

'Sit down,' he says, smoothing out the wrinkles in his trousers. 'Would you like a drink?'

'You've just settled, I'll get it,' Harry replies instinctively. Despite how he feels about the man, he can't watch an old person creak in and out of their chair when his own legs work perfectly well.

What must it be like to be so powerful for so long and then to find yourself weak? Harry is struck by a memory of his grandmother, days before she died, her milky eyes staring back at him as if his very existence was a marvel. Her final words to him: *Don't get old, Harry, there's no future in it.*

It happens to us all, if we are lucky, and yet the ravaging of time must hit so much harder for those who are used to living in a way that bolsters them against life's usual threats; protected by money and power and the submission of the people around them. Whoever you are, you can only be invincible for so long in this life.

'No need,' Clive says, calling out to his maid. Despite his physical appearance, he is not ready to relinquish power just yet. 'Aarti!'

The housemaid appears, setting down two glasses and a crystal decanter in front of them. Once she has left, Clive continues.

'So, Harry Dwyer . . .'

Clive leans forward and sips from his glass, considering Harry with an almost admiring expression. The brandy burns the back of Harry's throat.

'This isn't poisoned, I take it?' Harry quips and Clive narrows his eyes.

'Why would I want to poison you?'

'I could think of a couple of reasons.'

'Oh, really?' Clive's eyes widen in mock surprise. 'And what might they be?'

'Because I was paid to investigate you,' Harry says without hesitation. Honesty isn't just the smartest tactic, it's the only one. For Clive to have brought him here like this, he must already know something. Of course he does; he's been on to Anna so obviously he's on to Harry, too. But Harry still has leverage, and he's prepared to use it.

'I was working for a corporate investigations firm to investigate you and TradeSmart, and for the right price I'm willing to tell you who my client was. I think you'd like to know.'

Harry stops and waits for Clive to respond.

They sit like that for a few seconds, watching each other, and then Clive speaks again. 'It was Nguema.'

Clive keeps his eyes on Harry, enjoying the thrill of seeing him squirm, feeding off it.

'What, you thought I didn't know?' Clive sighs, as if by way of apology for letting him down. 'How frustrating for you. God, you must be starting to wonder why you got into all this in the first place. Complicated business, isn't it? *Nasty.* And it's always such a pain to learn you're not as clever as you think you are. So I tell you what, I'm going to let you into all of it, save you the indignity of thinking you know something when you don't. Here, let me top up your glass.'

'Jeff was the one who first introduced me to Francisco Nguema. It was via May, who had studied business at university with Francisco and remained friends with him after he moved back to Africa, and she went on to study law.

'In the early days, when I'd just started TradeSmart and Jeff was working as my accountant, Jeff mentioned he had a contact who was interested in us using his boats for the purpose of import/export. In return for our loyalty, Jeff said, he would do us a great price. So I went to Greece and met Nguema for the first time. He was charming, and as Jeff inferred, he was willing to cut a very good deal – too good, I might have thought if I wasn't so green around the gills. He also offered investment advice. The Eighties was a glorious time for Greece.'

Not everyone saw it that way, Harry resists commenting, thinking of those who had not benefited from the voting in of the Panhellenic Socialist Movement following the end of the military junta in the previous decade.

'The accession of Greece to the European Economic Community made it an attractive proposition for foreign investment, and really we got in there at just the right time. If I'd known, I might have invested more. But remember, I was just starting out. I had no idea what was to come. I had no idea about any of it – not least that our products were going to be used by Nguema as a cover to bring arms in and out of Africa, from Europe. I'm still not sure how much Jeff learnt, and when, but really it was May who was steering things. She could never have enough money, that one. And she was a gambler, in every respect. I admire her in many ways for that. But I blame her too, I suppose.

'Back then, I had such respect for May. I really valued her opinion. She was the brains, never Jeff. I'm not sure what she ever saw in him although I suppose it worked out nicely; her issuing the demands and him implementing them. She reaped the benefits and her hands were always clean – officially. Brilliant, really.'

Harry raises his eyebrows in acknowledgement.

'As the business grew, we needed more advice, more structure, and May offered to introduce us to a lawyer she'd trained with

– one James McCann. I had no reason to think anything of it until one day McCann, clearly convinced by May that we were looking for ways to diversify our portfolio, introduced us to a Russian by the name of Irena Vasiliev. Artemis was struggling and I suppose I slightly took my eye off the ball for a minute. Anyway, the next thing I knew, Jeff and May had embroiled us in a scam involving tax fraud, facilitated by different laws across EU member states. It was a money spinner, I will concede, but it was risky. Far too risky – and we didn't need it. We were making plenty through the business's legitimate strains – or so I thought, not realising then what Nguema was up to.'

Harry considers Clive, wondering at the extent to which he genuinely believes his own innocence. If you are running a company, it's your duty to know what is going on within it. If Clive truly wasn't aware of the side dealings that were happening in his name – and from which he was benefiting significantly – is ignorance really an excuse?

'May tried to convince me to stay in once I called time on it. She rang me one afternoon when David was young and tried to put the thumbscrews on me. I was livid. Who did she think she was? She had nothing to do with the business and yet she seemed to see herself as some unofficial broker. She wouldn't listen to reason when I explained that it was a one-off. After that, we didn't see each other for a while. Things seemed to calm down for a few years, and then one day, on David's seventh birthday, she started again. She said Nguema and Vasiliev had a new business opportunity that I'd be wise to listen to, and when I told her I didn't want to hear it, she handed over to Jeff.'

Clive shook his head in disbelief. 'Except this time, Jeff went behind my back. He went straight to Nguema and told him we were in. One day I got a letter at home from Vasiliev, thanking me for agreeing to register a company jointly – Jeff had instigated the whole thing without talking to me about it. What could I do? Vasiliev was hungry for the air of legitimacy our brand brought to the venture, and Nguema was intent on making it happen for reasons I didn't understand the extent of then. And I was so indebted to Nguema by this stage – he had invested so much and owned part of the business; if he decided to pull out . . .'

Clive's jaw tightened. 'Things had been very rocky for a while – I'd been facing bankruptcy. When you have as big a business as I had then, you're vulnerable. TradeSmart was one of the largest oil traders in the UK, handling around two million barrels of crude oil and oil products a day. One minute I had more money than I knew what to do with, and then the next . . . Jeff and I were at each other's throats. I suppose, if I'm honest, we got greedy; we'd begun to believe we were untouchable. By the time things went wrong we'd diversified into carbon trading and other green energies, and had our ethical foundation up and running. There was so much at stake.'

'Really? Because from what I heard the business was worth seventy-six billion dollars at the time of the chemical spillage.'

Clive's face darkens. 'That's because I made choices – difficult choices, but choices nonetheless. A few years ago we started purchasing heavy naphtha – I'm not proud of it, but it served a purpose. The naphtha was contaminated with a high content of sulphur compounds, known as mercaptans, but it was cheap and it could be made suitable as blendstock for petrol by washing it, as they say, with caustic soda. As I said, it was not a great time for us financially. Nguema had us over a barrel, and he knew it.'

'And you're telling me he then orchestrated the chemical spillage and made it look like you were responsible?'

'Yes,' Clive replies.

'Why?'

'Punishment. Revenge. A power-play. Call it what you want. With

'Anna, it's me. Open the door.'

As she does so, her expression churns, in just a split second, from confusion to anger to fear. 'What are you doing here?'

And then her eyes widen further as she sees the men step out from behind him, the hand moving over her mouth before she can scream. Harry turns away, walking quickly down the steps, hearing nothing but the door close behind him.

It is almost a physical tearing sensation as a part of himself leaves his body forever.

There is no discernible noise other than the faint distant rumble of a train as he steps onto the street and turns right towards the Heath. Perhaps she had known it was coming, perhaps she doesn't resist.

Reaching the entrance to the Heath at the top of Parliament Hill, Harry stumbles towards the nearest bush and vomits. Why hadn't she just left, months ago, when he told her to? She nearly had – it had been so close. She had got as far as Greece before Clive and his men lured her back under the pretence of David's death. At every stage, they had been one step ahead, waiting to make their final move.

He stands straight and reaches in his pocket for a cigarette, his gloved fingers trembling as he lights up. The colour is draining fast from the sky. Following his feet, he walks over the hill and pauses for a moment, drawing the fresh air deep into his lungs.

On the bench at the top of Kite Hill, he spots a young woman, her knees pulled up to her chest.

'Can I nick a ciggy?' she calls out.

The mundanity of her request catches him off-guard and he moves towards her, pausing briefly to pass her a cigarette before moving down the hill towards Highgate Road.

Around him, London is just as it was, the lights of the city starting to twinkle in the distance, couples walking arm-in-arm over the brow of the hill. But something inside him has shifted, and will likely never re-centre. As he reaches the tennis courts, his phone rings.

Clive's voice is calm. There is no hint of celebration, or even relief, in his tone.

'Is it done?'

'It's done,' Harry says, treading the butt of his cigarette into the grass. 'It's over.'

Meg had called it, that evening all those years ago in the flat in Bethnal Green. *You think you can do what you want and that there will be no consequences – you destroy everything that is good.* She had seethed at him, the rage pulsating through every part of her being.

She had been alluding to Harry's attempt to draw her into this world – there was no way she could have predicted anything more than that, back then – but perhaps she had seen in him a certain recklessness, the ability and ultimately the willingness to crush out a life.

It had happened slowly, discreetly, on the periphery of his vision while he had been busy looking elsewhere. And yet, he was not the only one who would have reason to pause at the sight of his own reflection. How easy it is to list one's intentions in a series of neat bullet points, to quantify, out of any context, the risks and chances one is willing to take; the values and beliefs one holds dear. *This is who I am and this is who I intend to be.*

But life takes place between the lines. In that space between the definable, the pure, the sacrosanct, that is where reality emerges: chaos born out of clarity; a murky cloud made up of the everyday choices we all make, the mistakes we have no way yet of knowing were mistakes – polluting the space between those absolute truths, the smell of the lead unnoticeable until it chokes us.

PART THREE

Madeleine

London, the inquest

Madeleine arrives last, standing at the back of the courtroom, near the exit. From here her eyes scan the backs of heads. It's busier than it was yesterday on the press benches, the sharks swarming in preparation for the final day, due to begin any moment.

The coroner rustles papers at the front of the room, ahead of the first witness statement of the morning. Why is she taking so long? This is partly why Madeleine hates coming to court; the whole bloody thing is so protracted. She should have finished her second coffee after all, but she had been worried she would be late. Again, she had struggled to sleep, thoughts rattling through her mind.

Her eyes move to the clock at the front of the room. Ten o'clock.

Time takes on new form in this room, and new meaning. Time is all they have, the dead whose final moments are sieved through and assessed in small, digestible pieces. Time and the prospect of justice, or – as often as not – no justice at all. Either way, whatever decisions are made in this room are only ever made after the fact, and what use is that to the dead?

As she looks away, a head turns from the press benches, and Madeleine blinks as though her eyes might be deceiving her.

Harry doesn't notice her and instinctively she feels herself lean back, out of view. What the hell is he doing here?

161

There is a rustling of papers as the coroner looks up and Madeleine's attention is drawn back towards the front of the room. 'The court will now hear from Sarah Marshall.'

The woman taking the stand is in her early forties. She is what might be described as frumpy, the very opposite of the image of Anna, the elusive socialite, depicted in the papers. But then friends don't have to be alike, do they? Madeleine's mind slides towards Gabriela. They'd had hardly anything in common, besides their jobs. But then look how that friendship had ended . . . She blinks, blotting out the image of the children. How could Gabriela have let it happen? How could she have drawn her family into something so devastating? She thinks, then, of Ivan, trying to imagine what he must be feeling in his jail cell, awaiting trial. Does he feel an inch of remorse for all of this? Something tells her he is not the sort of man who would accept blame for anything, even the loss of his own child, and her mother.

'Mrs Marshall,' the coroner says, as the woman facing the court finishes her oath. 'Could you please explain how you knew Anna Witherall?'

'Our daughters were friends from nursery. I, too, had lost my husband, a couple of years earlier. After Rose and Stella's father passed, I offered to help occasionally. Anna . . .' Sarah pushes a piece of hair away from her eyes. 'She didn't appear to have a huge number of friends . . .'

'And please could you tell us what happened the night Anna died.'

Sarah stops and closes her eyes, taking a moment to collect herself.

'Anna had something she needed to do in the day. I took the girls; it was only going to be for a couple of hours but when I spoke to her on the phone to check in on her, I offered to keep them a bit longer.'

'Check in on her?'

Sarah pauses. 'I mean, I just wanted to see if she was all right.'

The coroner waits encouragingly. 'And how did she seem?'

'She seemed . . . I don't know, I mean her husband had recently died and she had two young children to look after alone. I would say she seemed distracted, tired, maybe in shock?'

'And what happened next?'

'I offered to look after the girls a little longer and bring them home around six.' Her voice cracks.

'It's OK,' the coroner says. 'Take your time.'

'We live just on the other side of Hampstead, but it was freezing so I decided to drive. I didn't want to risk Rose and Stella catching a cold.' Sarah swallows at the memory of the girls, looking down at her hands.

'Please, take your time,' the coroner says.

'When we got to the house I left Mabel, my daughter, in the car. The lights were off, which I thought was a bit odd, I suppose.'

Sarah breathes deeply.

'I don't know how to explain it, but I felt something wasn't right as we approached the house so I told the girls to get back in the car with Mabel. I can't explain it. It was just a feeling. And then, I knocked on the door and there was no answer. When I tried Anna's phone, I could hear it ringing inside so I looked through the letter box to see if there was a light on in the kitchen or . . .'

There is silence as Sarah stops, moving her hand to her mouth. Tears stream down her cheeks and the coroner says nothing, leaving the witness to gather herself.

'I could see her, hanging from the stairs.'

She nods, as if confirming something to herself.

'If I hadn't offered to keep the girls later . . .' Her voice cracks and there is a cry from the front row that Madeleine can't place. 'I called the ambulance, but I could already see that it was too late.'

* * *

Madeleine waits outside the courtroom for Harry at recess while they prepare for the coroner's conclusion but he is nowhere to be found.

She hasn't seen him since Gabriela. They had spoken briefly on the phone but they hadn't met face-to-face: what would be the point? She knows exactly what happened to them, and she has told herself it is understandable that Harry would want to keep as much distance as possible from the case.

She tries his phone but it is off. As she slides the handset back into her bag she looks up and another face in the crowd catches her attention.

'Isobel?' The reporter looks up at Madeleine as she approaches, smiling in recognition.

'Madeleine? Oh wow. How are you doing? I didn't expect—'

Madeleine's mind returns to the article she had read in the *Camden News*, before Sean mentioned the connection between Vasiliev and Witherall. A month of digging later, they were hardly any further than they had been, though that was hardly surprising with a case such as this – everywhere they turned, walls seemed to rise up in front of them, blocking any kind of meaningful progress. Even with the testimony of Popov's maid, things weren't exactly progressing. Still, the years of work on breaking the phone encryption was at last appearing fruitful and if they could pull that off, there would be hope . . .

It is unlikely that Isobel will hold any meaningful answers, but it's worth a shot. From the little she knows of the young reporter, she is nothing if not tenacious.

'Would you be free for a chat later?' Madeleine asks.

'I can't today.' Isobel takes a drag of her roll-up. 'I'll have to run straight off to file my copy as soon as the conclusion is announced, but I can manage tomorrow. This is my card . . .'

'That's fine,' Madeleine replies. 'Actually, I've got to look for someone quickly—'

She is interrupted by the sound of the coroner's officer calling them inside.

'Oh,' Isobel says, grinding out her rollie with the sole of her Converse boot. 'Sounds like we're going back in.'

Artemis

London, the Nineties

It was one of those crisp mornings that London did so well, the sky beaming, the shoots in the trees signalling new possibility through every window in the house. But as Artemis stepped out of the front door she was stung by a bitter chill in the air.

Hearing the door click closed behind her, carried by a sudden gust of wind, she moved quickly down the steps. Without David, she felt naked. But now he was two and a half, he was potty-training and there was already plenty of opportunity for accidents without adding public toilets and a padded all-in-one to the mix. Besides, Clive could hardly complain about having his son there with him while she popped out to buy ingredients for a Rick Stein recipe the pair had selected for their monthly lunch with Jeff and May.

Still, he had complained. He was so snappy at the moment, so distracted with work, that even when he was in London it was like he was in another world. She scolded herself as she walked along Queen's Crescent. She should be grateful that he was working so hard to provide for his family, and she was, but she was allowed to be annoyed, too. Wasn't she?

The fishmonger looked up as she stepped into the shop, the smell instantly transporting her back to the island. Briefly, she faltered, picturing the drop from the mountain to the sea, the sky stretched out like a blanket.

The fishmonger's voice interrupted her thoughts and she was grateful for the distraction.

There was no point longing for something she couldn't have. Besides, she didn't want to go back there. Hadn't she been desperate to get away?

She walked home quickly, met by David's voice as soon as she let herself in the front door, watching him for a moment from the doorway of the living room, before stepping inside. He was using a collection of old toilet rolls sticky-taped together as an aeroplane, swooping it over his head with an extended hand. When she moved towards him, she saw that his trousers were sodden. As she approached, he started to cry.

Careful not to scold him – she knew more than anyone how easily accidents could happen – she stripped off the wet clothes, cursing Clive silently for having left him untended.

After just a moment's comforting, David calmed and returned his attention to his toys. Not wanting to disturb his game, Artemis left him there for a moment while she went to find clean trousers. As she reached the top step of the first flight of stairs, she heard Clive's voice from the study. He was strict about interruptions when he was on a call and even though she would have loved to throw open the door and reprimand him for working up here whilst David was left alone downstairs, something told her to remain quiet.

Slowing her movements, Artemis stepped carefully across the carpet, Clive's voice growing clearer with every pace.

'May, I'm not doing it,' she heard him say. 'I've told you. I'm not comfortable with any of this. I have a family to think of. You and I are not—'

Artemis turned sharply, the colour rising in her cheeks.

May?

The word repeated in her mind as she moved back down the hall, reaching for the bannister to lighten her impression on the floorboards which creaked below the emerald-green carpet. Clive's voice suddenly fell silent and Artemis picked up speed.

She was halfway back down the landing when she heard Clive coming out of the study.

'Artemis?'

His voice stopped her in her tracks. She turned slowly towards him.

'What are you doing?' His tone was suspicious.

'I was getting David some clothes. He wet himself.' As if on cue, she heard their child call for her from downstairs.

'Who were you talking to?' she managed after a moment.

Clive didn't miss a beat. 'Jeff. Why, is everything OK?'

She remained still for a moment, letting his lie sink in, and then she looked up, meeting his eye. 'Why wouldn't it be?'

'You look pale.'

'I'm tired, I didn't sleep much last night . . . David was upset just now,' she said tightly. 'He was soaking. I came upstairs to get him a clean outfit.'

Clive paused, not mentioning how she'd avoided answering his question. 'Where are the clothes?' he asked after a beat.

Artemis tensed, looking down at her empty hands, before lifting her eyes to meet his.

'I just remembered there's something for him outside on the line.' She turned away, feeling his eyes following her as she moved back downstairs to their son.

She was standing over the chopping board, slowly lifting a kitchen knife and piercing it through the flesh of the onion, occasionally tuning into the voices on the radio discussing the election of a new leader of the Labour party, when the doorbell rang later that evening.

'Will you get that?' Clive called out to her over the sizzling of fat, as if addressing a member of staff who was neglecting their duty.

Artemis pushed the blade firmly until she felt it lodge in the chopping board. She was inclined to argue. Since overhearing his call to May a few hours earlier, her shock had turned to despair and finally to quiet anger, which came and went in nauseating waves. When she looked up, Clive was grappling with a hot pan, finally getting to grips with domestic chores once an audience was expected. She thought briefly of the foundation he and Jeff had mooted, which would no doubt dominate conversation this evening. How much, she wondered, was it about doing good, and how much about being *seen* to be doing good?

'Artemis?' Clive said as the doorbell rang again. Losing the will to retort, Artemis left what she was doing, wiping her hands on her apron as she walked towards the hall.

The hallway was silent and she took a moment to observe the outline of two figures through the stained glass, enjoying making them wait, the swaying branches of the trees above their heads like dangling tentacles reminding her of the squid that lay splayed out on the port floor amidst the dead fish.

'Good evening,' Artemis said as she opened the door, an air of impatience hovering above the couple on the step.

'Gosh, I thought we were going to be left to die out here,' May replied, with a strained tone of joviality, her perfume thick and sweet as she passed, leaning in to kiss Artemis on the cheek. 'Something smells divine,' she added loudly for Clive's benefit, taking off her coat and moving past a gallery of framed photographs as though she owned the place. 'Sorry we're late, the babysitter is useless. Is Clive through here?'

'Artemis, you look beautiful as always,' Jeff beamed. Artemis smiled thinly back at him, his arm moving unnecessarily to her hip as he kissed her hello.

'Don't worry about her,' Jeff said, perhaps reading the energy coming off Artemis. 'She's just grumpy because she hasn't had a drink yet.'

'Right,' Artemis said, though Jeff wasn't listening, following his wife along the hall.

In the kitchen, May was taking a glass of wine from Clive. Turning, her sharp heels made impressions in the carpet as she moved from the kitchen through to the adjoining living room.

'Now where is David?' Her words trailed behind her and Artemis had a fleeting urge to run after her and grab her by the hair. How dare she say his name so casually?

'He's in bed,' she heard herself say, gripping the counter as she turned back towards the chopping board.

'She loves that boy as if he were her own,' Jeff said, to himself as much as to Artemis. *As much as the children she loves so much we never see them, left as they always are with one of a fleet of staff to whom the duties of motherhood are delegated,* Artemis let the thoughts form in her mind.

She heard the click of the glass Clive had been holding out in a private toast between the men.

'Yes, well, David loves her, too,' Clive said.

The thought dissolved into silence, the tears stinging her eyes nothing to do with the onions she was slicing into, her fingers gripped tight around the handle of the knife.

Artemis rang Athena the next day. Clive had offered to take David with him to have the car cleaned while Artemis tended to chores at the house. It was one of David's favourite things, to sit in the front passenger seat while the vehicle moved through the rotating foamy cylinders. She tried to suppress the jealousy that clawed through her as she watched him and Clive leave, through the living room window. But it hurt, how willingly he reached for his father's hand, how merrily he tried to move into step as they made their way towards the car. What little Clive did with David, he was always met with the sort of gratitude she couldn't help but feel he didn't deserve.

Shaking away her thoughts, she watched the Mercedes disappear at the end of the street before picking up the receiver and dialling Athena's number. Artemis was already mentally immersed in the conversation she was preparing to have with her oldest friend, confiding in her about the phone call she had overheard between Clive and May, and what it meant. But the moment Athena answered, Artemis could hear the distraction in her voice, baby Maria crying out in the background.

'Is everything OK?' Artemis asked. 'Shall I call another time?'

Athena shouted to Panos to close the door, muttering to herself irritably as she returned her attention to the phone.

'It's fine, she just won't stop bloody crying – all the time! I feed her, she cries, I put her outside, she cries, I bring her inside, she cries . . . How are you?'

'I'm OK,' Artemis replied hesitantly, put off her stride by the chaos at the other end of the line. 'Something strange happened, with Clive . . .' she started cautiously.

'Yes?' She heard Athena's interest pick up.

Artemis hesitated. 'Yesterday he was on a call to May – you know, that awful wife of his business part—'

'You do it!' Athena suddenly cried out, muffling the mouthpiece with her hand. 'Panos, I'm on the phone . . .'

'Listen, I'll call you back,' Artemis said, suddenly unsure of her words, her reserve exacerbated by the tension in Athena's voice, and the slight delay on the phone line. Besides, was Athena really the person to tell? Resentment lingered from the time she had tried to tell her about the rape. Artemis could ignore it most of the time, bury the hurt and the anger and the shame beneath the love she felt for her friend. But she felt its presence again now, crouched in the corner of the room, like a ghost. She had tried to tell her that afternoon, in the immediate aftermath, with the bruises at the tops of her legs newly-formed. The memory of his hands holding her down while she wrestled against him was still fresh – and yet after that conversation with Athena she came away asking herself if it had partly been her own fault, doubting herself rather than the boy who had been prepared to destroy her. She had agreed to go with him, hadn't she? How hard had she tried to resist? How firmly had she said no?

Hard enough, she reminded herself – more than she should have needed to.

And yet, even with that lucidity, the same sense of doubt crept up on her again now as she hung up the phone, muttering to Athena that she would call again later.

What had she actually heard Clive say, that day in the office? Perhaps she had imagined the word May, or, more likely, heard it out of context. Besides, that woman, with her too-orange perma-tan and grating manner, was hardly a romantic threat, was she?

Of course she wasn't, she told herself, silencing the voice that told her she wasn't a fool. She was simply being paranoid. Besides, she and Clive had a child together. Whatever she had or hadn't heard, they were a family and that was all that mattered. No one, certainly not May, would ruin that.

Madeleine

London, the inquest

'I would like to offer on behalf of the court my sincerest condolences to Ms Witherall's family, not least her mother and her daughters, Stella and Rose. The inquest is now closed.'

Death by suicide.

The words rattle through Madeleine's mind as the journalists move out of court ahead of the family and friends, each reporter desperate to be the first to file their piece.

Harry's face drops as she walks towards him, his fingers fidgeting with a cigarette outside the court. He has lost weight since the last time she saw him.

'Madeleine?' When he leans forward to kiss her on the cheek, his skin is sharp with stubble. 'Good to see you,' he says unconvincingly, his attention moving to the door.

'Why are you here?'

'I was about to ask you the same thing.'

'I knew Anna.' He inhales, looking away, releasing the smoke in a controlled line.

'Really? How—'

Harry interrupts, his voice urgent, as if the thought has been sitting there waiting to tumble out. 'I just can't believe it. Those children. Sadie, Callum . . . I wondered at first if it was staged—' He scratches his chest with his free hand, visibly upset. 'Do you suspect anyone?'

'Who do you think?'

He bites his lip, nodding thoughtfully. 'Fuck. I should have stayed with them longer. The girl, the older one, she asked me to stay. She . . .'

'There was nothing you could have done,' Madeleine says, more abruptly than she intends.

Harry looks over her shoulder, spotting someone out of the corner of his eye. His expression changes. 'Look, I have to go. It was good seeing you. You take care.' He pats her distractedly on the arm and moves quickly away, past the entrance to the court.

Madeleine turns and watches him moving towards the stairs leading to Granary Street and King's Cross station, beyond. She waits a few moments before following.

At the bottom of the stairs the road veers left towards Camden Road on one side, and to the other, sweeps under a small bridge towards the newly developed Coal Drops Yard and Granary Square.

She has barely taken a step onto the pavement when she spots a flicker of movement under the footbridge twenty or so metres away, followed by raised voices. Stopping, she instinctively takes a step back so that she is partially obscured by the wall. From here she watches the arguing figures. She can see them both clearly – Harry, and the red-headed woman from the family table at the front of the court. She is the one attendee Madeleine hasn't been able to identify in the nights she has spent trawling the internet for clues about the case.

There was Anna's mother, her father-in-law, Clive Witherall, and Anna's former boss, Clarissa Marceaux. But this woman, she could find no trace of.

After a moment, Harry disappears. Madeleine moves slowly towards the footbridge, and when she gets closer the woman leans against the wall and lights a cigarette.

'Are you OK?' Madeleine asks as she gets closer.

The eyes that look up at her are at once alert and remote, as if she has been disturbed in the deepest of thoughts.

'Hmm? Oh,' she says, realising Madeleine must have seen the argument. 'I'm fine. Thanks. Just having a catch-up with an old friend.'

'Right,' Madeleine says without moving, watching the woman's expression shift into vague recognition.

The woman inhales deeply, exhaling the smoke in a controlled line. 'When I say friend I mean total fucking arsehole.'

'It's an important distinction,' Madeleine nods.

'You were in court, weren't you?'

Madeleine nods.

'You're not a journalist?'

'No,' Madeleine replies, hesitating. 'I'm police.'

It's not strictly true, she reminds herself, but NCA officers often identify as such given the majority of the public wouldn't know what the National Crime Agency is, let alone what they do. Besides, they have the same policing powers – even if the old sweat officers would scoff at someone from the NCA calling themselves cops, not least someone like Madeleine.

'Police?' The woman lifts the cigarette to her lips and inhales again, looking away. 'Bit late, aren't you?'

'My name's Madeleine,' she says, ignoring the woman's tone.

'Meg,' the woman replies after a moment. 'So why were you in court, if Anna's death isn't being treated as a crime?'

Ignoring the question, Madeleine asks, 'What did you mean when you said we were a bit late?'

'Anna's already dead, isn't she?' Meg waits a moment. 'Is there a suggestion that Anna's death wasn't suicide?'

Madeleine's eyes narrow. 'Why would you say that?'

'Why else would you be here?'

Madeleine pauses, ignoring the question once again. 'The man you were arguing with just then . . .'

Meg exhales sharply, flicking away her cigarette and crossing her arms over herself, laughing sardonically. 'You wouldn't believe me if I told you.'

Madeleine doesn't flinch. 'Try me.'

Artemis

London, the Nineties

The day David started school, Artemis felt like someone had pulled the rug from under her world.

'He's in excellent hands,' the reception teacher assured her as they stood in the playground that first morning, her fingers gripped around his.

It was September and the trees swayed unsteadily above their heads. Artemis felt a flutter of nerves as she looked up. When was the last time those branches had been felled? People were killed by falling trees; even a smaller branch could damage a child if it landed on them from a height.

'I'm just not sure that he's ready,' Artemis replied, refusing to let go of her son's hand as the other children filed into the red-brick building where Clive had been educated, decades earlier.

The finest boys' school in London, Clive had said proudly once they received the letter to confirm his place, for which they would be paying more each month than Artemis could fathom. She thought back to her own school, the lessons held in the dusty playground, desks shared between pupils. The taunting.

This place, by contrast, with its cricket grounds and computer room, was not so much a school as an establishment. Another *institution* to which she somehow found herself inadvertently attached.

She should be happy for her son. It was a blessing to be able to afford such privilege. Unlike her, David would not have to scramble for books to learn another language; he wouldn't find himself derided for wanting to know more than the teacher had means to tell. But would he be happy?

She laughed at herself for that one. *You can be happy anywhere,* she had once heard Athena's mother tell her when she complained of being bored on the island, of wanting to get away, of wanting a more satisfying life. Yes, Artemis thought now. You could be happy anywhere, and you could be miserable anywhere, too. But how could she be sure David would be happy here? How would she know what went on behind closed doors? Her parents had never known what she endured each day when they sent her off to school.

'David will be absolutely fine,' the teacher said firmly, as if reading Artemis' thoughts.

She hadn't allowed herself to watch as he moved away from her, towards the next stage of his life, the doors closing behind him, stealing her son away in a world to which she had only the most limited access. As she walked home, the familiar streets of Hampstead contracted around her, squeezing her out, so that by the time she reached the bottom of her street, she felt like an outsider again.

She spent the morning on the Heath, trying to sketch to help pass the time before collecting David. But as she looked out at the birds sweeping in and out of the willow tree that hung resignedly over the pond, she felt her hand freeze up.

How long had it been since she had last taken pencil to paper? Something that was once second nature now jarred. It felt like another lifetime that Clive had promised her the gallery, once they were in London. She had never pushed the point, not even when he suggested she wait until she was further along in her pregnancy and then revisit the idea. She had lost her nerve; any faith she had in herself and her identity had drained away. She had lost whatever voice she'd had, and what was an artist with nothing to say?

She had better get home, she told herself, in case someone called from the school. David might need her. How had she not thought of it sooner? She ran the short distance, heading straight to the answerphone. When she found it blank she wasn't sure if she was relieved or disappointed.

As the months passed and Clive's business gathered momentum, the ratio of time he was spending in London to that which he spent abroad, at various meetings and conferences and heavens knows what else, diminished so that often Artemis felt like she was raising David alone. Not that she would have minded if David was actually there for her to look after – she might have relished it if that had been the case. But in the months since he had started school, everything had changed. Even though she knew it was selfish, she dreaded the time between dropping him off and picking him up again, pink-cheeked and full of all the exciting things they had done in class. It was an affront, of sorts, how easily he fell into his routine; while other children clung to their mothers, David would run into school happily.

'You're lucky that he's so keen to go,' one of the mums noted in the playground. 'He must feel very secure. Joel never wants to be more than a metre away from me.'

Artemis had spent the morning at a step aerobics class arranged as a fundraiser for a new computer suite for the school – as if the school didn't get enough donations on top of the already exorbitant fees. Slinking off as soon as she could, she made her way back through Hampstead with a sense of relief. It wasn't that she hadn't tried to like them – she had attempted to connect with the mothers of David's new friends, despite her instinctive aversion to their competitive socialising and unnecessarily obtrusive 4x4 cars with bull bars that would so easily break a child.

Dutifully, she turned up occasionally at the endless fundraisers or the coffee mornings where the teachers looked at her with an expression she could never quite read. But in the company of these women, her sense of loneliness was even more profound.

The sky was unusually bright this morning. Artemis nibbled at the corner of a chocolate bourbon she had snaffled from the tea tray on the way out. As she moved along Parliament Hill she cast her eyes over the houses that finally felt familiar, after more than five years. When she had first arrived here she had felt so claustrophobic inside the house, thinking of all the bodies wedged in their terraces along this street. But now, as she approached home, she longed for the feeling that she wasn't entirely alone.

As if by some projected response, the moment she moved into the hallway, she heard movement from the middle floor of the house. Feeling her heart lift to know Clive was home, she moved quickly upstairs to the bedroom. The moment she stepped inside, she saw the suitcase.

'You're not going away again?'

Without looking up, Clive continued to place neatly folded shirts into the open bag. 'You know I am. It's been in the diary for weeks. We have a big meeting in Asia. A whole new market is opening up and Francisco has brokered some meetings—'

Artemis felt her chest tighten. 'But I need you here.'

'Why?' He moved towards her, staring intensely as if he didn't understand the person who was standing in front of him. 'I don't understand, I go away all the time . . .'

'Exactly,' Artemis muttered under her breath. Either Clive didn't hear or he pretended not to.

'You're all sweaty,' he said, his eyes glistening as he pulled the strap of her vest-top from her shoulder.

'No,' she said, moving away from him. 'I'm serious. Maybe we could come with you?'

Clive laughed, as if it was the most preposterous thing he'd ever heard. 'Artemis, I'm going now. It's Tuesday, David's at school.'

'We could pick him up. He's still our child,' she snapped.

'Look,' he said kindly, 'whatever is happening, whatever's going on in your head, I wonder if you should talk to someone. I spoke to Athena – she's worried too, after your last conversation.'

Artemis paused. 'You spoke to Athena, about me?'

'Don't look so surprised. She rang and you were out and . . . Well, she mentioned you'd been distressed when you called her last week.'

'I wasn't distressed,' Artemis snapped, her hands opening and closing like a clam. She tried to think back on what she had said, but nothing sprang to mind. She might have mentioned that she missed her friend, and her parents, but she wasn't distressed as such. She was lonely. She was allowed to be lonely, wasn't she? 'Why would Athena say that?'

'Because she cares about you and she's worried. To be honest, she's not the only one.' He took her hand and she recoiled at his touch. Clive carried on regardless, as if addressing a wary animal, staying calm so as not to spook it. *Not so worried that you'd consider actually spending time at home*, she wanted to shout back at him, but he interrupted her thoughts.

'She mentioned what happened to your sister, in the earthquake—'

Artemis took a step back. 'I don't want to talk about that with you. How dare you talk about me behind my back?' Her face was stinging with heat, as if she had been slapped.

How could Athena do that to her? If she had wanted Clive to know about Helena then *she* would have told him. So why hadn't she? What sort of marriage involved one partner withholding such a key fact from the other?

'Go! Go and leave us *again*, I don't give a shit!' she said, suddenly furious, though she couldn't say exactly why or who she was angry at. Marching out of the bedroom and into the hallway, she ran down the stairs and back out the front door, slamming it behind her, the whole house quivering with what was to come.

Madeleine

They meet at the Wenlock Arms, off Essex Road – a pub far enough from the office that Madeleine is unlikely to bump into anyone she knows. This is not a meeting she wants to declare.

Isobel is already waiting at a table opposite the bar. She looks more composed, and healthier, than when they first met a couple of months earlier at the women's refuge, though she still seems outrageously young – or perhaps this is merely another sign that Madeleine really is past it.

'Isobel, thank you for meeting me,' she says, with a smile. 'Can I get you a drink?'

'I'm fine with water,' Isobel replies, indicating the glass in front of her.

Madeleine takes a seat, placing her bag on the table and signalling to the barman for a coffee. Presumably there was a day when ordering an espresso in a place like this would have been as frowned upon as the notion of table service, but those days are sadly gone. It would seem that she has somehow managed to be born both too early and too late.

'I appreciate your time; I realise you must be incredibly busy . . . I read your piece this morning on the inquest.'

Isobel raises her eyebrows. 'It's a pleasure. It's good that you're interested in the story.'

Madeleine smiles wryly. 'To me it's not a story, it's a case.'

'Same thing,' Isobel replies, taking a sip of her water. 'Except a case presumably ends when the judgement is made, but a story doesn't.'

Madeleine thinks of the first time she had seen Isobel, how she had blatantly smelt of booze. Giving her the benefit of the doubt, Madeleine had told herself it was probably a hangover rather than her drinking on the job in the middle of the day.

'That's a pretty deep assessment for ten a.m.,' Madeleine says, smiling. 'So you don't think this story is finished— Oh, thank you so much, please add it to the tab,' she says, turning to the barman as he sets down her drink.

Isobel leans back in her chair. 'I suppose I'm interested in why the NCA is interested in it,' she says, once the barman has left.

'First I should say that everything we discuss here is off the record.' Madeleine looks at Isobel's phone, which is on the table between them.

'I'm not recording,' Isobel says, picking it up and showing her the blank screen. 'And of course, off the record is fine.'

'You look well, by the way,' Madeleine says, hoping to start again, on a better footing.

'Thanks,' Isobel smiles coyly. 'I was having a bit of a stressful time when we last met. I really appreciated your – Dana's – help.'

'I'm glad,' Madeleine says. 'Did you find her, the missing woman?'

Isobel's face tightens. 'Yes. It wasn't quite what I'd thought. She's in prison.'

'Wow, I'm sorry to hear that.' Madeleine unwraps the biscuit on the side of her saucer. 'I read your piece about Anna Witherall's death, when it first happened. It was very thorough.'

Isobel scoffs. 'Yeah, well, it would have been more thorough if it hadn't been heavily cut.'

'What do you mean?'

She exhales sharply. 'I mean, as a local paper we don't have the resources to make allegations that bigger papers might be prepared to make, if they had enough evidence, and later see through in court.' She pauses. 'Let's just say, the story involving Eva, which I've been looking into for months, isn't as straightforward as I hoped it would be, and there are ties that connect that case and this.'

Madeleine's eyes narrow. 'In your piece, you mention the family business, TradeSmart.'

She sits back slightly and observes the young woman.

After a moment, Isobel nods. 'If you come back to my flat, I have some things you might be interested to see.'

Madeleine hails a cab and they sit in silence for a while after Isobel gives the address, a part of Hackney she has only heard of vaguely and even then, only in newspaper reports on trends in gentrification.

'I don't think it was suicide,' Isobel says after a while, her gaze fixed on the streets outside as they move along Essex Road.

'Why not?'

'Lots of reasons. There are inconsistencies that don't seem to have been picked up on or looked at. According to the scrapings under the fingernails, there was no blood or skin or anything else to suggest any sort of skirmish. There was also little evidence of bruising to suggest that she had been hauled up there. The crime scene shows no signs of forced entry or disturbance – no obvious wounds on the body. But it also appears the scene wasn't properly preserved. Usually, to check the implications of the ligature and marks around the neck, it would be proper to cut down a hanging victim using a cut above the knot, which preserves the item for forensics. Right? Knots usually involve a high degree of movement in their creation, leading to plenty of forensic opportunities for DNA profiles at a later stage . . .'

Isobel's voice gathers momentum, as if she has been waiting to share this for some time.

'From that you can ask, what do the marks around the neck show you? Is it just bruising following a similar pattern to the ridges on the rope used? That would be pretty normal and may be consistent with suicide. If there are other marks, alarm bells might start ringing . . .'

Madeleine nods. 'I have also read the Dummies' Guide to Forensics.'

'Ha,' Isobel says. 'But in this instance the knot wasn't cut properly, so either way, the evidence simply isn't there.'

'How do you know this? None of it was mentioned in court.'

'It was in the initial police report, which wasn't read out in full at the inquest.'

'Right, and you've seen this how . . .?'

'I have contacts, it's my job. This happened on my patch.' Isobel shrugs. 'And it's just as well seeing as no one else appears to want to look into it properly. There wasn't even a post-mortem.'

'That's not that unusual,' Madeleine says, playing devil's advocate. 'Without reason to suggest foul play . . .'

'Except how do you know if there was foul play or not unless every aspect is looked into – including a post-mortem?'

'Do you know what it would involve to investigate every suicide?'

'But this wasn't every suicide,' Isobel says, glancing at the light on the door to make sure the speaker transmitting their conversation to the driver's part of the cab isn't on. It isn't, but she holds her tongue nonetheless as the car turns onto St Paul's Road.

'This is it,' Isobel says a few moments later as they turn onto a residential street with tall Georgian houses lining one side, a wall bridging the pavement and a railway on the other. Madeleine pays with cash and waits a moment for a receipt.

'It's the top-floor flat,' Isobel says, as they move inside a metal gate that hangs from only one hinge.

'No problem,' Madeleine replies, before looking up at the incline of the staircase. 'I take that back.'

By the time they reach the top, Madeleine's breath is ragged. 'Christ, no wonder you're so thin.'

Isobel laughs. 'I haven't lived here long, still haven't got around to unpacking properly,' she says as they move through the tiny hallway and into a bright living room with high ceilings and large, rickety sash windows overlooking the train-line. The room is sparsely furnished, a couple of boxes stacked up against one wall.

'No need to apologise,' Madeleine replies. 'It's a lovely place.'

Isobel smiles appreciatively. 'It is. Especially compared to my last flat. Do you want a drink? I have tea or only instant coffee, I'm afraid.'

'I'm fine,' Madeleine replies, her attention settling on the wall that divides the living space from a galley kitchen.

Isobel clears her throat. 'I realise this makes me look a bit like a serial killer.'

'Actually it makes me feel very at home,' Madeleine says. 'May I?'

'Of course.' There is a glint in Isobel's eye as she watches Madeleine move towards the wall, which is covered in printouts of newspaper articles, internet clippings and, at the centre, a photograph of Anna Witherall. 'What I was leading to in the cab is that one of the paramedics who was on duty that night said that the psychiatrist showed up at the hospital and kept asking questions. Doesn't that seem strange to you?'

'Not necessarily.'

'Tough crowd.' Isobel shrugs, pulling out her rolling tobacco. 'That's Eva,' she says, pointing to a photo of a young woman with piercing blue eyes. Eva was the woman whose disappearance had originally brought Madeleine and the reporter into contact, and here she was again, this time her picture on a wall alongside the wife of the heir of the company that Gabriela's boyfriend was in business with.

'You saw her being attacked on Hampstead Heath, is that right?'

Isobel pauses. 'Yeah, that's what I thought I saw. And in a way it was true – it was her who was being attacked, by the guy who had trafficked her to England – initially. But she hit him back, with a rock.'

'Oh,' Madeleine says.

'Yeah, oh.'

'Was he badly hurt?'

'He died.'

'Right.'

'And now she's in prison,' Isobel continues. 'Because I wouldn't let the case go and in the process of thinking I was avenging her death, I managed to get her put in jail for defending herself against a man who—' She cut herself off. 'Anyway, it's all pretty fucked up.'

'Presumably she hasn't been tried yet?' Madeleine asks.

'Not yet. I'm hoping there will be leniency, or perhaps she could do some sort of plea deal . . . If she had information that was useful . . .'

Madeleine shrugs. 'Possibly. So tell me more about this.' She indicates the pages stuck to the wall.

Isobel clears her throat, pulling out a Rizla and filling it with tobacco, licking the paper before rolling it between her fingers. 'After I saw what I thought was Eva being attacked on the Heath, I started doing some digging. I found a building near Tottenham Court Road which was being used to film porn.' Holding the unlit roll-up between her fingers, she points to another piece of paper, with information about a business scrawled in illegible writing. 'The building is registered to a company called PKI Ltd, and when I looked into them it turns out it's a shell company, owned by another company called the Stan Group, which is registered to the British Virgin Islands – the signatory on both companies is a lawyer named James McCann.'

Lighting up, Isobel moves her fingers between various names tacked to the wall in a bid to illustrate the web she is unpicking.

'This lawyer, it's almost impossible to find out anything about his business online other than it's a law firm, McCann and Partners, based in Queen Square – but when I Googled him, what I did find was a photo. It was taken at a party, and in the picture he was there suited and booted necking champagne with a couple of "philan-thropists", according to the caption. When I Googled their names, it turned out the first man in the picture was Anna Witherall's father-in-law, Clive Witherall, the owner of a seemingly legit inter-national trading company called TradeSmart. The other . . .'

Madeleine's eyes have already moved on to what Isobel is about to reveal next.

'The other,' Isobel continues regardless, 'was a Russian by the name of—'

'Irena Vasiliev,' Madeleine interrupts.

'You know her?'

'Know of her,' Madeleine says. 'Please, carry on.'

'So I'm sure you know she is wanted by various countries for supporting violent regimes in Africa, as well as money laundering and financial terrorism.'

Madeleine takes a step closer. 'What's this?' She is pointing to an article from one of the leading newspapers, printed up on A3 paper.

In a letter exclusively obtained by this newspaper, Witherall, heir to the leading trading company TradeSmart, admitted he and his wife, magazine editor Anna Witherall, had masterminded the chemical dump in a bid to avoid necessary treatment costs to dispose of the toxic waste product.

The CEO and heir to the TradeSmart business, which was worth $76 billion at the time of the dump, hired a small local firm to illegally dispose of raw toxic waste, near a children's play-ground in a residential area of Equatorial Guinea, along with his then-girlfriend.

Organised by the pair when they were in their early twenties, while living together in the Witherall family home in Hampstead where they hosted frequent parties, more than 300 tons of the deadly chemical compound mercaptan, referred to in emails between the company's staff as 'slops' and 'crap', was offloaded in a residential area in Bata. As a result, 22 died and hundreds more suffered symptoms including burns and respiratory problems. The case has also been linked to a spate of miscarriages in the surrounding area.

Clive Witherall, who is in the late stages of an aggressive form of cancer, has denied all knowledge of the dump, and has passed on copies of correspondence between his son and daughter-in-law. A receipt for the cargo, which was erroneously abandoned near a playground by local delivery drivers after they panicked over the smell of the toxic waste, has been handed to police along with a letter hand-written by David Witherall not long before he died, after being hit by a car moving at high speed.

The former magazine editor and mother-of-two, Anna Witherall, has battled mental health problems since childhood when she underwent professional treatment following the loss of her brother, and suffered extreme postnatal depression after the birth of her twin daughters in 2016.

In an interview with this paper, Clive Witherall, who only has months to live, also claimed an investigation would be launched into David's death, which he believes could have been arranged by those wishing to silence him once it became clear he planned to hand himself in to police.

In a statement yesterday, Mrs Witherall's former boss Clarissa Marceaux told this newspaper she was shocked by the revelations, and confirmed that Anna Witherall would no longer be employed by the company.

Clive Witherall added: 'It is with great regret that I accept a degree of responsibility for the actions of my company, TradeSmart. Although I had no knowledge of it at the time, it is only right that I recognise that I failed to prevent this terrible misdemeanour, leading to the tragic loss of innocent lives.

'I have always said that corporate responsibility stands at the heart of, and has been the driver for, all that we do at TradeSmart.

In my years as a businessman I have always strived to hold the highest standards of corporate responsibility, not just through our own behaviours but through our foundation and our sponsorship programme.

'It is with great personal remorse that I must tell you that in the weeks following the death of my son, David, I received a letter from him, confessing to what had become to him a very heavy burden. In the letter, David revealed that under a degree of pressure from his wife, who I have since learnt had been duping my son from the moment they first met, the pair hired a local firm in Equatorial Guinea to dispose of waste materials, to avoid costs.

'My son accepted he acted with terrible misjudgement after falling for the charms of his wife, who entered our lives under a veil of deceit – and he was subsequently plagued by the ramifications of his actions in the years leading to his untimely death.'

Isobel looks back at Madeleine. 'It's an as-yet unpublished article written for *The Times* . . . by Clive Witherall.'

Artemis

London, the Nineties

There was a message on the answer machine. It was a few days after Clive had left and Artemis had just got home from dropping David off at school.

'This is Dr Blackman. I wondered if you could call me when you get this message. My number is 071 . . .'

She scribbled down the details on a pad she kept on the side table in the hall, not recognising the number beyond the London area code. Why was a doctor calling? Her first thought was David. What if he had been ill and Clive had taken him to see someone without telling her? It's possible that he didn't want to worry her. But then why would she be addressed in the message rather than Clive, if he had been the one who—

Her thoughts were cut off by a woman's voice. 'Good morning. Dr Blackman's office.'

'Oh hello, this is Artemis Witherall. I had a message from Dr Blackman,' Artemis said, her voice tense.

'Please hold, Mrs Witherall. I'll see if he's available.' There was a pause and then she came back on the line, 'I'm going to put you through now.'

'Mrs Witherall, thank you for calling back.' The voice at the other end of the line was convivial, as if speaking to an old friend rather than someone he had never met. 'I am an old friend of Clive's; he's been in touch, from Asia—'

'Is he sick?' Artemis was struck by a wave of guilt. She hadn't considered for a moment that it might be Clive who was ill.

'No, no, nothing like that. Please don't worry. Actually, it was you he was concerned about.' The doctor paused, letting his words sink in.

'I'm sorry?'

'Clive tells me you've been struggling.' He said it as a matter of fact, not requiring either confirmation or denial. From his manner it was hard to believe he had never even met the person he was talking to, but this level of self-belief, this unwavering certainty in what he was saying, was a trait she had noticed in so many of the people in Clive's life – her life, now. From the teachers at David's school, who spoke about her son as if it was they, not she, who had raised him, to the friends who came to the soirees he insisted on hosting at the house, denouncing the Prime Minister's ability to govern on the basis of his accent; they all seemed to have an opinion, on everything. And their confidence in their own assertions was such that there was no point trying to persuade them otherwise.

'It would be much better if we spoke face-to-face,' Dr Blackman rattled on. 'You could come to my office next week. I have an appointment available on—'

'Look, I'm not sure what Clive has told you, but there must be some confusion – I'm not sick,' Artemis interjected.

Dr Blackman paused. When he resumed, his voice had a patient authority. 'I understand. And nobody is saying that you're ill, necessarily. But with trauma can come long-lasting consequences, and sometimes it's best we seek help for these. There's nothing shameful in it. I think if we're honest, the concern here isn't just for you – it's for David.'

'David?' Artemis held a hand to her head, trying to make sense of what was being said.

'Now look, it's much better to speak face-to-face. I'll hand you back to Daisy at reception and she will book you in with an appointment, OK? I'm just on Harley Street, very central, easy to get to. I look forward to meeting you, Mrs Witherall.'

Artemis dropped David at school the following Monday and headed straight to the tube station, letting her mind go blank as the wind surged through the train carriages, the rattling motion of the Northern Line soothing her as she waited to get off at Euston, where it was just two more stops to Oxford Circus.

She was early for her appointment. She had hardly slept the night before and she stopped at Benjys, ordering a takeaway coffee which arrived in a cup so large she had to hold it with two hands as she walked towards Cavendish Square. On the other side of the square a couple of school-aged girls smoked cigarettes on a bench, screeching with laughter. There was a dishonesty to their display – no girl of fourteen or fifteen truly felt that free and at ease – and there was something saddening about watching them, wondering what they were hiding, from themselves and from each other. One day David would be their age. For a moment Artemis wondered whether she had instilled enough goodness in her son that he never became the reason girls like these cried in their beds at night. She closed her eyes and breathed in, picturing his eyes, the flecks of amber against a darker brown, the way he tipped his head back when he laughed so that his neck was exposed. David was good, of that she could be sure.

Dr Blackman's office was on the ground floor of one of the townhouses that lined Harley Street. There were bars on the windows, and as she was buzzed in she wondered if they had been designed to keep people in or out.

'Artemis, thank you for coming to see me. Do take a seat,' Dr Blackman said, indicating one of the chairs that lined the office.

Artemis hesitated for a moment before perching at the edge of the chair. The room was neutrally furnished, without so much as a bookcase to reveal anything about the inhabitant.

'I don't really know why I came,' she said.

Dr Blackman concentrated on her face with a neutral expression.

'Is that so?' He waited a while, to ascertain that she wasn't going to offer anything else, sat, hands interlinked on his desk, making no attempt to fill the silence. She focused on his upturned nose, the spectacles that might have been for show – he struck her as that sort of man. He didn't flinch under her assessment and she looked away first.

Almost a minute passed before he said, 'I think you do know. I think you came because you love your son very much and you would do anything to make sure that you are the best version of yourself so that you can be the person he needs.'

Artemis said nothing, looking down at her fingers.

'I understand you've never spoken before, about what happened to you.'

'It was a long time ago.' Still she didn't look at him.

'So maybe now you're ready to talk?'

'I don't see the point.'

Dr Blackman cleared his throat. 'But you came here today, so maybe part of you does see a point?'

'I came because I was curious, because I was concerned that my husband is talking about me to random psychologists without my consent—'

'I'm not a psychologist, Artemis. I'm sorry, I should have explained. I'm a psychiatrist.'

'Right,' she said. 'Well I think my point remains.'

Dr Blackman breathed evenly. 'Clive came to me because we have known each other a long time. He is worried about you, about David.'

Artemis looked back at him for the first time, a fierceness in her voice, 'I'm sorry, what are you suggesting about my son?'

'I'm not suggesting anything about David, other than that a child responds intuitively to a parent's emotions. If a mother is struggling then it stands to reason that their child . . .' Seeing her expression, he changed tack. 'There is nothing shameful about struggling, Artemis. From what I've gathered, you had early trauma and, undealt with, that trauma lingers. I can't make you do or say anything, but I can tell you that I can help you. If you let me.'

'Why didn't Clive come to me first?' She was asking herself more than him, but he replied.

'Maybe he felt you would respond better to a professional. These things can be just as hard, in a way, for the family. For partners, for children . . .'

Why did he keep bringing up David? She tightened her fingers around the base of her seat.

Sensing her reaction, he continued, unabashed. 'There is no shame here, Artemis. If you hurt your foot, you go to a doctor – you do not limp on because you are too embarrassed to ask for medication. It's no different when the wound is internal.'

'You want to put me on pills?' Artemis said.

'Not necessarily,' Dr Blackman replied evenly. 'Sometimes it can help, in the short term.'

'What sort of medication?'

'It depends. There are a number of different anti-depressants, depending on what suits various factors in your life. There are things if you're having trouble sleeping . . .'

Defensively, Artemis touched her hand to her face. She knew she looked terrible. The toll of endless sleepless nights was evident in the puffy lids and the dark rings that circled her eyes.

'Nothing is set in stone. Nothing has to be permanent. Sometimes in life we all need an extra hand, until we are strong enough to hold the weight alone.'

Madeleine

London, present day

'I was there for a job interview,' Isobel explains, removing the article from the wall and handing it to Madeleine. 'The editor approached me and asked if I'd consider coming to work for them.'

Madeleine looks down at the paper in her hand, reading again from start to finish as Isobel speaks.

'I ummed and ahhed for a while about whether or not to go to the meeting, for various reasons, and then eventually I decided I would. It was with the main editor – I already knew the news editor, so I guess the idea was that I was getting a vetting more than anything. Anyway, the meeting was in his office. It was just the two of us, and a few minutes in, there was a problem with one of the pages so someone came in and called him out for a minute.

'I wasn't snooping, I literally just cast my eye over his desk from where I was sitting and I saw this at the top of a pile of papers. It's an unpublished article – the main body of text is the real piece – but the standfirst is still dummy copy, you see? And the slug in the corner of the paper . . .'

Madeleine follows Isobel's finger and reads the words 'ANNA WITHERALL EXCL. Byline CW'.

'CW.' Isobel says aloud what Madeleine is already thinking. 'This feels like a strange piece to write about your recently deceased son and daughter-in-law, even if Clive did feel wronged by them . . . why would he go to the press?'

Madeleine shakes her head confusedly. 'I don't know. There's something almost too emphatic about the whole thing, too performative.'

'Almost as if he's trying too hard to push the point,' Isobel agrees.

Madeleine turns to face her. 'But why would he want to do that? I suppose if he was desperate to protect his image . . .'

'Yeah. Or if he wanted to set someone up.'

Artemis

London, the Nineties

It was David's seventh birthday, a Friday. Artemis had spent the morning finishing the cake and running errands ahead of supper to be held at theirs after school. They would be celebrating the following day with a few of David's friends, at the cinema in South End Green followed by lunch at Ed's Diner in the village, but tonight was for close family friends, which meant Jeff and May, and Clive's old university pal Clarissa together with her new girlfriend, Eliza. Clarissa and Eliza had been trying to conceive, unsuccessfully, through IVF, and May had decided, in an uncharacteristic show of empathy, that it would be fairer on them if she and Jeff left their children at home.

The decision struck Artemis as odd, but so much about May baffled her that she didn't think to question it. Not today of all days. David's birthday was a time for family and celebration, and she wouldn't let May ruin that. Artemis had worked hard over the years to push aside the feeling of unease she had initially felt after that overheard phone call, and, perhaps in part thanks to the sessions she had been doing with Dr Blackman, it had paid off. It had been a misunderstanding, that was all – one she had never bothered, or perhaps dared, raise with Clive.

It had been a perfect morning, in many ways. Artemis had slept well, as she often did now, thanks to the cocktail of pills that Dr Blackman prescribed, pills she relied on a little more liberally, perhaps, than he intended. She had risen first, blowing up a bag of balloons with which she filled the kitchen: green and red – David's favourite colours – and the sight of them cheered her as she listened to the birds through the window, preparing pancakes and fruit and coffee for a family breakfast.

For once, Clive had taken the day off work, and the easy sound of domestic co-existence rang through the house: the putting away of cutlery in drawers, the radio drifting out from the bedroom, reminding Artemis, for all its flaws, of the world they had created together. She held high hopes that the party would go well, everything just as planned.

May arrived early, an enormous gift tucked under her arm, clearly intent on demonstrating her best godmotherly behaviour when it counted, her lips plastered a startling shade of orangey-red, blue eye shadow smudged effectively around small, piercing eyes. Jeff would join them once he'd escaped the shackles of the office, she joked.

'Don't worry, you head off. I'll help Clive with these,' she added, pointing to a half-finished tray of canapés which Artemis had prepared with the help of the Nigel Slater cookbook Clive had given her for Christmas. 'You don't want to keep David waiting at the school gates.'

Artemis paused only for a split second before stepping out of the house. The sky was a perfect blue, a single trail of cloud like the trace of a bullet running over the top of the house.

Walking down the hill, Artemis breathed through her nostrils, enjoying the coolness of the air as it reached her chest. She thought of David's face that morning shining with glee at the sight of his presents stacked neatly on the table. She had been unsure what to buy him. He was growing up so quickly and the toy selection at Woolworths on Kentish Town Road no longer seemed sufficient to Clive, who was willing to throw in snarky comments about her choices but not offer any proactive suggestions. In the end she had settled on a red Power Ranger, which she found at Hamleys on Regent Street. She didn't want to raise a brat, not that David displayed any brattish tendencies, despite all his privilege, and this present, she felt, struck the right balance. It was such a relief when he opened it and it was instantly clear that he couldn't have loved it more.

The tips of the trees were turning brittle again, she noticed as she skirted the Heath next to the Freemasons Arms. David was such a kind boy, thoughtful in a way that made her proud, but he was also sensitive, which made him both vulnerable and aware of other people. One of the first things he had said after opening the red Power Ranger was that his friend, Irfan, would like to play with it, too.

Shit.

Artemis stopped in her tracks, remembering the conversation from earlier that morning. David had pleaded with her to let him take his new present to school and she had refused, on the grounds that pupils weren't allowed to take toys in. He had been so cross with her, the depth of his rage surprising, and she had promised she would bring it with her at the end of the day, to show to Irfan.

David would be devastated if she let him down. But it was OK, she told herself – she was only a few minutes away from the house; she still had time to go back home and make it to the school before the final bell rang. Picking up her pace, she turned and walked briskly towards home. Rushing up the front steps, she fiddled with the key in the lock and when the door finally opened, she left it ajar while she ran quickly inside. The Power Ranger was in the living room and she would only be a second, after all.

Turning left into the living room, she spotted the toy and leaned down to pick it up.

She was about to call out to Clive that it was only her, that she was heading straight out again, when she looked up and saw them through the open doorway into the kitchen: her husband and May, her hands on his shoulders, their faces inches apart.

She stood there in the living room for a moment, watching them, her feet soldered to the spot. It was as though time had stopped; she felt her breath drag through her lungs, unable to pull her eyes away. And then she felt herself move backwards, slowly, stealthily, as if away from a dog that would pounce if she dared break eye contact, her hand still clutching the Power Ranger.

In the hallway, the front door to the street was wide open.

Stepping out, she gulped at the air, holding her hand against the doorway to steady herself. Across the street, she saw the flicker of a net curtain from the upstairs window and she turned, as if part of a performance, to shut the front door behind her. She pulled it to quietly, sealing it with such precision that she might have been trapping a spider under a glass. Leaving it there to consider later, once she had worked out how it might be safely released.

Moving quite calmly down the tiled steps, she turned left again. This time as she passed the Freemasons Arms and onto the high street, nothing had changed. There was the Coffee Cup on one side, still with its burgundy reds and creams, mothers with prams double-parked outside. Opposite, in the window of Morgan de Toi, pistachio-green lycra and silver hooped earrings clung to emaciated mannequins. They looked dead, she thought, their bodies contorted and featureless, like staged corpses left out as warnings to others by some despotic regime.

*   *   *

She was amazed by her own performance the evening of the party as she welcomed her husband's guests, watching David's face light up as he received his presents.

May. She allowed herself the thought only once she was a safe distance from the house. She had been right. All these years since that phone call, she had convinced herself she'd imagined it and now here it was, the evidence she couldn't ignore.

David's grin stretched from ear to ear. Her heart wrenched as she leaned down and kissed her son, breathing in the scent of him as he took the Power Ranger from her hands and ran towards his best friend. By the time they left the playground, David's rucksack bobbing against his back slightly in front of her, she knew she wouldn't say anything to Clive. What good would come of it? She couldn't think of a single thing, though she could think of plenty of bad. How could she risk him leaving her? This wasn't about her and her feelings, it was about David. He deserved a better family life than the one she'd had, and she would let nothing put that in jeopardy.

That evening at the party, she moved through the room as if the volume had been turned down, sipping from a single glass of champagne. The scene in the living room was slowed down to the point of contortion, bared teeth frozen as laughter rippled across the table. David, dressed in a bright red polo shirt, moved in real time, his face in tight focus, happy and awkward in the manner of a child who didn't understand the jokes and was doing his best to mimic the reactions of the grown-ups. Only when he looked up at her did his face break into a proper smile.

Clive and May remained on different sides of the room for the rest of the party. It wasn't until David had gone to bed that she allowed the image to form again in her memory. Once it did, it stayed there, exactly where she left it, not daring to poke at it for fear of what else might crumble around her if she did.

Madeleine

'Can I keep this?' Madeleine asks.

'Of course,' Isobel says, her eyes dancing with energy. 'It's just a printout. I still have the original photo I took of the article on my phone. What are you going to do with it?'

'I need to go back to the office,' Madeleine says, pulling on her coat.

Isobel looks reluctant to let her leave. 'I'll walk you down.'

Before opening the door, Isobel turns again to Madeleine. 'Why were you there, at the inquest? I thought you worked in human trafficking?'

Madeleine nods. 'I do.'

'Right,' she says, acknowledging that Madeleine is not willing to share anything more with her. Madeleine feels bad, like she has betrayed a trust that was growing between them. But no matter how helpful Isobel has been, she is a journalist, and there's too much at stake.

'I'm sorry,' Madeleine says as they step out onto the landing. 'I really appreciate your help, though, it's extremely useful.'

Isobel leans down to retrieve the post from the doormat as they reach the entrance to the street. Madeleine hears her mutter under her breath as she looks down at the envelopes in her hand.

'Is everything OK?'

'Wow. Yes, I mean . . . I don't know. It's Eva, I applied for a visiting order to visit her in prison. I assumed she would reject it, but it's been approved . . . I can visit this Friday.'

Madeleine pauses, studying Isobel's face. 'Perhaps I could come with you?'

Artemis

Greece, the Nineties

Artemis listened to her son's shallow breathing as the plane took off at Heathrow, pushing up into a glistening summer sky. David's head was pressed reassuringly against her arm, one of his hands resting on her lap, the other clutching the same red Power Ranger he had been given a year earlier, his love for it yet to be eclipsed by another toy.

Clive had already been gone for a few days, on a working trip to Moscow, and was due to meet them on the island a week or so later. Something had been going on with his work over the previous months so that when he was home, Clive was largely holed up in his study, the door closed against the outside world. When Artemis thought of the house now, the paintings of her previous life hanging like remnants of another world, goading her every time she passed, she felt a shiver.

She breathed deeply, a wave of freedom rushing over her. She didn't have to think about the house, not now; she was on her way home.

Artemis ran a hand through David's hair as he leaned against her shoulder on the Dolphin boat from Skiathos to the island, watching the sun dance on the surface of the water.

Markos and Rena met them at the port, armed with freshly baked snacks. David guzzled hungrily, flaky pastry clinging to his lips as they made their way from the jetty to her parents' front door. Rena held David's hand, merrily chatting away to her grandson in Greek, so happy to have him there that she was oblivious to his almost total incomprehension. Artemis had tried talking to him in her mother tongue at home, but over the years it had become increasingly difficult, David looking embarrassed in front of his friends if they were in public, or claiming to be too tired to think in another language when he got home after a long day at school. When he was there, Clive discouraged it, too, as though wary of any form of secret code between them. For someone with little interest in the day-to-day business of parenting, he could be remarkably possessive.

They stayed at her parents' that first night. There was no need to head up to the house in the old village just yet. Artemis slept well, thanks to the extra pill she had taken just in case, she and David side-by-side in her old bed. There was no point risking a return of the nightmares now that she was back in her childhood home.

'You look exhausted,' Rena said the following morning, handing Artemis a coffee. She breathed in the aroma gratefully. Coffee in London was awful, so thin and insipid.

'Do I?'

'I bet you haven't had a proper cup in months,' Rena said, echoing her thoughts, taking a seat opposite her daughter at the kitchen table while David entertained Markos with the new Mario Kart game Clarissa had given him for his birthday.

'Don't be ridiculous,' Artemis said defensively. 'We have coffee in London. There are plenty of quite charming cafés on the high street just next to us, as you would know if you ever visited.'

Rena snorted. 'London? You have to be joking. Anyway, it's nice for David to come here, to see his grandparents in his mother's home.'

Artemis smiled, taking a sip. She couldn't stay angry with Rena for long. Besides, she was right, she was never coming to London and Artemis was relieved. This way, she could paint a picture of her life to show her parents from a distance, without risking her seeing the cracks that were impossible to miss up close.

'How's Athena?' Artemis asked, changing the subject, taking a sip of coffee and closing her eyes, savouring the taste.

'You haven't spoken to her?'

'Not for a few weeks.' Actually, when she thought of it, it had been well over a month. They always had their ups and downs, made worse since Clive told Artemis that he and Athena had been talking about her behind her back. But Athena always called on David's birthday and this year there had been no word.

'Panos has left,' Rena replied.

'What?' Artemis felt like she had been punched. Her best friend's husband had walked out on her and she'd had no idea. 'Why didn't you tell me earlier?'

'I thought you knew.'

Artemis stood. 'Can I leave David with you for an hour or so?'

'Of course,' Rena said. 'You know we love to have him here as often as we possibly can.'

The house Athena and Panos had moved into not long after she became pregnant with Maria stood at the top of the mountain, on the cusp of the old village, just before the cliff gave way to the water.

Through the kitchen window, she could see Athena standing at the sink. It was clearly her, but Artemis thought how different she looked, frail in a way that was impossible to pinpoint.

Artemis knocked on the door and waited a moment. She heard running footsteps and then the door opened wide, Maria's face falling as she saw who was there.

'What did I tell you, Maria? It won't be your father, he's not coming ba—'

Athena's voice was moving towards the door.

She stopped when she saw Artemis, the dishcloth she had been using to dry a pot falling from her hands.

*   *   *

'Now, what is your favourite food to eat, if you could eat anything in the world?' Artemis asked, swinging Maria's arm gently as they moved down the hill later that day. Maria thought for a while, her little face concentrating hard on the question. At six, she had grown even more like her father, albeit a far prettier version. She had the same dark, intense features, the same look of concentration.

'Chicken,' she said after a while.

'Chicken?' Artemis sounded impressed. 'I love chicken, too, and so does David. He's going to be so happy to see you.'

'Where are we going? We shouldn't leave Mummy when she's sad,' Maria said, her voice growing small.

Artemis stopped and crouched down so that she and Maria were on eye level. 'You're going to stay with us for a few nights, while Mama sorts a few things out and has a little rest. Does that sound OK?'

Maria nodded reluctantly.

'Good.' Artemis squeezed her hand. 'David and I are going to take very good care of you. You're like family to us. You know that, don't you?'

Artemis heard the diggers as she stepped out of the taxi, holding the door open for David and Maria to follow her onto the side of the road next to the house. Her hands gripped theirs more tightly as they walked up the dirt path towards the olive grove where earth came up in clouds of dust, like smoke.

'What are you doing?' she called out to the men, who turned nonchalantly from their tools, the metal claws chewing up the foundations of the land.

'Who are you?' the nearest replied, taking a step towards them.

Artemis felt David pull at her arm. 'Mama, it's OK.'

She ignored him, continuing to address the builder. 'This is my house.'

'Then you'll have to speak to your husband, the Englishman,' he shrugged, turning away.

Artemis' fingers trembled as she hurried through the front door, moving to the house phone and dialling Clive's mobile number. She had no idea what time it would be in Moscow and she didn't care.

'Clive, there are men digging up the garden,' she shouted down the line when he answered.

'Oh yes,' he said, as if the thought had just occurred to him.

Now she remembered, Moscow was only one hour ahead of Greece. And yet already Clive sounded drunk. Listening harder, she heard the clatter of cutlery in the background. She wouldn't ask him where he was – she didn't care where, or who he was with.

'Why are they here?' She tried not to sound agitated in front of the children.

'They're building a pool.'

'I'm sorry?'

'A pool. You know, those things you swim in?'

She heard him put a hand over the phone, saying something to whoever he was with.

'Why didn't you tell me?'

'It was supposed to be a surprise.' He moved his hand away so that his voice became clearer. 'David and I thought—'

'David knew?' She turned to look at her son. Since when did David and Clive have secrets? Irrationally, she flinched at the thought of the two of them conspiring against her. Yet it was hardly a conspiracy. Clive said it himself – it was supposed to be something nice. A surprise. Artemis had a sudden image of Clive and May in the kitchen.

When she pictured it, in hindsight, the image mutated so that at one minute it was a passionate embrace, the next a form of combat. Her throat constricted as she recalled the intimacy of what she had seen – her husband and his best friend's wife turned in on one another in her kitchen surrounded by her son's birthday balloons.

Blinking, the image of Jorgos formed in its place, his face towering over her as he held open the door of her wedding car.

How many more surprises would there be?

Madeleine

She hasn't eaten since breakfast. Following the map on her phone, she walks the twenty minutes or so from Isobel's flat to Highbury Corner, stopping at a tiny café near the tube station. It is the kind of place she has only discovered in adulthood, after years of refined restaurants and stuffy hotels with her parents, and she still relishes the sound of cheap meat sizzling on the griddle.

'I'll have a bacon roll, please, and a chocolate muffin,' she says.

'Hot drink with that?' the woman behind the bar asks.

Madeleine's eyes survey the foam cups and industrial size pot of Nescafé.

What is wrong with people? 'No, thanks,' she says. She won't go that far.

Taking a seat while she waits for her order to be called, Madeleine's mind drifts back to Isobel, and the question she had asked about Madeleine's reason for being at the inquest. She would have liked to tell her about Sean asking Madeleine to join the team based on information initially supplied by an old MI6 friend of his, suggesting a tertiary link between the Witherall family and Ivan Popov and Irena Vasiliev, whose frankly polymathic endeavours – including their human trafficking operation and tax evasion, with plenty more between – meant that what had started as one investigation had quickly morphed into another. But that's not how things work and Isobel knows it. Besides, it was almost embarrassing, how little progress had been made since Ivan Popov had been detained. They had Gabriela's testimony alongside information obtained by his maid, Polina. He would be charged with something, that was for sure, but how much they could make stick was another matter. Not least if he ended up refusing to testify against Irena Vasiliev – though the way things were going it was unlikely Interpol or Europol could get at her, and if they did it would be a tussle. The whole thing could take months if not years. Unless they could just break that bloody EncroChat.

'Bacon roll, chocolate muffin?'

By the time Madeleine tunes into the hum of the café, she can tell from the woman's face and the volume of her voice this is not the first time she has called out her order.

'Thank you,' Madeleine says, taking her food. 'I don't need a bag.'

Artemis

Greece, the Nineties

Artemis had forgotten how long the days were on the island compared to London.

Every morning that summer she, Maria and David would rise early, walking into town for fresh fruit and bread before coming home, the children watching the builders while Artemis made breakfast. They spent most afternoons on the beach, music drifting out from the restaurant on the edge of the cliffs, at the top of a steep path, staying until early evening when the sea-salt formed crystals on David's back, catching a lift back up the hill with one of the waiters.

When Clive arrived from Moscow on the Saturday, he was distracted with work, immediately casting a cloud over a near-perfect scene.

'I've been thinking, I want to stay in Greece,' Artemis announced one evening at the house, once David had gone to bed. Maria was back at home with her mother, Athena having had time to come to terms with what was happening and start looking for a job now that Panos was gone, taking with him their only form of income. Not that Artemis could entirely blame him, given that he had caught Athena in bed with another man.

Athena had been furious, blaming everyone but herself, her rage swinging from one target to the next, so that for a moment she spoke as if it was Artemis who had been responsible for what had happened. It was unfathomable to Artemis how her friend could have cheated on him – Panos had always been so generous. He was the only boy who had ever tried, gently, to comfort her at school when things got too much. As they'd grown older, he remained attentive and polite, always asking about her life – and actually listening – when she turned up at the house and Athena wasn't home. From what Artemis had seen, he was a loving father, thoughtful in a way that most men weren't. It was hard to believe that Athena would jeopardise what they had. And yet to walk out on their child? Artemis shuddered. Maybe he was as bad as the rest of them, underneath it all. Whatever happened in her own marriage, she could never leave her son.

'Sorry?' Clive looked up from what he was doing. He had been head-down in papers ever since he had arrived on the island, distracted with work. Always so damn distracted.

She fixed him with her gaze. 'I want to stay here. There's an international school in Skiathos David can join—'

He laughed. 'Is this a joke?'

'Why would I joke about something like this?' She was calm. 'Besides, I can't see that it would make much difference to you. You're rarely in London these days and when you are, you're working. You could come and stay with us here. I want to be close to my family and my friends – I don't see why it's that surprising to you. You know how lonely I've been . . .'

'Artemis, what the hell are you talking about?' He took off his glasses. 'What . . . I don't even know where to start.'

'It might make things more convenient, for you and May.'

She didn't know where it had come from, only that once she had said the words, it felt like a release. The silence that followed was loaded.

'I beg your pardon?'

'She could come over when you're in London, stay the night. You wouldn't have to pussyfoot around me.'

His jaw clenched. Suddenly he saw where this was going. For a while, he didn't speak.

'Well at least you're not denying it,' she said after a beat.

'There's nothing to deny. I'm trying to process what you're saying, what you're insinuating—'

'Oh please . . .' Artemis put up her hands to stop him. She was calm, her voice even.

'You know what? The thing is that I don't even care. Since I saw you two together – oh, almost over a year ago now – I've tried so hard to make myself feel some specific emotion – to feel angry or sad or . . . But I don't. I've felt detached, yes, I've felt *mad*. And now, being home this time, I realise I wasn't mad, I was lost. *This* is where I need to be. I'm not even angry with you, this isn't a punishment. I just know that this is what I'm attached to – this place, my people.'

What choice did she have but to redraw her own history?

Clive was visibly shaking.

Artemis looked away from him. 'I'm not breaking up with you. I'm not even telling you to stop—' Her voice was almost kindly.

'You're not telling me to stop what, Artemis? What are you even talking about? What is it that you think you've seen?'

'David's birthday, last year. I went out to pick him up and left you and her together at home, except I had to pop back for something and I saw you both—'

'Oh my God.' Clive covered his face briefly with the palms of his hands.

Artemis ignored his scorn. 'I don't know how long it's been going on or if Jeff—'

Clive moved forward suddenly in his seat. 'You know *nothing*.'

'So Jeff doesn't know.' She bit her lip, watching him for a moment. 'In that case, I won't tell him. If you agree to let me stay here without kicking up a fuss, I won't tell your best friend and business partner that you've been *fucking* his wife.'

Clive stood up, thrusting his chair backwards. As he moved towards her, Artemis arched away from him.

'You know *nothing*. Don't you dare threaten me.' He was so close that she could see the pores on his nose. When had he started to look so much older? He was barely forty and yet he could have passed for ten years more. But he was strong.

Artemis shifted back further.

'Do you really think I'd let you take my child away from me? Do you really think that you can *blackmail* me and then move *my* son to some provincial little island and that I will pay for him to go to a school inferior to the one he is at now while you fanny around in *my* house? And with your history of depen—'

'Excuse me?'

Clive shook his head. 'Do you think I don't know?'

'What are you talking about?'

'The pills. Do you think I don't notice how quickly you get through the medication Dr Blackman prescribes you? He hasn't said anything to me, for obvious reasons, but I have eyes, Artemis.'

Artemis sneered. 'You're accusing me of having a problem? Who is it that prescribes them, Clive? And who is responsible for me going to him in the first—'

'Because I wanted to *help* you, Artemis.'

'Oh yes, I forget how helpful you've always been. How you helped bring me to a country where I know no one; how you helped me with the promise of a gallery that you've since done everything in your power to prevent me from having; how you helped me by leaving me alone for weeks on end while you travel the world, occasionally coming home to fuck your best friend's *wife!*'

He stood straight again, smiling. 'You're madder than I thought.'

'We don't need your money,' Artemis snarled at him.

'Ha! I think we both know that's a lie, my darling. Have you seen Athena recently? Do you know what it's like being a single mother in a place like this? What are you going to do, Artemis? I mean, what are you really going to do? Go and live with your parents? Go back to work in the bakery?'

She clenched her jaw, her palms starting to open and close. It wouldn't be so bad. At least she would be living her own life.

'And David? What, he will go to the school you went to? The one where he has no friends and where he barely speaks the language? You'd do that to him? You'd take him out of the school he loves, away from his home, where he has more opportunities than he could ever hope for, away from his friends? For what, so you can feel a bit more . . . *you*?' Clive looked at her with disappointment in his eyes. 'Of all the things, I never thought you would put your own happiness above David's.'

He turned, disgust written over his face. 'I can't even look at you.'

Artemis charged from the front door, taking the pitch-black footpath to Athena's, on the other side of the old village, in strides. Summer was coming to an end and the sound of the wind coming up off the water rippled through the trees, reminding her of her childhood.

Maria was playing outside, piling blocks on a precarious tower with a look of intense concentration. She startled at the sound of footsteps, her face breaking into a smile when she saw who it was.

'Is David coming?'

Artemis touched Maria's hair on the way past, too angry to stop and talk, not bothering to knock before marching into the kitchen, where Athena was washing dishes.

'What's wrong?'

Artemis struggled to remain still. 'I can't do it any more.'

'Do what?' Athena turned off the tap and moved to the table, pulling out a chair. 'Sit down.'

Artemis stayed standing, the energy crackling off her. 'Clive, London, all of it . . . He's been sleeping with his best friend's wife.'

'What?' Athena's face darkened.

'I saw them. A year ago, in our home. David's birthday.'

Athena shook her head. 'Clive wouldn't do that.'

'How can you say that? I just told you I saw them.' Artemis

paused, and then the words started tumbling from her mouth, the ones she'd held in for so long. 'Oh God, you're jealous.'

'What?'

She sat down and looked at her friend, as if really considering the situation for the first time. 'You're jealous because Clive is sleeping with someone else and it's not you.'

Athena's fingers gripped the edge of the table, her voice quiet. 'How dare you. I've just lost my husband.'

'Yes, but you never wanted him, did you, Athena? You wanted *my* husband, and Panos knew it. He was never enough for you. You didn't *lose* Panos, you threw him away!'

'Don't you dare talk about Panos—'

'You have no idea what it's like to lose everything,' Artemis stormed on.

'Oh please. Not this. You were five years old, Artemis! Helena died in the earthquake and that's terrible, but you aren't the only one who lost someone that day – though your family acts like you were. And you? You're still letting that single event define you three decades later? Get over yourself. You don't want to be happy. You never have.'

'I don't want to be happy?' Artemis' voice trembled. 'You have no idea what it has been like for me, growing up here. I was taunted for years – *years* – and you did nothing to help me . . .'

'I did nothing? I was your only friend. I was the only one who would talk to you. You were an outcast and I brought you in!'

'You brought me in?' Artemis was lost for words. 'You did nothing for me. You were never a good friend. I tried to tell you what happened with Jorgos and you laughed at me. And now, I am the one who has done something with my life and it kills you – and you have lost everything because it was never enough for you. You always wanted what you couldn't have—'

'What *I* couldn't have? This is your fault. Me and Panos, it was because of *you* . . .'

There was a noise from across the room. When Artemis turned, Maria was staring back at them from the doorway.

Artemis' face dropped.

'Get out.' Athena's voice was a hiss. 'Get out of my house.'

Their argument left Artemis not so much with a sense of catharsis, but a feeling of resignation – she had committed the perfect act of self-sabotage. In standing up to Athena, she had lost her only friend. In attempting to stand up to Clive, she had unwittingly invited him to pull his trump card: their son.

The worst part was that he was right. She couldn't disrupt David's life for the sake of her own happiness. Besides, who did she have left on the island other than her parents, now? And they were hardly in a position to support their daughter and grandson. Without Clive's financial support, she and David had nothing. Without Athena, she didn't even have a friend.

They left the island the following day, the image of Maria's face as Artemis fled the house the night before scored onto her memory.

The journey back to London passed largely in silence, the rumble of the jet's engines interspersed with the occasional discordant beep from David's Game Boy.

At home, neither of them mentioned the argument again, returning to a semi-convincing version of family life with remarkable ease, talking to each other through their son when necessary, otherwise barely exchanging a word. After walking on glass for so long, Artemis knew the fragility of the land that lay between them. But she didn't hear it crack until it was too late.

The leaves were turning, changing their suits in preparation for autumn. Despite her aversion to the cold, she liked this time of year when the air sharpened, the paths on the Heath emptying of its fair-weather friends.

Clive had been working late again the night before and she hadn't heard him come to bed. He was still sleep when she left to walk David to school the following morning.

They held hands, she and David, as they passed the Holly Bush pub, catching the scent of smoke from one of the pub's first open fires of the season.

She watched David disappear into school with a proud yearning, turning and walking back the way she'd come, the high street coming to life around her. She could tell Clive was awake the moment she got home, his voice filtering downstairs from the office as she stepped through the front door.

She was in the kitchen an hour later when he appeared.

'I'm leaving now.'

She turned to him briefly, noting the perfect suit, the slight paunch that had developed over the years, straining the buttons.

'Fine, have a good day,' she replied.

He paused as though he might move forward to kiss her, but then he turned and left, the house falling into renewed silence in his absence.

Artemis spent the rest of the morning preparing food for David's supper. At lunchtime she picked up a pile of clean clothes and headed upstairs, pausing briefly as she passed Clive's study. She had rarely been inside without him there, and she half-expected the door to be locked as she grasped the round brass handle, but the mechanism gave way instantly.

The smell of Clive hung thick in the air as she looked from the roll-top desk with its dark green leather lining to the bookcase.

She moved cautiously, like a child trespassing, the thrill of the danger urging her on. Walking behind the desk, she let her hand hover over the telephone. Who had her husband been talking to? What did it matter? She sighed, taking a step away from the desk, spotting the paper scrunched into a ball by the side of the wastepaper bin as if Clive had attempted to throw it away and had missed.

Leaning down, Artemis saw that it was an envelope. Inside was a letter, which she removed carefully, flattening out the page carefully with her fingers.

Dear Clive,
I hear from our mutual friend that you are happy to accept my offer.
It is a great pleasure to be doing further business with you, and I look forward to meeting in the coming weeks to discuss further the creation of the Stan Group.
Yours sincerely,
Irena Vasiliev

Artemis felt rather than heard Clive's presence in the hallway outside. Dropping the paper, she moved across the study. Her heartbeat inexplicably sped up as she stepped outside and came face-to-face with her husband – what reason did she have to be nervous?

'I was just doing some cleaning and I thought I'd check if there were any cups . . . There weren't,' she said, looking away from him towards the stairs, imagining for a split second a shadow on the bannisters.

'You're home early,' she continued.

His demeanour shifted. 'Yes. I'm going to be working here for the rest of the day – please don't disturb me.'

'Of course,' she said, walking towards the stairs, looking up at him as she took her first step down to the ground floor.

He looked back at her as though he wanted to say something more but thought better of it. Instead, he simply nodded and stepped inside his office, closing the door behind him.

Madeleine

London, present day

The prison is in Kent, an hour or so east of London. It makes sense for Madeleine to meet Isobel at her place first, not least since she has offered to drive. Although the moment she sees Isobel's car, she wishes she had suggested she get them a cab.

'It hasn't broken down once since I bought it,' Isobel says, noticing Madeleine's expression as she opens the passenger door as if handling an unknown reptile.

'And that was when, 1980?' she says, deadpan, picking up a couple of cassette tapes discarded on the seat and tucking her legs under the dash. 'I'm joking, it's very evocative. What is it?'

'A Renault five,' Isobel says. 'Anyway, at least I have a car.'

'Touché.'

The visiting room is large and open-plan, a space designed to be inclusive and welcoming, to help convey the prison's mantra, 'Our aim is to change lives for the better.' As if sterile design and a snazzy tagline can distract from the lack of staff training and access to legal advice that are among the perils of an increasing number of privatised prisons like these.

'Thank you so much for agreeing to see me,' Isobel says, taking the lead as they sit opposite Eva. The woman looks younger than twenty-two, and Madeleine's first thought is of the child she knows Eva gave birth to less than a year ago. Madeleine checked when she made her application to visit and Eva isn't being held in the Mother and Baby Unit.

'Eva, this is Madeleine—' Isobel says.

'I know your friend Dana,' Madeleine interjects gently, sensing Eva's understandable wariness. Her eyes narrow with interest. Once satisfied that she is listening, Madeleine continues.

'I work for the National Crime Agency, specifically investigating human trafficking. Dana is among a number of women I have met through my work.' It is not strictly ethical, let alone legal, for Madeleine to be sharing details of an informant with anyone outside the agency, but seeing as Dana put herself forward to Isobel, via Maureen, and Dana and Eva were victims of the same gang, it seems like extenuating circumstances. Or at least, if Eva can help them bring the traffickers to justice then the ends will surely justify the means.

Eva looks to Isobel for confirmation, and Isobel nods.

'I hope you don't mind me bringing Madeleine with me.' She pauses. 'But first, I wanted to say how sorry I am, for all of this.'

'It's not your fault,' Eva says, matter-of-fact. 'It was me who killed Vedad, not you.'

'Yeah, but he deserved it,' Isobel says. 'I just . . . If I hadn't pursued you, you wouldn't be here.'

Madeleine senses it is time to step in. She speaks gently, guiding Isobel back to less emotive territory.

'I asked Isobel if I could come with her because we think you might be able to help us catch some of the people responsible for a number of crimes.' Madeleine lets her words settle, before sitting forward. 'What do you think?'

Artemis

London, the Nineties

The following year, the family didn't return to the island. Neither Artemis nor Clive even mooted the idea as the prospect of another school holiday loomed, as if to even mention the place where the fight had happened, while the repercussions were still being felt, threatened to throw off balance the careful dance that their relationship had become.

For her part, Artemis was simply relieved not to have to make a decision on whether or not to go home to Greece, where the threat of seeing Athena again loomed large. She had expected David to ask when he would be going back to visit his grandparents that year. But as he turned nine, the thrill of spending time with Artemis' mother and father in the bakery and occasional days out to the beach with Maria – who for all David's fondness towards her was ultimately still a girl, two years younger than himself – diminished in the face of the prospect of a summer in London, hanging out with friends his own age. The fact was that her son was getting older. One day her boy would be a man. She tried to picture it: David, with his obsession with catching woodworms to keep as pets; the way he subconsciously closed one eye when he tried, unconvincingly, to tell a lie; David who giggled uncontrollably as he showed his friends how he could push almost his whole tongue through the gaps where his teeth had fallen out – as a man. The truth was, he was already changing. The older he got, the more interested he became in hanging out with Clive, and the more Clive rejected him, the more vehemently he seemed to crave his father's attention.

Inevitably, when his requests were rejected by Clive, she was the one David seemed to blame, moping around the house, rebutting his mother's attempts to cajole him out of his mood with offers of the cinema or the zoo.

When, at the last minute, Clive suggested they spend the last few weeks of the summer in France that year, scoping out a picturesque village in Provence where he was interested in buying a property, David was enthusiastic in a way that Artemis was certain he wouldn't have been if she had been the one to suggest it. With the promise of a swimming pool and daily ice creams, David was lured away from days spent playing football on the Heath with his friends, playing Sega into the evening.

The smell of lavender clung to the village that August. It wafted over the wall of the garden, scenting the air as Artemis and David whiled away the hours reading in the shade, dipping in and out of the swimming pool, while Clive looked at houses. In the late afternoons, once the day had slightly cooled, the three of them would stroll to the boulangerie for supplies, the smell of pastries reminding Artemis of her childhood.

Maria would be turning seven that summer. The thought struck Artemis one afternoon, with a tug of sadness. She bought a card from a boutique in town with a kitten on the front and signed it from her and David, with the message *We hope you have a wonderful day. Can't wait to see you again* written inside, holding her breath as she wrote it. Would she ever see Maria again? She and Athena hadn't spoken since their fight. Artemis had considered calling, but what would be the point? Besides, Athena was the one who should be eaten up with remorse. *She* needed to make the call, not that she would. Athena had no concept of being in the wrong, ever.

Artemis was lazing by the pool, lost in thought, when Clive returned later that afternoon with a triumphant look on his face. 'I've found it,' he said, leaning down and kissing her hard on the forehead.

'Really?'

'Just you wait. It's an old chateau, in need of plenty of work, hence the price . . .' He walked over to the pool where David was practising his diving. David's face stretched into a smile when he looked up and saw his father pulling off his clothes and jumping in in his boxer shorts.

'Tomorrow we'll drive to Nice,' Clive said, catching his breath after a few laps. His arms crossed over the edge of the pool, he looked playful, childlike, his skin glistening in the afternoon sun, reminding Artemis of those early days in Greece. 'David, I'll take you to the casino. Make a man of you. What do you think?'

Something about the sound of her son squealing with excitement as she walked away unnerved her. She hated these flickers of jealousy she felt watching David bask in the sporadic attention of his father. But she felt powerless to stop them.

For so many years – as she watched him suckle milk, his tiny fingers desperately searching for and then clinging to hers, holding his hand while he shuffled along one of the fallen logs on the Heath, listening to him painstakingly sound out letters from an illustrated phonics chart – it had felt like she was the only person David would ever need. Suddenly, she had the feeling he didn't need her at all.

They took the Côte d'Azur coastal road towards Nice the following day, rolling back the roof of their rented Audi TT, sea stretching out on one side, the sky a hazy blue above their heads.

When she looked at him in profile, it was still there, an impression of the young man she had seen that day on the boat, the ambitious would-be entrepreneur intent on changing the world, but so faintly now that when she blinked it was gone.

Turning, Artemis caught a flash of herself in the wing mirror;

her face was less defined than it had been. She was still beautiful, though not in the way that made fools of men. That was partly why Clive's infatuation, in those early days, had been so peculiar, so meaningful; he had seen something in her that others couldn't. Had he loved her, then?

It occurred to her that she wasn't sure she had ever really loved him, or anyone, before David.

She felt a sudden intense ache at the nape of her neck, the sea air chilling the back of her head.

'So what do you think of the house, from the brochure?' Clive asked, interrupting her thoughts.

'I think it's beautiful,' she replied, touching her hand to her neck, watching him for a moment longer before tilting her head to look out of the window.

They checked in for the night at the Negresco, Clive pulling out his wallet and handing a card to the receptionist. She rarely thought about the mechanics of the inordinate growth of Clive's company, how it had gone so quickly from wary start-up to something lucrative enough to enable the purchase of plush second homes. If she had she might have reasoned it was the result of canny self-belief combined with the financial freedom of having inherited a house, and no small sum of cash, shortly before they met.

'Bit bloody gaudy, but all part of the experience,' Clive said, indicating around the hotel reception before slipping his card back into his wallet. 'I suggest we put our bags in the room and then go for lunch.'

'I'm not hungry, I want to go to the casino like you said,' David replied sulkily.

Clive gave him a reproving look and Artemis felt a pang of hurt on David's behalf. 'I can take him, I'm not that hungry yet either,' she said quickly.

'We have a lunch date, we can go to the casino after that,' Clive repeated firmly.

'With who?' Artemis asked, confused. He hadn't mentioned they would be meeting anyone.

'Jeff and May. They happened to be staying down the road and Jeff and I have a few things to discuss.'

Artemis felt a scream rise inside her. How dare he? After everything . . .

'Sound good, David? Your godparents are looking forward to having you.'

Intentionally, he avoided Artemis' gaze, holding out his hand to his son, who took it gratefully. 'Come on then . . . Let's not keep them waiting.'

Clive gave the perfect performance of someone having an ordinary lunch with friends. He and Jeff sat at one end of the table, the women at the other. Artemis, whose whole body trembled with obsolete rage beneath linen trousers, a white V-neck T-shirt and espadrilles, beside May in a lurid green summer dress and spiked heels. David sat between them, distracted by the sticker album May had presented him with.

May, either oblivious or indifferent to the air of tension that rang between Clive and Artemis as they approached the dining hall, drilled on as usual, giving an equally impressive show of nothing being off. And it wasn't, was it? Nothing had changed. As May rattled on about the spa facilities at their hotel ('honestly, so naff') Artemis' attention turned to the restaurant tables, raucous groups and coiffed couples of a certain age sitting in cool silence. She thought of Yannis' bar on the island, of the rows of dusty old bottles, the impassioned conversation and gentle bickering that rang between the tables.

Her mind slipping back into the room, Artemis' attention was caught by Clive's more clipped tones. 'Francisco's still going on about it. I've told him I'm not interested – and I thought you had done the same.'

'Well, I—' Jeff began.

'You need to rein this in—' Clive cut him off.

'I need the toilet,' David's voice blotted out his father's words. Artemis pushed back her chair.

'Let's go,' she said, holding out her hand to him, but he slipped past without looking back. 'I can go on my own, I don't need you.'

Madeleine

'Vedad was the son of my mother's best friend, Ariana. We grew up together. He was a few years older than me, the same age as my sister, Sabina, but we all spent lots of time together when we were small. Their house was the one along from ours. Where I come from, in the mountains, it is not like London, you understand. It was a good place to live, the families in the village looked after one another.' Eva's posture softens as she retreats into the memory.

'Every Saturday night when Sabina and I were small, my mother would take us to the square in the village to listen to the music that filled the streets. Together, my mother and Sabina would dance the kolo. They always asked me to join them, but I was too shy so I would sit on the wall opposite and watch them, swinging my legs to the beat. I thought these were happy days but later I started to feel the cloud that loomed over everything. I wasn't even born when war broke out, but what it left behind was everywhere.'

Madeleine knows their time is limited but she cannot risk urging Eva along in her story. Besides, it's impossible to know what details will prove fruitful, at the time. If she has learnt one thing in this job, it's that you have to pay attention to all of it.

'My father's brother, Uncle Arizote, was killed, attacked in our village along with several other men. At first, Ariana told me later, my father kept himself busy trying to get the case investigated by the United Nations Mission in Kosovo who had arrived at the end of the war; she said he nearly drove himself mad trying to convince them that Albanian gangs were to blame. When it became clear that those who attacked Arizote and the other men did so with the support of the foreign Kosovo Forces who were brought in to help keep the peace after the war had officially ended, my father . . . he gave up.'

Eva pauses. 'Anyway, it wasn't so bad when my mother was there. She would tell us stories and shield us from my father's tempers, but when she left to find work in Belgrade . . . There was no work and no money. My mother said she would come back. She sent money for me and Sabina every month, but my father kept it. It wasn't very much. She never came back.'

Her voice dips and Isobel leans forward, proffering a white plastic cup.

'Would you like a drink of water?'

Eva nods, taking a sip before returning the cup to the table between them. She closes her eyes and composes herself. 'After my mother left, Ariana started to look after us, Sabina and me. I had a crush on Vedad, I suppose, but as we got older he wasn't interested in playing with me, only Sabina. I found them once together in the barn when they were fifteen. You know . . .'

Eva blushes with shame, looking away before focusing on her hands. 'And then a few months later, just after Sabina's sixteenth birthday, Ariana told me that Vedad was taking Sabina to England, that he had found her work.'

Madeleine rearranged her legs beneath the table, sitting forward slightly in her chair.

'My father was so angry, I was never allowed to say Sabina's name again after she left. My father could do that; if he wanted to put something out of his mind, he could simply cut it out and he would never mention it again. It's what he did with my mother, too. I don't know if Sabina tried to get in touch but I never heard from her, for years. And then one day Ariana came to the house, when my father was out, and told me that Vedad had found work for me too. She said Usuf would help drive me to the port in the middle of the night when my father was asleep.'

'Who is Usuf?' Madeleine asks gently.

'He is Ariana's husband. He was a good man, I think.'

'Do you think you could tell us about that night?' Madeleine asks, glancing up at the clock.

'Usuf was waiting in his truck for me. When I got in the back, I saw there was another man in the front passenger seat. But he didn't say anything. I was scared even though I was excited because I was going to another country, and I couldn't even say goodbye to my father. But Ariana had some cake for me and she hugged me and told me it would be OK, that Vedad and Sabina would be waiting for me in London.'

Eva wipes her nose on her sleeve. 'It was so cold as the car took off, and eventually I fell asleep, wrapped in a small rug I had stolen from the foot of my father's chair while he slept. I kept thinking he would wake up and tell me I couldn't go, but the truth was he had been so comatose from drink that he wouldn't have noticed if the house had been on fire. I don't remember the journey too clearly. I remember the weight of the rucksack pressed against my knees, the truck making a roaring noise as it bumped along in the darkness, the smell of salt rising to meet the gasoline from the boats as we reached the port. Usuf slowed the truck and pulled into a queue of tankers and cars, and then for the first time, he turned and spoke to me. He said the man next to him would look after me and that I should do as he said.'

'Five minutes,' the guard at the front of the room announces and Madeleine feels Isobel bristle beside her.

Understanding time was running out, now that she has finally caught her stride, Eva speaks more quickly. 'Once Usuf had driven away, I followed the man over to a café set back a little from the dock. There was another man at a table outside the café. He was wearing a denim jacket and had long hair pulled back into a pony-tail. They spoke for a few minutes a little away from me so that I couldn't hear, and then the man with the ponytail told me to go with him, in English. He took me into the back of a truck sealed with panels of wood. There was another girl in there, who looked younger than me. I think she was happy to see me, she was shivering it was so cold. She said she was from Braşov, a town in Romania, and she was going to Greece to work in a café as a waitress. She said she was going to stay in Thessaloniki, which was where the boat was headed, and I was confused because I was going to London, but I thought maybe this was just how people travelled.'

Eva laughs at the absurdity of her own suggestion and then carries on.

'Just before the truck boarded the boat, the man with the ponytail stepped inside and gave us both a glass and told us to drink. After that I fell asleep and when I woke up there were men shouting and heaving things about outside and daylight was coming in through cracks in the panel of the truck, and the other girl had gone.'

The guard at the front of the room starts to walk towards them, signalling that they must leave.

'It's OK,' Madeleine leans towards Eva reassuringly. 'I'm a police officer, I can arrange to come in the next couple of days and inter-view you formally and you can tell me everything.'

Eva nods, her jaw clenched. 'I loved Vedad,' she says, matter-of-fact. 'I didn't mean to kill him. I was confused and he said he would make me go back. I couldn't go back – you don't understand what it was like. Every day they would make me have sex with men and they would film me. And Goran, he would . . .'

Madeleine turns to the guard, showing him her identification, knowing that even without official authorisation this will be enough to stall him at least for a few moments.

'Who is Goran?' Madeleine asks, remembering one of the names pinned to Isobel's wall.

'He ran the *studio*, as he called it. It was this building near Tottenham Court Road where they made us work, and they sold drugs from there, too,' Eva says.

'Goran Petrović,' Isobel interjects.

'How did you know?' Eva looks shocked but continues, understanding that the guard will be back in a moment and then she will have to wait until Madeleine returns. 'Goran liked me. Sometimes he would let me sit out for hours at a time just to talk to him while the other girls worked. I think it pained him to see other men having sex with me. He never said anything to Vedad, of course, and when the bosses were due to visit he would make me go back in – and he always made me do enough that it wouldn't be obvious when the films were watched back that I wasn't pulling my wei—'

'What other men?' Isobel cut in.

'I don't know all their names,' Eva says, flustered. 'But there was one. A Greek, he was the one who brought me over. The one with the ponytail. His name was Jorgos.' Eva looks away as she says his name. 'He used to watch, and sometimes he would join in. I don't know his surname.'

'Eva,' Isobel says. 'Have you spoken to the police about this?'

Eva snorts. 'What, the police who put me in here for trying to protect my baby? The ones who did nothing to help me when I was being raped every day for three years?'

The guard returns. 'I'm sorry, I've spoken to my senior and—'

'It's fine,' Madeleine says, looking at Eva. 'I will come back. We'll fix this. OK?'

Artemis

London, the Nineties

Artemis was curled up on the sofa in the living room, a copy of the *Camden News* spread over her knees, a fire crackling in the grate. It had been more about the distraction of lighting it, a comforting process that helped kill the hours, rather than needing the warmth of the fire itself. It was the Easter holidays and spring had brought with it a lift in temperature, though London to her was only ever a spectrum of varying degrees of cold, to which she could never acclimatise.

She heard the front door open before Clive walked in. 'What are you doing?'

She paused for a second, not so much meaning to ambush him with her plan as to tell him in a rare moment when she had his attention. 'I'm thinking of getting a job.'

Clive laughed as if she had made a joke, taking off his suit jacket and laying it over an armchair. 'God, this place is feeling tired. We should have some work done. Where's David?'

She paused before glancing up at him. 'He's at Irfan's, I'm collecting him in an hour.'

He looked cross, as if some plan of his had been changed without his permission, though it was hours before he usually got home from the office.

'I'm serious about the job,' Artemis said, closing the classified pages, which had, if she was honest, been completely useless.

'What sort of job?' Clive asked, incredulity in his voice.

'I don't know.' She wracked her brain for an answer more purposeful than the one she wanted to give, *anything to get me out of this fucking house*. 'There are lots of things I could do. I was thinking of asking at the library or one of the coffee shops on the high-street, perhaps—'

His expression silenced her.

'What?'

'A coffee shop?' He looked genuinely perplexed. 'Do you have any idea—' He broke off as though to finish his sentence would validate a suggestion too ludicrous to even consider.

The insolence in his voice was what she needed, something to rub up against.

'Why not?' she said, rearranging her feet.

'Why not? For a start, our son needs you at home.' He couldn't bring himself to name the real reason: his own pride; the horror of Clive Witherall's wife serving the mothers of the other boys at David's school, the suggestion that she needed or even wanted to work, as if what he gave her wasn't sufficient.

'No, he doesn't,' Artemis snapped, standing and looking at Clive. 'He doesn't need me at all. Neither of you do. All I do is sit around in this house, and clean, and—'

'For the love of God, Artemis, how many times do I have to tell you to hire a cleaner! I mean, Christ, we can afford one. And to be honest, I'm pretty sure she would do a better job.'

She slapped him. The sound rang through the room followed by a moment's silence and then the crack of firewood from the grate.

Clive stood perfectly still for a moment and then spoke quietly. 'You ungrateful bitch.'

His face was red with fury but he didn't move an inch, his voice slow and deliberate. 'Do you have any idea how much I do for you and David, how hard I work without ever asking anything from you? We don't even have sex—'

'*We* don't have sex? No, but that doesn't mean *you* don't have sex,' she hissed back at him.

Clive's stature changed then, softening, as if he was stepping out of costume and into a familiar coat.

'Oh, not this again, for God's sake! Change the record, Artemis. Nothing happened!' He looked at her, appalled. 'Though God knows, no one could have blamed me for looking elsewhere. The moment you had David, you and I ceased to exist . . . *You* ceased to exist.'

He let the words hang there. 'If it wasn't for our son I would have left years ago.'

The nightmares, which for the past few years had become sporadic, returned to her in engulfing waves that drowned her dreams in the weeks that followed, occasionally crashing into her waking hours.

'Disturbed sleep is one of the known side effects of paroxetine, but as you know, everything comes at a price.' Dr Blackman said it as if it was an unavoidable fact. 'You have the sleeping pills I gave you?'

'Yes,' she replied, not knowing what else to say. 'Should I try something else, adjust the dose?'

'Could do,' he said, his expression suggesting that it was anyone's guess. 'But to be honest, with drugs there is always a risk. Bad dreams, well, unless they're stopping you sleeping to the point where you're physically ill . . . Maybe it's not worth quibbling over?'

Quibbling. It was one of those curious English words designed to make the accused feel like what they really lacked was a stiff upper lip.

'How often are you taking the sleeping pills? Not too often, I hope,' he added obliquely. Satisfied that he'd answered his own question, he moved on. 'Now when it comes to the paroxetine, what you absolutely mustn't do is come off them too suddenly. It can have terrible side effects.'

Artemis wasn't listening, her mind already moving elsewhere.

*   *   *

238

It wasn't so much despair as a sense of emptiness that subsumed her in the weeks that followed. She found it hard to settle in the house in the hours when David was at school, finding herself in the same spot for hours, staring at nothing. Her son was growing up, wanting to spend more time with his friends, or with Clive when he was home. Artemis had defined her whole identity, her whole life, around him and soon he would be gone, and what then?

Even the prospect of time on the island couldn't raise any joy. Some nights she barely slept at all; when she did she would wake suddenly, convinced that something terrible was about to happen.

'You look awful,' Clive told her when he returned from his latest business trip, just in time for them all to travel to Greece as a family for the holidays.

'I am having trouble sleeping,' she replied.

He was frustrated rather than sympathetic. 'Artemis, this can't go on. You need to go back to Dr Blackman. Why don't I call him, make an appointment?'

'No,' she replied plainly. 'I'm fine. I am already following his instructions to come off the pills gradually. I just have insomnia.'

She was lying. The truth was, she didn't trust him. She had followed his instructions at first, that much was true, but how could she trust him? Clive had sent her to him, she reminded herself as she sat in the middle of the night, after several days with barely a few hours' sleep, once again paralysed at the kitchen table waiting for light to creep in. What if they were poisoning her? Dr Blackman and Clive could be working together. It was ludicrous, she knew that – she was paranoid. She thought of the words emblazoned across a T-shirt hanging from one of endless racks stacked up across Camden Market: *Just because you're paranoid doesn't mean they're not out to get you.*

She was an albatross, a dead weight. Clive had said it himself; if it wasn't for David he would have left her years earlier. Perhaps this was his way of getting her out of the picture, making way for a new life with May. May loved David as her own, didn't she?

Over the following days she started to experiment, taking a few pills and then noting how she felt. It was hard, though, to calculate – to separate the exhaustion from any other observable effect.

The more she thought about it, the more sense it made. Clive never so much as tried to touch her; there was no love there. How could she have been so naive? She was onto them – all she could do right now was stay vigilant, for David's sake if not her own.

She felt her spine straighten as she padded barefoot up the stairs towards the bathroom, the dawn light beginning to peer in through the hallway window. Locking the door behind her, she looked at her reflection for a moment before popping out the pills, one by one, letting them gather in the clammy grooves of her hand. She paused for a moment, observing them properly for the first time, each a compressed block of chemicals, so innocuous-looking. Each one a web of pollutants ready to filter out into her bloodstream and alter the make-up of her body and her mind. And for whose benefit?

Turning, picturing Dr Blackman's face – the thin line of his mouth as he doled out instructions – she took a few steps towards the toilet and held her hands in front of her, letting the pills fall into the bowl. Her fingers lingered for a moment on the handle before pressing down, enjoying the sound of the sucking motion dragging each pill below the water.

Her palms itched as the plane took off, a sense of unease tightening around her chest within minutes of the seven-hour journey to Athens, as if her body instinctively understood what was going to happen. As if pulling back and giving in at the same time.

'Are you OK?' Clive asked irritably. 'You've been up and down the whole bloody flight.'

'Fine,' she said, meeting his eyes. 'I'm fine.'

* * *

Compared to the house in France, which Clive had paid for in cash the day before they left Provence the previous summer, the little cottage on top of the mountain in Greece felt reassuringly compact. The smell of the wood, heated within the locked shutters, was exactly the same as the first day she came here. Everything around them had shifted and changed, but this house was a constant. She felt safe within these walls, she realised as she made her way upstairs, watching David duck through the space from the landing where she and Clive had slept that first night together, into the adjoining bedroom. He had outgrown it now – he and Clive both had – but for her it remained the perfect fit.

The time she spent alone in the house, on those rare days Clive wasn't working and so took David for a ride on the back of his motorbike, the two of them disappearing in a plume of dust, Artemis revelled in the smallness of the place, the manageability of it, the sense of security it gave her. She loved how the walls seemed to prop her up.

She hated the excess of space in London, her whole body seeming to rattle with it while David was at school; both the scale of the city and their home reminding her of her own insignificance. She felt equally disconnected to the house in the South of France, where she and David had joined Clive for various half-terms in the inter-vening year since he'd bought the place. It wasn't that she hadn't had fun there; she didn't hate the houses in London and Provence – she just didn't care about them. In a way she felt they had nothing to do with her.

The reason she loved this place so much, she realised now, was that even if it did belong to Clive, the memories surrounding this house were her own. Up here, amidst the olive trees, the view that stretched away from the island towards a horizon had been hers long before it was ever Clive's. Her own childhood memories lingered, just out of sight, close enough that she could hold them in place, but not so close that she couldn't run from them if she needed to. The walls of the house in Hampstead were steeped in other people's memories, their ghosts accompanying her along the landing as she moved from one room to another, reminding her of how fleeting her time there would be, of all the lives that were yet to inhabit the space once she was gone.

'Why haven't we seen Maria yet?' David asked one afternoon as they sat on the shore. She was looking out at the sea while he absent-mindedly shovelled stones into a plastic bucket. Clive, never able to sit still on the beach, had gone to get them all drinks from the restaurant.

Artemis tensed. She had been warily anticipating this question from David ever since their arrival two weeks earlier.

'I'll call Athena later,' she lied and sensed her son looking at her in a way that suggested he wasn't fooled.

She returned her attention to the sea. There were no waves, everything about the beach was still and yet she felt sick. Even in the height of summer only a handful of tourists were stretched out on towels, idly applying sunscreen, flicking through the pages of books in foreign titles.

Maybe she was just dehydrated.

'Did you buy water?' Artemis asked when Clive returned from the restaurant.

'You didn't ask for one,' he said bluntly, and Artemis took the beer he handed her, drinking hungrily, as if something inside her sensed time was running out.

'Slow down,' he said, watching her, uncertainly.

'Alexander!' David shot up and ran to meet the older French boy he had befriended the week before, who was making his way across the beach, his parents settled at the foot of the restaurant.

When he turned to his mother to check it was OK, Artemis smiled, encouraging him to play, but it took everything in her not to reach forward and pull him back to her.

'David, don't go too far, make sure I can see you,' she called after them as he and the other boy started tossing stones into their buckets.

'You remember we're having lunch with Francisco tomorrow?' Clive said, once David was out of earshot. 'We should get the boat across to Skiathos at around eleven.'

Artemis felt a tightening around her throat. She was so thirsty. 'Sure,' she replied, looking out at the water. 'David and I are going to see my parents tonight . . .'

'Fine. I'd better prepare, there are things I need to discuss with Francisco.'

A storm was brewing as they reached the port. Artemis watched the island disappear behind them through the window of the boat as Skiathos appeared on the horizon, the smell of someone's cigarette drifting in from the deck.

David was sulking in the seat opposite, annoyed to be pulled away from his new friend, who would be at the beach again today, expecting to play with him.

'Can I go and see him when we get home? I know where he's staying.'

His voice was whiney, plucking at Artemis' nerves. She felt herself wanting to snap at him, to lean forward and shout into his face for him to be quiet. She never felt like this with David; she never took him for granted even when he was in a bad mood or pleading at her for something she'd already told him he couldn't have. Having witnessed the aftermath of Helena's death, she knew too well how precious a child was, how easily a life could be ripped away.

Today she couldn't settle. She was tired but it was more than that; she felt frayed. *Frayed/afraid*, the words suddenly interchanged in her mind. Yet there was no reason to be fearful. Not any more.

'What time are we meeting him?' Artemis asked as they stepped onto the port, which was so much busier than it had been in the days when she and her parents would take the boat to visit her uncle. The cafés and bars parallel to the water advertised in English and French, bored-looking waiters leaning against the façade waiting for an influx of lunchtime trade.

'He'll be waiting there when we arrive,' Clive replied, leading them to a car and holding open the door. The driver stepped out, a heavy-shouldered man with a long ponytail.

Clive grinned at him before turning to Artemis. 'You remember Jorgos, don't you?'

The lunch passed in waves of conversation, Artemis refusing to look at him, determined not to let him know how uneasy his presence was making her. David's eyes bulged with delight when Artemis stood to use the bathroom and Jorgos reached into his pocket and pulled out a coin which he gave to David to buy a lollipop from the adjoining bar.

'Do you want me to come with you?' Artemis asked quickly and her little boy batted her away, scooting off as she moved uneasily in the other direction, turning only once and spotting the men's heads moving closer in her and David's absence.

In the bathroom, Artemis held onto the sink, breathing deeply. She just had to get through lunch, that was all. He couldn't get to her. Not now.

Except if she knew that to be true then why was she shaking?

When Artemis returned a few minutes later, the conversation stopped. Clive's face, when she studied it, was etched with emotions she couldn't read.

They parted company with the men at the door of the restaurant and were nearly back at the port when Artemis remembered the sunglasses she had left on the table. She should leave them, they were only sunglasses, but the thought of not having them made her tense. Or maybe she'd wanted another reason to go back.

'I won't be a minute,' she said to Clive, ignoring his look of intense frustration.

Instinctively, Artemis slowed down as she spotted the men lingering in front of the restaurant door. She stayed where she was for a moment, on the other side of the road, imagining what she would do if she'd had the nerve – what she would shout at him, right here, in front of all these people. Moving away slightly and crossing further up, she made her approach just out of their sightline.

She was building herself up as she walked towards them, working through the words in her mind. *Rapist.* Clive would never forgive her, but what did it matter? She was moving in behind, so close that she could have reached out and touched him, when she heard Nguema speak.

'We don't need him, Jorgos. Not any more.'

Artemis slowed, pulling back, tuning into Nguema's words. 'The man is a dead weight. I've made arrangements with Jeff.'

At the sound of their voices, any bravado washed away. What was she doing? She turned, moving slowly away, but before she could take another step out of view, to safety, she heard Jorgos calling out to her in Greek.

'Everything OK?' His voice struck her between the shoulder blades. For a moment she imagined herself on the floor, his weight pressing against her.

'Fine,' she said, a sudden wind catching her so that she held onto the wall for balance. Turning to face the men, she spoke more steadily. 'I just left my sunglasses at the restaurant.'

When she looked at Nguema, avoiding Jorgos' stare, his expression was impenetrable.

'They've just closed for the afternoon,' Nguema replied.

'It's fine, I'll get them another time.' She turned, suddenly desperate to be away from there, to be anywhere else.

Jorgos' voice called after her. '*Ta léme argótera.*' See you later.

* * *

She felt her husband watching her as the boat transported them back towards the smaller island.

'You're drinking a lot,' he commented, returning from the bar holding the beer she had asked for.

'Not really. I just fancied one.'

She refused to catch his eye.

'Should you be drinking, with the medication—'

'I'm not a child,' she barked back at him and David looked up from his game. She glanced reassuringly at her son and he looked down again.

'I need to talk to you,' she said under her breath to Clive as they arrived back at the house.

'Later,' he replied, brushing her off. 'I promised I'd take David out. Anyway, you look like you need a lie-down.'

Despite her remonstrations to the contrary, she did feel drunk. In the weeks since they had arrived, she'd been increasingly anxious, and combined with the wine from lunch – and the rest she'd consumed once Clive and David went down to the beach without her – it was making her woozy. She thought briefly about Dr Blackman's warning about coming off the drugs too quickly. But that could easily have been what he wanted her to think. Besides, she'd felt strange when she was back in London, before the cold turkey. Maybe there it had been the house, the spectres that shrouded it – apparitions of a life that wasn't hers – that was making her mad. Did she really believe Clive and Dr Blackman were conspiring against her? Truly, she didn't know what she thought. She was too tired to think. Tiredness made people insane, didn't it? Or at least it could make you feel as if you were. How was anyone to know the difference?

It was only five o'clock but she needed a nap. Except when she closed her eyes, she saw the men's faces staring back at her outside the restaurant; there was something in Nguema's eye that caused her to sit up again, her breath sharpening.

Standing and walking to the bathroom, she rummaged through her washbag in search of face wipes. She was so hot. If she couldn't sleep, she could at least try to freshen herself up, to feel less deranged than she was feeling now. She felt her fingers move over a packet of sleeping pills she kept for emergencies. Physically relieved by the prospect of sleep, she popped out a pill, her fingers lingering over the packet for a moment before taking out another for good measure.

They weren't supposed to be mixed with alcohol, but the instructions always said that. And she hadn't drunk that much. Clive loved to make her feel she was less in control than she was. He had been exaggerating. She wasn't so drunk, she just needed rest.

Her eyelids felt heavy when she was stirred back into full consciousness by the sound of tapping at the door. For a moment she thought she must have been dreaming, that the sound was the build-up to the earthquake she felt tearing about the house in her subconscious. But then it came again, more clearly this time.

The house was in darkness and when Artemis reached for the bedside lamp, it didn't turn on. It wasn't unusual for bursts of weather to bring down the power lines – they were so exposed up here – and Artemis kept a stash of candles and matches in the drawer.

She fumbled with the match before the room came partially into focus, the light of the flame soft at the edges. She moved slowly down the stairs, the storm gathering pace outside, her muscles tensing, as she thought of David outside, alone. And yet there was no way that would be the case. There had been talk of David going to see his little French friend, Alexander, in their rented house on the other side of the mountain, but Clive would never have left him to walk home alone after dark. There was no way it was Clive at the door, either. He could hardly bear to be in the house these days, as if the place served to remind him of something he'd rather forget. He would have gone to the bar to wait while David played, or perhaps he would have taken him for something to eat by now. She didn't even know what time it was. All she knew was that she was alone, apart from the person who was knocking on the other side of the door.

'Who is it?' she asked, imagining Carolina or another neighbour coming to discuss the generator, but there was no answer. Pulling the door open a fraction, she felt a foot jam in the crack and the force of it, together with the wind, pushing it open. There in front of her was Jorgos.

Madeleine

London, present day

They sit in silence for a while, the motorway slowly giving way to a series of roundabouts and junctions as London appears on the horizon.

'I wonder where the baby is,' Madeleine says after a while.

'It's with her sister,' Isobel replies, looking out the window. 'She chose to separate while she is inside.'

Madeleine looks at Isobel sidelong. 'I'm not going to even ask how you know that.'

Isobel shrugs, a small smile briefly on her lips, and then her forehead furrows again as she moves deeper into thought. 'Did you mean that, about coming back to speak to her again? Do you really think you can get her out of prison?'

'I don't know about that. The next step from here is to refer Eva to the National Referral Mechanism as a potential victim of trafficking. It's a different department at the NCA, but I'm entitled to assist her self-defence case, if she raises one. She still killed a man, regardless of the reason. But if we can prove she was traumatised and she didn't mean to kill him, that she was defending herself against the person who had perpetually abused her, who had threatened to take her baby away unless she went back to sex-work, which is her official statement . . . And if she can help us find the men who trafficked her to the UK . . . I can't say anything for sure, but I'm hopeful.'

Isobel says nothing and Madeleine watches her, the resolve coming off her in waves. Isobel's eyes are fixed on the road but it is clear her mind is simultaneously working on something else.

'Hey,' Madeleine says. 'You know when you found the article in that editor's office?'

'Mmm.'

'You said you were there for a job interview.'

Isobel looks briefly back at her. 'Yeah, I was.'

'Did you get it?'

Isobel nods without any hint of celebration. 'I don't know if I'll take it.'

'Why not?'

'I'm not sure if it's for me any more. Journalism, it's . . . I don't know. I guess I'm having some sort of early mid-life crisis.'

Madeleine whistles. 'Pretty bloody early. What are you, fifteen?'

'Not quite,' Isobel laughs. 'It's been a weird time for me. A friend of mine died a year ago and I had a bit of a breakdown. I'm in Narcotics Anonymous at the moment. Coming off drugs and stopping drinking, all feels like I'm just starting to get my life together, and I guess I feel I'm at a crossroads.' She makes a face. 'I realise that sounds melodramatic, but . . . I don't know. Journalism just feels so constrained – so tied up in agendas and advertising revenue, and bullshit and more bullshit. I just don't know if it makes any difference. Any of it.'

Madeleine nods. 'I know what you mean.' She pauses, and then clears her throat. 'If you were looking for a change, the NCA recruits from across a range of backgrounds. I mean, I can't promise fewer constraints or agendas or less bullshit but . . . well, if you were looking for a change. We could do with proper investigators rather than more bloody pen-pushers.'

Isobel takes the turn off for Central London.

'Don't take me into town,' Madeleine says. 'I can make my own way back from yours.'

'Are you serious?'

'Of course. You don't want to get stuck in congestion—'

'I mean about the job.'

Madeleine nods. 'Abso-fucking-lutely. I happen to know there's a recruitment drive. With no previous police experience you would likely go in as a basic investigator – a G5, as they're known – after an initial training programme. You'd get a mentor. There would be a lot of acronyms to learn, lots of dull paperwork between the actual investigating, but the good news is there are plenty of numpties so you're likely to soar once you're in.'

She looks at Isobel. 'Seriously, though, I couldn't think of a better candidate – and that's a bigger compliment than I've made it sound.'

Artemis

Greece, the Nineties

Jorgos' words chased Artemis as she ran across the scrubland towards Athena's house, rain lashing against her legs.

Aside from a bolt of lightning, the island was pitch-black and Artemis felt rather than saw her way, falling against the door as she reached it, banging with her fists as if her life depended on it. In that moment, she believed it did.

Athena's face dropped when she saw her. 'What the—'

Artemis pushed her way into the house, oblivious to Maria hovering in the doorway of the kitchen.

'He's going to kill me – Athena, you have to believe me . . .'

Artemis' fists clenched convulsively, the image of Jorgos' face up in hers. *You need to be very careful. If you speak to anyone – and I mean anyone – I will kill you, and then I will kill your son.*

She was desperate for Athena to comfort her, to tell her it would be all right. But Athena said nothing, simply staring silently back at her oldest friend as if she didn't know her at all.

'You have to believe me, Athena, I know too much! I can see it in his eyes when he looks at me. The way he talks about me as if I'm mad . . .'

She pictured Jorgos waiting for her on the way home from school, he and another boy throwing stones at her. Hissing at her. *Treló korítsi.* Crazy girl.

'Please just promise me that if anything happens to me you will remember what I told you.'

The sound of a branch cracking on a tree outside caused the women to turn and spot Maria in the doorway, a toy rabbit hanging limply by her side.

Athena took a step towards her friend, reaching out a hand. 'Artemis . . .'

But Artemis stepped back, away from the disbelieving gaze.

She turned as she spoke, more quietly now. 'If you don't believe me, what hope do I have?'

The house was still empty when she returned. The storm had begun to run out of breath, moonlight spilling through the window on the landing above as Artemis moved back up the stairs without removing her wet clothes.

When she blinked, she could see the house just as it was the day she first came here, the bed in the corner, neatly made, the copy of the business book Clive was reading placed on the pillow. She felt Clive's eyes on her, then; the way she felt under the intensity of his gaze, the power he held over her even then; the power she felt in the reflected glory of what he seemed to see in her.

She felt herself sit, drawing the bedsheet up to her chest, her fingers clutching the cotton so that it was ruched in front of her, a ghost not yet unfurled.

Her fingers worked their way along the hem of the sheet. Soon the material was taut between her hands, her wrists twisting in opposite directions so that she was now holding a rope. She felt a portentous energy glide over her as she held it against herself, noticing the malleability of the cotton as she touched it briefly to her neck, against the amethyst necklace Clive had given her, in another lifetime.

Briefly, she thought of her sister, how she must have felt that night, seconds before the house crumbled above her. And then her mind moved to David, his little face dappled in sun spots as he looked up at her, like a buttercup basking in the final glow of summer.

This time when she heard the knock, she didn't move. She didn't need to, the door was already open. She closed her eyes as Jorgos stepped inside, closing the door behind him.

Madeleine

London, present day

She doesn't know what to expect as she waits in the room they have been allocated for the purposes of this interview. She has looked him up, obviously, after reading his file, trying to build as much of a picture as she can. Her interest in this particular suspect is more personal than it usually would be. She wants to see him from every angle, to understand as best she can *why*. But it's useless. How can anyone fully understand what attracts one person to another, what compels a person to make decisions that defy logic?

Ivan Popov is in his fifties, she has discovered. He was born in Kybyshev – now Samara – the ninth-biggest city in Russia. His parents, both active members in the Communist party, were engineers who worked making parts for naval ships. Ivan's first business was selling shoes. After making some money, according to the official story, he became interested in philanthropy and started working in charity. His association with Irena Vasiliev, although yet to be fully unveiled, would suggest a more circuitous path.

He moves between a townhouse in Richmond, South-West London, and a swanky Moscow apartment but is currently residing in an altogether different setting, courtesy of Her Majesty's Prison Service, awaiting trial. How long he will be here is yet to be ascertained.

What neither the file nor Madeleine's Google searches have mentioned is his demeanour: the way he moves through a room and owns it, even in a uniform prison-grey tracksuit, flanked by a guard.

He nods courteously as he sits in front of her, the power of his presence making her sit up straighter.

'I'm Madeleine,' she says.

'Ivan, but you know that already.' He pauses. 'I'm sorry I can't offer you a drink.'

There is a hint of something she can't quite read in his eyes as she takes in the empty room, the bare table between them. What is it: danger, amusement, pain? Sitting opposite him, she can understand, against her better judgement, what Gabriela might have seen in him.

'I'm here about Gabriela and Layla,' she continues without flinching, watching his jaw clench. She sees him brace, shifting his chair, a tiny slide away from her. She wonders for a moment if he might leave. This is not an official interview, not yet; he is not compelled to be here, certainly not without a lawyer present. If she's honest with herself, she hadn't even expected him to agree to meet her today. This meeting is for her, to help herself reset. After everything that has happened with Gabriela, she needs to see him face-to-face, to understand who this man is who took her friend's life, and those of her children, and tore them to shreds. She wants to look him in the eye and try to understand something that she knows she never will.

'I'm sorry for your loss,' Madeleine says quickly, watching his reaction carefully for traces of how much he knows. He looks down at his hands, twisting his fingers, and Madeleine's forehead furrows.

His pain is real, that much she can be sure of – not that this means anything.

He moves forward, lowering his voice though the guard appears not to be listening.

'I'm going to testify,' he says. 'Against Irena.'

Madeleine pauses, waiting for him to continue, but he sits back in his seat.

After a moment, she nods. 'That's good to know. We can offer protection—'

Popov laughs, looking away from her. 'You think you can protect me? Even after what happened to Gabriela, you still believe that?' His face twists. 'You think Vasiliev can't get to me, even from behind bars, if she wants to?'

What's left of a contorted smile fades. 'None of it matters, not now. I'll tell you what you need to know. I'll tell you everything. I want her to pay for what she did.'

He raises a hand to his chest, absent-mindedly, as if responding to a stab of pain, and his face hardens again. 'I have nothing to lose.'

By the time Madeleine gets back to the office, it's lunchtime. She has barely pulled the lid off her Tupperware, seated back at her desk, when her phone rings.

'No!' She slams her fist tragically on her desk. Not now, for the love of God, she is starving. The temptation of the lasagne in front of her is such that she is minded to ignore her phone, but when she looks down and sees the name, she smiles. Taking a mouthful and chewing quickly, she answers, her voice distorted by the food.

'Isobel, how are you doing?'

'Madeleine, can you talk?' Isobel's voice is urgent. Madeleine dabs her mouth with a tissue, sitting forward in her chair.

'Of course, is everything OK?'

'You're not going to believe this,' Isobel says. 'I've just had a call from a woman called Maria. I don't know how else to say this – she says she's in the Maldives, with David Witherall . . .'

PART FOUR

Maria

Greece, the Noughties

The funeral was small but too big to comprehend, and Maria watched David across the church, clinging to his father's side in the same way he used to do with his mother when she was alive – the way he had done the last time Maria had seen him, two summers ago, just after her own papa, Panos, had left for good.

She felt a rush of guilt, a ball of moths rotating in her tummy, trying to imagine how she might have felt if it had been her own mother's body nailed inside that box. She couldn't imagine that she would have felt any worse than she did now if it had been Athena, rather than Artemis, about to be lowered into soil crawling with the insects she and David used to poke at with sticks.

The toes of her shoes don't reach the floor and she stretches out her legs, trying to think of something else, but she can't.

What would David say if he knew what she was thinking? She had tried to talk to him, to tell him what she had seen, but she didn't know what to say or how to say it. He wasn't the person to tell, and who else could she speak to? There was no way she could rely on her mother, and the whole thing had happened so quickly. The night of the storm felt increasingly like a dream, or a nightmare; when she tried to picture it now her memories tossed about like the branches of the trees that had lain scattered the following morning, once it had settled.

It all happened so quickly, and then Artemis was gone, and it wasn't as though anyone had come to talk to her. No one had asked any questions at all, as far as she could tell. Sometimes she felt like she was the only person in the world who cared about getting answers. If her father was still here, she could have spoken to him. He was always the one to listen, encouraging her to read and to think and ask questions. But Panos wasn't here, and he wasn't coming back. Maria had no one.

She didn't cry throughout the service, even while her mother, Athena, wept beside her. At one point she looked up and caught eyes with Clive, who was seated beside Jorgos his driver, and some other men she recognised from the house. She looked down again, her cheeks burning, the way they did when all her feelings came up at once. David was on the other side of his father. Even though he was a whole two years older than Maria, he looked younger than he had the summer before, his whole body shrunken so that it was as though he wanted to follow his mother into the ground.

'I'll leave flowers at the grave for you, when you go back to England,' she told him later as they sat under the shade of a tree, their parents engaged in conversation on the other side of the graveyard, perched at the edge of the cliff.

David said nothing and eventually when Maria was called away by her mother, she leaned forward and wrapped her arms briefly around her friend before walking away, ashamed, wishing she could say more. One day, she told herself, as she scuffed the toe of her shoe along the path. One day they would pay for what they did.

It was a Saturday, the summer after Artemis' funeral, and Maria and her mother were gathering supplies at Carolina's store at the top of the village when Carolina's daughter, Sofia, who had taken over the family business, mentioned Clive's return to the island. Maria had been idly fiddling with an elasticated bracelet she had been given for her recent ninth birthday, made up of pink and yellow plastic stars, when she heard David's name.

'Did Sofia say David is here?' Maria asked, struggling to keep pace as Athena made her way out of the store, a bag of fruit weighing down her left arm.

'She certainly did!' Athena replied, her tone brighter than Maria had heard it in months as she guided them in the direction of the Witherall house.

Maria felt a shiver as they approached the path. 'Should we not ring first?' she said, her eyes casting around as if on the lookout for ghouls.

'Oh, come on, Clive is never too busy for us, Maria. I told you, we are the closest thing they have to family now. Artemis and I, we were . . . She was like a sister to me.'

Clive must have been watching them through the camera pointed down at their heads, as he greeted Athena by name through the newly installed intercom before she even had a chance to ring the bell. Maria had to resist the temptation to burst into a run, picturing herself fleeing down the hill, away from the memories, as Clive's voice crackled through the speaker. The new gate reminded her of a prison, though it was unclear to her whether the locks were designed to guard against people coming in or going out.

Athena jumped briefly before gathering herself, adopting the voice she reserved especially for her dead best friend's husband.

'See, I told you he'd be pleased to see us,' she mouthed to Maria, straightening her dress as they waited for the lock to click open.

'Can I get you both a drink?' he asked smoothly, as he led them towards the house, which had changed in ways Maria couldn't quite pinpoint since she had last been inside.

Maria shook her head to say she wasn't thirsty and was relieved when she was instructed to go and find David by the pool.

The last words she heard before she turned were her mother's desperately transparent plea. 'Maria and I, we are . . . As you may know, Panos left us penniless. Until now, we survived but, well, I think I will have to sell the house . . . Unless I can find work . . .'

Maria spotted David seated at the edge of the water, the paleness of his skin highlighted by the red of his swimming trunks. He smiled when he looked up and saw her approaching. Only a year had passed since she had last seen him, but at eleven, he was suddenly much taller. Even with him sitting down she could see that. And there was something different about his manner, something cooler. It was as if this was a different boy to the one she had left crouched by his mother's grave, the soil beside him still dented with the marks of the shovel.

'Hey,' she said, keen to show off her newly acquired American vernacular, perfected with a detailed study of a video of The Baby-Sitters Club which one of the girls at school had let her borrow.

'Hi,' David replied, his expression serious.

'Can I sit?'

'Sure.'

Pulling off her sandals, Maria lowered herself onto the side of the pool, noticing the chips in the sparkly pink nail polish on her toes, which were coated in dust from the path.

'How long are you here for?' Maria asked, struggling for things to say, wishing for a return to the way they used to be. What a stupid thing to think – nothing would ever be the same again.

'Dunno, depends how long the building work takes.'

For a split second she felt overcome once more with the need to tell him, to confess exactly what she had seen. *Your mama*, she imagined herself saying. But the moment she pictured the man's face she knew she couldn't do it. What good would it do? How could she articulate the words, and let him be left with the same mental image she had been fending off ever since the night Artemis died? And what could he do? They were just children.

'What building?' she asked, looking away.

David shrugged. 'My dad's extending the house.'

'Cool,' she said, not trusting herself to say anything more, and hating herself for knowing that she didn't dare.

* * *

The building work barely stopped once Clive and David were back in London. Athena was taken on as housekeeper, which seemed crazy to Maria given that the Witheralls barely spent two months of the year here and surely could have got away with just shutting the place up while they were gone.

On the days when Maria came up here to help her mother, she would watch the machinery clawing at the house Artemis had loved, the diggers and cranes like the wolves in one of the less comforting stories her father would read her when she was young, tearing apart their kill.

In the years after Artemis' death, the house took on a new lease of life, as if it had sucked the beating heart from her body and used it to fuel its own gruesome metamorphosis.

Across the island, you could hear the delighted shrieks of the guests at the elaborate parties Clive held in the summer months when he and David arrived, with Clive's ever-growing entourage. Parties attended by an *international* crowd who cruised in and out especially for the occasion, according to Athena who loved nothing more than to proudly regale her daughter with details of the outfits and the food on display, as though it was her own party she was describing.

On one such night, while Athena was at work, Maria was sitting on a chair in the yard area at the front of her house. She was reading a book when she heard a noise and looked up to see David, his eyes red with tears. He was thirteen and Maria was eleven, and he pulled a single cigarette from his pocket, lit it and coughed.

'I didn't know you smoked.'

David shrugged. 'My godmother May gave it to me at the party.'

Maria nodded, not knowing what else to say.

'Do you want to walk?' David asked. 'Your mum won't be back for hours – the band has only just started and everyone's getting wasted.'

'Won't your dad wonder where you are?' she asked, following David onto the path which descended into darkness as they moved away from the house.

David snorted. 'Trust me, he won't notice. He's got his business mates there, he's busy.'

There was resentment in his voice and Maria wanted to comfort him so she took his hand, leading him through the paths she knew as well as the back of her hand. For a moment as their skin touched, there was a flash of memory, and she pictured herself following Artemis from a distance along the path towards her house, the sound of the wind whipping at the leaves.

'I miss my mum,' David said, as if reading her mind, and Maria stopped, the tempo of the cicadas seeming to slow down around them.

'Me too. David, I have something I need to—' But before she had time to confess, he leaned forward, so quickly that she didn't know what was happening until she felt his kiss on her cheek.

Maria hadn't slept, rolling the memory of the kiss over and over in her mind, her breath sitting high in her chest as she replayed the scene. When she heard her mother leave for work the following morning, she got up, spending the rest of the morning holding a Penelope Delta novel in front of her face in the shade of the tree. She tried to read but found herself unable to concentrate, her mind drifting back to the previous evening, to the sound of the insects as they moved along the mountain path, the faint smell of cigarette smoke that briefly enveloped her as David's lips touched her cheek.

He had lost his nerve as quickly as he'd found it, pulling away and sheepishly turning, parting ways with the briefest of goodbyes once they were back at her house. And for a moment Maria wondered if he could taste the betrayal on her skin.

When lunchtime came, Maria made herself bread and cheese,

which she picked at before giving up and moving into the bathroom. Plaiting her hair into two braids on either side of her face, she paused in front of the mirror for a moment to study her own reflection. Some girls her age had started to look different, their bodies and faces developing in a way that made them hold themselves self-consciously. But Maria showed no signs of that. She was still skinny, childlike, and ordinarily she liked how it made her feel comparatively inconspicuous, invisible to boys her age.

As her eyes moved over her own features, her father's dark complexion and almond-shaped eyes staring back at her, she imagined the kiss David had left on her cheek once more and pushed away any doubts. He had left because he was embarrassed. But she had had her first kiss, and it was with David. In that moment she felt nothing but contentment, the lines of her mouth lifting into a tentative smile.

Heat radiated from the newly planted trees that lined the entrance to the Witherall house once she finally worked up the courage to head over there later that day. She had been here thousands of times before, both with David and also in the winter months when he and Clive were back in London and Athena looked after the house, overseeing the maintenance of the pool and dusting the paintings that lined the halls. Yet today felt different, nerves gnawing at her tummy as she stepped inside the main gate.

Athena was making herself coffee in the kitchen when Maria approached. 'I thought you were staying at home today?'

'I was going to but . . .' Maria scrabbled around for an excuse, though she'd never needed one before.

'You came at the right time. I was about to strip down all the beds; you can help me,' Athena rattled on with her usual fervour, oblivious to her daughter's peculiar mood. Maria looked confused. Athena had changed the bedding two days before – surely it didn't need to be done again.

'Clive was called back to London for a meeting, so they left this morning,' she continued, and Maria felt the butterflies in her stomach turn to dust.

It was another year before she saw David again, the following summer: four years since Artemis' death. Athena spent a week in the run-up to their return at the house, fluffing pillows and rewashing hand towels, a giddy excitement following her from room to room.

The day they arrived, Maria was playing in the main square, concealed in shadow as the car pulled past, Jorgos in the driving seat, Clive in the back, another man she didn't recognise in the passenger seat of the car. A shiver swept over the back of Maria's neck and she pulled herself instinctively further out of sight.

She stayed away for the first two weeks after that initial sighting. Clive was working flat out, according to Athena who loved the opportunity to make herself indispensable at the house, cooking and cleaning while Jorgos watched on, Clive holding meetings with colleagues who flew in from all corners of the globe and who would partake in his now infamous parties, any complaints from the island's inhabitants quashed by the bouquets of flowers and crates of champagne he had shipped in to thank them for their tolerance, not to mention the large amounts of cash he sank at any number of the island's restaurants and bars.

'You wouldn't believe the outfits, Maria, and the money! People from all over the world. Russia, Africa . . .' Athena was flushed with excitement as she buzzed around their tiny kitchen, filling Maria in on every detail of Clive's social schedule, reconfiguring every event to place herself at the centre.

'He is so busy, I don't know what he'd do without me. Every day, there are more meetings that need catering for, more meals, more beds to be dressed down.'

Maria knew her mother was exaggerating the importance of her role. She had seen Clive's cohorts down at the port, prowling from restaurant to bar. It wasn't that Maria was spying; the island was simply so small that you'd have to be actively looking away not to notice them, with their incongruous suits and watchful eyes.

Maria shuddered. Whatever her mother might say, the men surrounding Clive were more than capable of looking after their own interests without the help of Athena.

Despite her refusal to go to the house when her mother suggested she join them there, Maria was almost as desperate to see David as she was to avoid being brought face-to-face with Clive and his entourage, waiting with increasing impatience for him to seek her out. She made it easy, hanging around in the main square in the village with the girls from school, walking to the beach nearest his house at the bottom of the mountain. On one occasion she even took the circuitous route home via the path that led past the gates with their glass eyes monitoring every person who came and went. But David was nowhere to be found.

'How's David?' Maria blurted to her mother over dinner one evening, out of pure frustration.

Athena paused in a way that was out of character, shaking her head as if considering something sad. 'He's been very quiet. You should go to see him, get him to go to the beach. I don't understand why you won't be a friend to him. He's so pale, that boy. He needs sunlight. He misses his mother, I can see it in his eyes.'

Maria took a mouthful of bread, the food expanding in her mouth as she chewed, postponing answering long enough that Athena had inevitably steered the conversation back towards Clive.

The following night, Maria dreamt of Artemis. Waking in a cold sweat, she got straight out of bed, slipped on a pair of denim shorts and a vest top and hopped on the push-bike she'd been given for her twelfth birthday. Following the road down towards the cemetery, she closed her eyes for a moment, daring herself to be guided by the undulations of the path, a light early morning wind brushing soothingly against her cheeks, blowing away the memory of Artemis' face the night of the storm.

She spotted David from the path as soon as she jumped off the saddle, on the other side of the graveyard, his hair falling in front of his face, casting a shadow across the tightly held line of his mouth. Withdrawing slightly so that he wouldn't see her, she watched him pressing the tip of a stick into a hard knoll of dirt, seeing how much pressure it would take before it snapped.

At fourteen, he had filled out since the previous year. Something about his appearance shocked her. It wasn't just his size, but his whole being seemed to radiate an energy he couldn't contain.

For the first time when she looked at him, she saw a glimpse of his mother – the woman who had treated her like one of her own. The one Maria had betrayed . . . Turning, suddenly unable to look at him and not tell him everything, she turned, pedalling furiously back towards the house, her heart thumping in her chest.

* * *

She hadn't intended to seek him out later that night, but an intuition – a nervous fluttering, like a bird lodged somewhere in her chest – made her go looking. Or perhaps she had been subconsciously preparing to tell him what she knew about Artemis' death. Perhaps in that moment, she was finally brave enough to do the right thing. The top of the mountain was black as she approached, the squeal of the brake on her push-bike the only sound as it slowed to a halt.

The gate was wedged open, as if preparing for visitors, and yet she knew Clive wasn't home. She had seen his car at the port a while earlier, and then spotted him with the same man she had seen in the passenger seat of the car the day he arrived, and a woman, seated at a restaurant overlooking the water. There was a casualness to their performance that appalled her: Clive, Jorgos and the rest of them, laughing and drinking on the island where Artemis had died, as if they hadn't a care in the world; as if it wasn't their fault. She stood for a while watching as Clive ingratiated himself with his crowd, just as he had with her mother, and the rest of the villagers whose affection had been bought with a donation towards a new library – another fact Athena had fed her daughter with such pride.

'He's so *giving*, a real *philanthropist*,' Athena had beamed, and Maria couldn't be sure whether the sense of pride derived from being one of the recipients of Clive's generosity or the fact that she had been party to these insights about his character.

Maria breathed deeply before taking a step towards the partially opened gate which gave way to a pristine gravel drive.

This part of the mountain felt like its own separate universe and Maria suddenly felt exposed as she made her way down the path, imagining the eyes of the CCTV cameras following her every step. She could see a light was shining deep inside one of the extended parts of the house, as she moved closer.

'David?' She called his name, hesitating for a moment before turning the handle of the back door. There was no answer though she sensed movement somewhere in the far end of the house.

Quickening her pace, she moved through the hallway to the stairs, calling out his name until she heard a reply. Following the voice, she pushed a door open tentatively and saw that it was a study. She had never been in this room before, in all the time she'd spent in the house while Athena worked, and there was a look on David's face that she didn't recognise either.

He was sitting on a swivel chair. When she stared more closely, she saw that he had been crying; from the overextended movement of his limbs and the way his vowels curled on his tongue as he said her name, she could see that he was drunk or high or something else that she was too inexperienced to be able to clearly label.

And then she saw the gun.

* * *

Running from the house, she felt their words chasing her, her own voice sounding childlike compared to his.

'Maria . . . You know I've always loved you, don't you?' His eyes had been almost unrecognisable.

'What are you doing, David? For God's sake, put it down! Are you crazy?'

'They said my mum was crazy, do you know that?'

Years later, she would replay this moment in her mind on loop: the moment at which she should have intervened, her opportunity to come clean, to clear the cloud of shame that hung over Artemis' name . . . But then she pictured their faces, and the scene lost its clarity, and once more she told herself she couldn't be sure what she had seen.

Again, she fixed her attention on David. Tears were rolling down his face but his jaw was clenched, his mouth hardly moving as he spoke. 'Why would you hang yourself, though? I don't mean why would you kill yourself, I mean why *hang* yourself, specifically?'

'Please, you're scaring me.' She was so scared, how could she not be? There were so many reasons to be frightened.

It was as if he couldn't hear her. 'You know, I've been thinking. If it were me I'd use a gun.'

He held it up, the barrel dipping slightly in the uncertainty of his grip.

'Please, David.'

The words poured from him, hot and volcanic. 'Do you know how many times I've seen him cry over his wife? Over how her body was swinging from the bannisters outside my bedroom. Why did she have to do it there?' He pointed towards the landing. 'Do you think she wanted me to find her? Do you think she hated me?'

It was only when she felt the tears rolling down her cheeks that she realised she was crying, too.

Maria didn't stop to collect her bike as she ran from the house, leaving David alone, letting him down for the second time in their short lives. Her feet hardly touched the ground as she ran back into the pitch-black night, away from him, away from the memory of the barrel held against his temple. She felt like she was trapped within the walls of a strange dream, coming to only when a car's headlights swept across the road, catching her in their beam, the glare of the metal on the Mercedes emblem causing her to squint.

As she ran Maria could feel Clive's eyes following her through the car window as it passed.

It was ten years before Maria saw David again, the night of the party. Ten years managed partly by pointed avoidance on both their parts, and partly by summers David chose to spend in the family house in Provence, or holidaying with friends elsewhere rather than Greece, according to her mother's unsolicited updates. David was fine – better than that, David was thriving. Whilst she passed her teenage years in the place she had lived her whole life, barely going further than Skiathos, a couple of islands along from here, finally applying for a place at university in Athens, David was off exploring the world, following the path his father had carved out for him.

As time passed, Maria's guilt turned into denial that she ever could have helped. After all, she was a child. She couldn't be sure of what she had seen, or whether it had any real bearing on what had happened to Artemis that night. What good would a vague recounting do for David other than to make him more confused? Besides, she was scared. What she had seen had terrified her, even if she couldn't be sure exactly what it was. It wasn't her fault, not really. She couldn't have stopped it. And David was OK, he was leading a great life, the kind of life she could only have dreamed of for herself.

Eventually denial settled into a different kind of guilt. Without the immediacy of what had passed, she found herself able to sit with what had happened and process it in a way that had previously been impossible. David had needed her and she had run in the other direction, quite literally. He had been her friend and he had believed he'd loved her, whether or not he knew what love was, and Maria hadn't tried hard enough to help him deal with the pain of finding his mother dead, even if for the reason that she was so young and his pain was so big, so raw, and that she had been scared.

No, she hadn't done the right thing, but she'd been a child and she wasn't to blame for Artemis' death. Clive was.

It was exactly a decade after the night when she had come across David holding the gun in his father's study that she saw him again. Maria was home from university in Athens. Clive was hosting a party, her mother said, as if smelling her new-found weakness, presenting it not so much as a suggestion as a fait accompli.

'Maria, I never ask anything of you. Please. How long has it been? Clive always asks after you and they know you are back from Athens. You don't have to stay long.'

In the intervening years, the house had changed almost beyond recognition. The dark stone kitchen had been replaced by Carrara marble and brass fittings; an infinity pool stood in the place of the one where she and David would throw in pennies and then race to see who could dive in and pull them out first.

The moment she stepped inside the house, she regretted it. Despite everything Clive had done to crush the memories of what had happened on this very spot, this was where Artemis had died.

And then she saw him. David – a man in place of the boy. And with him, a woman. Anna.

Maria had left the party as quickly as she could, but not before her mother had told David and his girlfriend about Maria's plans to study in London. Maria had squirmed as Athena spoke, wishing the ground would swallow her whole, and David's reaction had been so sweet, his offer of renewed friendship so genuine that the sense of guilt that sat in her gut once again sharpened into a blade.

'If you need somewhere to stay, or . . . If you ever need anything . . . It would be lovely to see you.'

She had toyed with the idea for a moment. Maybe it would be nice to see him again; she had felt a rush of affection amidst the remorse as he stood in front of her, grinning in his ridiculously formal shirt, the sort his father would have worn. But what would be the point? This was no longer the boy she had known, just as she wasn't the same girl. Too much time had passed. Besides, from the look Anna gave her, she could tell his girlfriend wouldn't appreciate having an old family friend around.

Maria had felt it, like a jolt of electricity as he'd kissed her goodbye on the cheek. And for a split second it was like no time had passed since that night on the track, but then they pulled away and her eyes briefly met his and she struggled to hold his gaze, the swell of emotions rising up in her once more.

No, there would be no point pursuing a friendship with David. She could see, even then, that it wouldn't end well. Though she couldn't have foreseen exactly how, or how badly.

The move to London, a few months later, was supposed to be the big thing that happened in her life, the chance to start again, but somehow Clive managed to ruin that, too. She should have run for her life the moment she heard mention of his name on her mother's lips in relation to her planned year abroad, but she didn't.

'Clive was asking after you, as he always does, and I told him about your plan to study in London for a year and— What? I happened to mention it while I was on my break and he said straight away that you can stay at his flat for as long as you like.'

Maria felt a pulsing in her chest at the mention of it. Was it excitement or revulsion? It was of course possible to feel both at once.

'He won't be there much. He's working abroad for months and when he is there, you would have your own room, of course. Oh Maria, it's so lovely. He showed me pictures. Right in the middle of Central London, on this grand square. The apartment is beautiful.'

'And what does he want in return?'

'Maria, he doesn't want anything. What more does he need? He is a rich man, and we are like family to him . . . I'm telling you, Maria, I know you don't want to believe it, but Clive Witherall is a good man. Artemis wasn't well when she said those things. Do you understand me? Anyone who can do that to themselves . . . To her son . . . Well, she wasn't right, in the end. She was sick.' Athena cupped her daughter's chin with her hand. 'Maria, Artemis was my best friend and I loved her like a sister, but the woman was paranoid.'

No matter how tempting it might have been, Maria declined Clive's offer. No amount of money could have forced her to take that man's charity. But when the opportunity came up for the job as a nanny to newborn twins Stella and Rose, within weeks of her landing in London and finding herself holed up in a grubby room above a shop on Green Lanes, paying the rent by scraping fat off the fryer at a local burger joint, Maria felt herself say yes. It had come as a shock, at first, to find out that Anna was pregnant. She hadn't been showing at the party so she must have been in the very early stages. And then a moment of jealousy, which quickly faded. And how slippery her moral high ground had been; how easily the justifications had slid off her tongue: it wasn't David's fault, what his father was like. It wasn't David's children who were to blame. Besides, she owed it to their grandmother, didn't she, to help in any way she could? Perhaps this was the chance to make up for never having told David what she knew about Clive and what had happened that night.

Ultimately, she wasn't in a position to pass up a well-paid job. It would only be for a year and then, once she had saved up some money, she would return to her course. She had no way of knowing, before the fact, the true nature of the work she was going to undertake, or the price they would all pay. If she had, she would have barricaded herself within the safety of the island.

Maria

London, a few years ago

Felicity's approach, when it came, had been seamless. Had they been watching her and Athena in Greece for years, and overheard their conversations about Clive? Had they been listening in when she rang home from the house when David and Anna were at work, and inferred Maria's feelings about David's father, when her mother asked after him? Maria could never be sure, but what was certain was that the offer when it came felt like a chance for atonement. The opportunity she had been waiting for, for years.

David and Anna had taken the girls to visit their grandfather, leaving Maria to head off to the British Library for the day, the clouds hanging low overhead as she made her way from King's Cross tube station along the Euston Road. She had been living at the house for a month by now, since deferring her course in order to work and save up money as a nanny to babies Stella and Rose. If she was ever going to go back to her degree in Political Science and International Relations, she would need to keep up with her studies.

Without a valid student card, she couldn't access the readers' rooms and instead was sitting on one of the single tables lining the wall in the coffee shop of the library, her notes spread in front of her, when a woman approached.

'Do you mind? Don't worry, I won't be long,' she had said with that insincerely apologetic manner British women would often affect before doing exactly what they pleased.

Maria had smiled that it was no problem and the woman had gestured towards a particularly dense textbook on the political economy of good government, brimming with Post-it notes, which she had bought with her first pay cheque from David.

'Gosh, that looks intense,' the woman said.

'Intense is one word for it,' Maria replied, the conversation then moving back and forth so easily that by the time Felicity showed up again, a few weeks later, and again, before finally making her intentions known, Maria had already been drawn in. It wasn't David who MI6 was interested in, Felicity made that clear – it was Clive. Spying on David, and subsequently Anna, was merely a means to an end – an end that none of them, including Maria, could ever have foreseen.

In the initial weeks after Maria's arrival at the house in London, Anna barely left her room other than occasional trips to the bathroom where Artemis' old perfume bottles were laid out like artefacts in a mausoleum. The lingering smell of David's mother, which had caused Maria to jolt when she first noticed it, became a bolstering presence, reminding Maria of what Clive had done.

Despite Anna's coolness towards everyone and everything, including the girls, it was hard not to feel sorry for her, Maria found as the weeks rolled on. What at first appeared as an aloof uninterest in the world around her revealed itself as a kind of absence, as if her spirit was somewhere else, her body left behind, useless to the young daughters it should have been able to nurture. To call it postpartum depression, as the health visitors had, conferring as they left the house, out of earshot of Anna, seemed too simplistic. At first Maria couldn't recognise what she was seeing, but eventually it came to her: it was fear.

Some days, Maria would sense a pair of eyes on her as she rocked the girls to sleep in the nursery and she would look up to find Anna hovering in the doorway, as if scared to step inside. With time, though, Anna grew more confident, taking the girls out by herself for periods in the double buggy. It was on one of these days, as she performed her usual sweep of the house, armed with a bottle of multi-purpose spray and a cloth in case anyone should find her and ask what she was doing, that Maria found Anna's second phone at the back of the cupboard in the bathroom. At first she wondered if it was a trap. It had almost been too easy. Was Anna really so stupid as to hide it there, barely encrypted and logging every piece of correspondence she and Harry shared – information Maria had been able to take right back to Felicity at MI6? But time and again, Maria's suspicions were confirmed. Anna wasn't terrible, she was something far more dangerous. Anna was vulnerable, and she was careless.

It was only a matter of time until she was found out.

That October, the family travelled to Provence. Maria tended to wake early with the girls, the soft autumn light drifting through the shutters. Anna seemed to be up half the night – Maria could hear her padding along the hallway to the bathroom, as she often did at home in those early days after the twins were born. But unlike the hallway there, which felt hemmed in despite the elaborate work that had been done on the house the Christmas after the girls were born – the interiors transformed into the sort of place they featured in the luxury magazine where Anna worked – the house in France was light and airy, the horizon from every window reminding Maria of home.

It was an old farmhouse renovated in soft pale stone, surrounded by lavender fields. Maria was sitting at the edge of the pool, her bare feet skimming the surface of the water as she watched the girls teeter on the grass on unsteady legs, when David emerged from the entrance of the house. She could feel his eyes on her as he made his way down the grass bank. He smiled as he approached, standing for a while, both of them watching Stella and Rose, who were building a tower out of blocks. After a moment, Stella watched Rose add a brick, and then, waiting for her sister's back to turn, pushed the whole tower over.

Rose turned and burst into tears and Maria frowned, holding open her arms. Rose bustled towards her, seeking comfort in her arms while David gently chastised Stella who cried out furiously.

Maria laughed, winking reassuringly at David. 'Don't take it personally. It's just their age – the terrible twos, you say in England?'

Holding Rose gently against her chest, she called out, 'Stella, be kind,' in her mother tongue.

'You're teaching them Greek?' David said and Maria flushed, releasing Rose and encouraging her to go and play with her sister.

'Sorry, I thought it would be . . .'

'Don't apologise,' David said. 'It's excellent for them to have the basis of another language when they're so young. If you stay around long enough, hopefully they will learn it thoroughly.'

He held her eye until she looked away.

'Do you remember the pool at the house in Greece, when we were kids?' he said after a moment once the girls were happily playing again, their fracas already forgotten.

Maria paused, something inside her shifting. 'Of course.'

'They were happy days, weren't they?' David said, more of a question than a statement of fact.

'They were.' She nodded and when she looked up, his eyes moved away from hers. She swallowed, the silence between them throbbing, and then David spoke again, wiping his face with his sleeve sharply, as if dabbing at invisible tears, his voice like that of a different person.

Maria looked up and from the corner of her eye saw Clive standing on the terrace, looking down at them, though she couldn't make out his expression.

'So, I wondered if you could take the girls out for the day?' David said, composed now.

'Really? But I thought Anna wanted to spend time with them—'

'Perhaps you could take them into town?' he continued, as if he hadn't heard. 'Anna's sleeping in late again, and Jeff and May will be over soon.'

'Of course.' Feeling the dynamics between them adjust back to the role of employer and hired help, Maria lifted her feet out of the pool, her jaw clenched.

She stood without looking at him. 'Come on, girls,' she said, tidying away the blocks. As she turned back towards the house, David's hand brushed against hers. 'Thank you for being here,' he said, so quietly that it was almost a whisper.

Maria woke the girls, who had napped in the buggy, as they returned to the house later that afternoon. There were no cars parked in the front drive and from the silence she assumed everyone was out. She put nursery rhymes on the television in the main living room and kept an eye on the twins through the glass door as she moved through into the connecting kitchen. She had been frustrated not to be here while Jeff and May were around, their lips loosened by the inevitable drink, so that she might have had a chance of over-hearing something she could take back to Felicity.

She filled the kettle, allowing her eyes to move freely around the room. There were no bags or coats left discarded downstairs and she could hardly go searching upstairs while the girls were awake. Pulling a cup from the cupboard, she searched for a cafetière. Clive always insisted on being in charge of coffee-making while they were in France, making a show of this rare act of generosity, and her hands moved between the cupboards until she felt her fingers run over a box tucked in the far back corner.

Pulling it out, she looked at the box of sleeping pills, turning it over and reading David's name stuck on the front. What was David doing with sleeping pills? If there was one thing she knew, from the nights when she lay awake listening to Anna rustling through the house, David's light snoring emanating from the open bedroom door, it was that he had no problem with insomnia. Of course, the heavy sleeping could have been the result of taking the pills, and yet the flash of memory was so immediate, so instinctive, it was as if her brain had intentionally held it there within easy reach, waiting for her to connect the dots: David, at the kitchen counter the night before, having insisted on serving up dinner, despite Maria's insistence that she could do it. He had flinched when she came in again a moment later, turning and holding something behind his back, his expression as if he had been caught in the middle of some illicit act.

But this was David, she reminded herself. He couldn't have been lacing Anna's food. And yet the more she let the possibility sink in, the more it made dreadful sense.

Anna had drunk wine over the course of the afternoon, but still it was unsettling how woozy she had seemed before excusing herself from the table and heading up to bed early, the previous evening. Unusually, there had been no sound of her in the night, and she had still been out cold when Maria went out this morning with the twins.

Maria's fingers trembled slightly as she replaced the packet of pills, gently closing the cupboard door as if suddenly aware that she might be being watched. She turned slowly so that her back was against the counter, jumping as she spotted the outline of Anna's body sprawled across the middle of the garden, through the glass doors.

Heartbeat rising, Maria moved towards the closed back door. As she approached, the image became clearer – Anna was not injured or collapsed but simply dozing under a tree. Hurrying back to the living room, she turned off the television, her chest straining with the possible implications of the stash of pills.

Stella wriggled off the sofa, Rose following more cautiously, and Maria took her hand as they moved through the house. 'Look,

Mummy's outside,' she said, opening the back door and leading the twins towards their mother, an empty glass of wine on the grass beside her.

Maria cleared her throat and slowed down, letting Anna come to as the girls moved ahead of her, Stella calling out, 'Mama!'

'Hello, darling . . . Have you had a lovely day?' Anna pulled herself up into a sitting position as Stella sat on her knee.

'Maria?' She turned and Anna continued. 'I'd rather you didn't take the girls out for the day without asking me.'

Maria smarted. 'I'm sorry. David asked me to, and I—'

'He what?' Something in Anna's voice made her backpedal.

'I mean, he . . . Or maybe it was me. I'm sorry if it wasn't what you were hoping for today.'

'David asked you to take them out?'

'I'm sorry, I really can't remember whose idea it was, maybe it was mine. But I will ask next time. I won't do it again.'

Maria tried to smile reassuringly, while her mind worked it out: David was drugging his wife and lying to her. He wanted her to think she was losing it. Was that really what was happening? Instantly, her mind moved to Artemis, her words to Athena the night of the storm: *You have to believe me, Athena, I know too much! I can see it in his eyes when he looks at me. The way he talks about me, as if I'm mad or . . . Please just promise me that if anything happens to me you will remember what I told you.*

Anna was working late at the office one evening, not long after they returned from Provence. Maria tucked the girls in their beds, lingering in the doorway, watching their tiny bodies rise and fall beneath the sheets. It was hard to look at the twins and not feel a burning resentment towards Anna for what she was putting them through, even if Stella and Rose were, for now, oblivious to the cradle of lies.

How could she do it to her children? Maria understood why she herself was in this: Clive had been responsible for the death of Artemis, and it had turned out that was far from all he was guilty of. How could Maria not have relished the chance to finally make him and his men pay? At the risk of being melodramatic, it was possible to believe this was her *raison d'être*, as if a higher force had brought her to London for this single purpose: a chance to avenge and atone in one fell swoop. And Maria wasn't betraying David – or at least not without just cause.

She moved away from the door and across the landing. She didn't feel guilty. But Anna? She had consciously made a family with a man she couldn't have loved, with the specific purpose of betraying him. David had no idea, Maria was certain of that. How could he? And yet, he had been feeding her sleeping pills, hadn't he? He had been intentionally telling her lies, presumably with the intention of making her question herself.

She stopped dead in the doorway to the kitchen, at the sight of him there, a rush of fear as she imagined him tapping into her thoughts. But he hardly moved, let alone reacted to her presence.

For a moment she felt like she was intruding. She hadn't known anyone was home and it was unnerving to find him here, alone, a whisky bottle hanging from one hand, a letter unfolded in front of him. There was a strange energy to the way he held himself, some- thing about the scene that made her want to back away. But she knew he must have already heard her and so she stepped into the room, moving behind him and casting a glance at the words on the page. All she could make out was the girls' names printed in a column under official-looking text.

'Is everything OK?' she asked, praying the trepidation didn't show in her voice.

'No, it's not. I've just . . . Never mind . . .' He closed his eyes. 'Maria, I'm so sorry. I don't know what came over me. That night, in Greece, I . . .'

Instantly she knew what he was referring to. It was the first time he had mentioned the incident with the gun in all these years, and the reference to their shared childhood caught her off-guard. She could still picture the night perfectly, feeling the breath catching in her lungs as she ran from the house, past Clive's car returning from the port.

Maria shook her head now, pulling a chair next to him and taking his hand. She was so moved by this flash of the old David, her friend – so reassured by the reminder of their shared history – that she momentarily forgot herself. It was impossible to reconcile the scared, bereaved boy she had observed that night with the image of the calculating, gaslighting husband that had been building in her mind moments earlier.

'Stop,' she said, comforting him. 'It's OK. I know, you had lost your mother. You were a child. I shouldn't have reacted so . . .'

He pulled away from her. 'Don't do that, Maria.'

She stood hurriedly, moving to the sink. 'Do what?'

'Don't be disingenuous. Don't lie to me. I've had enough of people *lying.*'

He took another swig from the bottle of whisky and Maria felt herself freeze.

'I wouldn't have done it.' He stood, crossing the room in silence, the tension loosening a little as she realised what he was referring to. There was something in his voice, though, that made her wary and she kept her eyes on the floor as she felt him move towards her. He paused, their faces a breath apart, and for a moment she was transported back to the house on the island, the thrill of the faint smell of cigarette smoke on his lips as he moved in to kiss her.

And then she felt it again, his lips, this time touching her mouth. For a second she leaned into it, parting her mouth, feeling for his tongue, and then, as keenly as he had moved forward she pulled back.

'I . . .' She was about to speak when the space between them was shattered by the jingle of keys in the lock. Pushing her hair away from her face, Maria moved quickly out of the room, seconds before Anna appeared at the door.

Maria

The rain has already started by the time Maria arrives back at the hotel on Portland Place.

Looking at her watch, she approaches the entrance, nodding courteously at the doorman as she steps inside, her mind on Anna, who will be arriving home from the lawyer's office at any moment. Maria pictures her, her face ashen in the back of the taxi as it carries her home from McCann's office on Queen Square, where she and Clive's lawyer had been due to discuss David's will.

Maria closes her eyes, feeling once again the finality with which she had closed the door behind her for the last time on the house where it had all happened, allowing the surge of emotion to overcome her. Would she see the girls again? Of course she would. She wouldn't allow herself to imagine the alternative. Instead, she imagines Anna finding the words Maria had left there, propped on the table; Anna's fingers still shaking with the shock of the meeting at the lawyer's office as she opened the envelope, pulling out Maria's letter.

> *David is alive. He and Clive are planning to have you killed, just as Clive did with his own wife, when she started to question the business. They will make it look like suicide and they will tell everyone that you were mad . . . I have made contact with Harry and together we will make sure of everything else. You can trust us.*

288

The hotel foyer is relatively empty. The soles of Maria's Converse squeak as she moves towards the staircase, heading for the room David has booked her into. She still has time to change into the heeled sandals and mid-length shirt dress he has bought for her, before the pre-booked car arrives. A car not a taxi. The circle of trust has grown tighter and tighter so that it is a wonder any of them can still breathe. Given the significance of where she is headed, and why, he has been sparse on details. Nothing could be discussed, David had once again stressed, unless done through EncroChat, the encrypted messaging service downloaded to the phone David had given her the last time they had seen each other, before he left.

Their last conversation had been brief. *If we're going to do this, you have to understand that you're giving up everything. You can never speak to anyone apart from your mum ever again.* 'David, I don't have any friends, apart from you. Athena has no interest in where I am or what I'm doing, you know that as well as I do.'

It's true. Apart from Stella and Rose, Maria has no one.

There is no time to shower. She throws her belongings into the small bag David has sanctioned for the trip, with its single change of clothes and basic toiletries. Nothing else to give away the world they are leaving behind.

A sheen of sweat glistens on her brow as she takes a final look around the room, avoiding her own reflection before heading towards the lift, the sound of the wheels of her suitcase on the carpet following her inside. When the doors open on the ground floor of The Langham, she steps out onto the marble, the clattering of her heels echoing above the discreet strains of classical music. Keeping her head focused forwards, refusing to turn towards the voices that goad her from either side of her mind, she walks purposefully towards the desk and out into the night.

The city she has lived in for the past three and a half years is unrecognisable as she waits under the porch for the car. Tonight, the world has shifted. Through sideways rain, she looks across at All Souls Church, a cluster of tents erected under the shelter of its porch. From inside, the strains of the choir practising for their Christmas concert drifts over sleeping bodies, their harmonies bleeding into the sky.

Briefly, Maria recalls the day she boarded the flight from Skiathos to London, intent on *making something* of her life. She can almost hear the explosion of noise that greeted her as she stepped off the bus for the first time, onto Green Lanes where her bedsit awaited above one of the grocery stores that dominated this seemingly endless stretch of road. Inside the doorway, the light was too sharp, highlighting the scuffed carpets and precarious light fittings as she placed her suitcase beside the narrow single bed.

Bedding down for the night, she had forced herself not to think of her university room in Athens, overlooking the Acropolis, or the bed in her mother's house on the island with its views across the water. This was her choice, she told herself then; she had wanted this and now she had it, and she would not wish it away. No matter what.

Breathing in a lungful of cold November air, she exhales, letting the steam rise in front of her face as a pair of headlights momentarily blind her. The car sweeps up to the hotel and she has to steady herself against the urge to run as the driver steps out and approaches, taking her single bag and locking it in the boot. Moving away from the portico, towards him, Maria attempts a smile as she ducks into smooth leather seats, the chill of the air-con rippling over her skin.

The man in the driving seat says nothing at first as the car pulls off.

After a moment, he speaks. 'Please can you pass me your phone?' From his tone she senses this is not a negotiable question.

Maria tenses and the man attempts to reassure her. 'It's just protocol.'

'Of course,' Maria says, leaning forward, her hand hovering for a moment behind the handbrake as he reaches back to take it from her. He must be in his twenties, Maria observes: smartly dressed, the sleeves of his shirt rolled up slightly to reveal a flex of muscles as his fingers close around the handset, pressing the power button with one hand.

Maria locks her attention on the outside world as they move along Euston Road, willing herself to remain calm. There are flashes of Regent's Park on one side, where she had once taken the twins, and Marylebone on the other, where she would occasionally accompany the family to lunch at an Italian restaurant Clive loved.

They move onto the Westway, following signs for Heathrow. Picking up speed, the driver opens his window, the sound of the wind rushing through the car as he tosses the phone onto one of the railings.

He watches Maria in his mirror as he closes the window again, judging her expression. She holds his eye, seemingly undaunted, as he returns his attention to the road ahead.

Feeling her heartbeat thump in her chest, Maria closes her eyes for a split second and prays. She still went to church most weeks, in London, to the Greek Orthodox mass near the house. It was near there that Felicity had approached her the time she finally revealed herself, moving up alongside Maria as she made her way home along Holly Walk. Refusing to let herself even think of that now, fearful that she will somehow give herself away, Maria returns her attention to the here and now. The car changes lanes, the engine revving, and Maria imagines the tyres skidding beneath them – the bliss of near-oblivion as she visualises the vehicle flipping, turning in slow motion, the impact hitting her in an instant as it finally lands.

They drive for almost an hour, the occasional roar of a low-flying jet causing Maria to hold her breath. Briefly, she plays out an alternative reality, one in which the choices she has made had been different – one in which she had walked away the first time Felicity tried to bump her. One in which she had long ago boarded a different plane, back to the island, back to her mother and the safety of a world that she had longed to escape. David had been standing next to her, watching her lips move, as she made her final call to Athena a couple of days earlier. Her mother had sounded sulky when Maria apologised for the length of time since they last spoke – not that Athena had tried to get in touch with her only child, either. She had already heard about David, though not from her daughter, she stressed. No, she'd had to learn about his death in the shop, as if it was nothing to do with her. She sounded more wounded by the dent to her pride than about the death of her friend's son. But that wasn't fair and Maria knew it. Athena had cared about David, just as she had cared about Artemis. It was just complicated. She was complicated. But aren't we all?

'Wait, I think that was our turning,' Maria calls out to the driver as they speed past the exit for the airport.

'It's OK,' he replies calmly, and Maria flinches, her eyes moving to the door handle.

Sensing her unease, he watches her in the rear-view mirror. 'David is waiting for you,' he says, and Maria can't be sure if the use of David's name is a reassurance or a threat.

They are moving along country lanes, the headlights of their own car swerving ahead of them as they speed through dark tunnels of trees. Maria has never ventured into the British countryside since she arrived – the Witheralls preferring more far-flung destinations – and she has no idea where she is. Looking out of the window, she sees stars for the first time in England and something about the sight fills her with longing for home.

What is she doing here? Once again her eyes move to the door handles, not that she could get away even if she did manage to escape. They would find her. There is no way out of this, not now. She breathes in sharply, picturing Stella and Rose. She is here for them, and for Anna.

Anna. Maria jolts at the thought of her.

If only there had been more time to prepare the plan, but it had all happened so quickly. She had barely had time to make contact with Harry. Back in London, she had felt so bold in what she was doing, so convinced she could pull this off. Now is not the time to start second-guessing. She has to trust they can do this. Whatever comes next, there is no going back.

Closing her eyes, Maria pictures herself back in the Maldives, three years earlier. It was Christmas and her bones had ached as they stepped off the seaplane, the sand moving unsteadily underfoot as she reached the shore. Rose had fallen asleep in her lap during the final leg of the journey from London, Anna and David sitting separately at the front of the plane.

It was a few days later, whilst pushing the girls in their buggy along one of the pathways behind the beach, that she overheard David on the phone to Clive.

I'm doing it tonight at dinner . . . I know! For God's sake, Dad. Do you think I don't know that? I love her.

Maria had been unaware then that she was overhearing David agree that this would be the night that he would propose to Anna, presenting her with the ring that was a physical manifestation of the circle that would draw tighter and tighter around her, until she could no longer breathe.

As the car slows, somewhere in the depths of the British countryside, Maria pictures the wooden walkway perched above the sea which led to their suites, the glittering turquoise surface deflecting from the endless black beneath. When she thinks of it now, she imagines it as a pirate's plank, the sharks circling out of sight.

The car slows, turning without indication. It's so dark out here, away from any streetlamp, that it is impossible to make out the world beyond the window. From the juddering movements of the car, Maria believes they are on a track; one thing is for sure, they aren't heading for an airport.

Whatever happens next, she cannot afford to panic. She has come this far, and David trusts her.

The car stops. The driver switches off the engine but he doesn't move.

'Is David here?' Maria looks beyond the windshield, where she can make out the outline of a building. She hears voices and then two men appear from the darkness, walking closer, until she sees Jorgos and another man opening the car door.

She shifts back in her seat at the sight of the men, Jorgos' head lit up from behind by a flush of moonlight as the clouds briefly part.

These are Clive's hangmen, come to kill her – come to do to Maria what they had done to Artemis, and what was lined up for Anna, too. For a moment, she is sure of that. They, or someone close to them, had been watching her when she went to meet Harry. They must have seen and heard every word. Someone had followed her to Anna's house the night she left the letters, pausing for a moment to tuck one back inside her handbag.

And yet she had been so careful, there is no way anyone had been tailing her. She had been so quick, and she was watching out the whole time for signs that she was being followed.

The fear that rushes through her nonetheless, as she looks up at the men, is a flood, and she struggles to keep her head above water. Panic is the most common reason people drown, she remembers her father telling her whilst teaching her to swim; if you find yourself out of your depth, keep calm. She works hard to keep her thoughts on her father, pushing aside the image of

Artemis that lingers in the corner of her mind. Is this retribution? Maria's punishment for not having called for help the night Clive sent Jorgos to the house, the night Artemis died? She can feel now the same fear that rattled across the island the night of the storm.

No. Maria pulls herself out of the current. That was not her fault. Whatever happened – whether whatever Jorgos said or did pushed her to hang herself, or whether he helped her tie the knot – that was on Clive. He was the one who betrayed Artemis, and their child. Maria was a friend to David, and she loved his mother. David knows that, he trusts her – she is his confessor, and he has shared too much to doubt himself now.

She thinks back to the days after that illicit first adult kiss, the evening she had found him at the kitchen table with the DNA results confirming the girls weren't his. If Anna hadn't interrupted when she did it was impossible to know what would have happened that night. As it was, Maria avoided him for the next few days, David heading out early for work and returning late. A few days later, she saw him again. Anna had been out all day and the girls had just gone down for a nap when she heard the front door close. She could tell from the way his footsteps paused in the hallway that it was David. Maria knew the family's movements so well by then that she could picture him removing his suit jacket and hanging it over the newel-post.

He said nothing as he stepped into the room, walking up behind her where she stood at the sink, swilling a plate. There was an inevitability to it, and she felt herself freeze, his breath against the back of her neck, his fingers moving gently under her T-shirt, and then sliding down beneath her knickers.

He didn't kiss her for at least a minute. She felt herself fall forward against the counter, giving in to his touch. It was such a relief to feel a man's hands on her after so long that for a while she could convince herself it was good, what was happening, as he finally moved his fingers back up and undid her trousers, and then tugged them down sharply.

Back in the car, forcing herself to meet Jorgos' eye, Maria swallows as he speaks.

'Hello, Maria.'

Maria

'Where's David?' Maria speaks in Greek, trying to establish a link between them, unable to stop her voice from shaking as the men guide her towards what she sees now is an old farmhouse.

The moon has receded once again behind the cloud and it is impossible to make out what lies on either side of the track, other than the building beyond.

If she runs, where will she end up? They might be surrounded by bog or open fields, offering the perfect view for her to be shot at, with the help of the flashlights the men are holding. Maria tries to map the route back to the main road in her mind, but they had driven for so long without signs of life before arriving here that she knows she will never outrun these men, even if she could get away.

'He's waiting for you,' Jorgos replies evenly.

They move inside the house, through a damp porch and into the kitchen, furnished with dark wooden furniture and old-fashioned light fittings.

'Where is the bathroom' Maria says, reverting to English. It is the only thing she can think of to buy herself time.

'After.' It is the first time the second man has spoken. He is heavyset with blond hair and slightly buck teeth, an accent she can't quite place.

After what?

'Please, I have my period and I really need to change my tampon,' she says, a little too desperately.

It is a cheap trick but she sees Jorgos flinch. Buoyed by his reaction, she presses on. 'I can do it in here if I have to . . .'

The men exchange a brief glance before Jorgos moves towards her, gesturing for her to take off her coat. 'The toilet is there. Give me your bag as well.'

Maria flinches. 'I need my tampons.'

Jorgos inhales, as if she is pushing her luck.

'They are in here?' He takes the bag from her and opens it, holding her eye for a moment before looking inside and spotting a small purple carton. Despite the cold, Maria feels a film of sweat on the top of her lip as Jorgos opens the packet and inspects the rows of sealed tampons.

He looks her up and down, her stomach tightening as his attention lingers over her breasts, and then he presses the box into her hand.

'Hurry up.'

Maria opens the door into the loo and closes it behind her, her heartbeat racing as if unleashed from its cage.

Her fingers shaking, she draws one of the tampons out and unwraps it, leaning over slightly, pulling down her pants with her other hand. Hearing Jorgos clear his throat on the other side of the door, she looks to her left and sees a flash of his head through the crack of the door. Whispering a prayer to herself, she leans forward a little, folding herself out of sight, obscuring her front from potential view as she quickly reaches inside her bra, pulls out the phone she had been given years ago by Felicity, and pushes it with a single shove up between her legs, dropping the unused tampon into the toilet and flushing.

Running her fingers for a moment under the tap, the water icy-cold, she feels her breath return to a more regular beat.

'I said quick!' Jorgos' voice is so close that Maria jumps.

'You didn't say you were using the toilet,' he adds as she opens the door and Maria's eye flickers.

'I had to get rid of the old one.'

They look at each other for a moment and then the second man speaks from his position on the other side of the kitchen, his back against the counter.

'Take off your clothes.'

Maria shakes her head and Jorgos pulls himself up at her show of resistance, reminding her that she has no choice other than to do what the men say. She is throbbing inside where she inserted the phone and she doesn't let her mind imagine what is coming next. Though if they planned to rape her, why would they let her change her tampon first?

She just needs to comply, that's all.

Taking another step back into the kitchen, Maria removes her top layers and stands there, the men watching her shiver in her bra and knickers.

The cold pricks her skin but she doesn't move, apart from her eyes which briefly cast around the counter behind Jorgos' sidekick, for anything she might use as a weapon if she can get close enough.

'Keep going,' Jorgos says and she looks at him.

'What are you going to do to me?' she asks, and he cocks his eyebrow.

'Why are you afraid, Maria? We are doing our job. Just as you have been.'

There is contempt in his voice and Maria's jaw tightens. 'David is not going to like this,' she says more firmly, convincing herself that David is still on her side.

'David understands,' Jorgos says. 'Take off the rest.'

Hans moves behind her. Closing her eyes briefly, Maria unclips her bra, letting it fall to the ground, and then her knickers, not looking down at the pale mauve cotton that lies crumpled at her feet.

She stands there for a moment, her humiliation complete, or so she thinks.

'Turn around,' Jorgos says.

Turning slowly, Maria feels the men's eyes on her body. Her instinct is to lift her arms to hide her nipples hardening against the cold, but she keeps them by her side, waiting for one of the men to move forward.

They are silent for what feels like a minute and then the second man speaks.

'Open your legs.'

Maria feels a rush of silent horror, picturing the foreign object stuffed inside her, willing away tears which suddenly ambush her as she slowly complies, shifting her feet into the second position the twins learnt at the ballet classes she sometimes took them to at her local church in Hampstead.

'Bend over,' Jorgos says and Maria hesitates, long enough for Hans to stand a little straighter. She breathes in, knowing that it is all over, understanding instinctively what comes next, once the device is inevitably discovered.

'Jorgos.'

The voice makes her cry out in shock, the handle of the door turning a split second before, and a third man steps in, dressed in uniform. 'We have to go now, or the Captain says we'll miss our flight path.'

Maria stays there a moment, frozen, and then Jorgos calls out, as if for the benefit of someone not in the room. 'She's clean. Right, let's go. Now.'

Maria hears the roar of the engines outside as soon as they start to move towards the back door of the farmhouse, the jet screaming to life as she lets herself be led towards the steps to the plane.

She is in shock, reminding herself that she is safe now, that the men didn't touch her, that they had turned their backs in some ludicrous show of respect as she hurriedly dressed herself again, moments after their thwarted search.

There is no one else on the plane as they step inside, met by pristine leather armchairs and classical music playing over the speakers.

'Where is David?' Maria asks again, more quietly this time, casting around the otherwise empty aircraft.

Jorgos indicates for her to sit by the window and settles himself beside her, his mate sitting opposite.

'He went ahead,' Jorgos replies without looking at her and Maria feels the plane start to lurch down the private runway, and across the point of no return.

Maria

Maria doesn't know how or when she falls asleep but when she awakes, she feels the plane descending towards its final destination, the familiar expanse of turquoise water dotted with sparkling atolls.

'Do you need something to drink?' the man opposite asks, noticing her come to.

'Water, please,' she says.

He stands and heads towards a bar on the other side of the jet.

Maria is acutely aware of Jorgos' presence beside her.

'Is this Malé?' she asks, not expecting an answer, but he shakes his head.

Maria feels her chest tighten. 'But this is the Maldives?'

'Yes.' There is an amused look in Jorgos' eye, as if he is enjoying her lack of power, feeding off the control it gives him. For a second, she pictures him approaching Artemis' house the night she died and Maria feels a burst of barely containable rage. She wants to grab him by the throat, to gouge out his eyes. But instead she sits in her seat, her fingers entwined.

'Is David here?'

'He's at the house,' Jorgos replies and Maria's mind holds onto this snippet of information.

'The house?'

When David said they were going to the Maldives she had assumed he had meant the same resort she had been to with the family that Christmas.

Jorgos looks back at her, refusing to elaborate, and Maria looks away.

Something about this alternative plan troubles her. She had pictured it all so differently, and yet what had she expected, that they would be hanging out with honeymooners, eating from the buffet at a public hotel? Had she really pictured it at all? If she had, she wonders if she would be here now.

'Thank you,' she says, taking the bottle of water from the tall blond man. 'What's your name?'

'Hans,' he replies, resuming his seat and looking out of the window as the plane approaches a tiny island. Maria watches as they descend towards a purpose-built runway that juts out of the island, which is occupied by a series of three villas, all white with terracotta slates on the roofs, flanked by palm trees.

From above, she can see that on the other side of the island there is a jetty and a tiny boat tethered to the boardwalk; aside from the buildings and an area of garden leading towards the shore, she can see nothing but sea and sky.

Interrupting her thoughts, Jorgos turns to her and smiles for the first time.

'Here we are. Home sweet home.'

Maria

The Maldives, the day Anna dies

There is something about David that she can't place as she walks down the stairs towards the glistening tarmac. Then she sees it, the likeness to his father as he steps forward in his pressed trousers and short-sleeved shirt, slipping so easily into Clive's shoes.

'You made it,' he says, kissing her in a way that feels unnatural in front of Jorgos and Hans, after everything that has just happened. 'Did you manage to sleep?'

'Yes,' Maria says, forcing a smile. She has no phone to check the time but she knows the flight is around thirteen hours so she imagines it must be mid-morning. The sleep on the plane had been deep, considering everything that she had been through, and she wonders if her body had let her pass out in an act of self-preservation.

'I'm sorry I couldn't travel with you. It was deemed safer this way. Just in case.'

In case his father's men had discovered she was a mole, and had to kill her? Except, with Clive so ill and David due to take over the helm, these are no longer Clive's men. They are David's.

Maria looks down. 'I understand.'

David takes her hand, speaking brightly though his palms are damp in a way that suggests he is nervous. 'Come and have a look around. This place is all ours, for as long as we need it. We're safe together here.'

* * *

'So this is our villa,' David says, guiding her towards the main residence, with false jollity.

'Who do the other two belong to?' she asks as he opens the door into an airy kitchen with veneered pine cupboards, leading through to a dining room at one end and a large double bedroom at the other.

'Jorgos and Hans are in one of them. The third is for the staff who run the place, and security.'

Maria's mind moves to the cameras she noted pointing in, and out, at various points, as they landed.

'Where's the bathroom?' she asks and David leads her towards the plainly furnished master bedroom, pointing at the *en suite* beyond an open door.

'I might have a shower if that's OK, freshen up after the flight.'

'As you wish,' David says and she smiles, stepping inside and locking the door.

She unzips her bag and takes out her washbag, scanning around for cameras before reminding herself this is David's domain. They won't be watching her in here. They aren't watching her at all. The thing with the phone and the search was a necessary final test – a test she had anticipated and prepared for, transferring everything she needed from her original phone to the second hidden device, which she had always planned to transfer back to her handbag after it had been checked. She hadn't anticipated the second part, though, and the memory of the strip-search chips at her, even if she under-stands why they had to do it. She had anticipated them thinking that her phone might have been bugged by someone else. Somehow she hadn't anticipated that they would suspect she herself was a conscious security risk. Except after Anna, she would be naive to assume they would trust her.

Maria's mind moves to Harry. It is too risky to try to contact him straight away. Instead, she undresses and steps inside the shower, turning on the water and then stepping out again. Bracing herself, she bends over and moves her fingers inside herself, fiddling around for the phone. It had been much easier putting it in than it is attempting to take it out, and Maria feels panic set in, imagining this foreign object moving further inside her. If she can't get it out, she will die. There will be no choice but to tell David that she needs to go to hospital. Perhaps she can feign appendicitis or an extreme urinary infection. But there is no way that will work. She has to do this on her own. Pressing her eyes tight against the pain, refusing to cry out with David just on the other side of the door, she reminds herself that women give birth to babies many times the size of the object that she needs to prise from her body.

She squeezes her pelvic floor, catching a corner of the plastic with her forefinger and thumb, tugging until she manages to get a grip around the handset and giving it a final pull. She stays there for a moment, bent over, before moving to the see-through washbag containing soap and a flannel, and mini shampoos and conditioner, which she had chosen believing they would be flying from Heathrow together, with only hand luggage.

She quickly wraps the phone inside the flannel, and tucks it into the washbag before ducking into the shower, collapsing with relief against the white tiles.

'Better?' David asks, when she emerges back into the bedroom fifteen minutes later, having lathered herself with soothing lavender-scented body lotion, and wrapping her wet hair in a towel.

She smiles at him. 'Much.'

'Good,' he says, stepping towards her and pulling off the towel wrapped around her body.

Later that evening, Maria is lying on the sofa in the living area of the villa, resting her eyes, when Jorgos enters the room unannounced. Gasping, she sits up.

'You frightened me.'

Jorgos barely seems to register her presence. 'David?' he calls out and David enters from the bedroom, apparently unbothered to see Jorgos here without invitation.

'It's done.' Jorgos doesn't say another word but Maria knows instantly from David's reaction, the way he leans against the door-frame for support, exactly what he is referring to.

When Maria thinks of David now, she sees him as two separate people: on one side there is her childhood friend, the boy she loved like a brother. It is as though the image is a jigsaw which has been smashed apart and put back together, with all the pieces in the wrong places so that here he is, the other David – a man she barely recognises, a man capable of killing his wife.

Maria

Maria can't sleep. She doesn't cry, either. It's not her loss to bear. But the girls . . . As her mind moves to Rose and Stella there is a wrenching in her chest, like the cracking open of bone.

Anna is dead. David's words move on repeat in her mind between cold sheets, her gaze fixed to the ceiling of the bedroom as she lies awake, following the circling of the blades of the fan above her head.

It is too late. The only thought she can cling onto now is the girls who have lost both the man they believed was their father, and now, just months later, their mother, too.

David doesn't come to bed, and she is glad not to have to pretend to comfort him right now, scared of what her touch will say.

Anna is dead.

At some point Maria finally falls asleep and when she wakes up the space beside her is still empty. Pulling on a cardigan, she moves through the empty kitchen, outside where a light wind blows through the palms.

Following the deck towards the grass which rolls down to the shore, she spots David, barefoot in the sand, looking out to sea. She says nothing, moving beside him and looking out at the water. His eyes are red from crying and she slips her hand in his, reminded of the night some fifteen years earlier when they walked together along the path beside her house, back in Greece, before David had given her their first kiss.

When she turns to face David now, she seems someone else entirely.

'Are you OK?' she asks finally, still not knowing the right thing to say to him, when it counts.

'Yes,' he says simply, turning back to the house. 'I'll have them make breakfast.'

'Do you want me to call the girls, see how they are?' Maria asks a couple of days later as they sit opposite one another at the kitchen table, both glassy-eyed from continued lack of sleep.

The words feel brittle on her lips. She has to be careful of what she says next, every word a potential fracture line – and yet, she would ask that, wouldn't she? The Maria David knows has spent the whole of the children's lives devoted to them, looking after Stella and Rose with a singular dedication. How could she possibly hear what has happened to their mother and not automatically turn her thoughts to them?

David's jaw tightens at the mention of Stella and Rose, the children who think he is dead, the man they still believe to be their father.

He turns away from her. 'Why would I want that?' Maria flinches, and after a moment his expression softens slightly. 'They'll be fine. They're with their grandmother.'

He places the emphasis on *their*, reminding himself as well as her that the children are no longer his concern – as if he could so easily spirit away his love for the twin girls he had raised for three years as his own.

For the first time, Maria wonders whether Harry knows the girls are his. Had Anna told him? There are so many things Maria can't be sure of; so much is staked on instinct, feeling about for who to trust. And yet where had instinct got Anna?

Later that week, she spends the morning walking the modest length of beach alone, while David and Jorgos sit hunched opposite one another at a table and chairs under the portico that runs between the two main villas. She can see from here that they are deep in conversation. She watches them, oblivious, wishing there was a way of listening in on what they are saying, but every time she has gone near them since her arrival, the men have fallen into silence. It is a moment before she sees the third figure, Hans, seated a few metres from the other men, looking back at her.

Turning away from his intense gaze, Maria moves back to the house.

There is something unsettling about the presence of the staff who suddenly appear, making up the beds unasked, swilling dishes, silently laying out food at the kitchen table three times a day, and then retreating again.

'Lunch is ready,' one of the maids says as Maria enters the villa, still picturing Hans' inscrutable expression.

'Thank you, I'll fetch David,' Maria replies and the maid indicates for her to sit.

'He has asked not to be disturbed. He will join you in five minutes.'

Maria wonders what this woman must think of her, unaware as she is that until recently she, too, was the hired help.

'This looks delicious,' David announces, sauntering into the room with an unconvincing show of ease as the maid sets to work at the lobster at the centre of the table, with a cracker and picker. The crunch of the shell is like breaking bone, and Maria winces as David fills their glasses from the bottle of Chablis.

'What have you been working on?' Maria asks, once the woman has excused herself.

David has already finished his wine, and she watches him pour himself another glass.

She is about to suggest he slows down, but she thinks better of it. In the week or so since Anna's death, David has grown increasingly tetchy. There is something performative about this newly cavalier persona – something unpredictable, and untrusting – and she has felt the soothing effect she has always had on him slipping from her grasp. Perhaps a few glasses of wine to loosen him up is exactly what he needs.

'Same old,' David says, just as she was beginning to wonder if he had actually heard her, leaning forward to refill the small amount of wine she has drunk.

'Have you spoken to your father again?' she asks a while later, once David has knocked back more than half the bottle.

'Why do you ask?' he snaps, as if she has no business uttering Clive's name.

'I just . . .' She takes a deep breath. 'He's not getting any better, David. The doctors—'

'The doctors are fucking quacks, the lot of them.' He cuts her off, taking a long sip of his wine and laughing slightly to himself as he returns it to the table.

'What's so funny?'

'I was just thinking,' David says.

'About what?'

'About Anna.'

'Thinking what?'

'I was just thinking how she thought she was so bloody clever, but she got everything wrong. Everything. She didn't even know where my mum died.'

David looks up at her, holding her eye, and Maria feels the mouthful of lobster catch in her throat.

'What do you mean?'

David's expression changes. 'Nothing.' He takes a bite and chews thoughtfully. 'Just that Clarissa told her about my mother dying, about me being the one to find the body, and she assumed it had happened at the house in London . . .'

He flinches at the memory, and then looks up. 'Anyway. It's interesting how you think you know someone but then it turns out you don't know them at all.'

'How long are we planning to stay here?' Maria asks over dinner one evening. David has spent the afternoon once again discussing business at the other house, returning with a look of frustration.

'Why, are you bored?' he snaps.

'No. But, well, it's not a long-term plan, is it? I'm just wondering what—'

'Look, I can't discuss this with you now. I need some peace to think. I have a call with Jeff in a minute.'

There is a note of disdain in his inflection when he mentions his father's business partner.

'I'm sorry,' she says. 'Is something wrong, work-wise?'

David pauses, as if he is about to say something, and then Jorgos walks into the room, calling him away.

David is further distracted when he comes back from his meeting, his foot thrumming at the base of his chair as he pours himself another drink.

'Are you all right, David?'

'Hmm?'

'You seem . . . Are you having second thoughts, about asking me to come with you?'

David leans forward, genuinely engaged with her for the first time in days. 'Of course not. I'm sorry I've been so short with you, it's just so much stress. You know? Everything, and now Jeff—'

'David, could I speak to you for a moment?' Jorgos puts his head round the door.

'Sure,' David says, beckoning him into the room. 'Come in.'

Jorgos pauses. 'Can we speak in private? It's about the meeting earlier.'

David stands up, unsteady from the wine, apologising to Maria.

'You go to bed, I'll be back as soon as I can.'

Maria waits up for him, dressed in a silk nightdress. She pours two glasses of brandy and sets them on the small round copper table in the corner of the room.

She is genuinely intrigued by who would own a villa like this, with its outdated kitchen and ready-made art pulled straight from the pages of a timeshare catalogue. It must cost so much money to own and run, and yet it's as though no one ever really visits. Except as soon as she thinks it, she knows exactly what an island like this is used for. It isn't a holiday retreat; this is a meeting place for people who want privacy, a space in the middle of the ocean where they can get away with murder.

By the time David arrives back, Maria is drifting off in one of the chairs, but she pulls herself awake at the sound of the door. Automatically, she feels for the phone by her feet, inside the bag.

Maria smiles up at him, and David's expression softens, his eyes appraising her outfit approvingly.

'Come, have a drink with me,' she says and he joins her, visibly relaxing at her touch as she waits for him to take his glass and then moves behind him and begins to massage his shoulders.

'Mmmm, that's good,' he says, closing his eyes, letting Maria work her hands around his shoulders and down his back. He takes another swig and makes approving noises as she kneads away at areas of tension.

'Come here,' he says, pulling her in front of him, pouring himself another drink and sipping at it before pulling her on top of him and lifting up her nightdress.

As he does so, his body visibly relaxes and he calls out, 'Yes, Anna.'

Maria tenses, waiting for him to flinch at his own mistake, but he just continues to push himself into her, unaware of what he's said.

Maria

It is the height of the dry season and Maria imagines other nearby islands, bustling with tourists, as she walks the length of the beach the next morning. As she moves towards the jetty, she sees a boat; food supplies being unloaded by a couple of the workers who share the third villa. For a moment she pictures herself creeping aboard, convincing the boatman to take her somewhere far from here. At that moment one of the maids looks up at her, and Maria turns away.

David had woken first but he is not at his usual place on the porch of the second villa, where Jorgos and Hans are staying. She looks around, the windows of the connecting villa glistening down at her, the glass reflecting the sunlight so that she has no idea who is inside, and who's looking out.

Maria's phone is by her side in her linen tote bag, which is where she keeps it at all times, wary not just of David but of the workers who bustle in and out without a moment's warning, their eyes everywhere. She reads a book on the beach for a while, turning the pages occasionally for the benefit of the cameras that lean in overhead. Who knows who is watching, and how close up they can move, whether they capture the wary movements of her eyes as they scan the page, willing a reply to the message she sent Harry from her phone, forwarding the picture of where in the ocean they are, in the dead of night.

There is no reply when Maria checks her phone the next day, or the one after that.

For all she knows, Harry might be dead.

A month on the island passes painfully slowly, her toes sinking further into the sand with every step. The rum cocktails that at first tasted sweet and reassuring become sharp and sit heavy in her gut.

Every day she checks her phone for a reply from Harry, and then one day it comes.

'I've spoken to my woman, she needs more than this. Has David mentioned Anna?'

Frustrated at the lack of meaningful information, Maria inhales sharply as she types: *'I'll try to call in the next few days. Please answer.'*

In the days leading up to Anna's inquest, Maria hears David waking early, heading out and pacing the beach until either Jorgos or Hans come down to get him, leading him, childlike, back to the villa where they feed him coffee and then spirits, as the day progresses while they toil over papers.

'I want to speak to my father before I make any kind of decision,' she hears David tell them pleadingly one afternoon as she passes along the beach below.

'It's not possible,' Jorgos says simply. 'It's not safe. Clive knows about this; he and Jeff have discussed—'

As if sensing they are being overheard, Jorgos lowers his voice and the conversation continues out of hearing range.

That afternoon, Maria takes a swim and when she returns to the house, David is sitting completely still at the breakfast bar with his iPad next to him. Moving behind him, Maria sees the whisky and then the article open on the screen, the headline reporting the inquest verdict.

Socialite hanging: Death by Suicide.

Maria expects David's nerves to calm once the verdict is announced, but the moment they learn of the coroner's conclusion, his restlessness turns to listlessness, as if rather than feeling he has got away with it, he has simply given up.

There is no sign of him when Maria awakes, a couple of days later. None of the men are to be found; presumably they have tucked themselves inside the other villa, wishing to discuss whatever it is that has been bothering David in a more private setting.

Taking the opportunity to check whether Harry has been back in touch, Maria turns on her phone, her mind going back to the day Felicity revealed herself, and MI6's interest in TradeSmart: 'Arms dealing, people trafficking, a child brothel frequented by older men at a very high price.' The investigations had been going on for years, she said, but they were finally reaching a critical stage. An inside man, one of Clive's closest colleagues, was helping to bring the whole thing down. But they needed more. They needed her.

Maria had questioned Felicity at once. 'Inside man? Who, Jeff? Jorgos?'

It could have been either of them, or someone else entirely. None of them were to be trusted. Felicity's face had given nothing away. 'I'm afraid I can't tell you any more than that.'

Maria slips the phone back into her washbag, which she returns to her tote, putting a towel and book on top, and leaves the bathroom holding the bag over her arm. When she opens the door and looks up, David is standing directly in front of her, his expression glass-like.

'David! You scared me,' she says and then takes a step forward, noticing the blotchy skin around his eyes. 'What—'

'It's Dad,' he says. 'He's dead.'

Maria

The day Clive dies

They sit for hours, side-by-side, without talking, the day Clive dies, just as they had the day of Artemis' funeral, two decades earlier.

'It might help to talk about it,' Maria tries for a second time, breaking the interminable stretch of silence, the only sound the occasional swig of David drinking whisky straight from the bottle.

He doesn't reply and Maria tries again. 'Perhaps we could send flowers?'

David finally turns to face her. 'Flowers?'

'It's your father's funeral, David, and you can't be there. I thought you might like—'

He laughs, as if she has just told the funniest joke. 'Oh yes, great idea. I'll just ring Interflora, ask them to send a bouquet reading "With love from your dead son, David".'

Maria blushes. 'I didn't mean . . . I just thought if there was a way of discreetly . . . But you do have a new phone here – isn't that risky?'

He stops laughing then. 'It would be if it was registered to my name, or in any way traceable to me. It's only for using the proper messaging system, not for chit-chat, not for ordering bloody lilies.'

'You mean the EncroChat you mentioned?' Maria asks.

He looks at her for a moment. 'Christ, what is this, the Spanish bloody inquisition?'

'David, I'm just talking to you. It's not like we have anything else to talk about, is it? It's not like I do anything other than—'

'I see,' David says. 'Are you regretting coming here with me?'

'I don't know.'

Her honesty cuts him dead.

Neither of them speaks again for almost a minute and then Maria continues, more quietly. 'I'm just lonely. There's nothing for me here. You're working all the time. You hardly talk to me.' She inhales. 'I suppose it's not how I imagined it.'

'So you wish you hadn't come?'

'I didn't say that,' she replies, taking the bottle from him and drinking, appreciating the burn of the whisky in her throat.

'I'm sorry,' David says after a moment and Maria feels a tug of guilt.

'It's not your fault,' she says.

'Is there anything I can do, to make things easier?' he asks and Maria pauses, before taking another drink.

'I would like to speak to my mother.'

'You know you can't do that.'

'Why?' she asks plainly, the frustration making her bold.

'We spoke about this, Maria. This is not a game. It's too risky. You agreed to cut off all contact, at least for the time being, until we're more settled.'

'Settled where? *How?*' Maria feels her voice rise. 'Don't you think it's stranger if I don't call, ever? It will be Christmas soon. There is no reason why anyone would be listening in to my mother's calls. Everyone thinks you're dead, David, and I'm just the *nanny*. The only person who is likely to be suspicious that something is wrong, to raise any kind of alarm, is my mother. If I don't call—'

'Jorgos wouldn't like it,' David says sharply.

'Jorgos?' Maria sneers. 'Who is in charge here, David? I have given up everything to be here with you, with no friends, nothing to do, for what, be your mistress – someone to have sex with at the end of another long day of meetings? And still you don't trust me?'

'It's not just about me,' David says, his voice quieter. 'Things are complicated with the business right now.'

'Complicated how?'

'It's Jeff,' he pauses. 'He wants to take the business in directions I'm not sure of.'

'You've just lost your father, I'm not sure that's the best time to be making any kind of major decisions.'

David snorts derisively. 'I'm not really in a position to be taking compassionate leave.'

Maria doesn't rise to the bait. 'What does Jorgos say?'

'It's nothing to do with Jorgos,' David snaps, his voice less controlled.

'I agree. But does he?'

'What do you mean?'

'I mean, it seems to me that Jorgos is keeping an eye on us, as much as he is protecting us.'

Her words hang there as David considers what she's just said. For a moment Maria wonders if he is questioning the use of the word 'us'. Does he even see them as a unit in this?

She presses on. 'What if – and I'm not saying this is necessarily the case – but what if Jeff and Jorgos are in cahoots. With your father gone, if Jeff wanted to make a play for a bigger part of the business . . .'

She lets her words sit there for a while as they circle back towards the house, neither of them acknowledging Jorgos and Hans seated on the porch.

'Look, I'm sorry,' she says a while later, as they sit at the table, David fiddling with his phone. 'I shouldn't be putting pressure on you right now; it's just that I'm worried about you. But I understand things are complicated.' She leans over and touches his hand. 'I'm so sorry about your dad, and Anna—'

'Anna?'

There is venom in his voice as David slams his phone on the table. He regards her a moment with contempt and then he stands, and moves towards the kitchen to get another bottle. Maria's eyes fix on the unlocked phone as he casts around the kitchen.

'David, just because of how things ended doesn't mean you're not going to feel upset. You loved her and she betrayed you, but that doesn't mean—'

She doesn't have time to doubt herself. She keeps one eye on him as he moves between cupboards with his back to her, unsteady on his feet. Reaching forward, glancing briefly back up at him, she turns the phone over and scrolls past the apps until she finds Voice Memos.

Pressing 'record' she returns the phone to its face-down position as David begins to move back towards her.

'You think I'm upset about *Anna*? You think I feel remorse for what we did?' His words are so matter-of-fact, she can hardly believe she is hearing them. 'Getting rid of Anna was the best thing I've ever done in my pathetic life.' His eyes are shining with a sort of furious glee. 'Knowing she suffered, just as she made me suffer, is only bettered by the fact that she will have known that *he* was the one who betrayed her. After everything she did for him – after the things she put me through in order to help him: after making me raise his babies, believing them to be mine . . .' He nods, reassuring himself more than her. 'When she died she will have looked him in the eyes and she will have known that he was complicit in her death.'

Maria's throat is dry, her voice rasping when she speaks. 'Who, David?'

'Harry bloody Dwyer! The man she was fucking,' he announces triumphantly. 'He was the one who got her to open the door to the men who—' His face falls. Maria can no longer be sure if it is David swaying with nausea, or her.

'Harry Dwyer. Our very own Trojan Horse.'

* * *

Maria's head is swimming as she leaves the villa. There is nowhere to go. She wants to scream. The whole island seems to be growing smaller and smaller by the day until she feels she will suffocate.

Harry was in on it. Harry *knew* they were going to kill Anna? Her mind tilts one way and then the other, finally settling on David's phone.

She waits until the dead of night, for his snore to grow loud enough that she knows he won't wake again, then she picks up her phone and moves outside, silently pulling the front door closed behind her.

A cool sea breeze follows as she moves, barefoot, towards the shoreline, keeping to the shadows, avoiding the sightline of the second villa as best she can. When she glances up at it, she sees the lights are on, but there are no signs of life inside, or on the terrace. She stops and listens, waiting until she is sure it is quiet before she carries on.

Crouching behind the narrow trunk of a palm tree, she scrolls through her address book until she reaches a number she hasn't dialled before, one she secreted from Anna's phone in the early days and passed on to Felicity, along with everything else, not long before Felicity cut her off once and for good.

It is late both here and in England and the phone rings several times before Anna's mother answers. She sounds older than she must be, and understandably perturbed by the unexpected call in the middle of the night.

'Yes?' she says and Maria clears her throat, talking as quietly as she can whilst still making herself heard.

'I am so sorry to bother you. I know it's late and you don't know me, but I am a friend of Anna's and I need to talk to you.'

'Isobel Mason, is that you? Trying to stir things up with your suggestions that my daughter's death was not suicide?' Her voice is a mixture of anger and fear.

'No, it's not Isobel,' Maria said quietly, trying to sound reassuring.

'So you're another journalist, bothering me in the middle of the night when there are children asleep upstairs? Like I told Isobel, I am not interested in telling my story—'

Maria whimpers at the mention of the twins. 'Diane, I am not a journalist, I promise you. My name is Maria, I was the nanny to Stella and Rose. That's why I'm ringing, to check on the girls. I wanted to—'

'Maria?' Diane's voice is calmer now.

'Anna mentioned me?' She looks up, noticing the lights inside the villas are now off.

'No. But she left something for you . . . in her will. A letter.'

'For me?' Maria says, her fingers stretching into the sand. 'Are you sure?'

'Quite sure,' she says. 'It's with the lawyer. Only you are allowed to collect it, in person. Anna's instructions were very clear.'

Diane's voice breaks, and Maria feels a pang of sadness for the woman who by all accounts couldn't find enough warmth in her heart to be a proper mother to Anna whilst she was still alive.

As if reading Maria's thoughts, Diane clears her throat. 'I was a terrible mother. After Thomas died I blamed her, and she knew it. I blamed her because she was supposed to be watching him and she didn't, when he fell from the roof. Do you have any idea what it's like to lose not one but two children?'

'I have no idea how you must be feeling,' Maria tries to comfort her, her attention pricked by a shadow on the terrace. She ducks down, further out of sight, but when she looks again it is completely dark.

'I'm so sorry, but I have to be quick. Please can I have the details of the solicitor?'

Committing the number and the address to memory, Maria ends the call, asking Diane to send her love to the girls and promising to ring again soon.

'I can't have them here forever,' Diane says plainly before the call ends, and any tenderness Maria was beginning to feel towards the woman hardens. What kind of woman rejects her own grieving grandchildren?

'You won't have to,' she says. 'But please look after them until something can be worked out. I'll call again soon. Diane . . .'

'Yes?'

'Can I have the number of the journalist – Isobel Mason?'

'Why?'

'I'll get her to leave you alone. It's not right that the girls should have to risk having her call again, upsetting you at this time.'

Diane sniffs. 'People have no idea how hard this has been for me.'

Maria swallows. 'I know. I'll speak to her. I'll sort it out.'

Maria's fingers are shaking as she dials again. The voice at the end of the line, when it answers just two rings later, sounds younger than she had imagined.

'Is that Isobel Mason?'

'Speaking. Who's this?' the woman replies, clearly still awake.

'My name's Maria. I'm . . . I am— I *was* the nanny for Anna Witherall and her children. Her mother, Diane, gave me your number – she said that you'd been going to the house. She said that you were asking questions about Anna's death. She said that you were unconvinced that it was suicide.'

'Oh,' the woman says, flustered but keen to keep her on the line. 'Yes, I'm Isobel. I'm a reporter, I'd love to talk—'

Maria breathes deeply before carrying on, knowing she is taking a risk by talking to this person, who could be anyone, though she has no other option. 'I need your help.'

It's hazy when Maria wakes the next day, David's side of the bed already empty beside her. Instinctively, she reaches down the side of her bed for her tote bag, which is just where she left it. She is about to pick it up when she hears movement in the kitchen.

Freezing, she sits up slowly and kicks the bag more discreetly under the bed.

'Did you sleep well?' Jorgos asks in Greek, from his position at the kitchen table, as she enters the room.

'Yes, thank you,' she replies in English, not looking at him as she moves to the counter and fills the kettle, the sound of the water hitting metal rising above the tapping of her own heartbeat. 'Where's David?'

'He just went to get something.'

'Are you working in here today?'

He doesn't respond and she places the kettle on its stand, moving to the fridge. The cool air hits her face and she stands for a moment, letting it soothe the heat rising in her cheeks. What is he doing here? She closes the fridge door, gripping it briefly before turning to face him, telling herself he doesn't know anything.

'Would you like coffee?' She makes herself half-smile at him.

'Mmm,' he says. 'Your mother used to make me coffee at Clive's house in Greece, when she was his cleaner.'

Something about hearing him refer to her mother makes Maria bristle. 'She wasn't exactly a cleaner,' she responds, her tone lighter than she feels.

'It wasn't a slight,' Jorgos says. 'I liked Athena. I still do. She was a good friend, loyal.'

Maria says nothing, scooping three spoons of coffee into the cafetiere, before picking up the kettle, tipping it and watching the boiling water cascade onto the granules.

When she hears his voice again it is right behind her. 'Not like her friend.'

Maria pulls herself closer to the counter, away from him, holding herself there. 'You remember Artemis, don't you?' Jorgos says, his voice a whisper, taking a step closer, so close that Maria dare not exhale for fear she will touch him. She feels the breath expanding in her lungs until her chest aches.

She is suddenly aware of the kettle still grasped between her fingers, feeling her arm lift a little when the door clatters open.

'Maria?'

'David.' She turns quickly, the hot water splashing out and catching Jorgos' shoulder as he also turns towards the sound of David's voice.

'*Malaka*,' he cries out, grabbing his shoulder and stepping away from her.

'Sorry, I didn't mean—' she says, as David steps forward.

'Jorgos, are you all right?'

'I'm fine,' he says, lifting his hand, trying to suppress the pain in his expression. 'Maria was just making us coffee. She needs to learn to be more careful.'

The men take their coffee to the other villa, and Maria moves straight into the bedroom, rifling for her phone and moving into the bathroom before the maid arrives. She is shaking as she waits for it to come on. When it does, the message is waiting for her: '*My name is Madeleine. Isobel contacted me, I can help you.*'

Maria

'How was Jorgos' shoulder?' Maria asks later, once they are seated on the shore overlooking the water, which unfolds, uninterrupted, into an unbroken blue sky.

'Hmm?' David is distracted again, taking a second to register her question before answering. 'Oh, fine.'

'David.' She takes his hand, willing him to look at her. 'I think we need to leave.'

'Leave? What are you talking about?'

Maria speaks slowly, keeping her voice calm. 'I don't trust them.'

'Trust who?'

'Jorgos, and that meathead, Hans. I don't think they have our best interests at heart.'

'Why would you say that?' He pulls his hand away from her defensively.

'You said it yourself, Jorgos is clearly siding with Jeff.'

'This isn't primary school, Maria, there aren't *sides*.'

'No,' Maria says, her voice losing its patience. 'It's a multi-billion dollar company that Clive and you have a major stake in – now with Clive gone, don't you think it's possible that . . . I don't know, David, maybe they're trying to control you?'

David shakes his head, less confidently this time, and so she presses on.

'With Clive gone, and Jeff pushing for things you're not comfortable with, isn't it possible that Jeff has charged Jorgos with watching you, controlling you, under the guise of protection?'

'I don't understand what you're saying,' David says, childlike, though she can see he is listening.

'I'm saying we need to go somewhere – just you and me. Anywhere we like, within reason. The point is to get you somewhere where you can be autonomous, start the conversations you need to have with your other business partners, without Jeff as a constant intermediary.'

She reaches again for David's hand and this time he doesn't resist. 'Look, I don't like saying this, but they're trying to push you out. Without your father, they think you're weak. How long do you expect to stay here, under their watch? They're not keeping you safe, they're keeping you where they can monitor you. We're their prisoners, David.'

Maria lowers her voice, aware of one of the maids cleaning down the sun loungers at the edge of the garden. She focuses on the thought of Madeleine's message, and then continues. 'Where we go is up to you. You could instruct your pilot to take us straight there. *Without* Jorgos. It has to be dictated by your job, by where makes sense for the business. You have to step up, before they crush you.'

After lunch, Maria goes to bed for a nap, leaving David to head outside with his phone. She is awoken by the sound of movement in the bedroom.

'What are you doing?' she asks, sitting up in bed.

'I'm packing,' David replies, without looking up.

'What?'

'You're right. We need to get out of here. Tomorrow . . .'

'Tomorrow?' Maria sits up. 'What? I don't understand . . .'

'I've arranged it all.' David doesn't look at her. 'The pilot is coming to collect us at noon.'

'Noon?'

'What's the matter? I thought you'd be pleased.'

'I am, it's just . . . Where are we going?'

Maria

A silence descends as Maria and David board the seaplane for the first leg of the journey, as if the whole island is holding its breath.

Jorgos and Hans stand at the shore, watching them, neither attempting to stop them leaving. For the first time in as long as she can remember, David is calm beside her in his seat. She thinks of his body the night before, tossing and turning for what felt like hours before it finally succumbed to a peaceful rhythm.

Still she had waited until she could hear him snoring before moving across the room towards the chair over which his trousers were slung. She only paused for a second, looking back at him as she gingerly reached inside the pocket and pulled out his phone.

As the plane takes off, Maria feels the same pressure tightening in her chest that she'd felt as she moved in front of David's sleeping body on the bed, muttering a prayer and then pressing the screen-lock on his phone against his thumb. At first the contact was too light, so she had to hold his wrist and press more firmly until the screen finally lit up.

'We're refuelling in Dubai, right?' Maria says and David considers her words as he uncorks the bottle of champagne he has retrieved from the fridge, pouring each of them a glass. Not that it matters. She had sent Madeleine a screenshot of their location from the Maps on his phone, alongside the recording she had made, before deleting both as well as the Sent message.

Wherever they stop, someone will surely be waiting.

'Why do you want to know,' David says, the question taking her by surprise.

'I'm just asking,' she replies, the leather of the seats beneath her turning moist. 'I know we have two stops to refuel before Dominica so I just wondered which was first.'

David thinks for a moment, the tiny movements of his eyes suggesting a thousand possibilities. 'You sound nervous. Are you scared?'

She shakes her head. 'Maybe a little. I don't like flying.'

'It's OK, I'll look after you.' David takes her hand, and she thinks of the night he first kissed her, their fingers entwined as she guided him along the dark path by her house.

'Whatever happens, I'll always look after you.'

They fly for what feels like an eternity, Maria closing her eyes for much of the journey so as to avoid having to look at him.

When the plane finally starts to dip towards the tarmac, she doesn't dare speak, her fingernails pressing into the armrests on either side of her seat.

'Are you OK?' David asks and Maria shakes her head.

She feels his eyes on her face as the plane descends, as if he can't bring himself to look outside.

When he does, he pulls away from her. 'No. No, no, no . . .' He stands, pulling at his seat belt, and moves towards the cockpit, calling to the captain not to land.

The pilot doesn't look back, continuing his course to the runway where the officers await, just as Madeleine had promised.

All the while, David holds onto the handle to the cockpit, his eyes trained on Maria. 'Please no, please no.'

He sounds like a child and Maria feels her head shaking. 'I'm so sorry,' she tries to say but no words come, her mouth quivering as the wheels clatter onto the runway.

Maria

London, a month after the inquest

It's a short taxi ride from Guildford station to the cul-de-sac. Maria lets her eyes travel over the buildings and trees, the sense of clarity offered by the cloud somehow reassuring after the unwieldy expanse of the Maldivian sky.

'Please wait here,' she says to the driver before stepping out of the car.

She stands for a minute in front of Anna's childhood home, taking in the sycamore tree overlooking the red-brick house with its detached flat-roofed garage. A picture of orderly middle-England.

Until she knocks at the door, Maria hasn't even considered what Anna's mother might look like. In the flesh she is small and brittle, older looking than her years. For a moment, Maria thinks of her own mother, and tears unexpectedly prickle in the grooves of her eyes.

'Maria, where have you been?' Stella says, moving into the hallway behind her grandmother, addressing Maria as though she might have just popped out to the shops for a pint of milk. Maria crouches down and waits for both girls to run over and throw their arms around her neck, their unquestioning acceptance of their new situation almost breaking her heart. They insist on showing her their new shoes as they dress to follow her into the taxi, Diane joining last.

'Where are we going?' Stella asks.

'We're going back to London for a few days. And then you'll

come back to Granny's house for a while, until you're allowed to come and live with me.'

Diane nods in tacit agreement.

'Mummy and Daddy won't be there,' Rose says and Maria looks up. It is the first full sentence she has ever heard Rose say.

There is a pull at her chest. 'No. But I will be there and then you'll come back to Granny's for a little while and then I'll never go anywhere without you again. OK?'

The flat they have rented for a few days is not far from the chapel on Rosslyn Hill where David's funeral was held.

'Will she be able to hear us when we say goodbye?' Rose asks the morning of their mother's funeral, as Maria ties a ribbon around one of her pigtails.

Maria pauses. 'I don't know, darling.' Rose looks away, her lip wobbling, and Maria leans forward. 'Hey, you know what? She will hear you. Absolutely. She will always hear you and she will always love you. You will never be alone. You understand?'

Rose nods and Maria leans in to kiss her head. 'I'm so sorry you have to do this.'

Maria takes the girls' hands in hers as the music plays, Diane walking behind them in a navy-blue hat. The church is bathed in light. Settling on the bench in the front row, Maria's eyes scan the room. Other than a few familiar faces, which she recognises as mothers from the school, and a throng of women who might have been Anna's former colleagues at the magazine, there are not many guests.

Feeling a hand on her shoulder, Maria turns. The woman with long red curls smiles.

'You must be Maria. I'm Meg . . .'

Without faltering Meg smiles brightly at each girl in turn. 'And you must be Stella and Rose.'

The girls nod and Meg holds their eyes, sniffing away the tears as they form. 'I've been so looking forward to meeting you.'

The organ starts up and Meg says, 'Maria, I'd love to stay in touch, if that's OK?'

'Of course.' She reaches out a hand. She is about to turn to the front when the doors at the back of the church open and a woman in a double-breasted coat marches along the central aisle, flanked by policemen. 'I'm sorry,' she says, holding up a piece of paper at the priest. 'We have reason to prevent the funeral taking place today.'

Maria bristles with nervous energy as she and the girls settle on a bench at the top of the hill, overlooking the pond, the leaves of the weeping willow skirting the water. She has managed to distract them from the police intrusion at the funeral the previous day, but she wonders how much will remain there, lodged in their subconscious memory.

Leaning in to kiss each of the girls on the head in turn, she sits back and watches Stella jump off the bench, taking Rose's hand and leading her to the edge of the water, tossing in a stick and marvelling as she watches it glide towards a band of coots.

Smiling to herself, Maria looks up and nods in acknowledgement at the woman from the adoption services who is supervising the visit from a respectful distance. Though she can't say officially yet, the woman has mooted the likelihood that the adoption order will be granted. There are no other claimants.

'Hey.'

When Maria looks up, she sees Harry walking towards her. He is fidgety, looking over his shoulder.

'Hey.' She smiles at him. 'How are you?'

'I'm good,' he says, settling next to her on the bench, a copy of the morning paper under his arm.

'Are you going somewhere?' Maria asks, noting the small suitcase by his feet.

'For a bit. I'm sorry I couldn't make it to the funeral yesterday . . . I heard it was broken up – what was that about?' His left eye flickers as he pulls out a cigarette, looking up sharply as the girls run back towards them, each trailing a stick. Stella looks up and smiles.

'Come here, there's someone I want you to meet,' Maria beckons to the twins.

When she turns to Harry, she sees recognition in his expression and she nods. Stella is the spit of him.

'It's OK,' she says. 'We don't need you. And I won't tell them. One day, maybe, but we'll see.'

Her phone pings and she reaches into her pocket, pulling out the handset, reading the message:

Ready. Madeleine. 'Right, it's time for us to go,' she says, standing and calling to the girls. She won't risk them, or the adoption official, seeing what happens next. As they walk away, leaving Harry in stunned silence, they pass one of the surrounding police officers who are situated at various points in the park, preparing to swoop.

She can't believe he came, really, but she's learnt to expect the unexpected. Besides, he had no reason to believe he was in immediate danger. Nothing had been explicitly stated as to why the funeral had been postponed. Harry might have thought that if he was under suspicion, the police could have come for him at home, straight away. And he might have assumed that there was no reason for anyone to suspect him. Men like Harry simply got away with things, didn't they? Until they didn't.

Maria

Now

'Are you sure you don't mind watching the girls?' Maria asks, and Meg smiles back at her.

'I told you, it's a pleasure.'

'Thank you so much – I won't be long. And if you need anything, you have my mobile—'

'It's fine, honestly! We're going to head to the playground and then maybe go for a hot chocolate. It will be fun.'

The solicitor's office is above a shop on Euston Road. Maria follows the map on her phone until she finds herself outside the address she is looking for. Once she is buzzed upstairs, she approaches the desk. 'Do you have an appointment?' the receptionist smiles.

'Yes,' Maria nods. 'I do.'

'Anna's will specified that this envelope must be given only to you,' the solicitor says over cheap spectacles hanging from a string around her neck.

Maria feels her cheeks grow hot. 'What is it?'

'Here you go,' the lawyer says, the letter in her hand.

Maria stands, her whole body bristling with nervous excitement as she moves back down the stairs, her fingers clasping the letter, shivering as she is met by a bitter blast of cold air.

Maria sits on the steps of an old bank, a few buildings down, the sound of traffic and bustling commuters fading away as she opens the envelope, Anna's cursive script staring back at her.

Dear Maria,
If you are reading this then I am gone and I was right to worry.
   I want you to know that I knew about you and David. I saw you together, one night in the kitchen. I suppose even before then I understood there was something between you. I forgive you, and I also need you to understand that I am not who you think I am, and David is not who you think he is.
   There is too much to explain, some of which will come to light, but one thing I know is that however much you might love him, you love the girls more – you are the only person on earth who cares as much about Stella and Rose as I do. There is no one else I can trust to help them now, and to help me. You have been a better mother to my daughters than I could ever be, and I am grateful to you for being the person I didn't have the strength to become.
   Below are the details of an offshore bank account with money I have been putting aside for the girls. In total, £500,000, which they will inherit when they are 18. There is also enough for you to look after them until then, and some for yourself for your trouble.
   Please look after them. I don't doubt that David loves you, but the girls love and need you more than David ever could.
   Be well.
   Anna

The words grow blurred through her tears as she reads them again, before standing and moving towards the crossing. As she reaches King's Cross station, she sees David, his face staring back at her from the front page of the *Evening Standard*.
Fake Death Inmate Found Hanged in Cell.

Maria

Months earlier

They had spent the morning in their usual spot, seated at the back of one of the chain coffee shops on Caledonian Road. It was a stone's throw from the football pitches where David played on Saturday mornings, and a short walk from the library where Maria had spent the past two hours staring at a blank page, no longer interested in the pile of books in her backpack, passing the time before David's weekly football was over and they would take their usual place opposite one another under the strip-lighting illuminating the Formica countertop.

It was the sort of place David could count on not being discovered by anyone he knew, and his hand rested on hers, his thumb moving back and forth against her knuckle.

He had been distant all morning. Driving from the house he remained silent, without so much as attempting to stroke her knee. By the time he finally joined her at the coffee shop, she was terrified of what might be on his mind. But then, with only the slightest prompting, the floodgates opened. If ever she needed proof that she was his confidante, this was it. As soon as he had started to speak, he could not stop.

'I didn't believe my father at first, when he told me. We had gone for dinner, the three of us, to celebrate Anna's promotion. It was the loveliest night, and then she went home early and my dad and I went on for a drink at his club. We'd just found out Anna was pregnant and I knew she didn't want me to say anything, but I couldn't stop myself. I was so bloody excited.

'As soon as we were in the cab on the way there, I felt him change. I assumed, at first, he was distracted by work or something else. We got to the club, we ordered drinks and as soon as they arrived, I told him. I blurted it out. Anna was pregnant. We were having a baby. I didn't know then, that there were two of them. But it turns out that was the least of the things I didn't know.'

David let out a laugh and shifted slightly in his seat, silent for a moment before continuing. 'When I told him, he didn't say anything at first. It was as if he hadn't heard me; he just answered that he had something important to tell me. I remember his words exactly. He said, "David, I'm not sure how else to say this, but your friend, Anna, she's not who you think she is."'

The movements of David's thumb stopped and he looked up at Maria, his eyes almost glazed.

'It was the night of my father's party in Greece that they had found out. The one where I finally saw you again. The funny thing was, he already knew there was a mole. He'd got wind of it from one of his contacts, but he thought it was Jeff. Jeff was always a loose cannon, and my father assumed he was the one selling him out. So he had Jorgos follow him, and Jorgos caught her coming out of the study. After that, my father checked the camera, and it was all there. My girlfriend, *the love of my life*, snooping around in his office.'

David shook his head, laughing to himself, before biting his lip.

'And you know, I still didn't believe him. Despite everything. I convinced myself it was an honest mistake, that she had just been looking for a pen or . . .' He shook his head. 'I know, fucking ridiculous. But what . . . I was supposed to believe that she was a *spy*? I was supposed to believe the woman I was in love with, the woman carrying my baby, was using me to . . .'

His voice trailed off, and then started again.

'For a while I blamed Jeff. I thought he and Jorgos must have been in on it together . . . setting Anna up in order to cover their own tracks.'

Maria's throat was constricting. For want of something to distract her hands, she reached for her cup and took a sip, the coffee unexpectedly hot, scalding her lip.

'But my dad, he wouldn't give up; he wouldn't stop going on and on about how she was a fraud. He had seen her passport. She wasn't born in Wiltshire at the airbase at Boscombe Down, like she told us; she was born in Surrey, and that was where she grew up. An unremarkable life in an unremarkable family, as she stayed until she met me . . . Her mother wasn't even dead.'

His fingers were pressed against the side of the table, his knuckles white, his voice wavering with disbelief rather than anger.

'But even then, I kept thinking there's got to be an explanation. For months, I believed there had to be an explanation. But my dad wouldn't drop it, so eventually, I set a trap. A few weeks before she was due to give birth, I went out and left my father's laptop on the table next to my bed. And I actually felt bad. Even doing that, doubting her just for a second. Then I came home, and it was the day she went into labour – in our room. I came back and her waters had broken, and next to her was the computer, under the duvet on the floor, and it was on. And when I looked at her, her face . . . That was it. I knew.'

Unaffected by Maria's silence, David had hardly paused for breath, something inside him having opened that could not easily be closed again before purging years' worth of stale, festering emotions. And then he stopped.

For several minutes they sat in silence, his eyes set somewhere in the distance while the memories churned around his head, until once more the words spilled out.

The coffee in front of her was cold and grey by the time he spoke again.

'You know, I might have felt like a fool, if it hadn't also been made clear that she had no idea who she was actually working for.

All of this, and she hadn't even bothered to check. Can you imagine that?'

Maria felt a prickle of hairs along her arms.

'That man, that reject journalist scum she was fucking – did I tell you that bit? No? Oh yeah, she was bending over for him at the same time as taking every penny my family ever gave her, lapping up every opportunity we offered. And the girls, they—'

He looked up, and then something stopped him continuing with his sentence. He picked up the stirrer and moved it absent-mindedly around in his cup.

'You know, sometimes I try to picture her face the moment the penny drops at how she's been played. Oh, to be a fly on the wall the moment she discovers that all along she was actually working for one of the biggest crooks in Central Africa.'

He was talking to himself now. Whether or not Maria was present was neither here nor there. She was the one into whose arms he fell, believing he had already been more betrayed than he could ever be.

Maria

The day before Anna dies

The day before Maria is due to meet David at the airport, she takes a short walk from her hotel to Regent's Park. She already knows from her Google searches what to expect as she approaches the stretch of Nash buildings behind her, along the path that curves towards the bench where she had insisted they meet. She recognises his face from the photographs online, the unnaturally blue eyes the computer screen had failed to do justice.

'Harry?'

He looks up, his eyes narrowing sharply as they meet hers before looking around, instinctively, for signs of company.

She could not be sure that he would come, after her call from the phone box the day after Felicity 'let her go'. She had stolen his number from Anna's phone with such ease that she wondered how Anna had ever thought she was fooling anyone.

Taking a seat, Maria holds out her hand.

'My name is Maria. Like I said on the phone, I'm a friend of Anna's. I also believe we have another person in common.'

'Another person in common, you say?' His accent is soft and she can instantly see from the way he holds his face, the intensity of the eyes, what had drawn Anna in; though she will not be making that mistake.

Harry raises his cigarette to his lips and inhales, the paper burning at the edges.

'Yes. I think until now, you and I have been working from different angles, towards the same common goal. And I think we could help each other, if we joined forces.'

Something clicks, a look of intent forming at the corners of his mouth.

'Is that right?'

Unnerved by the depth of his stare, she looks down for a moment and then lifts her head.

'If you're anything like me, you're not going to want to see him get away with it. After everything we've given to bringing them to justice?'

'We?'

'Yes, we . . .'

'What are we talking about here?'

Harry keeps his expression cool, taking another drag of his cigarette as he looks out across sculpted hedges circling an ornamental fountain.

'I assume you've heard about David.'

Harry raises an eyebrow, his voice measured. 'I read something about it. The funeral was a few days ago, wasn't it?'

'David's not dead.'

She watches his face turn towards her, and she smiles.

'Now you're listening? David is alive and is fleeing to the Maldives – tomorrow evening – where, as I'm sure you know, there is no extradition treaty, so once he is there, he's free. MI6, they're no longer interested. The African authorities, from what I gather, because of Nguema's involvement and how much influence he has there, they aren't in a hurry to prosecute. If anyone does try to fit him up for it, there is a plan to lay the blame on Anna. So the way I see it, there are only two people left on this earth who care about bringing Clive to justice. And one of us has been asked to accompany David to the Maldives, as his mistress.'

Harry cocks his head, exhaling a long line of smoke, his face breaking into a smile.

'Well, I certainly didn't get the memo. OK, now I'm listening.'

'Anna is due to meet with Clive's solicitors about the will. David and I are meeting at the airport, tomorrow afternoon. He wanted to be sure everything went smoothly in terms of Anna's reaction to the meeting she is due to have with his father's solicitors, tomorrow morning, so he has been lying low at his father's flat, "getting his ducks in order", that's what you say. Right?'

'I definitely don't say that.'

Maria pauses then, unable to stop herself. 'Why did you do it?'

'Do what?' His expression is one of genuine bemusement.

'All of it. I mean, there must have been easier ways to make money . . .'

Harry raises a hand at this, as if the idea of being in it for the money offends him.

'Seriously, I'm intrigued. I know why I did it, but I can't work out . . .'

Harry smiles then, as if considering something for the first time.

'But life's not like that, is it? It's not that straightforward. You must know that as well as I do. You make decisions as and when situations arise; you take steps and you never really know where they will take you. You just do what you think is right in that moment; sometimes you're right, and sometimes—' His voice stopped abruptly. 'Well, maybe I was right, maybe I was wrong. Maybe we all were. It just depends what angle you're looking at it from.'

Maria looks away, taking a moment to let his words sink in. He's right, about this point at least. Sometimes you're already so far into something that there's no other way out. Sometimes the 'right thing' in its purest form is no longer an option.

'Should one of us try to warn her?' Harry says, after a moment.

'I'll do it,' Maria replies. 'It will be better coming from me.'

*   *   *

That is part of what the meeting had been about, of course – as well as finding herself an ally who will help her get David arrested. But as much as that, she needs to ensure Harry doesn't go directly to Anna himself, to warn her of what Clive and David have planned, before the fact. In order for Maria's plan to work, Harry has to believe that Maria will do this herself – and Maria is nothing if not persuasive.

But she isn't as clever as she thinks, she realises much later. Because saving Anna had never been Harry's intention at all – she knows that now. Harry knew exactly what Clive had planned, and he wouldn't have warned Anna off, whether Maria had intercepted or not. Saving Anna had been the furthest thing from his mind.

She had completely underestimated what Harry was capable of – but then he had underestimated her, too.

Maria

Maria's flight is booked for the day after she meets Harry in Regent's Park. The car David has arranged to take her to the airport is due to pick her up at the hotel at 1 p.m., and she will be back by then, dressed in the demure button-down tunic dress he bought for her at one of the boutiques on the high street, together with a pair of pretty leather sandals; one of a number of parcels she'd found stashed in the cupboards or under her pillow over the past months. Her final transformation into the image of the woman with whom he intends to live out the rest of his life is almost complete.

She has stayed the night in the room Anna booked her into by way of atoning for her untimely dismissal, after David died. Anna had meant well in asking her to leave and Maria respected her for it. She wanted to be a good mother to those girls. The strength it must have required to tell Maria to go gave her some hope for Anna's future – at this point Maria was still able to tell herself the future had not yet been set in stone.

She takes some comfort in that as she brushes out her hair at the dressing table in front of the window overlooking the church on Portland Place; its presence has to be an omen of sorts, though whether good or bad, she cannot yet be sure.

There is no need to bring anything with her, David has explained. There will be a suitcase full of clothes waiting for her when they

344

meet at the airport. For a moment she wonders whether if, in the days to come, Anna will wander along the high street and notice the shoes she gave her for her birthday in the window of the charity shop, where she had deposited her belongings on her way from the house.

Maria stops herself. What a foolish thought. Anna will have no time for window-shopping after her appointment with the lawyer. But it is imperative that she still thinks of her as someone with a future. At this point, she cannot allow herself to engage with the alternative.

She leaves her hotel room at 8 a.m., giving herself enough time to do what she has to and still get back in time for the driver David has arranged to collect her from reception.

But for now, she ducks into her first taxi, the one about which David knows nothing. The one that forms the first stepping stone on the final journey to salvation.

As the car turns in a wide U before sweeping along Portland Place, towards Regent's Park, she thinks of those first days in London, having been brought in as much to watch over Anna as to care for her daughters.

'You'll be our eyes and ears, Maria. Anna, she's . . . volatile.' Clive had taken Maria aside one afternoon in the Maldives, talking to her like an old friend. 'We have our concerns. I know you can be trusted. You're like family to David and me.'

She had gripped the side of her shorts with her fists to stop her fingers from trembling.

At this time of morning it takes just twenty minutes to reach Hampstead Heath. As Maria steps out of the taxi, approaching the house on foot, the key she has secretly had duplicated pressed in her pocket, she thinks of the first time David touched her, in that room just there, the girls asleep upstairs.

Given this is the last time she will ever be here, Maria allows herself a moment to take it all in: the wisteria creeping up perfectly formed London bricks, the curve of the iron railing that lines the steps. To the random passer-by, this is London at its most pictur-esque. Few could imagine what secrets lie beyond these perfect windows.

It is 8.45 a.m. as she makes her way up the front steps of the house. By now Anna will already be on her way to see Clive's lawyer, as David has proudly made her aware. Yet still her eyes scan for signs of life within as she climbs one tread at a time, stopping for a moment before knocking tentatively at the front door, pushing her fingers through the letterbox and checking for any hints that she is not alone.

Only once she is sure it is safe to enter does she slide the key from her pocket and turn it in the lock.

Knowing she has to be as quick as possible, Maria only allows herself a moment to linger in front of the photo of Stella and Rose, the girls who she raised from birth; the girls whose lives will be destroyed along with their mother's. Unless . . .

Breathing deeply, she walks towards the kitchen and pulls two notes from her pocket. The first is in her own handwriting. She has deliberated for hours over the wording, but in the end she tells Anna as much as she knows. However she says it, it sounds incred-ible. How she wishes that it was.

Anna.
I know this will be hard for you to accept but David is alive. He and Clive are planning to have you killed, just as Clive did with his own wife, when she started to question the business. They will make it look like suicide and they will tell everyone that you were mad. You must leave the house immediately. You are not safe here. Please, as soon as you have read this letter you must burn it – if you don't I will be uncovered and I will not be able to finish what we started. So please, burn the letter, take the girls, and run. I

*have made contact with Harry and together we will make sure of
everything else. You can trust us.*
  Love, Maria

When she plays the moment back in her mind later, she will tell
herself that at this point she still hadn't made up her mind – that
there was still a chance she might have left her own note along with
his. Just as she told herself it wasn't her fault what had happened
to Artemis the night of the storm. And it wasn't, not really: she was
a child; she was so young and her dad had left and it was Artemis'
fault. She had heard Athena shouting this at Artemis one night
when she found them arguing in the kitchen not long after her
father left. From then on she had been so angry with Artemis. If
her father hadn't been in love with David's mother then he would
never have left her.

And then, the night of the storm, when Artemis came to the
house, she was so upset and Maria hadn't known what to do. Maria
had been holding in all her anger at Artemis for so long; she had
said such bad things about her in her head. But when Artemis, who
was always so kind to her, came to the house crying and Athena
was so nasty to her, Maria's head spun. Even then, as a child, she
knew what her mother had said was wrong. Artemis was a good
person. After all the bad thoughts she'd had towards her, Maria
needed to say sorry; she needed to see that she was OK.

Plagued by guilt, she had snuck out of the house – not that
Athena would have noticed or cared whether she left or not. The
storm was raging and the rain was lashing from the sky as she
followed the path to Artemis' cottage.

Visibility was bad in the dark, the rain further blurring her vision,
and Maria sensed the man's presence before she saw his silhouette,
pulling open the door and stepping inside. When Maria heard the
screams, she moved instinctively towards the house, but she didn't
understand what she was witnessing. It was so dark, only a candle

on one side of the room, and on the other, Artemis was slumped over the table, the man thrusting from behind her. Instinctively, she took a step back. She had understood the violence of the scene in a way that was intuitive, even to a child who had no understanding of what she was witnessing.

It was only once she heard the man come back out, pulling up the zip of his trousers and walking away from the house, that she dared step back towards the window.

She had wanted to go to Artemis, to comfort her as she sat sobbing at the table, circling a white cloth in her hands, but she didn't know what to say. She didn't know what she had seen. She was a child. And yet if she had done something, gone in to her, Artemis would never have done what she did.

Instead she ran home, and before she opened the door, she heard Clive's voice from inside, followed by her mother's laughter. She walked in, and found them seated across from one another at the table.

'Clive just stopped by to see if David was here. You haven't seen him, have you, Maria?'

Maria's eyes moved between their wine glasses.

'No. Have you checked at the house?'

'I'm going there next, in a minute, once I've finished this. He said he was going to come and see you first, Maria. He'd swapped a toy with that French lad that he wanted to show you,' Clive boomed, so self-assured, so at home in his own skin, even here inside their house. Even with his son alone on the mountain in the middle of a storm, his wife at home—

She pushed the image of what she had seen out of her mind.

'Why wasn't he with you?' Maria said, her voice accusatory.

Athena's expression shifted. 'Maria, how dare you speak to Mr Witherall like that—'

'No, no,' he said. 'It's fine. I like her spirit. David got bored waiting for me after our dinner in the square, he promised he would run straight here. It's only a couple of minutes. And then your mother mentioned something about Artemis so I just stayed for a moment, and now I'm going to go home and see if David headed straight—'

He never finished his sentence, for at that moment David appeared in the doorway to the house, shaking, his face pale, his eyes perforated with the image of his mother hanging from the stairwell.

Standing in front of the table in the hallway of the house, Stella and Rose's scooters lined up along the wall, Maria feels a single tear run down her cheek. But it is too late for tears. Pain and remorse are useless to her now, without action. Finally, she has the chance to do something, even if the final act means sacrifice. And she has no choice. If she warns Anna of Clive and David's plan, she will be putting her own life in jeopardy. They will know exactly who tipped her off, and the chances are they will find Anna anyway. The truth is, the die has already been cast.

She bows her head as she thinks of Anna now. *I will look after them.* She speaks aloud, and there is a strength in her words that bolsters her.

Anna is incapable of protecting herself or the girls. She is a liability to them all, and at this stage, Stella and Rose are the only ones who matter. They are the innocents. If Maria doesn't save them, no one will.

Absent-mindedly picking up the post from the doormat – just one thick cream envelope, another condolence card, no doubt – she walks back to the kitchen. She puts the card on the kitchen table, setting Harry's letter on top of it, and slides her own note back into her handbag. There is a sense of resolution, amidst the bitter sadness. Anna will at least know the truth, at the end. In part.

By the time she gets back from lawyer's, the men will already be waiting for her, and there will be no time to run. She will read Harry's letter and then she will burn it because if there is one person

Anna will listen to, even after everything he has done to her, it is Harry. She will put her trust in him and she will believe that he is going to save her. In the end she will know that Harry had wanted to save her.

In that knowledge, Maria finds some peace.

PART FIVE

May

Christmas Eve. Two weeks after David's death

Christmas lights line the King's Road, casting a gentle hue over the early afternoon sky as May walks along, enjoying the sound of her heels against the pavement. She breathes in deeply, watching the steam rise up in front of her mouth as she exhales. She prefers to walk, even in deepest winter, enjoying the smells of open fires and mulled wine drifting out from the pubs which have been transformed beyond recognition over the years. She doesn't mind the cold, wrapping her pashmina around her neck as she admires the dressed trees framed in the windows, like scenes from a doll's house, on her favourite square.

People in Chelsea still make an effort, even if it's all a bit more gaudy now than it once was. May feels like one of the last few around here old enough to remember when the right address in this enclave signified a certain social standing. Nowadays some of the best properties are occupied by Chinese and Russians, of course. Not that she objects to Russian money. She smiles to herself, picturing Irena at their dinner at J Sheekey the previous week. Yes, after a few bumps, things are starting to shape up nicely.

It's been a funny old year, and the children will be descending soon with the grandchildren and there is still so much to sort out. Jeff won't be much help, she can be sure of that, and with the new business deals she has been overseeing, she has been distracted. But now is the time for family. May has always prided herself on her ability to compartmentalise, not least when it comes to work and family life. This is, she thinks, partly why she has been so successful. Knowing when to pull back and when to press ahead is a life skill, as far as she is concerned, but it is also inherent. Some people understand when to move forwards, and others simply don't.

A young couple push open the door to Peter Jones without holding it open and May curses them under her breath as she steps into the department store, removing her gloves. With Clive and David gone, she, Irena Vasiliev and Francisco Nguema – and Jeff, of course – are free to proceed without limitation. She stops briefly when she thinks of David, pausing at the foot of the escalator. Dear David. He was her godson and she loved him, but by God the man was a liability. And the Greek girlfriend – well, she had really done them a favour, leading David to the police like that. It solved a lot of problems, in the end. Jorgos had been ready to offer a swift alternative, as always, but it hadn't sat right with May. Not at first. Whatever happened with David, she wanted to believe she could save him. Besides, having Maria around complicated matters – if it was just David, no one would have been looking for him, given that he was already officially dead. But Maria – who knew who might start asking questions at some stage, if she suddenly disappeared? Though she had pushed her luck. Surely she must have known she would be watched like a hawk – what was she thinking, sneaking around in the dead of night like some low-rent Miss Marple, imagining she wasn't being listened to, kept an eye on? She thought she was clever. And yet people are surprising, aren't they? You can never really be sure.

May carries on up the escalator and finds herself thinking of David again. The truth is, she always knew he was wrong for this – always. He was too emotional, too damaged. And she blames herself in part for that, which is why she had tried to give him the benefit of the doubt, over the years. She regrets what happened to

Artemis; perhaps she had been hasty in that, but the woman was a liability. And it wasn't her decision alone. Nguema was to blame there, too. Either way, she felt bad about it – sufficiently so that she had tried to get David involved in the business, to *understand* the possibilities for new investment. But he was always resistant, just like his father. Bloody pig-headed. And to be taken in not once but twice? Anna, she could sort of understand – but the second woman? To fall for Maria's little act . . . Well, the boy was a bloody fool, to boot.

May wanted so badly to believe that he would have kept his mouth shut, but she had to be honest with herself, Irena made her realise that. Irena certainly wasn't taking no for an answer, and sometimes one has to do what is necessary. Sometimes these things are out of our control.

May moves between the perfumes, picking up various bottles. Picking one up, she gets a hint of amber and she flinches, not long enough that the girl at the perfume counter will notice.

Her mind brushes over David, one final time. No, it wasn't what she'd wanted, but it was what had to be.

It is a charade, the performance with the perfume, and she and the perfume girl both know it. May will sniff and muse, and imagine for a moment that she might take something else, something different to the scent she has been wearing for so many years. But she will leave with the same bottle she always has. And she likes this about herself: she knows who she is. It is a quality she admired in Clive, too.

Dear Clive. It was a sorry, sorry situation, the whole bloody thing. But at least he wasn't around to learn that his only son has committed suicide in prison. No, the cancer had been aggressive enough to put him out of his misery quickly. There would have been nothing more undignified for a man like Clive than to have gone down slowly. And putting aside her personal sadness for the loss of one of her oldest friends, May has to look to the future. None of them are getting any younger and she is not ready to give up the ghost just yet, thank you very much. It is simply a fact: without Clive, they are freer. For all his wisdom, he just never had the imagination, or the stomach, to try new things. It was May who was constantly having to push to get the business – Christ, without her, they would have gone under years ago. And to think that originally it was Clive and Jeff who had joined forces with Nguema, *her* friend! Though it had made sense; when the babies were young May was happy enough looking after them, until they started school and her feet started to itch. So many young women these days try to do everything at once, and where does it get them? No, one has to pace oneself. One can have it all, just not all at once – one has to bide one's time.

Of course, she had known everything about the business, she had been there from the start, sitting in on dinner meetings while she fed the boys, bringing the men Scotch whilst drinking in every detail of every deal. And so, slowly, and then with gusto, she had started to chip in. She had always been the one with the brains – and the beauty, as she and Jeff liked to joke. Once May came into the business, the whole thing had taken off. And she was always off the books. What would be the point of making herself visible? There were so many things one could get done from behind the scenes. That's the problem with people these days; everyone is always so keen to be *seen*.

Not that May is one to live in the past. You can't stay in the past; you have to embrace the future if you are to keep up with changing times. Apart from with perfume.

'I'll take this one.' May winks at the counter girl who smiles before turning her back and preparing the wrapping. May has barely taken out her purse when her phone rings.

Her expression drops the moment she sees James McCann's name flash on the screen. That bloody lawyer. What the hell is the point of them investing thousands of pounds on encrypted software if he's going to call her on her personal bloody mobile?

May presses answer and takes the outstretched bag from the shop assistant before speaking into the microphone.

'Hello.'

'We need to meet.'

McCann is waiting for her as she makes her way across Hyde Park, towards the horror of the final days of the Winter Wonderland.

'You look well,' McCann says in his usual sycophantic manner.

'James,' she says, moving alongside him towards the gates of the theme park, where the background noise of the crowds and the godforsaken jingles will provide a useful muffler for the conversation they are about to have. May would like to believe they are safe here, but given all that has happened it would be ludicrous to believe she is safe talking anywhere, or to anyone. No, no one is to be trusted, besides Jeff, who frankly doesn't have the wits to pull off that sort of betrayal. And the children. She can trust them implicitly on the basis that she has never told them.

May sighs, taking a sip of the coffee McCann passes her.

'So?' she says.

'David's friend,' McCann replies, lifting the cup in front of his mouth to obscure the movement of his lips for any potential observers. 'It's done.'

May exhales, nodding thoughtfully. 'I see.'

McCann sighs. 'Did we do the right thing? Those girls have already been through so much . . .'

'The girls will be fine. I'll see to that. They might not be flesh and blood but they don't deserve all this.' May looks back at him. 'Come on, don't be glum. It's Christmas. Besides, what choice did we have?'

Epilogue

Madeleine

Madeleine has nothing but a carry-on bag, expertly packed. After years of business travel, she knows what she is doing. Besides, she will only be staying one night, so she won't need much.

'G and T, please,' she smiles at the air hostess, taking the drink and swallowing gratefully. She won't have more than one; she has to drive when she reaches the other side, and mountain roads, after all, can be treacherous.

At Frankfurt airport she catches her connecting flight to Linz, exiting by the sign reading 'car transfer'. She pays for the vehicle in cash and takes the *A to Z* from her bag. She won't risk a GPS, which would be far too easy to trace.

Checking her rear-view mirror for any sign that she is being followed, Madeleine follows the map until she spots the exit sign for Steyr. She has never been to the house before, even though she is the one who arranged for them to have it, this part of Upper Austria being removed but conspicuous enough to facilitate the necessary hiding in plain sight. Besides, they are almost unrecognisable from the pictures in the news reports. The family photos Madeleine had issued to the press were intentionally old, and slightly anonymous, their faces caught in shadow. The photo only showed the four of them, anyway: no image of the baby has ever been released.

When Gabriela comes to the door, having been alerted to Madeleine's arrival by the sound of the wheels in the drive, she looks so different that Madeleine almost wonders whether she has the wrong house. Her hair is cut short and dyed a lighter chestnut brown; everything about her is faded.

Madeleine can't help but smile. 'Hello, you.'

Madeleine follows Gabriela through the house, looking around the rooms, taking in the details of family life: the unwashed cups, the discarded school bags on the dresser.

'The children are in the garden,' Gabriela says as they settle at the table in the kitchen, overlooking the matchbox lawn where Sadie is holding Layla in one arm, pushing Callum on a rusty swing with the other.

Gabriela pours out two glasses of whisky from the bottle Madeleine has produced from her bag.

'Where's Tom?' Madeleine asks.

'I'm not sure,' Gabriela replies, not meeting her eye. 'He spends a lot of the day away from the house.'

'How are things with you two?'

Gabriela shakes her head, taking a swig of her drink. 'As you'd expect. He's good with Layla, though, and the kids have adjusted to the idea. Or else, they're building it all up to have a total melt-down later in life . . . Have you spoken to Ivan?' The question rushes from Gabriela's lips and Madeleine looks at her, trying to understand how she could have given it all up for a man she hardly knew. But then she looks away.

'I went to see him in prison. He's going to testify, so he will probably get a leaner sentence,' she says, keeping it top-line. Gabriela doesn't deserve to be kept informed, not fully; besides, Madeleine doesn't trust her not to try to contact him or to jeopardise her family's life once again. 'The good news, as I mentioned, is that it looks like Vasiliev is going to be extradited as part of some trade-off between the UK and Russia. Turns out she's pissed off a few of the high-ups over there along the way, which is fucking excellent news for us. Once she's here, she'll be tried. Finally, we've cracked the encrypted messaging system they – and hundreds of other criminals – have been using . . . Turns out they had such faith in it, they talked about everything in such detail we have a lot of evidence, on a lot of things . . .'

There are things she doesn't want to go into. She doesn't mention that David Witherall was arrested in Dubai under an urgent Interpol Red Notice thanks to the swift work of the international liaison officers stationed there. She doesn't mention how Dubai was eager to assist after the Financial Action Task Force gave them a poor rating in their recent evaluation report. She doesn't mention, either, that no one had contested his extradition to the UK, which meant he was swiftly returned to the UK. And she doesn't mention how he was found swinging in his cell, despite having been on suicide watch.

Her mind turns briefly to Maria, trying not to picture her face as she fell. The British press had never caught wind of that one. What interest would such a story have to their audiences? A Greek woman stumbling off the edge of a cliff on an island somewhere in the Sporades, whilst out walking on a visit home to see her mother for Christmas, was nothing more than a tragic accident in a far-off land. The media had never managed to connect it to the Witherall family – the daughters themselves were of little interest these days, even if they hadn't been too young to legally report on.

Madeleine had checked in on Stella and Rose, out of a sense of guilt for what had happened, though she knew that it wasn't her fault. Given that she had assisted Maria in getting her and David to the UK, she feels partly responsible, even if she knows she isn't. Not really. Those children had lost everyone, and Madeleine had felt obliged to know what would become of them. It was some comfort to learn that David and Anna's old friend Meg, who had given her information on Harry, was applying to adopt them.

She thinks, then, of her and Meg's initial conversation, under the bridge after the inquest. The resentment in the woman's tone as she told Madeleine about how she had first met Harry, when she was an intern at the paper he wrote for – how he'd tried to recruit her to spy on David – had been palpable. She hadn't known that Harry had turned his sights on Anna, how he had manipulated her, once it became clear that Meg wouldn't be sucked in. She hadn't seen Anna for years, she said, not until David's funeral.

Madeleine could tell that Meg had felt a degree of remorse for what became of her old friend, of responsibility for not having been around to save Anna. She hadn't known Harry was involved in the way that Madeleine now knew, definitively – the way that the world would soon, once the trial was over – but she knew enough to sense something wasn't as it seemed. She had, in her own words, smelt a rat.

'Does he know that we're here?' Gabriela asks and Madeleine is momentarily confused by her drifting thoughts, but then she remembers and her expression hardens.

'Popov? Of course he doesn't. No one knows, apart from me and a couple of my colleagues from the Protected Persons Unit who helped facilitate the relocation. We can't risk anyone knowing, ever . . . You understand that, right?'

'Of course I do.' Gabriela looks away.

Madeleine doesn't mention the threats he has already received in prison. She doesn't mention the likelihood that one day they will no longer just be threats, given Vasiliev's web of contacts.

A few moments pass and then Gabriela speaks again. 'What about Harry, the guy who brought us here? I liked him.'

Madeleine takes another sip of her drink, unwilling to divulge the details of his arrest. 'I liked him too. So, what about you – do you have enough money?'

Gabriela nods. 'We have the rent from my mum's old house, which keeps us afloat, thanks to the account you set up for us. We're going to be OK, I think.'

Madeleine nods tentatively.

'I read the story in the *Mail*, the latest theory about the unexplained death of an English family in the French mountains,' Gabriela says. 'Did you arrange Saoirse's interview with them?'

Madeleine shakes her head. 'God, no.' The truth, though she wouldn't say it to Gabriela, is that it had been helpful, the implication from Gabriela's oldest friend that she had been depressed and had intentionally driven off the side of the cliff. In the end, the papers had moved on to something else, for the moment at least – the absence of bodies put down to wild boars.

'Do you think she really believes that I'd have done that?' Gabriela asks.

'I don't know,' Madeleine shrugs.

'In the interview, she didn't mention the baby,' Gabriela adds quietly.

'Perhaps she was trying to protect you.'

'Do you think she knows?' Gabriela says, and Madeleine frowns.

'Of course not. Unless you told her, which you didn't . . .'

'I didn't,' Gabriela replies. 'I just said I was in trouble and I needed her help.'

Madeleine reaches for her drink. 'So then she helped you.'

'Yes,' Gabriela says, as though working something out. Her gaze remains fixed at a point somewhere in the distance, her expression unchanging though her eyes finally fill with tears, which she makes no effort to wipe away.

Madeleine says nothing as Gabriela reaches for her hand. They sit for a while in silence, their fingers resting next to one another's, watching the children through the window.

'Thank you,' Gabriela says, after a while, as though the thought has just occurred to her. 'I don't think I said that before. You've been so good to us, you've saved our lives.'

Madeleine takes a final sip of her drink. She looks away. 'What choice did I have?'

Author's Note

The Second Woman is the third of three connected books, following on from *Part of the Family* and *A Double Life.* Each is a stand-alone novel that is also one in a series – not so much a trilogy as a triptych – that can be read in any order, with each book homing in on a strand of a larger, more complex web. I wanted to explore what happens when you look at the same crime from a number of perspectives, always with a woman at the centre of the story.

The genesis of this project was similarly manifold.

As with some of the best tales, it began in a pub, when a journalist friend told me about a trial he was reporting on involving a shipping company accused of dumping deadly toxic waste near a playground in a developing country. In the days that followed, as I read through the court transcripts, I knew I had my crime.

But for me, first as a news reporter and now as a writer of fiction, the most interesting thing about a crime is not the crime itself. In this sense, these books started to brew in my teens and early twenties, as I attempted to reconcile my own memories of the smiling grandfather I recalled faintly from childhood trips to Moscow with the public image of the double agent Kim Philby. As I considered his many faces – father, husband, friend, traitor, hero – questions began to emerge in my mind: How and why do we dupe the people we love; what is the impact on those we betray and on ourselves; and ultimately, what happens when the deceiver is a woman?

These books were inspired, in part, by some of my favourite espionage novels and political thrillers, and they deal, in various settings, with the elements of intelligence that interest me most. They are not traditional spy stories. Rather, they are an attempt to shift the focus so that we might reimagine a traditionally male world through a female lens.

Usually, when we think of women and criminality, we think of strong-armed accomplices or victims – and statistics around women in prison demonstrate that they often are. But not always. When a woman commits a crime that is typically thought of as 'male' – and in doing so, demonstrates the characteristics associated with that crime, often at odds with notions of femininity and motherhood – then her actions are almost always perceived, at least in part, through the prism of her domestic setting. She was a mother, a sister, a daughter – and look what she did.

I wanted to explore the distinct duality of roles that women face in their everyday lives and give each of my protagonists her own sense of agency, her own cross to bear and her own distinct flaws. So we have Anna, who must betray her family in order to protect them; we have Gabriela, who, in uncovering a double agent, finds herself living a double life; and we have Maria, bound and ultimately destroyed by loyalty.

I hope you find the books as entertaining, transportive and, dare I say, as exciting to read as I found them to write.

Acknowledgements

This book was finished whilst homeschooling in lockdown and I am wildly grateful to my husband, Barney, who was not only my first reader but who kept us all (relatively) sane during these turbulent times, and to my children who allowed themselves to be shouted at and stuck in front of the TV for hours on end whilst we attempted to work with everyone under one trembling roof.

Huge respect and gratitude to my inimitable editor, Ann Bissell, for her excellent guidance and patience; to Julia Silk, super-agent and occasional therapist; and to the brilliant team at Borough – Felicity Denham, Katy Blott, Izzy Coburn, Alice Gomer, Andrew Davies, et al. I'm so thankful for your support and talents.

Special thanks to my dear friend Hannah Foster for introducing me to the island of Alonnisos over the course of various summer holidays, first as teenagers, then as adults. It continues to occupy my thoughts. To my excellent police advisor, Richard H, for steering me away from glaring factual errors (any remaining are fully my own responsibility). To Vilma Nikolaidou – thank you, a million times, thank you. To my mum, who is a beacon of all things good, but not too good, because that would be boring. And finally to Xander, to whom this book is dedicated: good things come in threes!